"If you love me . . ."

"We'll live in Montmartre, Jenny," Marc said, holding her hand. "Jenny, we'll be happy."

A coldness crept over her. She wanted so much to be Marc's wife . . .

"Marc, I can't. Not yet. I can't leave my family until Danny's old enough to take over the shop. In two years—" *Let Marc wait two years for her. Please God, let him wait.*

Marc stared at her, hurt and anger in his eyes. "I thought you loved me."

"Marc, I do love you. But I support them. Without me, they have nothing." *Marc came from a different world—how could he understand what it meant to be poor?*

"Jenny, if you love me, you'll marry me," Marc said coldly. "Your family will manage."

"I can't, Marc. I'm sorry. I can't."

Blinded by tears, she spun away from him and ran off into the night.

Also by Julie Ellis from Pinnacle Books

EAST WIND

MAISON JENNIE

JULIE ELLIS

PINNACLE BOOKS NEW YORK

This novel is a work of fiction. Names, characters, places, and incidents are either the product of the author's imagination or are used fictitiously. Any resemblance to actual events or places or persons, living or dead, is entirely coincidental.

MAISON JENNIE

Copyright © 1984 by Julie Ellis

A Pinnacle Books edition. Reprinted by arrangement with Arbor House Publishing Company. All rights reserved.

Arbor House edition/July 1984
Pinnacle edition/September 1985

ISBN: 0-523-42357-8
Can. ISBN: 0-523-43360-3

Printed in the United States of America

PINNACLE BOOKS, INC.
1430 Broadway
New York, New York 10018

9   8   7   6   5   4   3   2   1

FOR ELENA AMOS—
a dear friend and "the hostess with the mostest"
of charm, imagination and creativity

ACKNOWLEDGMENTS

I WOULD like to express my deep thanks to Casey Edward Greene, Director, Library/Archives of the Dallas Historical Society of Dallas, Texas, and to the staffs of the New Orleans Historical Society and the New Orleans Public Library.

My gratitude, also, to the librarians at the New York Historical Society, the Museum of the City of New York and the various divisions of the New York Public Library, particularly the Drama Division of the Lincoln Center branch, the Historical Division of the Mid-Manhattan branch and the Genealogy Division at the main New York Public Library at Fifth Avenue.

My thanks to my son Richard for research on my behalf at the various libraries of Columbia University and to my daughter Susan for an able assist in research and copy editing.

MAISON
JENNIE

CHAPTER ONE

On a glorious sunlit afternoon in February of 1900, the streets of New Orleans were filled with the sounds of Mardi Gras. From the door of a modest little piece-goods shop two blocks off St. Charles Avenue, Jenny Straus watched the crowds who had gathered on the streets since early morning to catch a glimpse of the colorful floats.

It had been six years since Jenny had moved to New Orleans with her mother, father, two sisters and brother. After living on a farm fifty miles away, where the nearest town was so small the family saw the circuit-riding rabbi only once a month, New Orleans seemed to her a magical city.

"Jenny, don't hang out the door that way," her father said. "Without a mask no one should be on the street."

"But papa, look at the costume of that lady there. Did you ever see such beautiful velvet?"

"Too rich for our customers, child—but beautiful, yes."

It was Papa who had taught Jenny to love the feel of fine materials, the elegance of rich colors. At first she had been angry when her mother told her four months ago that she had to leave school to help out at the store—but now she loved helping the customers, keeping track of the inventory. Her sister Sophie, already eighteen and terrified of becoming an old maid, was going to marry Herman Goldwasser next month—he ran his own store—and Mama said that Sophie had to leave the store to go out to work so that she could earn money for the linens and blankets she should bring to her new husband. Jenny couldn't understand why

Sophie was marrying Herman—he was fat and old, already thirty-three. But Mama was pleased.

Jenny watched her father climb on a stool and put empty boxes on the top shelf. "Papa, what are you doing? What if somebody asks to see what's in those boxes?"

He chuckled. "What do I always do? The customers have to know we have so little stock in the shop? If they ask, I'll just say, 'that merchandise has been sold to a peddler who buys from me once a month.'"

Jenny knew her father hoped that one day they would have a magnificent store—like Maison Blanche or Goldman's Department Store, and she, too, dreamt that one day theirs would be a fine store. But how? She turned back to the streets.

"Papa, did they have Mardi Gras in Vienna?" Mr. Straus had left his family's farm for Vienna when he was twenty and Jenny loved to hear him tell about how he had met the beautiful Louise Solomon in a café, and had fallen in love with her instantly. Mama's parents had not felt the same enthusiasm for their daughter's penniless, uneducated suitor. Mr. Solomon had been the president of an important Vienna bank and even now Mama talked about their beautiful house and her fine clothes—almost as if she was sorry she had run off with papa to America.

Mr. Straus smiled. "Jenny, in no place in the world is there Mardi Gras except in New Orleans."

"Listen! I hear parade music again." Over the noise of the crowd she heard the strains of the triumphal march from the opera *Aida*—known throughout New Orleans as the "Mardi Gras March."

He laughed. "All right, my little love. So go already. Watch the parade for a couple of hours, then come on home. Nobody will buy today. We'll have an early supper—a nice Rahmbraten for Mardi Gras."

She ran behind the counter and grabbed her black mask.

"Mind you, behave yourself, Jenny. Remember, you are still my little girl."

"Thank you, papa." She threw her arms around him, thinking how Mama would have said she was being unladylike. "I love you."

"And I love *you*, my darling."

Of all his children—Sophie, Evvie, Daniel—she was the closest to his heart. "Remember, all masks come off by six. Mama will be serving supper early."

Jenny slipped out into the cobblestone street. Who cared that she wasn't wearing a costume? Her bright blue-green skirt and brilliant blue shirtwaist—she had made it herself from remnants in the store—were eye-catching enough.

Jenny could never understand her mother's fascination with the elegant private balls of Mardi Gras, attended by the cream of New Orleans society. She was always dropping hints that she might have been on those exclusive guest lists—if what? Jenny wondered. If she hadn't married papa?

She pushed her way through the throngs, ignoring the men who stopped to stare at her. Though only fourteen Jenny looked older, and with her lustrous black hair, curvaceous figure and ivory complexion, she was an arresting sight.

At Mardi Gras inhibitions are forgotten. Within minutes she had been swept into the arms of a handsome young man disguised as a steamboat captain, wearing a quarter-sized fake diamond stick-pin, and was waltzing with him to the strains of the "Merry Widow Waltz," played by a cluster of street musicians. Papa had taught her to waltz. Mama had not danced since she was a girl.

She wandered through the crowds, savoring the smells of popcorn, cotton candy, Creole frankfurters and beer, enjoying these moments alone. She drifted to North Claiborne where "Indians"—actually New Orleans blacks—and exquisite dark-skinned girls paraded in gaudy costumes, and then on to Royal and Bourbon Streets.

Five-thirty came too soon. Slowly, she began making her way through the bustling American section toward the narrow-fronted wooden house with a tiny balcony where the Straus family lived.

The crowd was now surging toward Royal Street to see the last parade of the season. Parents tugged reluctant but tired children home for supper. On Jenny's street a jazz band was playing, urged on by a cluster of onlookers.

Opening the door that led up the narrow, creaking stairs

to the Straus flat, Jenny froze at the sound of wailing from upstairs. It sounded like mama—but she would *never* cry in front of the children.

Her heart pounding, Jenny ran up the stairs and threw open the door to the kitchen.

Mrs. Straus sat in a chair by the table, moaning as she rocked back and forth. Sophie and Evvie, too, were crying. Daniel, his face ashen, stood in a corner. Jenny looked frantically from one to the next.

"Mama—"

"You!" Her mother looked up, her face twisted in rage. "Where were you, Jeannette Straus, when your father needed you? You killed him!"

Jenny looked at Sophie.

"It's true, Jenny. A thief came into the store to rob the cash box. Papa was alone. Now he's dead."

Mrs. Straus's voice cut through the air. "If you had been where you belonged, he would be alive."

Dazed, Jenny went about arranging for her father's funeral. At last she went to Rabbi Schul, who suggested that she go to one of the Jewish benevolent associations to get help with the money. What choice did she have? Then she remembered the emergency fund mama kept hidden under her mattress.

"My mother will pay, Rabbi Schul. That's the way papa would have wanted it."

The following day, as she stood next to mama, Evvie, Sophie and Danny in the Dispersed of Judah Cemetery while the rabbi conducted the Orthodox funeral, Jenny remembered her father's face that last day in the store . . . hadn't his last words to her been, *"I love you, my darling"*? How could she live without him? But what they had shared would live on. She wasn't alone.

Mama cried and clung to Sophie. Evvie held Daniel's hand and cried into her handkerchief. Who was there to comfort her? Her own family, it seemed, had rejected her.

The kaddish was said. Now, as was the custom in New Orleans—for a hundred years it had been unlawful to bury the dead in the ground because the water table was only three feet beneath the surface—the coffin was placed in a tiered receptacle. They left the synagogue and went back to the flat to sit shivah.

The fast was broken by the traditional mourners' meal of consolation, brought in by friends. As Jenny sat alone on a box at one side of the room papa's words came back to her: "The *Talmud* urges you not to mourn excessively or too self-tormentingly." But how could she do otherwise?

The seven days of shivah dragged on and Jenny found her thoughts wandering. How were they going to manage with papa gone? Clearly mama's "emergency fund" wouldn't be enough. Someone had to take charge.

On the eighth day, with the key to the store in her pocket, Jenny got up early, hurriedly dressed and grabbed a roll on her way out. She was met at the door by her mother.

"I know where you're going, Jenny, and you might as well forget it. A man is coming this morning to talk about buying the stock, and I'm going to listen to what he has to say."

"But, mama, *I* can run the shop—papa would have wanted it that way. Please—people will expect the store to be open this morning. We can't turn customers away."

"You're only a child, Jenny. What do you know about running a store?"

There was a knock at the door and Mrs. Straus stepped aside. "Evvie, answer it, please."

Jenny waited impatiently while mama and the nervous looking dark-haired man made small talk. Since they did not have a proper parlor, she brought a tea tray to them in the corner of the kitchen. At last the man stood by the door, his hat in his hand. Mama was smiling as she shook his hand. "I will give you my decision tomorrow, Mr. Buxton." Jenny bit her lip to keep from crying out. This robber was offering them one tenth of what papa had paid for the piece-goods and the threads. Didn't mama see how he was cheating them? If she accepted his offer, in two or three months all their money would be gone. The store would be gone. What would they do then?

There was a knock at the door. Jenny opened it, and a

coachman for the Weisses—a well-established old Jewish family in town—stood before her. In his hand was a message, a note of condolence from Mrs. Weiss. She had added a postscript:

> *My mother-in-law has moved here from New York and is afraid of the "schwartzes," so we've decided a white maid would make her feel more comfortable. Would you be interested in the position? Your presence would be required only from seven in the morning until six in the evening, leaving you free to care for your family.*

Mrs. Straus slapped the letter on the table.

"Imagine! Ruth Weiss expects me—Louise Solomon—to work as a maid. My God, the insolence of that woman!" Jenny smiled. Apparently mama didn't realize Mrs. Weiss meant only to help. But that was typical—with mama, pride was more important than anything.

"Mama, don't be so upset," Evvie pleaded.

Mrs. Straus brightened. "You're young and strong, Jennie, darling. Go right over and talk to Mrs. Weiss about this job. Mind you, don't let her cheat you on the wages."

Jenny hesitated. In New Orleans only colored girls and French girls who didn't know any better worked as maids. But at least this way she would be bringing home money every week.

"All right, mama. I'll go."

"Put up your hair and wear something nice. For God's sake, don't walk into the Weiss house in that gypsy outfit."

Jenny ran uptown to the Garden District. If she brought home money every week, then maybe mama wouldn't always be angry at her. But what would happen to the store?

At last she stood before the Weisses' tall, stately Georgian mansion. She hesitated at the door, mama's tirades against the "common" worker coming back to her. But if papa had taught her anything, it was to be practical. She rang the bell.

The houseman escorted Jenny into a small sitting room

and in a few moments Mrs. Weiss came in. The interview was brief. Mrs. Weiss was polite but firm. The job had been offered only to Jenny's mother—they wanted a woman—not a child.

At supper that night, Jenny toyed with her food, Evvie was quiet and even Danny—who usually chattered throughout the meal—sat in silence while Sophie and mama discussed the offer for the store. Apparently, Herman had already denounced the prospective buyer.

"He says the man's a *gonif*, mama," Sophie said as she passed Evvie a bowl of steaming *tsimmis*.

Mrs. Straus looked stricken. "But I'm a helpless widow. What else can I do?"

"Herman is sending a man over tomorrow who will buy not only the stock but the fixtures. He'll even pay for good will—he wants to take over the store and run it. And Herman's warned him he's not to take advantage of a widow who's a *landsman*."

"So what am I to do about the other man? Suppose Herman's friend changes his mind?"

"Herman says to hold him off. Tell him you have to talk about it with your future son-in-law."

"Oh dear Lord, this is too much—how am I to take care of myself and three children? A woman raised as I was . . ."

Evvie cleared her throat. "Maybe I could get a job."

Mrs. Straus looked horrified.

"My poor Evvie, what could you do?"

Jennie knew it was her chance.

"I could run the store, mama. Papa taught me everything."

Sophie stopped eating and put down her spoon. "Jenny! You're fourteen years old. What could you know about running a business? Stop bothering us with ridiculous ideas. Mama's got enough on her mind."

While Jenny was washing the breakfast dishes, Mr. Buxton arrived. Apparently he had been ready to close the deal, but the minute he heard that a prospective son-in-law had been consulted he lost interest.

"Forget it! I don't want your stock. It's a little nothing anyway—I'm an important man, you know—I don't have time to be toyed with like this. Never mind the tea. I'll see myself out."

As soon as the door closed Mrs. Straus turned to Jenny. "When did Herman say his friend would be here?"

"Mama, please . . . let me go open up the store, just so he can see that we're doing business. If he thinks you're not anxious, then he'll make us a better offer."

"Suppose another thief comes into the store? You're going to stop him from killing you and running off with the change?"

"It'll be different now that the Mardi Gras is over, mama. Nothing will happen to me—except maybe I'll do a little business. The rent is paid on the store. Let me try and see what stock we have."

Mrs. Straus sighed.

"All right, God help me, go ahead. I can't bear any more of this. Just leave me in peace."

Jenny hesitated by the door.

"Mama, I'll need some change for the cashbox—"

For the cashbox Papa had been killed . . .

Mrs. Straus looked at her for a long moment, her gaze wary.

"All right. Bring me my purse. And make sure you come home with what I give you."

Jenny hurried off to the store; but as she approached the tiny shop that had been papa's pride, she felt her throat tighten. Her hands trembled as she fumbled for the key. She opened the door and a blast of hot, musty air hit her. The store had been closed up since the day of the Mardi Gras. Tears filled Jenny's eyes as she remembered papa's dreams. Here, at least, for this moment, she was alone with him. Here, in their private world.

"Why, papa?" Her voice bounced eerily off the empty shelves.

All the sadness of the past few weeks flooded her, and

when she saw the dark stain on the floorboards—papa's blood—she dropped to her knees and wept.

"Papa, I didn't mean to let it happen. I didn't know."

Within an hour after she had opened for business, Jenny had made two sales. She wasn't alone—papa was beside her, telling her how to match wits with the customer, who of course always argued about the price. She remembered to ask a little more than she expected, to have room to "come down."

Late in the morning she noticed a man hovering in the doorway. Instantly she knew it was Herman's friend.

Rebellion surged through her. No matter what they said, she was not going to let someone else run the store. This store was all papa had left them. They just couldn't throw it away. She could make enough to keep a roof over their heads and food on the table.

She decided to act as though he were a regular customer.

He reached into his pocket and pulled out a cigar. "Good morning, miss. I'm just looking around this morning. Mister Goldwasser said I should come take a look."

"Oh." Jenny pretended to be disappointed. "I was hoping you were a customer."

"You must be the daughter who helped Mr. Straus—may he rest in peace." He paused solemnly.

"Papa didn't need me to help him. Who comes into our store when there's Maison Blanche just two blocks away? I just stayed to keep him company."

"Yes, my dear, but somehow he supported a family." He glanced at the shelves. "You keep a fair amount of stock in the store."

Jenny looked at him innocently. "That's very kind of you, sir, but do you see all those boxes on the top shelves? They're all empty. Look, I'll show you." She reached for the stool, climbed up, pulled out a box. "See? Papa kept hoping he'd be able to bring in more stock, but—"

"Look," he said nervously, "tell your mother Herman's friend stopped by. I don't think the store is what I'm lookin' for. Tell her I ain't interested."

Jenny watched the cool stranger go out the door and close

it behind him. Her hands trembled as she replaced the lid on the empty box and climbed on the stool. She had done what was right. What papa would have wanted of her. Now the store would stay in business. She would work hard to bring in enough money to take care of mama and Evvie and Daniel.

She wasn't a little girl anymore. She was a business woman. Papa always said she had a sharp business head, good Yiddish *kop*. Mama would understand now that there was nothing else to do but to let her take papa's place in the store.

CHAPTER TWO

WHILE SOPHIE COOKED dinner for the family, Jenny listened guiltily to her mother's cries that now, surely, they were destined for the poorhouse. Of course it wasn't Herman's fault that his friend had withdrawn his offer—he was Sophie's future husband. But what were they to do now?

"I'll have a nervous breakdown," she wailed. "They'll take me off to Touro's Infirmary. My poor Daniel—my baby—he'll go to the Jewish Orphans Home! And Evvie, what will become of you?"

"We'll manage, mama," Jenny said. "I'll run the store. Already today I made four sales."

Sophie watched Evvie hobble around the table, painstakingly setting down the utensils. "Mama, why don't you give Jenny a chance?" But she, too, was troubled. In three months she would be Herman's wife. She would have a husband to take care of her. But what about the rest of the family?

Last night she had talked to mama about postponing the wedding so that she could bring home money from her job at Mr. Fleming's ribbon shop. But mama wouldn't hear of it. Who knew when another Herman would come along? Let one child at least be married and secure.

Because she had no other alternative Mrs. Straus finally relented and let Jenny continue to run the store. Every night Jenny came home with the profits from the day's sales. The cost of the merchandise sold was put into a special envelope so that at the end of the week she could replace the stock that was gone.

11

Mrs. Straus was shocked when she saw Jenny slide the envelope under her mattress.

"You keep money from me! My own child!"

"It's for stock, mama. We can't have a store without something to sell. Papa did the same, remember? He brought the profits home to you and the rest he used for buying."

"But you didn't tell me. From now on you must tell me everything. How much you take in, how much you save for stock . . ."

Jenny sighed.

"Mama, I swear—I bring everything to you."

Jenny was the first to wake up every morning. She ate a biscuit and tea and hurried off to the store, opening even earlier than she had when papa was alive to catch any customers on their way to the French Market. She filled the two tiny windows with her prettiest fabrics and she was warm and friendly even to "lookers" because—who knows?—one day they might buy.

On a cloudy humid day in May Sophie and Herman were married, with only the family in attendance. Herman swaggered down the aisle, Sophie looked pleased with herself, and all mama could talk about was her older sister Clara's wedding in Vienna, where two hundred guests were lavishly entertained at a magnificent supper and an orchestra played waltzes by Johann Strauss.

Ten weeks after the wedding Sophie announced that she was pregnant, and from then on, mama never missed a chance to launch into a tirade about the horrors of childbirth. Once Jenny tried to persuade her mother to be less graphic—wasn't it enough that Sophie had such a bad time with morning sickness? But Mrs. Straus said, "Let Herman know what a woman goes through to give a man a child. The man wants the family, but it's the woman who goes through the pain. I ought to know—I've been through it four times. Well, I don't want to hear about this baby until it's all over. My nerves just won't take any more."

Insisting that Evvie was too fragile, Mrs. Straus told Sophie to send for Jenny when the time came.

Jenny watched Sophie's swelling belly with a fierce protectiveness, but she tried not to imagine her under the blankets with Herman. Sophie said nothing against him, but Jenny hated the way he was always criticizing the Viennese cooking Sophie had learned from mama, saying he preferred German-Jewish food. He seemed to enjoy embarrassing Sophie in front of the entire family with accusations of how much money she spent on food. If there was one thing mama had taught all her children, it was the value of every penny.

When Sophie was in her seventh month, Jenny started going to her flat on Sunday mornings to help with the cleaning. On Sunday mornings his store was closed, so Herman went off to play pinochle with his friend, Emmanuel Adler.

"Sophie, sit." Sophie was always on her hands and knees, scrubbing the floor. "Let the baby come when it's due—not early because you're killing yourself cleaning the flat."

On a chilly day in late January a small boy who lived in the flat below Sophie's came to the shop with a message. Without reading it Jenny knew instantly what it meant. Her hands trembling, she locked up the shop and ran the few blocks to the flat.

Sophie sat in a kitchen chair with hands clutching her enormous belly. Despite the day's chill, perspiration rolled down her neck.

"How long has it been?"

"About four hours," Sophie said between breaths. "I didn't want you to close the store until I was sure."

"You're sure? Then I'm going for the midwife."

"Jenny, first put up a pot of *tsimmis* for Herman. He'll need something to eat when he comes home."

"Sophie, for goodness sake—I'll put it up when the midwife's here with you. Your husband won't starve."

Seven hours later, while Herman sat at the kitchen table shoveling *tsimmis* into his mouth, Sophie pushed a large and oddly silent male infant into the world.

Jenny hovered over the midwife.

"Why is he so quiet?"

"Take him." The midwife cut the umbilical cord and handed the baby to Jenny. "I'm busy with your sister."

Trembling, Jenny took the baby and began wiping him clean. *Why was he so quiet?*

"The baby," Sophie whispered. "Something's wrong! Let me see my baby!"

"Wait, Sophie. Let me finish cleaning him." The baby's breath was coming out in rasping coughs. Jenny turned him face down and gave him a whack on his behind. He coughed up gray phlegm and burst into a lusty wail. "Thank God," Jenny whispered.

A moment later Herman threw the door open. "How dare you keep the father waiting! Well, tell me . . . is it a boy?"

On the first anniversary of her father's death Jenny sat at the dinner table and watched the *yourtsayt* candles glow in the window. For weeks she'd been thinking about using the storage area above the shop as the family's flat. With whitewash and paint it would be liveable—and the money that had to be handed over every month to Mr. Lieberman for rent could go to buy more stock.

Mrs. Straus didn't like the idea.

"Jenny, what are you talking about? Always with the crazy ideas. Evvie, tell her. Tell her she's driving me into a nervous breakdown."

But Jenny knew that eventually mama would give in—if only because she'd tire of arguing.

"Sales could double if we had the merchandise, mama. In two or three years we'll be making enough at the store to move somewhere nice."

"Oh, yes," Mrs. Straus said sarcastically, "we'll move all the way up to the Garden District."

"Mama, I'm getting the people who used to shop at Maison Blanche. They come to me now because if I don't have what they want, *I* try to get it for them. I give them service. That's the difference. Service."

"All right, all right. I'll talk to Herman." Mrs. Straus sighed, her fingertips pressed to her temples. You'd think Herman was the oracle, Jenny thought in annoyance. He was nothing more than a *salesman*.

On September 9, at Daniel's modest bar-mitzvah—three days after the assassination of President McKinley—Mrs.

Straus complained throughout the night about how she couldn't have done better by her only son. Sophie, Herman, and their son Karl were the only ones who seemed to be enjoying themselves. Jenny was grateful they were able to afford a bar-mitzvah at all. Papa would have been so proud to see how she had learned to haggle with her suppliers to get the best deals, to coax a sale from the most reluctant customer. She was doing everything he had taught her, and she had a flair with people that was all her own.

She worked furiously, always looking for new ways to increase sales. One day, as she watchd her mother sewing a tiny dayslip trimmed with lace ruffles and lace insertions, she had an idea . . .

Later that week she brought her mother a sketch of a trousseau gown she'd copied from one on sale at Goldman's Department Store and asked her to make up such a gown to sell in the store.

"Jenny, will it never end? Now you're asking me to do sewing for you?"

Evvie, always the soothing influence, stepped in.

"Now, mama, Jenny didn't mean that."

Jenny stood her ground. "I just need a model, mama. If I can get orders, then I'll be able to have a seamstress make them up. That way we can make a big profit."

"A profit she says! Do you know what it would cost? All that expensive silk and lace?"

"But it's an important investment. I wouldn't think of it except I know what a beautiful nightgown you made for Sophie when she married Herman. And the dayslip you just finished for Karl." Sophie's first child was mama's pride and joy. "Not even in Paris could anybody make something so beautiful."

Mrs. Straus hesitated. "All right. I'll try it. But I think it's foolish and I'm not even going to tell Herman. He'd have a fit. Look for silk that won't cost you too much. Take lace from the store." She sighed. "Somehow I'll find the time."

Jenny struggled to hide her impatience while mama took her time completing the sample. She kept the real cost of the silk and the fine French lace a secret, knowing that mama would have been furious had she known. But when she went out with the model in hand, despite her charm and enthusiasm and the genuine loveliness of the piece, no one was interested. Baffled, she inspected her mother's handiwork. The nightgown was exquisite. Why wasn't anyone interested?

Like all of New Orleans, Jenny knew about the "restricted" district—the greatest in all America—that had come to be known as Storyville. It had been legally established back in the summer of 1897, and was regulated by local government, much like European "red light" districts.

While no respectable woman would set foot in Storyville, the area catered to some of New Orleans' wealthiest men. There were constant whisperings about the opulent mansions with mirrored ceilings, Persian rugs, fine oil paintings, where a man might pay up to fifty dollars a night to be entertained by a girl who looked like a Mardi Gras queen. It was even said that the chamber pots were lined with gold.

Jenny knew that she could find customers in such a house.

She sat down and wrote letters to four of the best known madams in Storyville bordellos. Not trusting the post, she hired a messenger to deliver the letters, all carefully written on thick lavender paper and enclosed in lavender envelopes—a wickedly expensive venture, but worth it. Jenny knew the Storyville ladies would be impressed by such an extravagance.

Four days later Jenny was showing nightgowns to a well-known madam whose house on Basin Street received the top politicians in the state. Local gossip had it that this woman had personally entertained a congressman for the past ten years. She clucked and fluttered at the price—and promptly ordered six. She didn't even bat an eye when Jenny delicately asked for a deposit.

"I expect each one to be just as pretty as this," the madam said. "In my house nothing but the best." She gazed appraisingly at Jenny. "You know, a girl like you could make a fortune in my house."

Jenny felt the flush in her cheeks.

"I'm in a different business, ma'am," she said demurely.

The madam burst out laughing. But if mama ever knew the store was selling to a Storyville madam—even the fanciest, with a uniformed butler to admit her patrons . . .

"Jenny, I will not become your dressmaker. My nerves won't take it. It's different when I make little things for Karl."

"Then make some christening gowns. I'm sure I can sell them uptown—"

"Don't push me, Jenny. I won't allow my own child to drive me into a nervous breakdown. That's it—no more discussion."

With her "fine nightwear and lingerie" department launched, Jenny arranged a corner of the shop with a pair of dainty chairs and a cheval mirror where clients could sit and consult with her. Thanks to the gracious notes she and Danny had personally delivered to houses in the Garden District, her christening gowns were soon drawing the ladies of the New Orleans elite and within months these ladies were also buying Jenny's nightgowns and lingerie.

On a steamy summer afternoon a few weeks after Jenny's sixteenth birthday—a time when most well-placed New Orleanians were away at their lake houses, at eastern resorts or touring Europe—a tall, handsome young stranger appeared in the shop. His hair was dark and slightly unruly, his eyes were rebellious yet warm and a deep brown. He stood self-consciously before Jenny, his fingers nervously tapping the counter.

"May I help you, sir?"

"Yes. My mother asked me to pick up a package for her. Mrs. Goldman."

So . . . this must be one of Mrs. Goldman's sons—the very same Mrs. Goldman who owned the famous Goldman's Department Store. Jenny had been so proud when she had come in to buy two nightgowns a few weeks ago.

"Yes, her nightdresses are ready. Just let me wrap them up for you."

As she cut the wrapping paper, she tried to figure out which Goldman son this might be. The older son, Benedict, worked in the store all day, so this must be Marc, who was a student at Harvard. The family was in town, Mrs. Goldman had told Jenny, because Mr. Goldman's mother was seriously ill.

With the package under his arm, Marc hesitated at the door. "Your mother runs the shop?"

"I run it."

"Alone?"

"Sometimes my sister Evvie comes down for an hour to help out—but she's delicate, like my mother."

"So you must *like* running it."

"Oh yes, I love it, I—" Jenny stopped, blushing. "I used to help my father."

For a few mintues they talked about their families. Marc was feuding with his parents because he didn't want to go back to Harvard in the fall—he wanted to go to Paris to study painting. Four years ago Marc and his sister Nicole had, with his mother and the older Mrs. Goldman, taken a summer tour of Europe and Marc had fallen in love with Paris. But Mr. and Mrs. Goldman had not been exactly thrilled with his plans to become an artist.

"They just don't understand. They expect me to finish at Harvard, then come into the store, like Benedict. To them— even to my grandmother—being an artist somehow isn't quite respectable. My younger sister Nicky is the only one who understands."

"If you want to be an artist, then you should. People should be free to choose what kind of lives they want. Parents never seem to understand that times are changing."

Another customer came in and quickly Marc asked Jenny if he could see her again—away from the shop. When she explained that she opened the store in the morning and must remain until well in the evening, he persuaded her to meet him before she opened up.

"Tomorrow we'll go to the French Market for coffee and watch the early morning sun over the water. I go there every day to sketch."

"It will have to be very early." Jenny knew she couldn't mention this to her mother. But mama slept late every morning; if she left early enough she wouldn't be missed.

"Early it is, then." He smiled. "Shall I meet you here?"

* * *

The next morning, waiting in front of the store for Marc to appear, Jenny realized that he, too, wanted to keep their meeting a secret. Her spirits lifted at the sight of his tall, slender figure hurrying toward her. How handsome he was!—what mama would call aristocratic.

It was a mild, sunny morning, barely hinting at the heat that would embrace the city within a few hours. They walked downtown into the French Quarter, where the winding streets and strange little alleys were slowly coming to life, the scent of roses, magnolias and jasmine everywhere.

Negresses with large shallow baskets on their heads walked gracefully along the street, calling out their wares. The milk carts, tall green boxes set between large wheels, moved along the street with the driver standing to see the road and ringing a bell before the doors of regular patrons.

As they approached the French Market they were slowed by the busy rush of noisy wagons and carts. On every side was the clatter of voices in foreign tongues.

"Belle Callas! Tout chouds! Belle fromage! Chaurice! Belle des Figues!"

Marc slid a protective arm around Jenny's waist as they were jostled by the early morning shoppers and those who came to sip *café noir* and *café au lait* with a brioche or *cala*—a delectable doughnut of rice and flour.

"How do you like your coffee?" he asked as they lined up at a coffee stand. *"Café noir?"*

"Yes." Right now she would have agreed to anything. Here she was in the French Quarter with Marc Goldman, so handsome that he drew stares from passersby . . . but she didn't realize that the stares were for her, too.

The chicory-laced coffee was hot and savory. Jenny would never have admitted it, but this was only the second time she'd ever had coffee—except on special occasions, mama always served tea.

Marc was telling her about the scenes he especially enjoyed sketching. Like her, he was fascinated by the assortment of people in the Market. Here, Gascon butchers mingled with Spanish fruit sellers and German vegetable women. Moors fresh from the Holy Land, wearing strings of beads and crosses, bought goods from peddlers—

"rabais men"—with their tiny stores on wheels. It was a potpourri of humanity—Chinese and Hindu, French and Creole, Jew, Irish, English, Malay.

Jenny knew about *lagniappe*—the Spanish word for a gift that would be given with each purchase. In the French Quarter the *lagniappe* was usually a piece of candy, cake or fruit.

"I love to sketch the women there," Marc said, smiling at the sight of the old Creole Negresses in tignon and bandanas selling pralines, *pain potatoes*, and *calas*.

They each ordered another cup of coffee. The air was thick with the smell of coffee beans, wild herbs and woodland leaves. They stopped and stared at a papoose strapped to the back of his Choctaw Indian mother. The handful of Indians in the Market were the last remnant of the once mighty Choctaw tribe, who had owned the land on which New Orleans was built.

It was here that Jenny and Marc decided to meet secretly every morning. They would visit the French Market or walk along the levee, pausing in front of the fish market to watch the fishermen land their cargoes of oranges and oysters, fish and vegetables. Marc had often sketched the crew of traders as they unloaded and loaded their small vessels or loitered around the levee smoking cigarettes and cooking their meals over charcoal stoves.

Late at night, when everyone thought she was downstairs in the shop going over stock, Jenny would meet Marc in a fragrant park or sit with him in the dark shadows of a bistro. They went to May's on Canal Street for ice cream and on especially hot nights took the "belt ride" on the streetcar line. Marc poured out his heart to Jenny—about his family, his art . . . and she listened to every word, filled with wonder that he had come into her life.

At night she lay awake thinking of him. She loved his joy in living, his unshakable belief in his talents . . . and she knew from those few stolen kisses in the park that she wanted to spend the rest of her life with him. But what would happen when Marc left New Orleans, either for Harvard as his parents wished, or for Paris to study painting? Secretly, she hoped he would ask her to marry him—but all the while she knew she *couldn't* marry. *Who would support her family?*

Meanwhile, Sophie was already pregnant again—so she and Herman had their own problems. It was *her* responsibility to care for mama and Evvie and Daniel. Still, she couldn't help dreaming about life as Marc Goldman's wife . . .

One sultry, hot summer evening, as they strolled along St. Charles Avenue, he suddenly let go of her hand.

"Jenny, wait a minute. I'll be right back." He hurried toward a group of people coming out of the Young Men's Hebrew Association. Jenny watched as he talked to a pretty young girl with dark hair and a beautiful smile and she realized it had to be his sister Nicole—the resemblance was astonishing.

Tears of humiliation welled in her eyes as she waited for him. Apparently Marc Goldman, heir to the fine Goldman's Department Store, was ashamed to be seen with a little Jewess who ran a tiny shop on a side street.

"Sorry, Jenny, I had to talk to my sister Nicky for a minute." He laughed uneasily. "Forgive me for running off like that."

As always, Marc took Jenny home and waited until she was safely inside. Usually he would then take a carriage or a streetcar to the Goldman house in the handsome residential section of Canal Street beyond the bustling business area of the 170-foot-wide asphalt-paved boulevard.

But he had things to think about so tonight he decided to walk. He could tell Jenny had been hurt that he had not introduced her to Nicky. He felt guilty about that, but he wasn't ready to let his family know about her yet—and while Nicky would never knowingly hurt him, she was young and impulsive and one never knew what she was going to say. He could predict the reaction . . . His mother would launch into a speech about those Jews who married "beneath." She was always throwing socially accepted—and usually Christian—girls at him.

He couldn't bring himself to go back to Harvard. Somehow, he had to go to Paris to study. But without Jenny? Maybe he could persuade her to marry him and go with him. There wasn't much time left. Only three weeks . . .

* * *

Jenny, too, was aware of the days slipping by. She could feel Marc's turmoil, even while she was struggling with her own feelings. Much as she wanted to hear him ask her to marry him, she dreaded it because she knew what her answer had to be. Just one week before he was scheduled to board the train for Boston, he finally asked her.

"Maybe it's wrong to deceive my parents," he said gravely, holding her hand, "but they refuse to recognize that I must live my own life. They think I'll be leaving for school. Instead, we'll be married here, travel to New York and then sail for Paris. I have enough money to pay our passage and to live on until I find a job. We'll live in Montmartre in a cheap garret. Jenny, we'll be happy."

A coldness crept over her. She wanted so much to be Marc's wife . . . but her first duty was to her family.

"Marc, I can't. Not yet. I can't leave my family until Danny is old enough to take over the shop. In two years, when he's sixteen—" *Let Marc wait two years for her. Please God, let him wait.*

Marc stared at her, hurt and anger in his eyes. "I thought you loved me."

"Marc, I do love you. But I support them. That's been my responsibility since papa died. Without me they have nothing."

"You'd let me go to Paris, alone, then?"

"I can't let them starve—" She knew she sounded melodramatic. Marc came from an entirely different world—how could he understand what it meant to be poor? "If you go back to college for a year, maybe by then—"

"Jenny, I can't wait another year! I need to study painting *now*. If you love me, you'll marry me and come to Paris."

"I do love you—" Her voice trembled. "More than anything in the world."

"But not enough to leave your family?"

"Marc, I have responsibilities." She searched his face for some sign of understanding.

"If you love me, you'll marry me," he repeated coldly. "Your family will manage."

"I can't, Marc. I'm sorry. I can't."

Blinded by tears she spun away from him and ran off into the night. She couldn't go with him. Not yet. Papa's memory ran too deep.

CHAPTER THREE

EVERY DAY JENNY waited for Marc to come to the store. Alone, behind the counter for fourteen hours a day she prayed that he would understand, that he would come to her with a promise to wait for her.

Danny was bright—she could teach him to manage the store. Already—over mama's objections—she had him making deliveries after school to help out. In two years he would be out of school then mama would have no say in the matter.

But Marc never appeared. His painting, it seemed, came before her. She was hurt, she had moments of regret, but she understood his dedication and in a sense loved him all the more for it.

She knew she would never marry anybody else. How could she? But she would spend her life building the store, and someday it would be as fine as Goldman's. The store would be her husband, her children. Her life.

The days turned to weeks. Jenny awoke one hot sultry morning and realized that Marc would be leaving today. For a few moments she lay back against the pillow and let her thoughts drift back to the beautiful summer hours they had shared. She remembered the first time Marc kissed her. It had seemed so natural. They had been standing by a grand oak tree draped in gray Spanish moss . . .

Now in a few hours, he would be on a train to New York, where he would board a ship to France. He would be out of her life forever.

She forced herself to push aside the sheet, damp from

perspiration, and get out of her bed. She was the only person in the world who knew Marc was on his way to Paris—and he hadn't even come to say good-bye to her.

She dressed and hurried downstairs to the store before the others woke up. Life must go on. But she knew this would be a day of anguish, a day when each passing minute would make her more certain that the man she loved was lost to her forever.

Until the moment he boarded the train in New Orleans—plagued by guilt that he had not told his family about his plans—Marc had hoped that Jenny would change her mind. For days he had haunted all their familiar meeting places, hoping to catch sight of her. Twice he had even walked past her shop, imagining that he heard her voice calling out "Marc! Marc, of course, I'll marry you!"

He'd considered waiting for her. But he couldn't deny his talents for two more long, lonely years. Soon he would be twenty-one. It was time he embarked on the life that was meant for him. Couldn't Jenny understand that?

But throughout the long train journey to New York and the passage on the merchant ship to Cherbourg, Marc was haunted by the look on her face that last day . . .

When at last he arrived in Paris, he realized that the Paris he was to know was a different city from the one he had visited with his family when he was sixteen. His mother had favored the Café de Paris, Voison's, Foyot's, and Maxim's—he could afford neither these gourmet dining spots nor the fine hotels where his family had stayed.

Keenly aware of his limited resources—but grateful that at least he spoke fluent French, Marc quickly found himself a modest studio in an old slate-colored house on a steep, cobbled street in Montmartre. The light was good, it was cheap and the neighborhood was filled with inexpensive cafés. He could live here for three months before his money ran out. Within that time he would establish himself with a teacher and work part-time at a job that would help pay for food and art supplies.

He was enthralled with Paris . . . its broad boulevards and avenues lined with chestnut trees, the outdoor cafés and the Bois de Boulogne. Most of all he looked forward to living so close to artists and would-be artists. There were moments when he was overwhelmed with homesickness, moments when he was so lonely for Jenny he thought his heart would break. She had become so much a part of him. With her at his side he would have confidence in his talent. Somehow she always lifted his spirits, even in his darkest periods of self-doubt. What would his life be like without her?

He had been in Paris less than a month when at a Montmartre coffeehouse he met Paul and Eugenie Kaufman—a wealthy young American couple living in Europe for one year's fling. Their year was almost over and Paul was trying to prepare himself to return to America to join his father and uncles in a prestigious New York law firm.

Drawn to this handsome and charming young artist, the Kaufmans insisted he accompany them to a party at the home of another American expatriate, Mary Cassatt.

"Her father, you know, is president of the Pennsylvania Railroad," Paul said.

Marc was impressed. "Mary Cassatt, the artist?"

Eugenie shrugged. "Its gossiped all over Paris that she has been Degas's lover for years, but no one knows for sure. We only know that Degas is a nasty anti-Semite while Mary was loudly on the side of Dreyfus in those two ugly trials."

For a moment they were all silent, remembering that while Dreyfus had been pardoned by President Emile Loubet—when champions of justice throughout the world protested the unfairness meted out to the former French officer—he had not yet been declared innocent.

Eugenie drained her glass. "Come, let's go to Mary's house. She may be rude and brutally insulting, but she is the greatest living American painter. And she has fascinating people at her parties."

Marc was intrigued by the exciting world of Mary Cassatt, though he was put off when she said that American students in Paris were "café tramps." Within minutes he met the Countess Simone de Champlain. Widowed, beautiful and wealthy at forty, she was a witty and charming woman, sympathetic to the plight of young artists. Marc was delighted when the countess invited him to a dinner party at her house the following evening. Perhaps his life in Paris was looking up.

From Mary Cassatt's flat the Kaufmans took Marc to a party in a Montmartre studio. While neither Paul nor Eugenie possessed any real talent for painting, both appreciated the artistic spirit. Here the mood was young and electric, the conversation boisterous and stimulating, all revolving around the artist's world.

Immediately Marc was drawn to Colette, a vivacious little artist's model, who reminded him of Jenny.

"Would you like to paint me?" she asked pressing her high, full breasts against him. "For you no fee," she purred. "It will be a pleasure."

With Jenny he had never dared express his desire, but from what they had permitted themselves, he was convinced she was passionate. He remembered all the nights he had held her in his arms, his mouth clinging to hers, their bodies tense with denied satisfaction.

"I live quite near." Colette dropped a hand on his chest and slid two fingers between the buttons on his shirt. "Come home with me?"

"Right now." *Pretend this is Jenny.*

Over Colette's head he gestured to the Kaufmans that he was leaving. Paul grinned, nodded knowingly.

"You are so handsome," Colette murmured in the dark hallway outside the studio. "I knew the minute you walked in that we were to make love."

"Not here. Let's go to your flat."

Colette lived in a garret room overlooking a narrow street. She stood on the sidewalk before the ancient structure and pointed to a dormered window four stories above the street.

"This is where I live. Must we wait until we climb all those stairs?"

"This will do for now," Marc murmured, pulling her inside the dark entrance hall and bringing his mouth to hers.

Marc had been raised to respect the young ladies of his social set, but his father had taken him to the finest brothel in Storyville to learn about love. In his father's milieu it was accepted that many wives recoiled from the physical side of marriage.

Colette lifted her open mouth to his, and with a groan he swept her small, deliciously curved body to his while his tongue explored her warm mouth and his hands caressed her full breasts.

Reluctantly he pulled away.

"Do you have to live on top of all those stairs?"

She laughed. "You are young. You will still have strength."

At last they arrived, breathless, at Colette's door. She swore as she struggled with the key.

The instant they were inside the dimly lit flat Colette moved toward him. "Would you like some wine?"

"Later." He pulled her toward him. "All I want at this moment is to bury myself in that beautiful body."

"Am I really beautiful?"

Undressing in front of him, Colette goaded Marc into extravagant compliments, refusing to let him touch her until she stood naked in the soft lamplight. At last, when he could bear it no longer, he swept her into his arms and carried her to the unmade bed.

"Mon cher—" Colette reached for him.

Marc groaned and lifted himself above her.

"I knew you would be like this," she said exultantly while they moved together. "Such a man," she whispered, her hands roaming his muscular back. As Marc groaned and shuddered in release she cried out once, and then was silent.

He remained within her, knowing that in a few moments he would be ready again. Tonight a desperate hunger would be satisfied. It was almost like being with Jenny. Almost.

When he woke up late the next morning Colette had already left for a sitting. Along with the note she had left him a roll and some coffee on the stove. He ate the still-warm roll and sputtered over the coffee—nothing compared to the strong, vigorous New Orleans brew he'd shared so often with Jenny—and left, knowing he would never see Colette again. Under a warm early October sun he walked through the winding streets of Montmartre, the beauty of the morning heightening his homesickness. He walked for hours, contemplating his future.

If he returned to New Orleans, his parents would insist he finish college and go into the store. He shuddered at the thought of being sucked into the family business. No, he couldn't go home. He would stay in Paris. Not even Jenny could draw him back to New Orleans.

If she truly loved me, she would have married me and come to Paris. Here is where I belong. Here is where I can learn what I need to know. If it takes the rest of my life, I'll become an artist who'll live forever in the museums of the world.

Every morning, Jenny looked for a letter from Marc, but none came. It began to seem as if she'd never even been part of his life.

She buried herself in her work, badgering mama to let her place a small ad in the *Times-Picayune* announcing their line of handmade lingerie and christening gowns. Mrs. Straus went through her usual squawking and finally gave in, never guessing that the amount Jennie quoted was one quarter of the actual cost. Jennie had siphoned off small amounts for weeks in order to pay for the ad and she felt only the slightest guilt about it. Once the ad appeared fine carriages began lining up outside the shop.

Jenny had made the shop her whole life, telling herself to forget Marc. Clearly, he had forgotten her.

Six weeks after Marc had left New Orleans, Nicole Goldman came into the shop with an order from her mother. For Jenny it was like seeing Marc again—the same dark hair and eyes, the beautifully sculptured features and slender build, though Nicole was petite and Marc was tall.

Instantly Jenny knew that she wanted to become Nicole's friend and Nicole, too, was drawn to Jenny's warmth and energy, thrilled to have a friend whose life was so different from her own.

"Jenny, you wouldn't believe it. Mama and papa have cut Marc out of their lives—at least, they pretend to. But I've gotten letters from him. Poor fellow—he's having such a hard time in Paris."

Bored with the social scene in New Orleans—the upper echelons were closed to Jews—Nicky came often to the shop. She told Jenny of her secret dream to be named Queen of the Mardi Gras, but both of them knew that, though her family had the wealth and position to promote her, no Jewish daughter of New Orleans could ever win this title.

Jenny waited anxiously for a report of each new letter Nicky received from Marc. He was struggling to earn money to pay for studies and secretly Nicky was sending what she could. Much to her surprise, even her grandmother had refused to help.

"I don't know what it is, Jenny. Grandma has always been on Marc's side. I guess she's spoiled us shamelessly. But this time she's siding with mama and papa. She says that someday she wants to see Marc running the store." Nicky smiled. "Grandma worked side by side with grandpa to build the store into what it is today. She's not always happy with the way papa and Benedict run things—she thinks Marc is much smarter than the two of them put together. If she didn't want him home so badly, I'm sure she'd send him money. But this way they're all convinced Marc will come home in a few months."

Meanwhile, Jenny was building up a steady clientele. Profits were high enough to impress even her mother, though she would have died before she admitted it. But Jenny could tell she was pleased when, at the end of each week, they went over the expenses and receipts. Now at least she couldn't complain that the family would have to ask for charity.

Just when things seemed to be going smoothly, word reached Jenny that Daniel was secretly taking the tips he received from deliveries both to Storyville and to the Garden District to bet on the races. But with the way the business was expanding she couldn't afford to fire him, so she just gave him a scolding. She didn't tell her mother— mama would never believe her son would stoop to gambling.

Desperate for help in the shop, she talked her mother and Evvie into helping out at the cashbox for two hours every day during the busiest selling period. She herself worked endless hours, and she never received one word of encouragement or praise from her mother.

Instead, Mrs. Straus was busy trying to get Jennie to accept the attentions of Emmanuel Adler, who had moved to New Orleans from Phoenix and was to become a partner in Herman's store. Mannie and Herman had lived in the same small town in Germany before their families came to America on the same ship twenty years ago, when Mannie was eight.

"Jenny, why *are* you so stubborn? Mannie has no family anymore—he wants a home of his own. He's tired of living in cheap boardinghouses. He'll make you a good husband."

"I don't want to get married. I have the shop to run."

"Nonsense. Sophie wants us to come to supper Sunday night. Mannie will be there—you'll see he's a fine young man. Imagine, a young girl wanting to spend the rest of her life alone!"

"I won't have time to go to Sophie's—I have to change the windows on Sunday nights."

"You'll make time. You can leave the shop for two hours on a Sunday night. How many times do you have to change the windows?"

At Sophie's flat on Sunday night, while the *tsimmis* simmered on the stove, Herman and his friend sat in the tiny Victorian parlor playing pinochle. Jenny gritted her teeth in distaste as the squat, round-faced guest—dark hair shiny with pomade and belly already threatening to hang over his belt—jumped to his feet with a broad smile.

"Mama, you've met Mannie," Herman said expansively. "And Evvie. Now, Mannie, you'll meet the rest of the family. Danny—" he waved a hand at his brother-in-law. "And Jenny, who runs the store." The condescension in his voice brought fire to Jenny's eyes. How dare he! Her store was doing better than his. Even Sophie said so.

"Herman, you didn't tell me Jenny was a beauty." Mannie stuck out his hand, the fingers short and hairy. Jenny thought of Marc's large, graceful hands.

She hardly spoke through the meal. She knew that in mama's eyes Mannie was "a good business man like

Herman." She knew, too, through occasional remarks from Sophie, that there had been some fighting between Herman and Mannie—mama probably meant to settle that by bringing Mannie into *their* store.

After dinner, over coffee, mama invited Mannie to supper three nights later. Jenny was stunned. Mama, who never invited *anybody* into the house, who was always saying it was enough to talk to people in the street or from the piazza! If mama was so anxious to have Mannie for a son-in-law, then let Evvie marry him. What did it matter that Evvie had a slight limp? She was so pretty—like a cameo, Nicky had once said. She would probably lose her shyness once she was out from under the glare of mama's scrutiny. Mama seemed to assume that Evvie would be her lifetime companion, but perhaps with a husband Evvie could be an entirely different person.

But Mannie made it clear it was Jenny he wished to marry. Sophie and mama foiled her efforts to avoid him. Was Sophie so in love with being married that she wanted it for her too? Herman was already becoming a cantankerous old man—only his baby daughter, Carrie, seemed to make him happy.

Nicky visited Jenny in the store every day, avoiding the hours when mama and Evvie were there. She brought her books from the library, took her to the opera or the theater. Always, Marc came into their conversation.

Like Jenny's father, Mr. Goldman was interested in what was happening in the world. In her friendship with Nicky, Jenny found her own horizons expanding. Herman and Mannie seemed to be contemptuous of any sort of change. They even spoke of President Roosevelt with distaste.

"A rich man's son, a Harvard graduate," Herman jeered. "What does he know about being president? What does he know about storekeepers and workers and farmers? He don't deserve to be in the White House!"

But according to Nicky, her father admired Theodore Roosevelt even though he was a lifelong Democrat.

"Papa says Roosevelt is only a Republican because he knew that was the way to win in politics. But he also says Roosevelt means to bring about wonderful reforms for the country. Look how he's gone after the 'beef trusts.' And papa says it's only a beginning."

Secretly Jenny and Nicky attended meetings on women's suffrage, telling their mothers that they were taking ping-pong lessons—the new craze that was sweeping the country. Already in four states women were allowed to vote.

"Wyoming gave women the right to vote way back in 1869," Jenny said. "Why must Louisiana be so backward?"

One rainy October morning Marc woke up and realized that today marked his first year in Paris. He squinted at the peeling paint on the ceiling. What had he accomplished? He was surviving, little more. He had no money to pursue the study of his craft and he spent so much of his time chasing after small jobs to pay his room and board that he had little time left for painting.

Part of it was the mood of the times. This was a period in Paris when only the traditional artist was accepted and Marc was anything but traditional—he wanted to explore new avenues, initiate innovative styles. He had to admit that if it were not for Simone—who invited him for dinner or lunch at her masterpiece of a house on Rue de Marignam at least once a week—he would be struggling to eat.

From Nicky's letters he knew the family was waiting for him to admit defeat and come home. She wrote that all anger was forgotten, that he would be welcomed with open arms. And if he went home, he would marry Jenny—no matter what mama and papa said. He didn't even consider the possibility that Jenny may have found someone else.

He got up to make a cup of coffee. Only New Orleanians knew how to brew the real stuff, he thought nostalgically. As he dressed he remembered that today was Simone's birthday. Tonight she was giving a small dinner party at Maxim's—with its lush red velvet divans and mirrored walls—to celebrate. He was to be her escort.

It seemed incredible to him that Simone—the Countess Simone de Champlain—believed in his talents. Like all wealthy Parisian women, she had her "day" each week, between five and seven, when she entertained. Imperious but charming, she was trying to acquire a salon. He was beginning to realize how important this could be to his career.

As she had requested, Marc arrived at Simone's house well before the party. Her houseman escorted him to her small but elegant sitting room.

A few minutes later, Simone floated into the sitting room.

"Marc, how good to see you. God, I loathe birthdays." Tall and lovely, she stood before him in an ivory velvet creation edged with sable, designed by Jacques Doucet. "They make me feel so old."

"You'll never be old, Simone."

She laughed. "You're very kind, my love—even if you are a bit of a liar. By the way, *you're* looking very handsome tonight—not unlike the man in the de Roszke cigarette advertisements. Though, of course, it does make me feel just a bit decadent to be seen on your arm. I'm old enough to be your mother."

"I think of a mother in an entirely different mold. Someone slightly plump and unfashionably gowned and always urging me to eat." He refrained from admitting that his own mother was still slender and exquisitely dressed.

"Marc, I have something I'd like to discuss with you."

"Yes?"

"I want to talk about something I've been thinking about for weeks. I'm bored with my life as it is . . . the endless parties and shallow laughter. But unfortunately I have no special talents. So, I've decided that I'd like to devote myself to helping you become the important artist you should be." She spoke quickly, holding up a slender hand in a command for silence. "I'd like to see you studying with the finest masters. I'd like to care for your needs so that you can devote yourself entirely to painting." Marc stared in disbelief. Simone wanted to become his patroness? To subsidize him so that he could no nothing but study and paint? "But if I do this," she said with a wry smile, "everyone will believe we're lovers. I'm too proud to have people gossip about me, Marc. So what I'm offering you is marriage."

For a moment Marc simply stared.

"Simone, I—"

"You must not make a decision at this moment. If you decide to accept my offer, I will expect you to be faithful to me. I won't have people laughing at me behind my back."

"I—I never suspected you would do me such an honor."

"Well, we shall see. It is your decision." She smiled. "Now, there'll be no more talk about this tonight. In three or four days I'll expect you to come to me with your answer. I don't mind confessing it, Marc—I *would* adore showing off such a handsome young husband."

Marc was shocked. He knew that many older women in Paris took young lovers and, on occasion, young husbands. But Simone had never given any sign that she meant for theirs to be a romantic relationship.

Once they were settled in her carriage Simone took his arm and said, "I'm tired of living alone, darling. Tired of living without a purpose. By now you must know that I enjoy your company. With you my life would acquire new excitement."

The birthday dinner at Maxim's was a glamorous affair. Like most Frenchwomen, Simone made no secret of her age—only in private did she bemoan the years. The dinner was superb, the champagne the finest. Marc tried to relax, but his mind still whirled from Simone's proposal.

Late that night, after he had taken her back to her flat, he roamed the streets. If he declined the proposal their relationship would be over. Once again he'd be a lonely American in Paris, fighting to survive.

He paused before the huge Galeries Lafayette, remembering the day he stood here with his grandmother. In the silent, deserted street he could hear her voice.

"Marc, instead of gadding about Europe, you should have worked here this summer. Your father could have arranged it. It would have been a real education in running a store."

He couldn't go back to New Orleans. Painting was his dream—and Paris the only place to pursue it. Simone was right.

I'll marry her. I'll study with the best teachers; paint every possible minute. I'll become the artist we both wish me to be. Simone will be my salvation.

CHAPTER
FOUR

W ITH THE APPROACH of Hanukkah in 1903 Jenny encouraged mama to be extravagant in shopping for her grandchildren. Karl was three, Carrie—the image of Jenny—almost a year.

Jenny treasured her growing friendship with Nicky, who was teaching her about a whole new way of life—theater, art, fashion . . . Before papa died, she used to go twice a year to a play at the lovely cream-and-gold decorated Crescent Theater, always sitting in the cheapest seats. For fifteen cents, papa would say indulgently, let them enjoy themselves. Mama never went—she said all those stairs were too much for Evvie to climb.

Nicky regularly insisted that Jenny be her guest at the magnificent French Opera House on the fashionable Tuesday or Saturday nights, where they sat in the boxes with ladies and gentlemen in full evening dress—or at the elegant Tulane Theater. Jenny looked stunning in a gown she had copied from a Paris model.

Two days before the first night of Hanukkah Nicky burst into the store, her face glowing with excitement. She stood by impatiently while Jenny finished with a dawdling customer.

"Jenny, you'll never guess what's happened. I can't believe it. Nothing so fascinating has ever happened in this family."

"What is it?"

"Marc has just been married! To a countess! Even mama's impressed. Of course, the countess is lots older than

Marc. He says she's forty-one. But she's beautiful and terribly rich. And a *countess*, Jennie . . . I can't wait for them to visit—Marc says that they'll live in Paris."

Now Jenny realized that all this time she had been harboring a hope that one day Marc would come back to her.

She swallowed, trying to hold back the tears. So . . . her hope had been a foolish one. Marc had married a forty-one-year-old countess. He had forgotten her.

Jenny decided to stop battling mama's campaign to marry her off to Mannie and tried to think about his good points. He was kind to mama and to Sophie's children. Sometimes he was almost humble. Maybe she *could* grow accustomed to his abrasive manner, his fat, greasy looks.

On the first Friday in January Mannie came to supper at the Straus house along with Sophie and Herman and their children. While she helped Evvie serve the dessert, Jenny mentioned—at mama's instigation—the new play at the Crescent Theater.

"You want to see it?" Mannie asked eagerly. "I'll take you. Tonight."

All eyes turned to Jenny.

"I—I'd like that very much."

Mannie helped her into her coat and Mrs. Straus, beaming, pushed them out the door.

On the streetcar, Mannie launched into a monologue about his impoverished childhood in a small town in Germany.

"Here in America it's different," he said. "A man can make a living for his wife and his family. He can be a real *mensch*."

Later, sitting in the darkened theater, she barely heard what was being said on stage. The actors were shadows. During the third act Mannie reached cautiously for her hand, his clammy fingers encircling hers.

Maybe she *should* marry Mannie Adler. He would be a good provider. Mama wouldn't have to worry that she would end up an old maid. Mannie and Herman were friends—if Herman was good enough for Sophie, who was she to look down on Mannie?

As they left the theater, Jenny sensed that he, too, was thinking about their future together. From the way he had been acting, she had a feeling he'd already talked to mama about it.

When they approached the door to the Straus flat, he suddenly stopped and grabbed her hand.

"Jenny, I talked already to your mother—like in the old country I have respect for the parents. She agreed I should ask you to marry me. I'm not a rich man, but I can support a wife." He paused. "Well?"

Jenny hesitated. If she married Mannie maybe she could forget Marc. But first she had to take care of the family until Danny was old enough to take over.

"Mannie, there's something you have to understand. I think we should talk about this together with mama."

"Whatever is right for your family and you is all right with me, Jenny," he said magnanimously. "We'll talk."

"I've got fresh coffee ready," Mrs. Straus said as she opened the door. "Was the play good?"

"It was a fine play," Mannie said. "We both enjoyed it."

Jenny started to say she thought it was a silly play, but stopped herself. Over coffee she told Mannie that she planned to run the store until Danny was old enough to take over. Her mother looked uncomfortable but remained silent.

Mannie shrugged. "If you can handle it, fine."

Mama cleared her throat.

"Sophie says you two should eat with them for a while after you're married. That way you won't have to worry about running home from the store to cook supper."

"I—I suppose we'll delay starting a family for a few years," Jenny said, blushing.

Mrs. Straus smiled. "Come now, you're barely eighteen. There's plenty of time to start a family."

"So." Mannie looked straight at his future mother-in-law—not his bride-to-be. "When can we have the wedding? Living alone in a boardinghouse is no life for a man."

Jenny insisted on a date when she knew Nicky would be visiting in Palm Beach with her grandmother—she was embarrassed to have Nicky meet her new husband.

* * *

The task of telling Jenny about her wedding night went to Sophie. Actually, it was unnecessary—Nicky and Jenny had already discussed the subject in detail—with Nicky being the most candid.

"You can't grow up in New Orleans without knowing about Storyville and what happens there, Jenny. And if it's so much fun for the man, why shouldn't it be for the woman?"

Jenny told herself that her wedding night would be beautiful. Once they were married, Mannie would be different. At last she would be able to put Marc out of her mind forever.

Early in January, on a cold gray Sunday afternoon, Jenny and Mannie were married by the rabbi of the Orthodox synagogue in the parlor of the Strauses' new flat. Only the family attended. Jenny wore Sophie's wedding dress, shortened and taken in. When Mannie kissed her at the conclusion of the ceremony, she felt only the slight brush of wet lips.

Sophie and mama had been cooking for three days in preparation for the wedding supper. There was *gefilte* fish, a rich chicken soup with noodles, streaming plates of *tafelspitz*—boiled beef with vegetables, *nockerin*—wonderful Viennese dumplings served with a delicious sauce, apple strudel, and *palatschkinken*—feather-like sugared pancakes. And of course strong black coffee topped with freshly whipped cream.

Tonight mama was happy. She had married off two daughters. For once, Jenny thought wryly, *she* was responsible for mama's happiness.

As she sat silently next to Mannie at the table she tried to accept the fact that she was now Mrs. Emmanuel Adler. She would never be Mrs. Marc Goldman. In a little while Mannie would take her off to the tiny flat he had rented and furnished for them.

Up until now she had been too distracted by her anger at Marc to think about the consummation of her marriage. Now, she was nervous.

To her relief, Mannie seemed in no hurry to go to the marriage bed either, content instead to sit around the table and talk to Herman about the old days in Germany. At last he stood up, trying to appear casual and confident, and they said their good-byes.

They walked the short distance to their new home in strained silence, Jenny distracted by thoughts of how different tonight would be if she had married Marc.

Mannie proudly escorted her through the three tiny rooms of their flat, lighting a kerosene lamp in each and complaining about the high cost of kerosene. She gritted her teeth as he pointed out the cost of each piece of furniture. Why did he feel compelled to tell her the price of everything? Suddenly she felt trapped, a character in one of those melodramas at the Crescent Theater. *How had she let this happen?*

"It's late," he said, staring at the huge brass bed. "We both have to be up early in the morning."

"I'll wash up and be ready in a minute," she said, relieved that mama had arranged for her clothes to be brought over this morning—her nightgown and negligee were in the bottom of the dresser.

Mannie coughed.

"I think I'll have a cup of coffee before I go to sleep." He reached for the doorknob. "It don't matter that it's been sitting since breakfast."

He closed the door behind him. Jenny felt hot color rise in her throat as she walked into the tiny bathroom off the bedroom. Mannie's shaving equipment sat on a wooden shelf beside a discolored mirror. A dirty bar of soap was on the edge of the washbasin.

Jenny rinsed off the soap, washed and dried her hands and face, and then went back into the bedroom to change. She wanted to be in her nightgown and in bed when Mannie came in. The white silk and lace gown was cut indecorously low, providing a dangerous display of her high, full breasts. It embarrassed her. She tried to flatten the nipples that rose beneath the soft lace.

She placed the negligee across the foot of the bed and slid beneath the light blanket. Should she turn out the light? The door opened and Mannie walked into the room. Her throat went dry as he stared at her in the soft lamplight.

"What in the hell are you wearing?"

"My nightgown."

"Whores wear nightgowns like that! Not a wife! In fancy brothels women dress like that!" A vein throbbed in his forehead. "When you come to bed dressed like a wife, then I'll come to you."

He slammed the door behind him. Shocked, Jenny lay absolutely still. She sold these nightgowns to the high-class brothels, yes; but she sold them, also, to the fine ladies in the Garden District. Even Nicky wore them.

She heard Mannie fling himself on the narrow horsehair sofa in the sitting room. Clearly he meant to sleep there tonight. She turned off the lamp and pulled the covers around her shoulders. She couldn't talk about tonight to anybody—not even Nicky.

In the morning she was dressed and drinking coffee by the kitchen sink when Mannie came into the room. He avoided her gaze as he fixed himself a cup of coffee.

"Mannie, would you like some breakfast before you go?"

He glared at her.

"Tomorrow you'll make breakfast. Go to the store now."

The day dragged interminably. As mama suggested, she and Mannie were to eat at Sophie and Herman's every night. The men had made the financial arrangements and Sophie said she didn't mind cooking for two more.

Immediately after supper Jenny and Mannie left for their own flat. While Mannie helped himself to another cup of stale coffee, Jenny washed and changed into a flannel nightgown that covered her from her chin to her toes. In bed she reached to turn out the lamp.

Mannie didn't bother to knock. He walked into the bedroom, stood beside the bed and changed into a nightshirt. She stiffened as he lifted up the blankets and slid beneath them. A cold foot kicked her. A hand fumbled at her breasts. He didn't even try to kiss her.

"Pull up your gown."

She obeyed.

He lifted himself above her, heavy and perspiring despite the coolness of the night. She felt a growing hardness against her small flat belly while his hands moved roughly over her breasts. She closed her eyes and waited.

He reached down toward her thighs.

"Jenny, relax. It won't hurt."

She cried out once in pain as he entered her, then lay motionless while he began thrusting. At last he grunted in satisfaction and rolled over on his back. He got up and went into the bathroom, not bothering to close the door.

Jenny reached to pull down her nightgown and turned on her side. When he returned to the bed, she pretended to be asleep. Within a few moments Mannie was snoring.

She lay wide awake at the edge of the bed. Obviously, in Mannie's mind a wife submitted to a man only to become pregnant. She wasn't to enjoy it. It didn't even seem that *he* enjoyed it.

She realized now that this was not the time to become pregnant—not with the store and family responsibilities to consider. Mama had mentioned that there were ways to avoid having babies, but she hadn't elaborated. Tomorrow, when Josie from Storyville came into the shop, she would ask her how she could make sure she didn't become pregnant. A fancy madam would be wise about such a problem.

In the weeks that followed Jenny came to know a side of Mannie he had never shown before. He was overbearingly puritanical, given to bursts of temper within the privacy of their flat. He was unhappy at being Herman's partner, resentful—though he understood it was necessary—that she worked to help support her family. He considered himself a put-upon husband.

Every time Mannie had a fight with Herman Jenny knew he would come home and find fault with her. On the night of the first Seder, which they shared at Sophie's flat, Mannie was bad-mouthing Herman before they were even out of the house.

"And while we're talking about your family," he said,

"there's more. I hear that brother of yours is enjoying life in high style."

"What do you mean?"

"He's the darling of Storyville. You send him over there with deliveries, and the girls take him on three at a time."

Jenny winced at his crudeness. "How do you know? I don't believe it." But aware of Danny's charm, remembering some of Josie's remarks about "that handsome young brother of yours," she wondered.

"Men talk, Jenny. Some of the richest men in the city wish they were in his shoes. What would cost them a fortune Danny gets for nothing. No wonder he complains he's too tired to do his homework for school after he makes deliveries at Storyville."

"Then I'll make arrangements," Jenny said. Mama would never let her hear the end of it if she found out.

It didn't take Jenny long to figure out why Mannie knew that Danny was playing with the whores in Storyville. That's where *he* went the nights he talked about going back to the store "to check on the inventory."

It was only to Nicky that Jenny confided her disillusionment with her marriage. Nicky had accepted the proposal of an earnest young lawyer who "happens to be Jewish"— important to her grandmother but not her parents.

"I've known Armand for a long time, but I *never* expected him to ask me to marry him. The Lazars are one of the oldest and richest families in New Orleans, which of course pleases mama no end. Armand is their only child. Mama's annoyed that we're having such a short engagement; but that's so we can take six weeks to go to Europe for our honeymoon, when Armand won't be tied up in court."

Jenny had never once heard Nicky even mention Armand Lazar.

"Nicky, are you in love with him?"

"Oh no. I hardly know him. We've seen each other at parties, and I've flirted with him the way I flirt with every good-looking man at a party." She shrugged. "But Armand is handsome and charming and I'd love to be a young matron with a beautiful house of my own."

"There are other sides to being married, you know."

"You mean going to bed with him. Well, I won't mind that, though I'd never admit it to mama." She paused. "You know, Jennie, you shouldn't be upset that Mannie goes to brothels. It's just a man's way. I'm sure papa visits Storyville—but only the best houses, of course. Mama doesn't want to know about it. She says it doesn't concern her."

"I don't feel that way," Jenny said. "If a woman has to be faithful, why should it be different for a man?"

Jenny brought in an extra seamstress to supply lovely nightwear for Nicky's trousseau. She was pleased and touched that Nicky planned to invite Mannie and her to the wedding in spite of what she suspected would be objections from both families—ordinarily the fine families of New Orleans did not invite small storekeepers to their social events.

Although the wedding had to be arranged with a haste Nicky's mother deplored, it was one of the social triumphs of the year. The ceremony was performed at the beautiful Temple Sinai. The air was heavy with the scent of roses and jasmine. Though mid-May, the summer heat seemed to have let up for the day.

Mannie was appalled at the Reform services of the temple—conducted in English and with the sexes not separated as in the Orthodox synagogues.

"It's hardly Jewish at all," he muttered to Jenny in the middle of the ceremony. "I'll bet they serve pork at the wedding supper."

"Mannie, hush—" He was constantly embarrassing her. She had even been forced to enlist mama's help in persuading him to dress appropriately for the ceremony. Mama, of course, had been agreeable to everything, thrilled to be invited to such an elegant affair.

She decided to try to ignore Mannie. Nicky was a beautiful bride, her white satin gown was trimmed with Valenciennes lace, her train attached to a small cap of seed pearls.

She had been so proud when Nicky had insisted she come

to the house yesterday to see and approve the lovely gray flannel day suit, trimmed with green velvet buttons and mink collar, that she would wear on the train to New York.

At the lavish wedding banquet Jenny tried to hide her discomfort over Mannie's crude table manners. She was relieved when, before the dancing began, he insisted that they leave.

Maybe mama could get Mannie to behave. He seemed to respect her. When *she* had talked about the clothes he would need for Nicky's wedding, he only yelled at her, accusing her of being snooty. It was mama who had convinced him to borrow a suit from the stock in the store. But as it turned out Mannie solved her problem for her.

"Next time you go somewhere with your fancy friends, Jenny, go without me. I don't need them."

A few months after the wedding Jenny realized that her period was late. So much for Josie's advice. With Nicky gone she told Evvie, who was delighted at the prospect of yet another niece or nephew. Sophie was due to deliver any day.

"Why haven't you told mama, Jenny? She'll be so pleased."

Jenny laughed. "I haven't even told Mannie."

She had tried to put out of her mind the complications a pregnancy would bring into her life. But she was young and strong—she would be able to remain in the store almost until delivery. Mama and Evvie would have to put themselves out and fill in until she could come back. With what the business was earning she could afford a girl to help with the baby.

She was surprised at how happy she was to be carrying Mannie's child. Even though she secretly wished it was Marc's, she knew she would love this baby. If only papa were alive to enjoy his new grandchild.

Mannie was overjoyed. He walked around with a swagger, a smug smile on his face—and now it didn't bother him that Herman boasted constantly about his children; in a few months he, too, would be a father. He no longer bothered to reach for Jenny at night—apparently he felt that his mission had been accomplished.

Mama was thrilled, but Jenny knew that Sophie's children would always come first.

She told herself the baby would make her marriage worthwhile. Herman had insisted his children be named first for his mother and father and now the latest child—another boy—had been named for his brother. Jenny took special pleasure in the knowledge that her son would bear papa's name.

CHAPTER
FIVE

Marc waited impatiently at the busy Gâre Saint Lazare for the arrival of his sister and brother-in-law. While he continued to write regularly to Nicky, he had sensed a reticence in her since his marriage to Simone. Did she disapprove of his marrying a foreigner? Or was it the difference in their ages? It couldn't be that Simone wasn't Jewish—that would upset only his grandmother.

His face softened as he thought about Grandma Goldman. She was always on his side—and Nicky's—in any family battle. His marriage to a *shiksa*—even a countess—must have been a blow to her. She must realize, too, that he would never present her with a great-grandchild.

So he had disappointed Grandma twice. Once in rejecting the store and now in his marriage. But he had chosen the life that was right for him. She would understand that.

Marc reached into his vest pocket for his watch. As usual he had arrived at the station early. The Orient Express from Vienna was not scheduled to arrive for another twelve minutes. She was prompt by nature. Like Jenny . . .

He went to a kiosk and bought a newspaper. The war between Japan and Russia was going badly for the Russians. The Russian people didn't want to fight a war—rumors were rampant about a revolution in St. Petersburg.

Tossing aside the newspaper, Marc considered the changes in his life in these few months of marriage. Never before had he worked so hard or so well. He was impatient to make up for what he considered the wasted four years

46

behind him. Now he was studying under a teacher known to be one of the finest in the world.

Before he had met Simone her life had been ruled by the Parisian social calendar. From mid-December till early spring, along with the rest of French society, she had enjoyed the Little Season in Paris. In early spring she traveled to Cannes or Monte Carlo, returning to Paris for the Season, which began after Easter. In the summer she had gone to seashore resorts—either Deauville or Dinard. In the fall there were endless house parties.

Now Simone stayed with him in Paris most of the year, even during the hot summer, though occasionally they spent weekends at her white marble-trimmed three-story red brick house, surrounded by expansive gardens and towering trees on a fifty-acre estate. Sometimes she made brief trips alone, refusing to let him interrupt his studies. Since their quiet civil marriage she had made it clear that her only goal in life was to see him become a successful artist. Slowly she was creating a salon in their Paris home so that he could meet those who would be important to his career.

As much as he enjoyed Paris—he often felt an overwhelming nostalgia for home. For Jenny.

But he could not have her *and* his painting. He had made his choice.

"Marc!" Nicky's jubilant voice startled him. "Marc, how wonderful to see you!" She kissed him. "Well! You haven't changed at all."

He laughed. "What did you expect?"

"You beat me every time we played chess at the club, remember?" Armand said, extending his hand. "Your concentration was astonishing."

"Yes, I do, as a matter of fact," Marc said. "But as I recall you're quite a player yourself. Tell me your plans. Paris is hot and miserable already, but I assume you'll want to see the city. Simone and I would love it if you would come to the country house for the weekend."

Marc drove Nicky to the Hotel du Rhin on the Plâce Vendome—where they had a suite reserved—while Armand followed in a carriage with their luggage. Nicky squealed in delight as Marc handled the narrow, curving roads. While she told Marc about the new Olds she and Armand planned to buy, Marc could still feel the distance between them. It puzzled him.

"Nicky, you must understand that Simone is a wonderful woman."

"I'm sure she is." Nicky hesitated. "It's just that—well, we never expected you to marry a Frenchwoman—and somebody only a few years younger than mama." She paused. "But Jenny said I mustn't make judgments until I meet her."

Marc froze.

"Jenny?" *His* Jenny?

"My very best friend back home. You wouldn't know her. Jenny Straus."

His hands clenched the wheel.

"How do you know Jenny Straus?"

"Mama sent me to pick up a package at her shop—" Nicky stared at him curiously. "So you know Jenny. Why didn't she tell me? Why did she always let me go on talking about you without saying a word?"

"Maybe she wanted to forget she ever knew me." *Just when he thought he had himself in control Nicky came to Paris to talk about Jenny.*

"What?"

"One day that summer before I came to Paris, mama sent me to Jenny's shop. We began seeing each other. I asked her to marry me and come to Paris with me. She said she couldn't leave her family—they needed her. I needed her, too. We loved each other. But Jenny chose to stay with her family."

Nicky sat in silence for a few moments.

"Oh Marc, I'm so sorry. What a terrible choice to have to make. Poor Jenny."

"What about me?" he said quietly. "She was my whole life."

"No," Nicky said gently. "Painting was your life." There was a long pause.

"How is she?"

"She's married. Since January. Not long after I babbled

about your marrying a countess. Oh Marc, what a horrible mess!"

"Is she happy?"

"No. At least, not from what she tells me. Her husband is a stupid boor. She just married him to satisfy her mother. She still runs the shop, though. That makes her happy."

"So you'll go on being her friend?"

Nicky looked amazed.

"Of course. Jenny and I will always be best friends."

"Will you take her a small gift from me? It's just something I'd like her to have."

"Sure. What is it?"

"A painting of a live oak tree in the city park." His face was taut. "She'll understand."

Nicky, Armand, Marc and Simone ate dinner together that first night in Paris. Aware that Nicky and Armand were on their honeymoon Simone then insisted that she and Marc not intrude. The two couples would be together for three days at the country house. Only when Nicky telephoned and asked for advice about the Paris shops did Simone arrange for the four of them to have lunch at the fashionable Restaurant Julien, after which she personally escorted Nicky to the shops.

Marc consoled himself with the knowledge that Nicky admired and respected Simone. But Nicky *loved* Jenny like a sister—Jenny, who had so very nearly become her sister-in-law.

By the time Nicky returned to New Orleans, Jenny was visibly pregnant. Nicky hugged her.

"Jenny, you didn't tell me!"

Jenny laughed.

"When you left, I didn't know yet. I should have suspected, but I was so sure it wouldn't happen."

"I hope Josie does better by her girls." Nicky's face grew serious. "Are you happy?"

Jenny hesitated.

"Oh, Nicky, it's my baby, of course I'll love it. It's just that—I didn't expect it to happen so fast." Already Mannie and mama were conspiring to get her out of the store. Mannie was having ugly battles with Herman. Sophie was upset. But mama *couldn't* push Mannie into the store with her—it would be bad for business. Mannie didn't know how to handle the aristocratic ladies who had become the mainstay of her business.

"Jenny—" Nicky drew her into her arms. "I know about Marc and you. He told me."

Jenny stood immobile.

"What did he say?"

"That you and he had been in love. That he'd wanted to marry you—"

"But he wouldn't wait two years! Why didn't he understand that I couldn't walk out on my family? Mama and Evvie couldn't support themselves. Danny was still in school—"

"Marc never did have much patience," Nicky said. She reached inside her bag and brought out the rolled-up canvas. "He asked me to give you this."

Jenny unrolled the canvas, stared long at the sturdy oak embedded in moss. Their tree—where Marc first kissed her.

"Oh Nicky, thank you," she said. "It's lovely. I'll have it framed and hang it here in the shop. Is he happy with his wife?"

"Simone is a lovely, charming woman," Nicky said carefully. "Marc's not in love with her, but he has a special fondness for her. And she's terribly excited about his paintings."

When Jenny looked up there were tears in her eyes.

"Then it's good for him. Someday Marc will be a famous artist, Nicky. You'll see."

Because of the problems with Herman, Jenny and Mannie now went to Mrs. Straus's house for supper. Evvie insisted it was just as easy to cook for five as three. A woman came to the flat to clean twice a week and Evvie did the cooking, so mama was free to spend most of her days sitting on the piazza.

Drenched in perspiration as she climbed the stairs to her mother's flat, Jenny heard her mother and Mannie talking,

Mannie's voice agitated, mama's soothing. She tensed, anticipating trouble, and paused on the landing to catch her breath.

The hours in the store were long, but she sat whenever it was possible. The awful sleepiness of her first three months was at last fading and mercifully she had been spared the morning sickness that had paralyzed Sophie.

She knocked on the door. Abruptly, the conversation inside stopped. Mannie opened the door, frowning.

"You're early."

"My usual time." Jenny walked to the sofa, the back and arms covered with doilies mama had crocheted. Evvie was in the kitchen. Danny was not yet home from looking for work. "Did you see the children today, mama?"

"What a question. Of course. I see them everyday. They're fine, though Sophie says she thinks already Freddie is teething. It's not enough to have to put up with this heat," she said, reaching for her fan.

"You look tired, Jenny," Mannie said shortly.

"No more than usual." She turned to her mother. "I was talking to a man about those new electric fans that people are putting in their ceilings. I think you wouldn't feel the heat so much if you had one in the kitchen."

"Who can afford that?"

"*You* can." She herself took no money from the profits of the store, though Mannie often made nasty remarks about her not sharing in the proceeds. In truth, she resented being dependent on Mannie, but how could she ask mama to pay her a salary? "A fan could last twenty years."

She caught a guarded exchange between her mother and Mannie.

"This is not a time for new expenses," Mrs. Straus said firmly. "How much longer can you stay in the store? Never mind. Mannie and I think that in another four weeks it's time for you to stay at home and wait for the baby. Mannie will take over. He and I will have a partnership. Of course this means we'll all have to do with less—" she sighed, "but it's madness for you to go on working in the store."

"Mama, I can run the store until two weeks before the baby comes." So, *this* was what mama and Mannie had been plotting. "It's not like I'm working for strangers. When I'm tired, I sit down—"

"No. It's a disgrace to see a woman big with child working in a store. It—it's unladylike." She glared at Mannie and he rose awkwardly to his feet.

"It's so hot, I'll go down to the store to buy ice cream to go with supper."

Jenny was on her feet before Mannie was out the door. "Mama, I have to be in the store. I don't care what you two have decided. Mannie can't run it."

"Don't be ridiculous. You belong at home waiting for the baby."

"It's not disgraceful to be pregnant."

"It's advertising to the world what happened between you and your husband!" Mrs. Straus said blushing. "It's indecent to have strange men see you looking like that."

"But I'm needed in the store."

"Mannie will run it. He's not a business man?"

"Mannie runs a store with Herman. Mama, please . . . Mannie wouldn't know how to handle my customers. He'd kill the business."

"Sophie is having a terrible time because of the fights between Mannie and Herman. I want Mannie to take over. He and I will share the profits. With the business doing so well, we'll manage for the two families."

"Mama—"

"I've heard enough, Jenny. The store belongs to me. I make the decisions. In four weeks Mannie takes over. You'll stay home where you belong."

CHAPTER
SIX

JENNY STAYED IN the shop until she was well into her fifth month—mostly on the pretext that she had to teach Mannie the business. Her mother understood that selling in a men's shop was different, that Mannie needed grooming. At the same time, with Mannie's support, Jenny brought Danny into the store. Danny seemed unable to find work anywhere else in New Orleans.

Her first morning at home Jenny knew she would have to keep busy so she threw herself into cleaning the tiny flat until every corner was immaculate. She hated housecleaning, and had even suggested hiring a girl to clean one day a week.

"Who do you think you are?" Mannie had sneered. "One of the rich Goldmans? What else have you got to do? You'll clean and cook and take care of the baby. That's what a wife's for."

Ensconced in what was now "my store," Mannie began taking every opportunity to criticize her. She began hearing regularly about how *his* mother had kept a model house.

"When mama cleaned," he would say, "you could eat off the floors. And every night in the week she put a good Jewish meal on the table. Always a plate of meat and potatoes. *Flanken, gefilte* fish, *borscht*, chopped liver, *chav*. Not this crazy New Orleans Jambalaya . . . Bouillabaisse, red beans and rice—all *goyisha* junk."

He looked at her distastefully. "*You should put on weight. What kind of milk can you give the baby when you're so skinny? Herman says Sophie's gained twenty pounds since they got married.''

"Mannie, I don't *want* to gain twenty pounds."

"American wives," he scowled as he climbed into bed. "All they care about is their looks."

Every day Jenny read the local papers—anything to escape the boredom—and as she learned about the presidential campaigns she became increasingly annoyed that women were still denied the vote. Mannie didn't even bother to vote, but of course he didn't think women should be allowed to. Still, she had decided that Theodore Roosevelt had made a fine president and should be re-elected. Mannie insisted all Republicans were rich men who thought only about the lining of their own pockets.

Two afternoons a week Jenny went to sit for an hour on the piazza with her mother and Evvie. But she looked forward the most to her visits with Nicky—either at her own flat or at Nicky's lovely new house in Garden District.

For days Nicky did nothing but reminisce about her honeymoon, recounting every detail of the glorious week they spent in Vienna. When Jenny tried to tell her mother about Nicky's experiences in the land of the Blue Danube, she was cut off. Jenny wondered often about her mother's family in Vienna—how sad for mama to be cut off forever from her family.

The eternal romantic, Nicky shared each of Marc's letters with Jenny. Since Nicky had learned Marc's and Jenny's secret, a precious bond had formed between the three of them.

When mama had insisted she stay out of the store, Jenny had brought Marc's painting of "their" tree to hang in the parlor. She told Mannie the painting was something she had picked up in the French Market—he complained about her wasting money on junk.

Jenny was worried about what was happening in the store, but Mannie brushed aside her questions.

"You worry about the house, I'll worry about the store."

Mrs. Straus, too, refused to discuss it. One late November Friday night when Jenny and Mannie and she went to her house for supper along with Sophie and Herman, Jenny cornered Danny while the two men were playing pinochle and mama and Sophie were helping Evvie in the kitchen.

"Danny, what's going on in the store? How's business?"

Danny looked around the room uneasily.

"Well—Mannie fired the two seamstresses."

Those two old ladies had been so grateful for the work. Jenny was shocked. Danny shrugged. "I don't know, Jenny. He said the handmade stuff wasn't moving anymore."

The "handmade stuff" represented eighty percent of the profits!

"What do you mean, it isn't moving?"

"The carriages with the ladies stopped coming. What I mean is . . . the store isn't selling anymore to Story-ville."

"What? How can Mannie do this? He's ruining the business! Danny, that's everything I built up!"

"Look, Jenny, it's not my fault. Please don't tell him I told you."

No wonder Mannie constantly whined about how much money he could give her for the table each week—he'd driven away most of the customers. Mama must know— why didn't she say something?

Now there really was reason to worry . . . Two fami-lies had to live off this store, and clearly Mannie was running it into the ground. She didn't know what to do. Every time she mentioned it to her mother, she was cut off. After Mrs. Straus let the cleaning woman go, she went to Evvie.

"Mama would kill me if she knew I told you this," Evvie said, "but Jenny, *I'm* getting worried. She's been dipping into her savings every week and there can't be much left now. What'll we do if she runs out?"

"It's going to be all right, Evvie," Jenny said, fire in her eyes. "Once the baby is born, I'll come back into the store. I'm not going to let Mannie ruin what I worked so hard to build up. Just don't say anything to mama. Somehow I'll work it out."

* * *

On an early December morning, only minutes after Mannie had left for the store, Jenny felt her first labor pain. Clutching her swollen belly, she vowed that for this child she would work miracles. She would go back into the store. She would make it as important as Maison Blanche.

She felt her water break as she walked through the bedroom into the bathroom. Should she change into a nightgown? But the baby probably wouldn't be born for hours. She would feel ridiculous walking around in a nightgown. She decided to change only her underclothes.

For a moment, Jenny thought of calling for mama, but then she remembered mama's feeling about childbirth. She went back to the sink and finished the breakfast dishes. The doctor had told her to send for him when the pains were four or five minutes apart. She knew that with a first baby there would be a long labor.

The next pain was fourteen minutes later. She decided that before the next one she would go downstairs and use the phone in the store on the corner to call Nicky.

She went downstairs, walking carefully down each step. A maid answered the phone.

"Miz Lazar still sleepin'. You want me to wake her up?"

"No. But as soon as she's awake, tell her that Mrs. Adler called. Tell her I said 'it's time.'"

Jenny went back to the flat, pausing halfway up the stairs as she felt another pain. Slowly she made her way inside the flat again and sat on the horsechair sofa. But she was too nervous to sit still . . .

She got up and went into the kitchen. Mannie would expect to eat. Yesterday she had bought meat and carrots and prunes, so she prepared the *tsimmis*, and put it up to simmer.

There was a sharp knock on the door. Awkwardly Jenny stood up, walked across the room and pulled it open. It was Nicky, breathless from racing up the stairs.

"Why didn't you tell Arlette to wake me?"

"Because there's no real rush yet, silly." But she was relieved that Nicky was here—if she'd had to send for Evvie mama would find out. "I've had a grand total of six pains."

Nicky sniffed at the air.

"What were you doing? It smells like a restaurant in here."

"I put up *tsimmis* for Mannie's dinner."

"Oh, Jenny," Nicky said. "You *are* something. If you were still in the store, you'd be selling between pains."

Nicky helped Jenny into her nightgown and settled her into the bed. The pains were coming faster now and she, too, was getting nervous.

"Maybe I should go down and phone the doctor, honey— it looks like this baby's getting ready—"

"Not yet," Jenny said. "Dr. Cohen told me to wait until they were four or five minutes apart."

Nicky tried to divert Jenny with stories about her grandmother, an irrepressible old lady whom Jenny had met twice and had instantly liked. After about an hour the pains were coming one after another. Jenny was pale, breathing deeply.

"Nicky," she said, "I think it's time to call Dr. Cohen."

At two minutes past four in the afternoon Jenny gave birth to a seven-pound son. Tears filled her eyes as the doctor placed him in her arms. Carefully she inspected the tiny red face.

"My little Leon. He's the image of papa."

For a few weeks Jenny was so entranced with the baby that she had no room in her mind for anything else. She did notice that Mannie and mama were upset and she knew that meant that something was wrong in the store—but whenever she asked about it, Mannie was surly and uncommunicative.

She decided to ask Josie what had happened. If she could call on Josie when patrons were not being received in Storyville . . . she asked Evvie to sit with the baby so that she and Nicky could go for a drive in the Lazars' new Olds.

"I spoke to mama this morning, Jenny," Nicky said as Jenny stepped into the car. "She said the ladies she knows stopped buying from the store because they felt uncomfortable ordering intimate apparel from a man." Nicky hesitated. "And I'm afraid Mannie doesn't exactly make the best impression."

Mama prided herself on being genteel—how could she let coarse and crude Mannie come into the store when she knew they were selling now to high-class ladies? Even if he was her husband—and Leon's father—mama should be able to see Mannie for what he was. But mama had been so anxious to marry off her daughters, she had shut her eyes to their husbands' shortcomings. "Nicky," Jenny said, "do you think we'll have trouble driving into Storyville?"

"Definitely not. Tourists go there all the time now. Even women." She smiled mischievously. "Not at night, of course."

Josie received them in the luxuriously furnished private sitting room of her three-storied mansion with magnificent stained-glass windows. The house was rumored to be the most expensively furnished brothel in America. At this hour the residents of Storyville—except for Josie, who supposedly slept no more than four hours a day—were silent.

Josie listened carefully to Jenny's questions.

"Sugar, I don't know what to tell you. That man in the store—" She paused. "Well, he's got no class. He acted like I was something unclean when I came in to order nightgowns for my girls. When I spend my money, I expect to be treated like a lady. And I'm not the only one from Storyville who stopped buying." Her eyes met Jenny's. "Anytime you're back in that store, I'll buy again."

"Thank you, Josie."

Jenny stood up, her jaw set. "I'll be back, I promise. I'll drop you a note and let you know when."

After supper, with the dishes done, Jenny told Mannie that she was coming back into the store.

"The hell you are! You'll stay home where you belong."

"No. I'll come into the store, where I belong." His insistence that a woman's place was in the home absolutely infuriated her. How dare he. This was the twentieth century. Women went out to work in stores and offices. How many men knew how to operate a typewriter?

"Mannie, we can't live on what the store's bringing in. You're selling and not replacing the stock—" It was a wild guess, but she could tell by his expression that it was true.

"Danny told you that, the little bastard!"

"Danny told me nothing. I walked past the store this morning. I could see what's been happening. I talked to some of the ladies who used to buy from the shop. They stopped because they were embarrassed to buy from a man." She refrained from saying that it was this particular man. "I talked to Josie in Storyville—"

"You went to that whorehouse? My wife?"

"Nicky and I went, just like any tourists . . . Nobody recognized us. But Josie was my biggest customer. She says she'll come back the minute I'm in the store and I'm sure the other houses will start buying again, too, once I'm back."

All at once Mannie seemed cowed. How would he support his family if they lost customers?

"There's only one way I will let you back into the store. If we move into a house with your mother so the baby's grandmother and aunt can supervise. I won't allow my child to be turned over completely to a *schwartze*."

Jenny shuddered at the thought of living with her mother again. "How do you know she'll agree?"

"She will, that's all. Never mind why. Anyway, she won't have to lift a finger. Just be there. That's the only way."

She knew it was a terrible mistake for them all to live together. It would be an impossible situation, with mama always taking Mannie's side— "After all, Jenny, he is the man in the family." But Jenny gave in. She could run home to nurse Leon, but she couldn't afford to waste another day away from the store.

CHAPTER
SEVEN

I T TOOK JENNY several weeks to find a small, inexpensive house that both her mother and Mannie could agree upon. She supervised the move, and she and Danny did most of the packing and lifting—with Mannie showing up occasionally to issue instructions.

Jenny was in charge again at the store, though they all pretended Mannie was the boss and she was just helping out temporarily. She sent out charming little conciliatory notes to all the ladies who had once been her customers, and soon business was again flourishing.

One night when she had been back in the store a month, Danny cornered her shortly before closing.

"Jenny, I can't work here after this week. This fella I know is getting a promotion, and his boss said I could have his job if I want it clerking in a man's haberdashery. I need the money," he added defiantly. "I can pay for my board if I'm working."

"Danny, that's fine." Jenny understood his frustration— he received no wages from mama and was totally dependent on the pittance she doled out for spending money. Of course, he hated being treated like a little boy. With a job of his own—money of his own—he'd be independent.

"I guess mama's going to be mad."

"Probably. But I bet you'll make her understand." Danny had a certain charm that would turn the heads of a lot of girls—and mama was particularly susceptible.

"What'll you do about deliveries?"

Jenny paused. "I guess Mannie will have to handle

them." It was important to keep him busy—off the selling floor.

Over the next few weeks Jenny tried to ignore Mannie's complaining and focused on tiny Leon, who was her constant joy. Though the doctor had told her there were devices to pump her milk to give to Leon in bottles while she was at the store, Jenny insisted on going home for feedings. She cherished those sweet private moments as she held her son at her breast.

With the coming of summer, the threat of a possible yellow fever epidemic—which a group of concerned doctors warned would not be mild like that of eight years ago—brought fear into the hearts of all New Orleanians.

Nicky, her mother and grandmother prepared to leave for Saratoga Springs.

"Papa and Benedict have to stay to keep the store running," Nicky said while she and Jenny shared soda water and ice cream at May's on Canal Street the day before they were to leave. "But I just can't figure out why Armand persists in staying here when nothing really happens in the courts until September. I think he's just trying to pretend he's not scared of the fever."

"Well, *I'm* scared," Jenny said. "Especially for Leon." She remembered that people had laughed four years ago when Dr. Kohnke, the health officer, urged a serious crusade against mosquitoes. Ever since Dr. Reed's experiments in Cuba in 1899 everybody knew that mosquitoes carried the fever . . . "The only time Leon's not under the netting is when I feed him."

"Maybe you could send Leon away with your mother for a few weeks."

Jenny laughed. "Not likely . . . mama won't budge from the house. She won't even let Evvie come into the store now. And Sophie's really scared—she never leaves the house either. Baby Milton is just a few weeks old, so Herman brings food home—not, of course, without complaining bitterly that his wife is turning him into a servant."

On her way back to the store she tried to devise a plan. Most of her big customers were away for the summer, though they had left a few orders to be filled in their absence. Business from Storyville would keep them going through the summer. Maybe it would be best if mama and Evvie went away somewhere cheap—just take a room for themselves and Leon.

During the next three weeks a few isolated cases appeared. By July over a hundred cases were reported and twenty of those had already died. New Orleans was once again in the grips of a yellow fever epidemic.

Jenny ignored Mannie's and her mother's wails about the cost and hired workers to screen every window and door in the house. A screen door was put in at the store and everybody at the house was ordered to open and close doors quickly. At night she woke a dozen times and left the bed to make sure the netting around Leon's crib was well secured.

Hysteria erupted in the neighboring communities. Shotgun quarantines were set up around the city, shipments from New Orleans turned back. One town refused to accept mail from the plague-ridden city unless it had been fumigated. Fishing boats from Lake Pontchartrain were barred from entry into Lake Borgne.

Responding to the New Orleans officials' pleas for assistance, the government sent Dr. Joseph White, the assistant surgeon general, who ordered 60,000 cisterns screened, hundreds of miles of gutters and canals salted or oiled, houses screened, fumigated or provided with emergency medical treatment.

When Danny showed symptoms of the fever, Mrs. Straus became hysterical. Jenny insisted—on Dr. Cohen's suggestion—that he be moved to the hospital . . .

"They'll give him the treatment he needs at the hospital, mama. We can't do it here." What she didn't say was that Danny was a source of infection and she was not going to let mama put her son's life in jeopardy.

"You're just jealous of him!" mama sobbed. "You've always hated him. You can't send him away. I won't let you. He belongs here with me."

"No. The doctors say he needs to be in the hospital." Jenny turned to Evvie for support, but like mama, she was distraught—she had always worshipped Danny.

"I never understood you, Jenny." Mrs. Straus turned away. "You're just not like my other children."

If Danny died of the fever, she knew mama would never forgive her, but Dr. Cohen—and the other doctors in the city—agreed that patients should be treated in the hospitals.

Danny was taken to the contagious ward at the emergency hospital. After a week, the doctors told Jenny that it looked as though Danny was one of the lucky ones. Mama accepted the news quietly.

The citizens of New Orleans responded valiantly to the crisis. Volunteers worked side by side with professionals and funds to help in the effort poured in from local donors. The fatalities were kept far below any epidemic in the history of the city. It was declared that New Orleans—and in fact the rest of the South—would never again be menaced by yellow fever. By October 23 the last quarantine on the city was lifted.

The days turned to weeks. Nicky took Jenny to the theater or the opera whenever Armand was with a client. Jenny treasured these evenings with her dear friend.

Nicky wasn't happy. Bored with her life as a beautiful young society matron she spent most of her time buying clothes. Often she dragged Jenny away from the store for an hour just to help her choose between two dresses. Though continually astonished at the time and money Nicky—and other New Orleans ladies—spent on their wardrobes, Jenny, too, was acquiring a sense of style as well as an ease in meeting the rich. Late in the autumn she conceived a daring new image for the store.

She waited until her mother came into the kitchen for her final cup of tea for the night and Mannie was seated at the table with his coffee to bring up the subject.

"We'll enlarge our piece-goods stock to include the finest fabrics available, and we'll add a dressmaking department. You know how Maison Blanche and Goldman's always have the best dressmakers in the store coax their rich customers to buy from them instead of having clothes made to order in New York? Why can't the Straus store do the same—in a smaller way?" She looked first at Mannie, then at her mother, including Mannie only to soothe his ego—both of them knew that ultimately it would be Mama's decision.

Mannie laughed. "You're crazy, Jenny. We ain't Maison Blanche and we ain't Goldman's. You know the trouble with you? You're a snob—comes from running around with that Nicky Goldman. You're trying to be what you ain't."

"Don't be stupid, Mannie," Mrs. Straus said. "Jenny comes from as good as Nicky Goldman, but who's got the money for that kind of store? It would take a fortune."

"It's a wonderful investment, mama."

"That's fine for the rich. They have money for investments. Not Louise Straus. Anyway I'm tired of your fancy ideas."

But Jenny would not give up. She badgered her mother until Mrs. Straus capitulated—over Mannie's objections.

"It's because mama's put away in the bank so often, Jenny," Evvie explained. "She feels secure enough to take a small risk. Anyway, you exhausted her."

Jenny paused. "What's this about mama at the bank?"

"You know what I mean—her mattress savings . . . mama's saved quite a lot. And she figures you know what you're doing if you've managed this well so far."

But mama never gave any sign that she appreciated what was happening with the store. She never once said, "Jenny, you're doing a good job." Jenny knew it was childish, but she longed for just one word of praise.

In January of 1906 Jenny rented the store next to theirs. She had the wall between them knocked down, and gradually, under Nicky's tasteful decorating and Jenny's supervision, the store took on a gentle elegance. Only Evvie knew how extravagant they were being. Jenny had become an expert at keeping secrets and had long since stopped feeling guilty about it—she knew what was best for the store. Lately Evvie had been coming out of her shell. She seemed to enjoy her hours in the store, and insisted—despite mama's protestations—that working wasn't "too much for her." Jenny knew that what mama really worried about was losing Evvie's companionship.

One day a man came into the store and introduced himself as Sidney Wolfe. Jenny was busy with a customer and the seamstress who helped out with sales at the busy hours was also helping a customer. Rather than wait, because he was on an errand during his lunch hour, Sidney picked up two purses and asked Evvie for her opinion. Charming and gracious, Evvie advised him.

Jenny saw the touch of color in Evvie's cheeks when Sidney Wolfe came into the store the next day, despite a heavy rain, on the pretense of buying something else. He was polite, gentlemanly, extraordinarily good looking—and obviously interested in Evvie. She watched, her throat tightening, as Evvie deliberately emerged from behind the cash register—the old cashbox had gone along with the new image—so that Sidney could see that she was lame.

That same day Sidney asked if he could call on Evvie. Jenny prayed that her mother would not spoil this chance for Evvie to have a normal life. Except for Mannie everybody in the family liked Sidney. He was a bank clerk who talked eloquently about his high ambitions.

Sometimes, seeing how Evvie glowed when she was with Sidney, Jenny felt tears sting her eyes. She looked back on the wondrous summer she and Marc shared before he took off for Paris. Even now, four summers later, it hurt to remember.

But now she realized that even if they had waited for Danny to reach sixteen, she still could not have deserted her family. Danny wasn't responsible enough to handle the store. Whatever money he earned he immediately spent on himself, not even contributing to his own keep. Of course mama closed her eyes to this.

After only a seven-week courtship Sidney asked Evvie to marry him. Everyone was overjoyed that shy, sweet Evvie would at last have a husband to care for her. Sidney had a good future at the bank. His mother had died four years earlier and his father had died when he was a boy, so, like Mannie, he was without any close family. He often spoke of his regret that his parents would never know his bride.

It was decided that Evvie's wedding would be far more lavish than that of either of her sisters. Sophie was pregnant again so Jenny would be Evvie's matron of honor. The ceremony would be conducted in the synagogue, with a reception afterwards.

During Evvie's engagement, Jenny fought the disquieting feeling that Sidney wasn't telling them everything about his past. There were moments—unnoticed by the others—when she caught Sidney looking at her oddly, as if inspecting her. And he seemed to be always colliding with her when no one else was around. But maybe she was imagining it. Except for Mannie, everybody liked Sidney. Mannie was sure Sidney thought he was marrying an heiress.

"Don't be silly. What would Evvie inherit?" she'd ask whenever he made one of his snide remarks.

Three weeks before the wedding Danny lost his job and mama decided he could be put to work in the store at the cash register once Evvie was married. Jenny had to admit that Danny's charm and gallant manner could be an asset with the ladies.

On the Tuesday before the wedding Mrs. Straus came into the store—almost two hours before closing—and announced that Jenny had to go home to stay with the baby. Apparently the girl had not come in because of a death in the family and she and Evvie had to meet with the caterer for a final conference about the reception.

"I'll have Mannie stay with Leon, mama."

"No. You're the mother, you stay. Mannie never even changed a diaper. Something happened, how would he manage? Miss Emily can take care of customers." The gracious, aristocratic Miss Emily had been elevated to saleslady. "I left supper on the stove. When Mannie and Danny come home, feed them. Don't wait for us."

Mannie could have stayed with Leon for an hour, Jenny thought in annoyance. But mama always made a point of deferring to Mannie as the head of the household. Would it kill him to change one diaper? Any time Leon was sick—never anything serious, thank God, but teething or a cold—she was the one who stayed up with him. His loving father slept straight through the night. In the bed they might as well have had a dividing wall between her side and his.

She always knew when Mannie went to Storyville. Not a

fancy house such as Josie's—he would not have been comfortable there, nor could he pay her prices. He always made some excuse right after supper about going back to the store. An hour later he would return, a smug smile on his face, and take a nip from the bottle of schnapps he kept on a shelf in the kitchen. Even when he paid, Jenny thought grimly, he spent little time on passion.

She left the store and walked home with her mother. Evvie was waiting. Jenny couldn't help but notice how happy and pretty she looked.

"Mama, we have to hurry," she said, greeting them. "I've already fed Leon and put him to bed." Evvie loved taking care of Leon—she often said it was the next best thing to having a child of her own.

Jenny smiled. "Take your time, Evvie. Make sure everything is the way you want it to be."

After a flurry of last minute decisions Evvie and Mrs. Straus left and Jenny went upstairs to look in on Leon. He was asleep. For a few minutes she stood beside the crib, content just to watch his gentle breathing. At moments like this, alone with Leon, her life seemed full and secure.

She adjusted the mosquito netting around the crib and tiptoed from the room. Maybe a cup of tea would help her sleep. The house felt strange in its emptiness—she couldn't remember the last time she'd been here alone.

As she approached the stairs she thought she heard footsteps.

"Danny?"

"It's Sidney."

She smiled in relief.

"Oh, hello, Sidney. Evvie isn't here—"

"I know." As he smiled she couldn't help noticing how handsome he was. "They'll be gone at least two hours."

There was something about the look on his face that unnerved her.

"How did you get in?"

He chuckled.

"Who locks doors in New Orleans?"

"Would you like a cup of tea?"

"No, I would not." He reached for her hand.

"Sidney—" She forced the rising panic out of her voice. "Why don't you come back later when Evvie's here?"

"I can see Evvie any time. You're the one I want." She took a step back.

"What are you talking about?"

As she tried to draw her hand away from his he pulled her into his arms, one hand fondling her breasts.

"You're the only one in this family with tits." He smiled as a nipple hardened beneath his fingers.

"Let me go!"

"I've seen you with Mannie." His voice was low, triumphant. "You can't stand the bastard. How in hell did you ever bring yourself to marry him?"

"Let me go! I'll scream till the whole neighborhood hears!"

"No, you won't. That would be quite a disgrace to the family, wouldn't it?"

He clamped his mouth on hers and tried to push his tongue between her clenched teeth. Breathing heavily, he released her mouth, but his hands held her pinned against the banister.

"Let me go!" She kicked his ankle with all her strength.

"You little bitch!" he hissed, "you want it as much as me. You don't give a damn for that slob you married. He's always running after two-bit whores."

"You'll never marry Evvie." She tried to push him away but he was too strong for her. He picked her up and carried her into Danny's bedroom, kicking the door shut behind him.

He dropped her on the bed and crouched above her.

"Sidney," she said, "if you'll go away now, I won't tell anybody. I'll forget it ever happened—"

"You won't forget me. No woman forgets Sidney Wolfe."

"Then I'll scream." They both knew she wouldn't dare.

His hands fumbled at the buttons of her waist. Swearing, he ripped off her blouse and groped at her breasts. He dropped on top of her, thrusting against the poplinette of her skirt and she felt him harden as he fumbled with the buttons of his trousers.

"I've waited so long for you, sweet little sister," he said, his mouth at her throat. "Every time we've been in a room together I've imagined what it would be like with you. You've got fire in you, but I'll bet it's never been tested. Mannie would never know what to do with a woman like you."

He nipped at her breasts while his hands tugged at her skirt. In spite of her revulsion, Jenny felt the stirrings of her own passion.

"Men have been lynched for this, Sidney."

He pulled off her undergarments and lightly caressed her soft thighs.

"Enjoy it, sugar. You know you want it."

"No!" She felt sick as he entered her. "I hate you! I hate you!"

She lay motionless beneath him, trying to shut out the sounds of his voice as he begged her to move with him. She gritted her teeth, ashamed at the sounds of passion that welled up in her throat. *How could she feel this way with the man who was to marry her sister?*

At last she heard his groan of satisfaction. For a few minutes he lay still. Then he pulled away, swung himself from the bed and stood staring down at her.

"Why does Mannie run to whores when he has a woman like you at home?"

"You'll never marry Evvie," Jenny said. "I'll see to that."

"Yes I will."

"Not when I tell them you raped me."

"Don't bother to tell them, Jenny." Now he was the quiet, charming Sidney they had always known. "Nobody will believe you. With Storyville a walk away, why would I push myself on a married woman with a child?" His laugh was low and hollow. "They'll never believe you, Jenny."

CHAPTER
EIGHT

Trying to hold together her torn clothes, Jenny scooped up her undergarments and stood outside Danny's bedroom until she heard the front door close. Her heart still pounding, she went to check on Leon. He slept soundly.

She returned to Danny's room to straighten the rumpled bed and then hurried down to the kitchen to put up water, determined to wash away the filth of Sidney.

How could she bring herself to tell Evvie about the man she was to marry? Jenny thought as she scrubbed herself with soap and hot water. And what if she were pregnant? Mannie hadn't touched her in months, so she couldn't pretend it was his child. She would have to go to Josie. It wouldn't be a sin to rid herself of a child of rape.

She was out of the tub and dressed when she heard Mannie and Danny come home. She struggled to compose herself. She would have to go down to the kitchen and serve them supper. Later, when the others went to bed, she'd tell mama.

It was a steamy night. The electric fan that Jenny had insisted on having installed in the kitchen ceiling only circulated the hot, stale air. While the family sat at the table, Leon woke and began to cry. Jenny left the table and went upstairs to wash him down with cool water. She sat with him until he fell asleep.

She heard Mannie coming up the stairs. Danny was going out the front door.

Mrs. Straus sat bolt upright.

"Danny, where are you going? It's late."

"It's too hot to sleep, mama. Come with me for a ride on the streetcar. Everybody will think you're my girl."

"Danny," she said, giggling, "don't talk silly. Just don't stay out so late the neighbors all think you're a bum."

Jenny hurried downstairs to the kitchen. Her voice trembled with suppressed rage as she told her mother what had happened. Without a word Mrs. Straus went to the stove and turned off the boiling water. She poured it over the tea leaves and stood waiting for the tea to brew.

"Mama—" Jenny said in exasperation. "Didn't you hear what I told you?"

Her mother kept her back turned.

"Mama, don't you believe me?"

When at last Mrs. Straus spoke, her voice was low.

"You're not like your sisters. Where do you get your crazy ways? Something like that would never happen to Sophie or Evvie." She brought her cup of tea to the table and Jenny could see that her hands were shaking. "You must have led him on."

Jenny was appalled. *How could mama say such a thing?* "Mama, I never led him on. Sometimes I was uncomfortable, the way he looked at me, but I never gave him any reason to—to do that."

"We are not to do anything to disturb Evvie's happiness," Mrs. Straus said. "Do you understand what I'm saying, Jenny?"

"You'd let Evvie marry the man who raped me!" Jenny said, incredulous.

"It's not for us to understand what men do. Sidney must have thought you would not reject him. You have such forward ways, Jenny. Evvie may never have a chance to marry again. Who'll take care of her when I'm gone?"

"Mama—"

"You can't shame your husband. How would Mannie feel if people heard you claim that Sidney had raped you? Everybody knows that a woman who has been raped is forever shamed. Her husband is dishonored. Forget what you told me, Jenny. Forget it ever happened."

Through the night and the following day Jenny struggled

with her decision. Finally she forced herself to be realistic—exposing Sidney would hurt too many people . . .
but what about Evvie?

At last the wedding day arrived. Jenny walked down the
aisle in her lilac-gray silk, copied by the store seamstress
from a design by M. Felix of Paris. She could feel her
mother's anxious scrutiny, but she didn't say a word. Let
mama worry about whether she was going to let this
marriage go ahead.

As she watched the orthodox ceremony she saw only
Evvie's face, lovely in her happiness. She felt a pang of
regret. How long before Evvie discovered her husband for
what he truly was? Mama beamed, playing the role of the
mother of the bride to perfection. Jenny marveled at the
ease with which she could shut her eyes to ugly situations.

At last the evening was over and she could go home.
Sidney was taking Evvie for a one-night honeymoon at an
inn on Lake Pontchartrain. Tomorrow morning he would
report for work as usual. Had mama talked to Evvie about
the wedding night? The girl was so sheltered from life.

Long after the others were asleep, Jenny lay awake. At
least Evvie was in love with her husband—that was more
than Sophie or she could say.

She shuddered as she remembered the first night that
Mannie had come to her. Sophie's wedding night, too, had
probably been less than idyllic. But if Marc had been her
husband, she would have welcomed him with love. With
passion.

But tonight her heart ached only for Evvie, who loved a
man undeserving of any woman's love.

Jenny tried to convince herself that she was not pregnant
by Sidney. The odds were on her side. She confided in no
one, not even Nicky, though Nicky sensed something was
amiss and asked her about it.

"I'm worried about Evvie's marriage," she said. "Mannie and I are the only ones who believe that Sidney is no
good. I think he chases other women."

Nicky smiled knowingly. "So, he went after you."

"He tried."

"That wasn't very smart. He should at least be more discreet. I worry sometimes that Armand is having an affair with one of his clients. She's only seven or eight years older than he and so attractive." She sighed. "I tell myself I'd rather not know, what I don't know can't hurt me. And sometimes I think he loves me. If only I'd get pregnant! Then I'm sure Armand wouldn't go chasing after other women. What's wrong with me?"

"Nicky, it'll happen." *Let it not happen to her.* "At the right time you'll be pregnant."

"When's the right time?"

Jenny smiled. "Mama would say, 'when God wills it.'"

When she woke up the following morning with cramps, she murmured a prayer of gratitude. God had been good to her.

She was happy as she went into the store. After this she felt like she could cope with anything. Today the whole world seemed good. But at the end of the day, when she totaled up the sales, she knew something was drastically wrong.

She was alone, as usual. Carefully she added up the money in the register again, subtracted what had been put in this morning for change. She remembered one particularly large sale. In her mind she added up a rough estimate of Miss Emily's sales. Nobody touched the cash register except Danny. He must have siphoned off a good chunk of the day's receipts.

Jenny fretted through the evening. She didn't dare approach him at home because mama would take his side. She forced herself to wait until morning and created a pretext to bring him into the store half an hour earlier than usual.

"Danny, I know you've been taking from the cash register and I simply won't tolerate it."

"What are you talking about, Jenny?" he said. "Every time you bring a customer to me, I put the money into the register. I'll bet it's that hoity-toity Miss Emily."

"Miss Emily wouldn't take one cent that didn't belong to her. I'm putting you on warning, Danny. One more shortage and I'll have to tell mama." What was he doing with the money? Gambling again?

"Mama knows I wouldn't steal."

"I know better," Jenny shot back. "From now on, every time Miss Emily or I make a sale, we'll write the amount on a sheet of paper right here beside the register. If the register is short one dime, I'll tell mama. That will prove it to her."

"You better watch that Miss Emily," he muttered. "You ought to be ashamed, talking to me about stealing."

Danny wasn't shrewd enough to realize that she could never bring herself to tell mama he was helping himself from the register—it would hurt her too much. But maybe now he'd be scared enough to keep his hand out of the till.

On a sunny, warm morning shortly before the New Year Nicky charged into the shop in unusually high spirits. From the glow on her face Jenny guessed that she was pregnant.

"I'm taking you off for breakfast at Bégue's, Jenny. I've already reserved seats so you can't say no."

"But I can't leave the store." Jenny looked at Miss Emily, who was finishing up with a customer. Another customer was in the fitting room with the dressmaker.

"Miss Emily is almost finished with her customer," Nicky said. "Come on, she can manage for an hour without you. Danny can help too." She threw him a dazzling smile. "A woman always enjoys having a handsome young man in attendance."

"All right. If we aren't too long." Jenny sighed. She had never been to Bégue's, though it was celebrated around New Orleans for its Bohemian breakfasts, served every day at 11 A.M.

"We won't be. Get your coat. The car's out front. We'll drive to Decatur Street."

Nicky refused to divulge her news on the ride to the restaurant.

"I'll tell you once we've ordered, I promise."

"Come on Nicky, I'm dying of the suspense!"

"Never mind. Grandma's so excited that President Roosevelt has appointed Oscar Straus to be Secretary of Commerce and Labor. Mr. Straus is the first Jew in

American history to serve in the president's cabinet. The way she's carrying on, you'd think it was papa who had been appointed to the Cabinet."

Nicky told her that she was leaving for Palm Beach with her mother and grandmother in three weeks.

"Armand urged me to go with them. I think he's anxious to get me out of the city."

"He wants to see you enjoy yourself. Anyway, you love Palm Beach."

Nicky smiled. "I suppose you're right. Maybe I'm becoming a jealous wife. But enough of Armand. We're going to Bégue's for breakfast, and we'll have a marvelous time."

Directly across from the French Market, Bégue's was a single low-ceiling room one flight above the street. Patrons sat at a long table reaching back to the kitchen—in plain view and at a slightly higher level, where Madame Bégue and her assistants cooked amidst ropes of hanging garlic, red peppers and assorted game.

Jenny and Nicky were escorted to their seats at the table. Immediately, Negro waiters brought them a loaf of still-hot French bread and a bottle of claret.

Jenny waited impatiently for the waiters to disappear.

"Nicky, you're bursting with something special, and I'm dying of curiosity. Tell me."

"Well, okay. I had a letter from Marc this morning. He's having his first art show in Paris in four weeks and the critics will be coming to write about his work! Oh, Jenny, I've never been so excited in my life. I want to go to Paris for the show, but Armand says he can't get away from the office and he won't hear of me going to Paris alone. He has a heavy court schedule for the next three months." She sighed. "So I guess we'll have to be satisfied with reading about the show in the Paris newspapers. Marc will send us all the clippings."

Jenny hugged her.

"Why, Nicky, that's wonderful. We both know how hard Marc's worked for this."

Because of all of Marc's letters they had shared, Jenny felt a part of his life. While she listened as Nicky read his letter once again she felt a pang of regret, tried to tell herself that at least she had Leon. But she knew that for her life to be complete there had to be more, and Marc's success fanned her own ambitions.

Marc slept restlessly in his large, square, high-ceilinged bedroom and awakened instantly at the first light of a gray Paris dawn. Today his work would be formally presented to the public for the first time. Until today no one—except for his instructor and Simone—had been allowed to see his paintings.

He pulled a mound of silken pillows behind his head and considered the day's events. After his appearance at the salon, he would escort Simone to the dinner party she had arranged at Maxim's to celebrate his showing.

He had been in Paris only a little more than four years and he had studied with one of the greatest teachers on the continent. Bless Simone for supporting him when he broke away from tradition. While he was not yet one of the *fauves*—wild beasts, so called because their work was considered savage—he leaned strongly toward their style.

When he stood with Simone in the salon d'Automne October a year ago and saw the work by the *fauves* presented as a group he had been overwhelmed. But the critics ignored the "wild beasts of color"—Matisse, Braque, Rouault, Derain. In truth these artists were followers of Gauguin, Van Gogh, and Cézanne—like himself.

He was too excited to sleep. He threw back the covers, reached for his dressing gown laid across the foot of the bed and crossed the room to pull aside the burgundy damask drapes at a window that looked down upon the Rue de Marignan, deserted at this hour except for a handful of stragglers en route to work.

His family kept pleading with him to come home with Simone for a visit. They were impressed that their son had married a wealthy countess—even if she had forfeited her title when she married him, she was still known throughout Paris as Countess Simone. He couldn't return to New Orleans until he was recognized as an artist.

But could he ever return, knowing that Jenny was

married to another man? When would he be able to think of her without longing? He moved to the rosewood commode that sat between a pair of tall, narrow windows and reached into a drawer, rummaging for the miniature he had painted from memory.

A miniature of the only girl he would ever love—Jenny Straus, now Jenny Adler.

Simone was a Frenchwoman. She didn't ask questions about his past. She didn't demand that he love her as he loved Jenny. He gave Simone immense respect and a deep affection. She gave him the means to develop his talents. Encouragement when he suffered doubts. Comfort. It was greedy of him to expect more of life.

He started at the delicate tapping on the door between their bedrooms. Quickly he returned the miniature to its hiding place.

"Simone?"

"Yes, darling." She opened the door. "I thought I heard you moving about. I knew you'd have trouble sleeping. Why don't you come back to bed?"

She seemed no more than a slip of a girl in the gray early morning light, her delicate blue negligee buttoned loosely at her waist. "Simone," Marc said, "what would I do without you?"

He brought his mouth down to hers, his arms closing around her slender frame. He was making love to Jenny . . .

"Marc," Simone whispered, "close the drapes."

When he returned, she was beneath the covers, her negligee and nightgown lying beside the bed.

"You're tense," she said. "Let me help."

He lay immobile, knowing Simone enjoyed his passivity. Her mouth touched every inch of him until suddenly he could bear it no longer.

"Oh, Marc," she whispered. "There's never been anyone like you. Please, don't ever leave me."

CHAPTER
NINE

Annoyed by Herman's constant bragging about having three sons and a daughter and another one on the way, Mannie began dropping hints to Jenny about having a second child. In spite of her revulsion at the prospect of making love to him, she realized that Leon, already two, would probably like to have a younger sister or brother, and she hoped that a second child would quell her own silent dissatisfaction with her life. But she vowed this time she would not let Mannie push her from the store.

Another factor in her decision to have a second child was the fact that Nicky was at last pregnant. It would be nice if they each had a child the same age. She would have a girl, Nicky a boy. Maybe when the two grew up, they'd fall in love and marry.

For three interminable weeks, Jenny endured Mannie's crude lovemaking, and by late March she knew she was pregnant. By June he was again trying to push her from the store, as if he had forgotten what had happened the last time she was forced from the business.

She refused to lose her calm. "There's no reason for me to leave the store, Mannie. I look perfectly respectable in these tea gowns." She had copied the designs of the new maternity dresses brought back from New York by a patron, who had come to her to have more of the same made up. "They're being worn by very rich women in New York." Despite his frequent show of contempt for money, Mannie was fascinated by the rich. "A woman named Lane

Bryant—up in New York—is doing very well selling only clothes for pregnant women."

"I don't care what the rich women in New York are doing. It's shameful for a woman in your condition to flaunt herself in public. You'll leave the store at the end of the week. That's final."

"No, I won't. Times are bad throughout the country. We're moving into a depression. We can't take chances with our future."

"I'm the husband!" There was fear in Mannie's eyes. "I make the decisions in the family."

"Mannie, we have one child and another on the way," Jenny said. "We have to think about mama and Evvie. The newspapers talk about how bad things are—" Mannie paid little attention to the newspapers, except in the baseball season. "We'll do what's best for the store. I'm needed here, Mannie."

Jenny knew Mannie complained to her mother about her continued presence in the store, and while mama was sympathetic to his position, she made no outright demands that Jenny retire from the store. But one Friday night, with Sophie and Herman and the children over for dinner, mama announced that it was "unwomanly" of Jenny to appear in the store when she'd be giving birth in less than three months. Sophie disagreed.

"I don't see why Jenny can't keep on at the store," she said, ignoring Herman's disapproving stare. "She looks better pregnant than a lot of women who aren't pregnant. Besides, why should it be shameful for a woman to be carrying a child?"

"That's right," Jenny said. "Pregnant women don't hide at home anymore. Doctors and psychologists agree that they should live normal lives."

"Listen to my wife," Mannie sneered, "the great reader. The college professor."

"Mannie," Mrs. Straus said, "have some more of the boiled beef before it gets cold. Sophie, eat."

Jenny looked around the table. The world was changing, but men like Mannie and Herman weren't keeping pace. They lived in an earlier generation. The thought of women getting the vote terrified them, but *they* never bothered to go to the polls.

She was changing. Even Sophie was changing. Jenny looked at her mother. But not mama. She lived in a tight little world of memories that would never acknowledge progress.

Jenny set up a partitioned area at the rear of the shop where she saw customers in privacy and Miss Emily handled the other customers. On busy days Mrs. Straus now condescended to help out for two hours in the afternoon. Mama was constantly surprising Jenny. Here was a woman with a keen sense of business who chose to sit on the piazza for hours a day just pushing away her life.

Jenny knew that mama came in every afternoon only because she was lonely without Evvie, who spent the afternoons cleaning the house and preparing supper. Every morning she visited her mother.

Jenny made every possible excuse to avoid seeing Sidney. Whenever he came to mama's house for supper, she planned to be away. When Evvie invited them to her house, she was always involved in some crisis at the store. She couldn't brush aside the feeling that at any moment Evvie's marriage would crumble.

In July Nicky gave birth to a son, named Louis for his maternal grandfather. For Grandma Goldman Nicky insisted on an elaborately catered *briss*. Despite her advanced pregnancy Jenny attended as the baby's godmother. She didn't bother to ask Mannie to accompany her.

In late September Jenny was in the store talking to a customer about the hem on a wedding gown when she felt her first labor pain. Seven hours later she gave birth to a beautiful baby girl. She named her daughter Helene.

Once the glow of the birth had faded, Jenny faced reality. The country was in the grips of financial panic. She was worried about the rash of bank failures regularly reported in the *Times-Picayune*.

On a dreary November morning while the saleswomen gossiped over tea—it was too early for Jenny's wealthy customers to be in the store—Mannie arrived, pale and disheveled, with a package from a supplier.

"I want to talk to my wife in private." He gestured to Jenny to join him in the small area at the rear that had become her office. From behind the cash register Danny's curious eyes followed them.

"Mannie, what is it?" she asked. Had he been home? Had something happened to the children?

"I'll tell you what it is!" Mannie said grimly, closing the door behind them, though every word said above a murmur in the office could be heard in the rest of the store. "Our bank's just closed up! Nobody knows what's happening!"

"But I talked to them at the bank last week. They said they had no problems." Why hadn't she paid the bills last week? They had the money. As soon as the business began to grow, she had put all the receipts in a savings account in the name of the business until it was time to pay bills. The interest wasn't much, but it was found money.

Mannie gripped her arm. "All I know is that every cent we have is tied up in the bank. Not just the account for the store." Mama's money, Jenny thought, sick with shock. "Our own money. God knows if we'll ever see it again! Why didn't you move over to Sidney's bank when he asked you to? It would have looked good for him to bring in business. Sidney's bank didn't close!"

"You were the one who didn't want to move to Sidney's bank, Mannie."

"I told you we ought to invest our savings in a dry goods store I could run. What good was the money doing sitting in the bank?" Mannie had no inkling that she'd meant for the savings to contribute toward buying a house. "If you'd listened to me, we'd have a good investment instead of nothing! You think you're so smart. You've ruined us, that's what you've done! From now on—if we ever get our money back—I'm going to make the decisions about what to do with it."

Throughout the nation banks were closing. People lost their life savings. Jenny went to her creditors to plead with them to have patience. They reluctantly agreed to wait for payment, but Jenny knew she couldn't expect them to extend her further credit and the store needed merchandise.

She was astonished when her mother ordered Mannie to stop hammering at her.

"Jenny's responsible for the banks closing, Mannie? She could go to President Roosevelt and say, 'you have to keep the banks open because Mannie Adler is upset'?"

Business plummeted. Only the wealthiest of Jenny's customers seemed unaffected. The women who worked in the store feared for their jobs. Jenny saw the fear even in Danny's eyes—he had come to enjoy his position behind the cash register—he'd made quite a few friends among the ladies since his first day.

Knowing Jenny was upset about the state of business Nicky took her to the opera one Saturday night, two months after the closing of the bank. Armand was in Natchez on business. On Saturday nights Mannie played pinochle with Herman while Sophie visited with mama. Evvie, too, usually visited on Saturday nights. Sidney always seemed to have a pressing appointment.

Again Jenny was immersed in the opulent lives of New Orleans' upper class. This was what had pushed her into the line of fine lingerie and then into bringing in the French dressmaker. Now she tried to think of other ways to profit from her wealthy patronage.

Between acts, while they talked with a few ladies of Nicky's acquaintance in the *foyer*—the elegant salon used as a promenade—they heard about a new store that had recently opened in Dallas.

"It's called Neiman-Marcus, and it's on two floors at Elm and Murphy Streets. I wouldn't dare tell my husband how much I paid for the things I bought there, but everything they have is so elegant."

"And you know what else? It's all ready-made. Not just skirts and waists but dresses and coats, too."

"I heard they have a dressmaker in the store who makes sure whatever you buy fits perfectly. There's not a store like it anywhere in the South."

Jenny knew the moment to be daring had arrived. If only she could emulate the success of the new specialty store in Dallas! But Mama was shocked by the idea.

"Now, when we've lost all our money in the bank closing? When we don't know when the creditors will close us up?"

"They've given me a long extension. These people in Dallas are making a fortune with ready-to-wear. It's the new trend. We have to invest money in merchandise—we can't operate with empty shelves. At Neiman-Marcus—"

"Neiman-Marcus? They're Jewish?"

"Yes." Jenny knew her mother had enormous respect for the successful Jewish merchants.

"And they buy dresses all made up without knowing anybody's measurements?"

"They have a dressmaker on hand to alter. Maybe shorten or take in tucks. It goes so fast and the customers love it. They buy a dress or a coat and they can take it home in two or three days."

"That'll cost more than buying yard goods. Where will you find money for such an investment?"

Jenny took a deep breath.

"Extend a loan to the business, mama. In six months you'll have it all back, with interest."

"Buy my money is in the business. How can I make it a loan?"

"From your private bank."

Mama always pretended to be surprised that the children knew about the money she hid under the mattress, but actually she meant for them to know in case something happened to her. "Mama, it's our chance to make the store important in New Orleans. Nobody in New Orleans sells ready-to-wear. We'll sell only the most expensive clothes. That means a very high profit."

Mrs. Straus shook her head.

"Your ideas are too big. Why do you try for so much? We'll lose everything."

"No, we won't. In five years we'll be rich. Mama, it's the chance of a lifetime."

"Don't bother me with such craziness. How can I gamble with what little I have to keep a roof over our heads if, God forbid, the creditors take over the store?"

"They won't," Jenny said. "Business won't stay bad like this. All the experts say the depression will be over soon."

"The experts," Mrs. Straus mimicked. "What do they know? They make guesses like everybody else."

Over the next few days Jenny was relentless in her campaign. They both knew better than to talk to Mannie about it. Jenny brought Nicky to the house for dinner so that they could talk about it with an unbiased party outside the family.

At last mama relented.

"I know I'm going to regret this, Jenny, but I just can't take any more of your badgering." With a sigh she headed upstairs to "the bank."

Jenny smiled. She'd suspected all along that eventually mama would give in. Thank God Mannie had already gone to sleep—if he didn't play pinochle with Herman, then he went to bed right after supper. He'd carry on something awful when he discovered what she had planned—but it didn't matter; this was between mama and her.

Jenny finished drying the dishes and stacked them in the cupboard. She was about to pour herself a fresh cup of tea when she heard a scream from upstairs.

"Oh, my God! Who? Who could have done this?"

Jenny rushed out of the kitchen.

"Mama, what is it?" Tearing up the stairs she saw Mannie, yawning, coming out of their bedroom in his drawers.

"Jenny, I've been robbed." Ashen, Mrs. Straus stood in the doorway of her bedroom.

"Now, mama, don't jump to conclusions. Maybe you changed your hiding place." Jenny glanced at Mannie. Danny could have taken it.

"You're wrong!" Mrs. Straus's voice soared to a high thin wail. "In twenty-seven years I never put it any place but under the mattress. Who would steal a widow's last few dollars?"

"We'll look, mama. Don't upset yourself."

"Don't upset myself? With my life's savings gone?" Her hand fluttered to her chest. "I can't breathe. Call Dr. Cohen. I think I'm having a heart attack."

CHAPTER
TEN

Jenny sent Mannie downstairs to phone for Dr. Cohen and helped her mother into bed. She had never seen her so frightened.

"Why is Doctor Cohen taking so long?"

"Mannie just called him, mama. He'll be here very soon."

"Get me some water, Jenny. My throat's dry."

As Jenny hurried down to the kitchen for a glass of water, she wondered if her mother really *was* having a heart attack. Maybe she should call Sophie and Evvie.

By the time Mrs. Straus had drained her glass, Jenny heard Dr. Cohen's voice downstairs. She walked into the hall to meet him.

"She's had a bad shock, Dr. Cohen, now she thinks she's having a heart attack."

The doctor patted her arm and smiled. Mrs. Straus had been one of his first patients.

"We'll see about that, Jenny."

Jenny hovered beside the bed while Dr. Cohen examined his patient.

"You're fine, Mrs. Straus. Nothing to worry about. Just nerves." He turned to Jenny as he fished in his satchel. "Give her two of these pills. She'll go to sleep. In the morning she'll be good as new."

"Why does God do these things to me?" Mrs. Straus moaned. "I was a good wife, a good mother. Why do these things happen to me?" Dr. Cohen diplomatically remained silent and Jenny suspected he was well acquainted with

85

mama's nerves. Thank God her diagnosis was wrong. But wait till Danny got home—he'd have to answer to *her*. He was the only one who could have gone into mama's bedroom and stolen the money.

"Mannie, go back to sleep," Jennie said once Dr. Cohen had left and her mother had taken her medication. "I'll wait up for Danny."

"That young *momzer!* I'll give him a piece of my mind." For a moment Mannie was thoughtful. "How much do you think he took from mama?"

"Now, Mannie, let's be fair. We don't know for sure yet that he took anything. Let me talk to him alone. You need your sleep."

"No. I'll talk. All you women spoil him. Let him hear this from a man." How ridiculously pompous he sounded, Jenny thought; yet he was right about one thing—Danny had always been spoiled by the women in the family.

They sat down in the kitchen. Mannie began rummaging around for some coffee and Jenny put up a fresh pot. When *would* Danny come home? Mama had long since stopped waiting up for him.

"He's a young boy—" She would say, "why should we expect him to come home early like an old married man?"

Jenny sat at the kitchen table and half listened to Mannie rant about Danny.

"Shh, keep your voice low. You'll wake the children."

But she had to admit that this was one issue which she and Mannie could agree upon. It seemed that time and time again something happened to distract from the success of the store—now that she had finally convinced mama to put money into a ready-to-wear department, the money was gone. It would have been a tiny department because mama wouldn't have enough saved for a big splash—but it would have been a beginning. Now where would she find an investor? Even before she talked to mama, Nicky had tried to coax Armand into investing in the store but he had firmly rejected the idea. *There was nobody else.*

While Mannie dozed at the table, Jenny heard Danny come into the house and Mannie was jolted awake.

"Danny!" he thundered. "Come out to the kitchen."

As Jenny listened carefully to Mannie's attack and Danny's blustered denials, she became convinced that Danny was innocent. His defense was flimsy and uncalculated, and to her that meant he simply wasn't clever enough to have stolen the money.

"Both of you, quiet before you wake up mama and the children. He's telling the truth, Mannie."

"Then who did it?" Mannie demanded, frustrated at not having squeezed out a confession.

"It must have been the *schwartze*," he said. "She's alone with the children when mama comes into the store in the afternoons."

Jenny laughed. "Annie Lou wouldn't take a lump of sugar."

"Aren't you the grand lady," Mannie sneered, "always protecting the *schwartzes?* She's the only one who's been alone in the house—she must have seen mama put money under the mattress."

"Mannie, I don't care what you say—it wasn't Annie Lou. Somebody obviously got into the house without our knowing. Look, I'm tired. Let's talk about this in the morning."

Jenny reached over to quiet the alarm clock before it awakened Mannie. She cherished her half hour alone in the morning before the others woke up and Annie Lou arrived.

"Mawnin', Miz Jenny," Annie Lou greeted her as she put up the pot of coffee. "Looks like we're gonna have a real nice day."

All at once the morning stillness was punctured by a staccato banging on the door.

Jenny frowned. "Who's that at this hour? I'll get it, Annie Lou. You go up and look in on the children."

She hurried from the kitchen and down the hall to open the front door. Ashen, trembling, Evvie stood before her.

"Jenny, Sidney didn't come home last night. I was waiting up for him. I must have fallen asleep in my chair. When I woke up he still wasn't home. I looked in the closet and the dresser drawers. He had taken his clothes and left.

Jenny—" she broke into sobs. "My husband's left me. What am I going to do?"

As Jenny hugged Evvie, her heart went out to her sister. Sidney must have been the one who had helped himself to mama's nest egg. Then he had taken off. Evvie was right— he wouldn't come back.

It was tacitly agreed that no one would tell Evvie the truth about Sidney. Over mama's reproaches Jenny insisted Evvie come into the store to help out for a few hours a day to keep her from wallowing in her depression. The worst thing for Evvie would be to return to the role of the lame daughter. Evvie had built her own life—she could be a whole woman if mama wasn't allowed to smother her again.

Jenny tried to keep up the pretense that she could pull the business out of this crisis but the creditors were tapping their feet and she was beginning to feel desperate. If she couldn't come up with something soon, she would lose the store.

To her surprise it was Herman who finally came forward with the offer of a loan. The amount he proposed to provide, at the normal bank interest rates, was less than Jenny needed; but it was the only loan on the horizon, so she decided to consider it.

At a family conference, with Sophie grim and silent, Herman laid out the rules. Not a cent was to be distributed without his being consulted. Jenny knew Herman's miserliness and suddenly the prospect of the loan didn't seem so appealing.

"Jenny, you do like Herman says," mama ordered. "If he could save up so much money from a small tailoring shop, then he's a good business man."

"But we run a different kind of business," Jenny said. "Herman doesn't understand how we operate."

Herman scowled. "What's to understand? Business is business. How much profit you show at the end of the day tells the story. You come to me before you spend a cent. Take it or leave it."

"We take it," mama said, avoiding Jenny's eyes.

Nobody in the family—even Sophie—had ever guessed Herman had saved up so much cash.

"Let me talk to the people at the bank again," Jenny said desperately. "Maybe they'll—"

"I said we're taking Herman's offer," mama snapped. "Didn't you admit that already the creditors ask when they'll get paid? Now we know."

The night was cool and crisp, usually Sophie's favorite kind of weather. But tonight she was upset by what she had heard at her mother's house. She walked beside Herman in silence. How could he have stored away all that cash wihout a word to her?

Herman smiled smugly.

"Sophie, I guess you're worried that I'm investing in your mother's business, but it's okay—the money's safe. I know what they don't know. In six months, tops, the store's bank will reopen and they'll pay back every cent. I have a customer who's a bank officer. He told me."

Sophie pressed her lips together. So typical of Herman to completely misread her. Now he was playing the great benefactor. Why couldn't he have told Jenny the money was sure to be repaid, like the bank officers had promised and nobody believed?

As they approached the house, she saw the dim glow of the lamp in the parlor of their second floor flat. Herman complained about how much it cost to light the house, but he could lay out all that cash to pay off mama's creditors. For bank interest.

"It's a waste," he grumbled, reaching into his pocket for the key to the downstairs door. "Paying the girl to sit with the children every time we go to your mother's for supper."

"You pay her less than it would cost me to make supper for the two of us," Sophie snapped. Herman looked at her in surprise. It was unusual for Sophie to speak sharply to him.

Sophie could no longer contain her resentment. After all the years of penny-pinching, of mending clothes, of haggling over the price of a piece of meat or chicken—to learn he had been secretly laying money aside!

All along she had been telling herself Herman would always keep a roof over their head, food on the table. But shouldn't life be more than that? All that money he'd squirreled away . . . They hadn't been allowed to go even once a month to the Crescent Theater, whose upstairs you could sit in for fifteen cents. To the Grand Opera House, that showed plays for as little as a dime in the top seats. But now he handed out all that money to earn interest. Would the children and she ever see any of it? Maybe Carrie—for her, it seemed, Herman would do anything.

Once they were upstairs in the house they went through the nightly ritual Sophie detested—she was to distract the girl—a warm, humble woman in her sixties—with questions about the children—had they slept through without waking? Did they eat their dinners?—while Herman inspected her brown sewing bag. He was convinced that she would take from the kitchen.

Sophie looked in on the children and went into her bedroom to prepare for the night. She wasn't even twenty-six years old, and she felt as though her life was over. She loved the children, but she couldn't bear the thought of another pregnancy—wasn't it time already that Herman was satisfied with the size of their family?

She was tired of always being stuck at home with a baby at her breast. Jenny never had to cook or clean—she had Annie Lou. Jenny went to the theater, to the opera, the restaurants with her fancy friend Nicky. What was there ahead for *her* in life? More of Herman's complaining, cooking and cleaning and washing clothes . . .

Herman was in the parlor with the ever-present piece of paper and pencil, scribbling figures about the shop. Maybe he was calculating how much money he had in another bank account that she didn't know about, she thought bitterly while she changed into a flannel nightgown. Why, he was so cheap that even in the night chill he saw no need to put more coal into the stove once the children were asleep.

She curled up underneath the blankets. Tomorrow she would leave the children with mama for half an hour while she went to the library to get another book. Something else by Laura Jean Libbey. In books the girls were always beautiful and the men handsome. They fell in love and by the end of the book were married and sure to live happily ever after. Never mind that Herman made jokes about her reading—at least library books didn't cost him anything.

She heard Herman humming under his breath as he headed toward the bedroom. He was feeling good tonight because of the deal with Jenny. She turned on her side and pretended to be asleep while he stripped down to his drawers. Any time Herman thought he'd done something smart, he wanted to make love.

"Sophie?" The bed sagged under his weight.

She tried to breathe evenly so he'd think she was asleep. On nights like this she wished he was the kind who went over to whorehouses instead of bothering her.

"Sophie?" He thrust himself against her rump and snaked his hand around to fondle her breasts, still heavy with milk. As always, she lay absolutely still.

She murmured a faint protest when he pulled her roughly onto her back, pushing the flannel gown above her hips and shoving himself deep inside her. As he began to move in growing heat she realized that she felt like one of the whores in Storyville. Except that a whore knew she'd be paid.

Jenny pursued her plans to follow the lead of the new Dallas store. Her first step was to search for a new location. Determined to thwart her, Mannie and Herman convinced Mrs. Straus that Jenny would lose everything.

"Why should Herman make a loan to the store?" Mannie demanded. "He's willing to sell his own business and come in together with us. We'll put the business back on its feet. Not with fancy ideas. With good business sense. Times are bad. Everybody looks for bargains. I personally will go out to look for distress merchandise while Herman stays here in the store. It'll become a business that makes real money. You'll see, mama."

Jenny knew it was futile to fight Mannie and Herman when they were a team. Clearly their earlier troubles had been forgotten in their united front to push her into the role of saleswoman. Again, the line of handmade lingerie was discontinued and the store was to run on a bargain basement system. Mama insisted that Evvie stay home. Danny would be at the cash register.

Jenny was angry—but not surprised—that her mother had once again allowed herself to be manipulated by her sons-in-law. Had she forgotten that the store was nothing until she, Jenny, took it over and built it up? Apparently all mama remembered was that the bank had closed and her third son-in-law had stolen her remaining nest egg.

The delicate gray walls of the store were repainted a harsh white, the sheer lilac curtains separating the windows were taken down, and the chairs she had painstakingly reupholstered in gray and lilac damask were removed because, Mannie said, they didn't want "customers loafing around the store—let them buy and get out." Now it was Jenny who left at closing time every day while Mannie and Herman stayed late.

She found comfort in Nicky.

"They're turning the store into a junk shop, Nicky. All the rich customers I worked so hard to bring into the store are gone. What's there at Straus's for them to buy now? No refined lady would want to come into such an ugly place." She sighed. "I could have built another Neiman-Marcus."

"You know, Jenny," Nicky said, "Grandma thinks you're a wonderful businesswoman, and she's fascinated by what I've told her about Neiman-Marcus. It was started by three young people, one of them a woman. My brother Benedict told me. Carrie Neiman—she was a Marcus before she married, is twenty-four. Her husband Al is twenty-seven. And her brother, Herman Marcus, is twenty-nine. They opened it last September, with banks failing all over the country, and Benedict admits they're making money."

"It kills me the way mama turned her back on me. It wasn't my fault that the bank failed and we're in so heavy to the creditors—even she admits that. But Mannie and Herman talk to her and she listens. She doesn't even hear me."

Nicky's face lit up.

"Jenny, Grandma is coming over to my house for lunch one day next week. Could you come, too? She'd love to talk to you about what it was like when she worked in the store. You can get away, can't you?"

Jenny's laugh was hollow. "Oh, sure, I have all the time in the world." She wondered how long it would be before Mannie and Herman would drive her out of the store altogether.

"Friday?"

"Friday's fine."

On Friday Nicky arrived at 12:30 sharp. Jenny was relieved to leave behind the "bargain basement" for Nicky's exquisitely furnished brick house with its wide verandah and impressive white columns, set amid lavish gardens and towering chestnut trees.

The air was heavy with the scent of roses and jasmine as they approached the Garden District. Someday, Jenny told herself, she would own a house up here. Leon and Helene would grow up and go to college from that house—Leon at Tulane, Helene at Sophie Newcomb.

"Grandma's already here," Nicky said as she parked before the sprawling verandah. "She's upstairs in the nursery with Louis."

Jenny smiled. Mrs. Goldman adored her only great-grandchild. Benedict and his wife, after years of marriage, had not yet presented her with one and everyone assumed that Marc and Simone would never have children.

Nicky took Jenny upstairs to see Louis. Then the three women went downstairs for lunch, served in the English Regency dining room which was furnished with pieces by Duncan Phyfe and Sheraton. The tall narrow windows were curtained with fine lace, the highly polished floor covered with a lovely Aubusson rug.

Mrs. Goldman was delighted that Jenny had come. Though they saw each other only occasionally, over the course of the past few years they had developed a deep friendship. Mrs. Goldman loved to reminisce, and in Jenny she had found an enthusiastic listener.

"The good years, Jenny, were when I helped my husband—may he rest in peace—in the store. For years, even after the children were born, I worked there right beside him. The customers were delighted to be served by 'Mrs. G. herself.' My husband and I were treated like royalty. But now my son and daughter-in-law treat me as though I were some fragile flower." Her voice dropped to a whisper. "I know what they think. It doesn't look right for the wife of the founder of Goldman's Department Store to be working on the floor. But if I had my way, that's where I'd be right now."

"Grandma," Nicky reminded, "you know mama and papa worry about your health." Mrs. Goldman's two daughters had married and moved away, but every year, during Mardi Gras, they came to visit.

"So I was sick one summer six years ago." Mrs. Goldman shrugged. "That means I should stay in retirement forever?"

That was the summer she met Marc. Because of his grandmother's illness the family remained in New Orleans. If she had married Marc, this delightful old lady would have been her grandmother by marriage. Nicky would be her sister-in-law. *How different her life could have been.*

As soon as she returned to the store, she sensed that Mannie and Herman had been plotting against her. But they didn't say anything immediately, so she began to wonder if it was just her imagination. Finally, in the middle of the afternoon, Mannie sauntered into the parlor, a sly grin on his face.

"Jenny, me and Herman have been thinkin'. The store's no place for a woman—and anyway, this ain't a woman's shop anymore. Mama agrees. As of tomorrow you're to stay home and be a wife. Take care of the children. You won't need Annie Lou."

It took all of Jenny's self-control not to lash out at Mannie and wipe that satisfied smile off his face. But more than Mannie and Herman she blamed mama for letting this happen. *Where was her head?* What kind of profit did she think the sleazy new store was going to bring in? *How would they live?*

CHAPTER
ELEVEN

JENNY TRIED TO adjust to her new way of life, but the hours of every day dragged endlessly. Mama, too, had insisted that Annie Lou be let go, saying that she and Evvie would take care of the meals and Jenny would be responsible for cleaning the house and watching over her children. While she loved being with the children, very quickly she grew bored without the stimulation of working in the store.

The days grew hot and humid. The Goldman women left to spend a month at Saratoga Springs. Nicky wrote that it had been a long, hot train trip—but now they were cool and comfortable in their cottage.

Jenny tried to fill the hours reading. How did mama and Evvie sit out there on the piazza all day long, talking endlessly about nothing at all? Mama didn't even bother sewing for the children anymore. She was too busy crocheting doilies.

Sometimes while Leon and Helene napped, Jenny sat beside mama and Evvie in another of the line of bentwood rockers. Three or four times a week Sophie would come over with the children. Six-year-old Carrie was always picking fights with the usually sunny dispositioned Leon, and Mrs. Straus always took Carrie's side: "A little boy shouldn't fight with a little girl, Jenny, even at their ages. It's ungentlemanly."

At last Nicky returned from Saratoga Springs. While she changed for lunch with Nicky, Jenny heard her mother talking to Evvie on the piazza.

"Here comes that young Goldman woman in that fancy

car of hers. Who does she think she is, driving around alone like that? I would never trust any woman who ran around the city in her own car. It's not natural."

Jenny tried to put her mother's words out of her mind as she clambered into the car beside Nicky.

"I've got good news—" Nicky said. "Grandma's having lunch with us. Hey, what's wrong with you?" Nicky was wearing her pongee "sheath" dress—the newest fashion in Paris and New York—and she was in her usual high spirits. "Grandma thinks you're about the smartest—and prettiest—woman alive. Don't you want to see her?"

Jenny laughed.

"Sorry, Nicky. Of course I do. I love your grandmother. She's good for my morale. I'm just a little distracted today." Jenny was especially flattered that a woman with such a keen business mind would respect her judgment.

"I picked up a copy of that new book by Mary Roberts Rinehart—you know, *The Circular Staircase*. I'll lend it to you when I finish it. Everybody says it's awfully good."

"Has Armand made up his mind yet about running for district attorney?"

Nicky smiled.

"He's decided against it. I think Armand has made up his mind to bypass running for political office since he's sure a Jew will never be elected to the presidency. At least, not in this century. Now he wants to be the power behind the politicians."

When they arrived at the house, Jenny was taken up to the white and blue nursery to visit the little Louis, who was the image of his father. At moments like this she realized what a constant source of joy it was to her that she could be so close to a member of Marc's family.

Over lunch Mrs. Goldman reminisced about the old days when, fresh to New Orleans, she and her husband struggled to build their small shop into an important department store. Jenny listened carefully, tears filling her eyes . . . what Mrs. Goldman and her husband had accomplished, *she* had hoped to accomplish.

"Jenny, are you happy out of the store?" Mrs. Goldman

asked while they lingered over chicory-laced coffee and pralines.

"No, Mrs. Goldman, I'm not. I miss it terribly. I suppose it's unnatural for me to resent being tied to the house—of course I love the children. But must a woman's life after marriage be so limited? Is it so terrible that I want to do more with my life than clean the house and watch the children play?"

"For women like you and me, Jenny, it's the right thing to be in business," Mrs. Goldman said firmly. "My children were cheated out of nothing because I was at the store during the day. They knew I loved them. I was happy, and they shared in my happiness. Would it have been better to have a bored, cranky mother fussing over them?"

"Grandma, tell Jenny what you have in mind," Nicky coaxed.

"I like your ideas about business, Jenny," Mrs. Goldman said slowly. "And you have a wonderful feel for materials and lines. For style. I would like to go back into business myself—but as a silent partner." She paused. "With you. But you must promise that no one—not even your family— will know that I'm the investor. Only Nicky, you and I can know what's happening. And Armand. I'll sell stocks and real estate to finance the store. The family doesn't have to know. Armand will handle everything for us. As my attorney he has to keep everything confidential."

"Mrs. Goldman, I can't believe it. It's everything I've ever dreamed and yet I—"

Mrs. Goldman smiled. "Say yes, my dear. In time I expect the store to become as influential as Goldman's and I want you in full charge. We'll start off small, but you'll bring to New Orleans what Neiman-Marcus has brought to Dallas. The store will grow. I have complete confidence in you, Jenny." She hesitated. "Perhaps it's wrong of me to talk this way, but I know that Goldman's Department Store as run by my son and grandson does not have the power in this city that it held ten years ago. They just don't have that flair. I think you do."

As planned, Armand arrived to set up the necessary business arrangements. Jenny's starting salary was decided—a fortune by her standards, and she would share with Mrs. Goldman in the profits. Jenny sensed Armand was not comfortable in hiding his grandmother-in-law's financial dealings from her children, but he was an honorable man and would abide by his professional ethics. Jenny realized that this was the major turning point in her life. Nothing—*nothing*—would be allowed to interfere. Not Mannie. Not mama.

Jenny signed the necessary papers. Smiling indulgently, yet with misgivings, Armand wished her luck, and left to return to his office.

"As I've told you, Jenny, I want you to make decisions," Mrs. Goldman said, "but my instincts tell me that of course you will consult me in important matters." She sighed. "Getting old is not good if all you do is sit around and have folks wait on you. My husband—may he rest in peace— would not have let the children do this to me. But," she brightened, "now I'll have something to interest me. Our store."

As she listened to her new business partner, Jenny sensed that the new store was Mrs. Goldman's revenge on her family for not "tending the store"—and for neglecting their Jewish faith. Mrs. Goldman still attended services every Friday night at the temple and observed the holidays. Twice a year, on Rosh Hashanah and Yom Kippur, Mrs. Goldman's son went to temple. Sometimes his wife accompanied him.

"Let's see . . . what shall we call our store, Jenny?" Mrs. Goldman's brow furrowed in concentration. "We'll take your name—but we'll spell it 'Jennie'—that looks pretty. Why don't we call it Maison Jennie?" She smiled at Jenny's expression. "And in the store you'll wear an elegant black frock and a fresh gardenia. Customers will come to know it as your trademark—every morning a fresh gardenia from the French Market."

Before she went back to the house, Jenny went to Bucktown—the colored settlement of West End—to talk Annie Lou into coming back. Annie Lou had been reduced to taking in washing since she'd been let go.

"Oh Miz Jenny," she said, "you don't know how proud I am to come back to you. I sure miss them children."

And she was thrilled when Jenny increased her wages. That would be part of her business creed, Jenny promised herself. To pay help well. It was a good business practice, papa always used to say—though he was never in a position to hire help.

On the streetcar going home Jenny tried to brace herself for the inevitable battle with Mannie and mama. But it was time for her to take charge of her life. She no longer had to ask permission. She made the decisions. She was returning to the business world on her own terms.

She waited until after supper, after Leon and Helene had been put to bed, to announce her news. Mannie was outraged—until he heard her salary. Then he just stared in disbelief. Jenny said nothing about her partnership and the fact that she would be sharing in the profits.

"And who's setting up this fine store?" Mrs. Straus demanded.

Mannie laughed harshly.

"It won't last. Who pays a saleslady that kind of wage?"

"I'm the manager, Mannie. I'll be in complete control." Now that it was too late, mama appreciated what Jenny had accomplished for their store. "I know nothing about the investor. I can only say that Nicky's husband made the arrangements. They want me to set up a store like Neiman-Marcus in Dallas." She hesitated, gauging the conflicting reactions about the table. Evvie, bless her, was happy for her—she was the only one who realized how lost Jenny had been away from the store. Mama was skeptical. Mannie was torn between greed at the prospect of an exalted new family income and wounded pride that his wife was moving ahead. "The store is to be called Maison Jennie. I'm to wear an elegant black frock and a fresh gardenia every day."

Evvie's face was tender with affection.

"I think it's wonderful!"

"Wonderful for the children to lose their mother?" Mrs. Straus said coldly. "Better you should stay at home with Leon and Helene."

"I want to know who's paying the bills for this fancy store," Mannie blustered. "I bet there's somethin' goin' on behind my back."

"Mannie!" Mrs. Straus was indignant. "Jenny would do nothing improper. I don't approve of the mother of two children deserting them to go into business either, but to even imply anything else is digusting."

"Hold on," Mannie said. "As Jenny's husband don't I have a right to know who's running the business?"

Jenny refused to be baited.

"Armand Lazar knows. That's enough for all of us."

Mrs. Straus looked skeptical.

"I suppose you'll hire a girl again to look after the children and clean?"

"I've already talked to Annie Lou." Jenny saw Mannie bristle as he realized the whole deal had been a *fait accompli*. "She'll come back to us in the morning. I'm already on salary."

Jenny's first job was to find a location for the store and plan the decoration. Mrs. Goldman meant for Maison Jennie to be elegant, luxurious. Every day the two women met at Nicky's house, so that they wouldn't be under the scrutiny of the Goldman family.

"I know you won't throw money away, Jenny, so don't worry about cutting corners. This is to be a store to attract the wealthiest clientele in New Orleans. They'll eventually come to Maison Jennie from a hundred miles away."

"I wish we knew more about Neiman-Marcus," Jenny said wistfully. "Not that we'll copy what they've done, but they've established something the public clearly likes."

"Then go to Dallas. Take Nicky with you. You needn't look so shocked, my dear. This is the modern age—it's all right for women to travel. And Nicky will be glad for some diversion. Talk to her tonight and leave as soon as you can."

Nicky was thrilled at Jenny's plan.

"The children will survive for a few days without us," she said, "and I know exactly where we can stay—the

Oriental Hotel. That's where Armand stayed when he was in Dallas on business."

Of course mama and Mannie were shocked. Mama disapproved of two mothers leaving their children alone "just for business" and it was only greed that prevented Mannie from creating ugly scenes.

It would be Jenny's first time out of New Orleans since the Straus family first moved to the city when she was eight years old. She could barely contain her excitement. On a sunny October morning she and Nicky approached the new Terminal Station, its exterior of Bedford stone finished in a special matching gray brick. Escorted by Armand and followed by a porter carrying their luggage, they walked through the building's thirty-feet-high archway, marveling at the station's beauty.

"Now don't buy out Neiman-Marcus, ladies," Armand teased as he settled Nicky and Jenny in their plush compartment aboard the Dallas-bound train of the Houston & Texas Central Railroad.

Nicky laughed and kissed him with a passion that startled Jenny.

"I'll try not to."

Then they were alone in their luxurious red velour upholstered compartment, Nicky bubbling with excitement.

"Jenny, Armand said we must be sure to see the Sanger Brothers store and A. Harris and Company while we're in Dallas. And we're to take a drive—or a long walk—it's only a dozen blocks or so from the downtown business section, to see the residential area caled the Cedars. The Sangers live there in fabulous mansions."

Jenny smiled.

"My customers told me that Neiman-Marcus is right across the street from A. Harris and Company. At the corner of Elm and Murphy."

"Oh, Armand gave me a memo while I was dressing." Nicky dug into her Mark Cross purse. "He said we'd have plenty of time to look at it on the train. Things he uncovered about Neiman-Marcus."

"What kinds of things?"

Before the conductor came through to collect their

tickets, Jenny and Nicky had learned that Neiman-Marcus had thirty-five employees and that the yearly rental on their store was nine thousand dollars. It seemed overwhelming, but Jenny told herself that she must learn to think in these terms. Sometimes at night she woke up, terrified at the thought of how much Mrs. Goldman was investing in their store. It was more than papa had earned in a lifetime . . .

Once they'd arrived in Dallas, Jenny and Nicky took a carriage from the H & TC passenger depot at Central Avenue to the Oriental Hotel. Along the way Jenny noticed the narrow sidewalks and crosstown streets—some of which hadn't even been paved. But there were impressive stores and business buildings. According to Armand, Dallas had a population of 86,000—New Orleans had over 287,000 people.

The carriage deposited them in front of the entrance to the six-story Oriental Hotel, considered one of the finest in the area. It was a striking building, the lower sides painted gray, the upper reddish brown, the turret black. A pair of bellboys collected their luggage and escorted them like royalty into the large ornate lobby, its elaborate ceiling festooned with chandeliers.

Once settled in their suite, their valises unpacked, Jenny and Nicky went to visit Neiman-Marcus—though their initial plan had been to rest up, have dinner in the hotel dining room, and see the store the following morning.

Their first view of the two-story building that housed the famous store was disappointing.

"*This* is the fabulous Neiman-Marcus?" Nicky asked.

But the instant they stepped inside they were immersed in the most opulent surroundings they'd ever seen. The floor was covered with lush carpeting. The fixtures were red mahogany. They were welcomed by a smartly dressed, smiling saleswoman. In moments they were standing in a beautifully mirrored, flatteringly lighted dressing room and Nicky was trying on a carriage coat suit designed by Drecoll.

"It only needs to be shortened two inches," the saleswoman said. "Otherwise it fits perfectly."

Jenny eyed the hem of the suit.

"We'll be in Dallas for three days. Can it be altered before we leave?" Now she understood the appeal of the ready-to-wear lines, first introduced to Dallas by Neiman-Marcus.

"Oh, yes," the saleswoman said. "Madame Bartel will have the suit ready for delivery by tomorrow afternoon." She turned to Nicky. "If you wish, you may come back and try it on again to make sure the length is right. Or we'll have it sent to your hotel."

"We'll be doing more shopping," Nicky said. "So we can be in the store again tomorrow. I'll pick it up then."

They spent the rest of the afternoon inspecting the Neiman-Marcus merchandise. While Nicky tried on a gown designed by Sarah Bernhardt Jenny took notes, sending the saleswoman out to search for a purse to go with the gown.

Nicky twirled in front of the mirror.

"Soaking up information, Jenny?"

"You know I am!"

They spent the next morning sightseeing. Walking in the brilliant autumn sun, the air crisp and pleasant, they visited the elegant residential area close by known as the Cedars. From Armand's description they knew that the two grandest houses belonged to the Sanger brothers.

Standing before a huge house with a wide graceful verandah, a double stairway, attic turrets and flower entwined beige wood trellises, Jenny vowed that one day, soon, she would own a house like this.

CHAPTER
TWELVE

ON HER RETURN from Dallas Jenny focused on finding the proper location for the new store. At last she and Mrs. Goldman agreed on an available space, but substantial alterations would be necessary. While walls were being torn out and a second floor added to the area, Jenny designed the interior. She loved tracking down special wallpapers, just the right shade of carpeting, good reproductions of Louis XV chairs and tables that would lend the aura of a lovely home—she felt a little guilty to be drawing a substantial salary for doing what was such a pleasure.

When the alterations were within weeks of completion Mrs. Goldman told Jenny to go to New York to buy merchandise. Everything about Maison Jennie must have a personal touch.

Jenny was worried about the reception at home to yet another business trip. But Mannie and mama simply could not interfere. She should have anticipated it, but with all the decorating problems, she'd had no time to think ahead. Mrs. Goldman was adamant.

"Take Nicky with you, Jenny. Like you she has impeccable taste, a wonderful sense of style. She'll be helpful."

Nicky, excited at the prospect of another trip, was a bit piqued that Armand agreed so readily to let her go. Jenny delayed telling Mannie and her mother until a week before she was supposed to leave. She came home from the store earlier than usual to feed Leon and Helene and get them to bed before Mannie arrived. More than anything else, she looked forward to her time each day with the children.

Mannie usually avoided them, but he did like to brag about them to Herman.

She was coming downstairs when she heard Mannie throw himself into his usual chair in the parlor to read the newspaper. Mama and Evvie were in the kitchen. Danny was out with his friends. She took a deep breath and walked into the parlor. Quietly she explained about the trip.

"What do you mean, you're going to New York?" Mannie's jaw was set in a stubborn line. "Respectable women don't go running off to New York and leave their husbands and children at home."

"I have to go. Armand told me. I'm the only one who can do the buying." She felt a twinge of guilt, but she had to believe that the children would be fine. She'd promised to bring them each a present from New York.

"So," Mannie tossed aside the paper, "again the husband has nothing to say? I think I can do without supper here. I'll get somethin' outside." He picked up his jacket and stalked out of the parlor.

When Evvie called her in to the supper table, Jenny told her that Mannie had gone out.

"We had a fight." She knew she didn't have to elaborate—Evvie wouldn't pry.

While the three women were cleaning up the kitchen after supper, she told her mother about the trip. As she had anticipated Mrs. Straus disapproved.

"You put the business ahead of everything. Even the children. And you shouldn't be saddling me with them. You know how bad my nerves are. They'll drive me into a breakdown."

"Mama, I'm not *saddling* you with anyone. Annie Lou will be here. You won't have to lift a finger."

"All you care about is getting around to strange places with Nicky Lazar. You just got back a few weeks ago from Dallas. Now you're running off to New York. Soon it will be Paris. At this rate the children will forget they have a mother."

Jenny stiffened. Would she ever go to Paris? How could she, without seeing Marc?

"Mama," Jenny said, "we'll spend exactly four days in

New York, calling on the manufacturers. That's all." Put Paris out of her mind! She was lucky to have been in Dallas, and now New York was ahead of her. "It's not a social event, mama. It's business."

Right after New Year's of 1909—when buyers were heading for New York for their spring and summer lines, Armand took Jenny and Nicky to the Terminal Station and into a drawing room aboard the elegant pullman that was to carry them across the southland to Atlanta, where it would be hooked up to a northbound train.

"You girls take good care of yourselves now." He hugged Jenny, kissed Nicky and hurried out of the pullman as the warning was being sounded for the departure of nonpassengers. Nicky plunked down in her seat and stared sullenly out the window.

"Nicky," Jenny said, "where did you get that suit? And the fur? More gifts from your adoring husband?" She knew Nicky's mink coat had been a Christmas gift from Armand, chosen by Marc and Simone in Paris at Revillon Fréres.

Nicky's expression didn't change. "I'm furious with him. Did you notice how it seemed like he couldn't wait to get me out of town? The more I think about it the more I'm sure he's having an affair."

"You could be wrong—"

"I'm not. Jenny, it's wonderful at night when we're in bed together. Why does he have to go chasing after other women?"

"Maybe he's just trying to prove something to himself. Armand loves you, Nicky. And he adores Louis."

"Then why can't he stop playing these games?"

Jenny smiled sadly. "If I knew the answers to that I'd be the wisest lady around. Be happy with what you have, Nicky."

"Maybe you're right. To the devil with Armand's games." Chameleonlike, Nicky switched moods. "Hey! We're on our way to New York! And I'm going to make damn sure I have a marvelous time." She leaned forward and opened a suitcase. "I've brought along that Pierre Loti novel—*The Disenchanted*. And Mary Roberts Rinehart's newest mystery. Let's read until it's time for dinner."

Jenny tried to focus on *The Disenchanted*. Whenever she couldn't sleep at night she'd slip downstairs to read, leaving Mannie, snoring, sprawled across their bed. At times like this she caught herself wondering what it would be like to enjoy sleeping with her husband, and Nicky's references to hers and Armand's happy sex life highlighted her loneliness. Even with their problems, at least Nicky and Armand loved each other.

But for her and Mannie, the chasm between them seemed to widen with each passing year. Mannie had been in this country since he was eight years old, but—like Herman—he was a foreigner. He didn't understand New Orleans. He didn't love the city the way she loved it. They had nothing in common. But she was still determined—for the children and mama—to keep the marriage alive. Thank God he hadn't touched her since she'd been pregnant with Helene—he seemed to be satisfied to have fathered two children. Sometimes, late at night, she imagined what it would be like to make love with Marc. Did Simone know how lucky she was?

At Nicky's insistence they dressed up for dinner. Jenny wore one of the beautifully cut black crêpe dresses that had been made for her from a Paris design when the shop opened. Nicky wore the gray crêpe from Neiman-Marcus.

Jenny was aware of the admiring glances from the other passengers in the dining car as they gave their orders to the white-jacketed waiter standing at their table.

"You see those two men at the table just ahead of us?" Nicky whispered. "I'll bet they think we're buyers for some big store back in New Orleans."

Jenny giggled. "We are. We're going to New York to buy for Maison Jennie."

"You know what I mean. A lot of the men on the trains are drummers, store owners and professional men looking for excitement. Armand warned me—he says these men all think women buyers are fair game."

"Nicky!" Jenny was shocked. "Well, if that's true they'll find out fast enough they're wasting their time with us."

Nicky smiled mischievously. "Can you imagine trying to sneak a woman into an upper or lower berth? Of course, the man who's traveling in a compartment or drawing room wouldn't have much of a problem. I doubt the conductor is going to come knocking on doors to demand if he has a woman in his accommodations."

"God, Nicky, it all sounds so sordid."

"Maybe," Nicky said, "maybe not. It could be pretty romantic."

"Read Pierre Loti's novel tonight, Nicky." Jenny said sternly. "That'll be enough romantic adventuring for *you*."

"Jenny, does it bother you that you know Mannie runs around with whores?"

Quickly Jenny looked around to make sure no one had overheard. "Well, yes," she said. "It does. I guess I don't understand it." In truth, she hated sharing a bed with Mannie after he'd come home from one of his "inventory checks." "But we don't have a real married life. It's not like with you and Armand."

"So," Nicky said, "because Armand's a man it's all right for him to chase after other women? Why should it be any different for a woman?"

The waiter arrived with their soup and Jenny changed the subject. As on the trip to Dallas, the dining-car food was excellent.

While they lingered over coffee, Nicky whispered that the two men who had been watching them throughout dinner were moving toward their table.

"Come on, Jenny," she said, "it won't hurt to talk to them. We'll be traveling together for three days and nights."

"Excuse me," the taller of the two men—both well dressed and somewhere in their thirties, paused at their table, "but didn't we meet in Dallas recently?"

"You're buyers from Sanger Brothers, aren't you?" the other man asked.

Nicky smiled. "No, but we were in Dallas recently."

Now Jenny realized that the young men must have over-heard their conversation about Dallas.

Jenny tried to be polite but impersonal when Nicky invited the two men to join them at their table for another round of coffee. People on trains were friendly, she told herself—it was entirely innocent, just a way of passing time. And actually she was enjoying this unexpected male companionship. It made her realize, yet again, how far removed she had become from the world of her family.

Mannie's conversation revolved around his pinochle games with Herman, baseball and what happened in the store that day. Mama only wanted an ear for her endless list of minor complaints. Who knew what Evvie was thinking? She was mama's shadow. And Sophie talked only about the children and the house. Sometimes Jenny felt like a stranger in her own family.

"I think it's fascinating that Henry Ford has brought out a new car," Nicky was saying. "More women will begin driving. You'll see."

"Do you drive?" The older of the two seemed enthralled at the prospect of Nicky behind the wheel of a car.

"I adore driving. I wish I could have been in that car that drove from Peking to Paris two years ago. What an exciting adventure!" Jenny noticed the glint in the gentlemen's eyes and the girlish lilt in Nicky's voice. *Nicky wouldn't*. Would she?

She was shocked when Nicky and her admirer excused themselves to go to his compartment "to see a magazine article about the Savannah race won by a Fiat." A barely perceptible wink from Nicky told her not to worry if she didn't come back to their compartment that night. Instantly Jenny made it clear to the other man that she would not be following suit. He seemed disappointed but was enough of a gentleman not to press her.

Jenny lay sleepless while the train sped through open stretches of dark, silent country. It would have been so easy to have gone to Paul's compartment. He was easy to talk to and it felt good to be admired again. But would she have liked making love with him?

Paul was a store executive, accustomed to living well. No lower or upper berths for him. He moved in the kind of world where Mannie was uncomfortable. Did Paul have a wife? Children? Did his wife suspect he picked up women on his business trips?

If only she and Marc had shared more than a few chaste kisses. It had been more than six years since he had boarded that train. Did he still remember her? He *must*.

At the sound of a soft urgent knock she left her berth to unlock the drawing room door. It was Nicky.

"Oh, Jenny, you didn't have to wait up for me." As she stepped inside, Jenny could see that she was radiant, her hair slightly disheveled. "I'm not sorry, you know. I'm not in love with him, but I enjoy making love. That doesn't make me a whore. Why shouldn't women enjoy it? Anyway, I only did it because I was furious with Armand. I figured what's all right for the husband is all right for the wife." She smiled. "But you needn't look so stricken, darling. I won't make a habit of it."

To Jenny—whose travel had been limited thus far to the trip to Dallas—this journey across the southern states and up the eastern coast was a joy. During the day she sat by the window, absorbing the view. She and Nicky went to the dining car for long leisurely meals, which they shared with the two men they'd met at dinner on the first night. Both of them fended off any further invitations to bed. When they arrived in New York they exchanged pleasant good-byes and separated.

Nicky had been to New York at least a dozen times, either with her mother to shop or en route to Saratoga Springs or Europe. But to Jenny, being in this wonderful city was a miracle.

Nicky had warned her of the severe New York winters and insisted she borrow her Hudson seal coat.

"Now aren't you glad you're wearing my fur?"

Jenny laughed.

"I'd be an icicle without it." So this was the city papa had glowingly described to her—mama seemed to have only unpleasant memories of the four months she'd spent here.

"There's so much I'd love to see," Jenny said as they unpacked in their room at the new Plaza Hotel, rebuilt just two years before at the cost of twelve million dollars and furnished in dazzling baroque Louis XIV. "But we'll be busy with the manufacturers and the stores."

"Let's take one afternoon to run up to the Metropolitan Museum—just in passing you'll see a lot of the sights."

"The business is more important than anything right now, Nicky. It terrifies me to think that I'm to do all the buying for the store without your grandmother seeing even one piece."

"You'll do fine. Do you think she'd send you to do all this if she didn't trust you? And I'll help. After all," Nicky said, "everybody says I wear the smartest clothes in New Orleans, and you always help me choose. Armand moans about how much I spend, but he's proud of me. The only time he's angry is when I talk about working for women's suffrage."

"You know, Nicky, I really think that will come within the next ten years. It has to, with the way women are going out into the business world."

For the next few days, Jenny and Nicky visited manufacturers. Jenny had vowed to make this period an education in merchandising. In the mornings she would do the buying, selectively and with growing confidence—yet shivering at the thousands of dollars she was spending. She was just following Mrs. Goldman's orders, she told herself. In the afternoons—except for two hours they stole for visiting the splendid Metropolitan Museum, they haunted New York's most elegant shops and department stores.

Both of them were intrigued by the number of automobiles in New York—and particularly by the green and red motor "cabs" always waiting outside the hotel ready to whisk them to their destinations. They had breakfast every morning in the Plaza's dining room, which looked out directly on Central Park. Jenny was thrilled to see her first snow flurries from that window on their second morning in the city.

They were entertained royally every night by Maison Jennie's new suppliers. They dined at the Colony Club, Palm Garden and the Casino in the Park. They went to two Broadway plays and heard a fabulous new violinist named Mischa Elman at Carnegie Hall. Jenny felt guilty that she was having such a wonderful time when the children were two thousand miles away.

Back on the train, she felt at once impatient to be home and yet sure that she would miss the excitement of New York. But she was returning to New Orleans with a purpose. She was going to make Maison Jennie a success. When she heard that Carrie Neiman went to Paris to buy, she decided to start French lessons the minute she returned.

She did not dare admit even to herself that a major attraction in Paris was Marc.

When their train arrived at Terminal Station, Armand was there to meet them. Jenny was pleased to see how eagerly he greeted Nicky. They would have a warm reunion tonight. What would hers and Mannie's be like? She felt a wave of loneliness.

"I drove over," Armand told them, gesturing for a porter to collect the luggage. "We'll drive you home, Jenny."

He insisted on carrying Jenny's valise to her door.

"There's no need to wait, Armand. You take Nicky home. We've had quite a trip and she's got so much to tell you." Jenny doubted that there would ever be a repetition of Nicky's one-night affair. Not that Nicky regretted it—but it was more of an impulsive thing, her one gesture of the defiance against the double standard both she and Nicky deplored.

Jenny heard footsteps in the hall. Mannie would be asleep. Mama would be sitting in the parlor with her cup of tea. Leon and Helene would be asleep.

The door opened.

"So." Mrs. Straus stood before her, Mannie peering over

her shoulder. "The wife and mother has finally come home."

"This is when I was due to come home—" Jenny looked at Mannie. "What is it? Are the children all right?"

"What do you care?" Mannie jeered. "You're off buying for your store. What else do you care about except your precious store?"

"What's happened to the children?" She pushed past them toward the stairs.

"Don't disturb Leon!" Mama snapped. "The doctor wants him to sleep."

"The doctor?" Leon was sick and she wasn't here to be with him? "What's the matter with Leon?"

"Annie Lou didn't notice," Mannie said. "Your *schwartze* who's supposed to be so smart. The father saw he wasn't feeling right. The father sent for the doctor."

"Leon's all right." Evvie came out from the parlor. "Why are you trying to frighten Jenny?" She turned to Jenny. "He has a slight cold. The doctor said there was no reason to worry—half the children in New Orleans have colds right now."

Mrs. Straus pressed her palm to her forehead. "Evvie, go to the bathroom and get my nerve medicine. I can't take these responsibilities. Jenny, *you're* the mother. I've raised my children."

CHAPTER THIRTEEN

JENNY LIVED OUT her dreams in the creation of Maison Jennie, but she scrupulously avoided working beyond normal hours lest Mannie and her mother pounce on her for neglecting her family. She zealously guarded those special hours with Leon and Helene when everything was pushed from her mind. Only after she had put them to bed for the night did she allow her thoughts to return to the store.

Worried about how withdrawn Evvie had been since Sidney left, Jenny decided to talk to her about working in the store. She knew mama would have a fit, but there had to be more in life for Evvie than sitting on the piazza and helping with the meals.

"Evvie, it's important that I have someone on the register whom I can trust," she began one evening when mama had gone to Sophie's for supper and Mannie was already in bed. "How would you feel about coming into the store for the first few weeks until I have time to find somebody that's right for the job?"

Evvie's eyes widened.

"In such a fine store? Oh, Jenny, I'd be scared."

"It would be such a help to me, Evvie. All you have to do is sit there and take the cash and smile. You're always so gracious and pretty."

"Oh, no, I'm not." Evvie's face clouded.

"Yes you are," Jenny said. "We'll choose some pretty dresses from the stock for you to wear. You'll look lovely. And you will be helping me—now I won't have to worry that my boss is being robbed blind."

"All right. If it's that important to you." Evvie sighed. "I'll try."

Two weeks before the opening of Maison Jennie, a sullen Mannie sat at the supper table shoveling brisket and potatoes into his mouth. Why did they have Sophie and Herman to supper every week? Wasn't it enough he had to look at Herman all day long in the store?

"Everybody's waiting for the opening of the store," Sophie said with pride. Mannie ignored her. "I never saw so much excitement about a new store."

Mrs. Straus shook her head.

"It's a store, not a circus."

"Yeah." Crumbs spilled out of Mannie's mouth as he spoke. "Some rich fools playing games. I betcha this fancy store will close in six months." And when it did, he'd put his foot down. Let Jenny know who was boss in this family. His father would *never* have put up with this. A man went out to earn the living. The wife cooked and cleaned the house and raised the children. That was the way it was supposed to be. His mother would never have dared to leave her children at home to go out to work. Jenny was spoiled rotten. Always doing what *she* wanted to do. To the devil with the husband.

"Don't dismiss Maison Jennie so fast," Danny said, slicing into the brisket. "Jenny's bosses may have something good going there. You've got a smart wife, Mannie. She's earning more than anybody else here at this table."

Mannie flushed. It was only Jenny's salary that kept him from *ordering* her to stop work. It infuriated him that she wouldn't hand over her pay envelope to him each week. She kept saying it was the house money—she'd handle it.

"Yeah, my wife made a good connection for herself," he said sarcastically. He hated Nicky Goldman with her fancy clothes and her automobile. "It don't take brains for that."

"Watch yourself, Mannie," Herman said. "Folks in New Orleans will be calling you Mister Jenny."

"That's the day Jenny stops working." He'd thought he was doing good for himself when he married an American-

born girl. He should have married a girl from the old
country. They knew their place.

As usual, Sophie took it upon herself to lighten the
atmosphere.

"Mama, what are we having for dessert? I know I gain
three pounds every time we eat here, but nobody bakes like
you."

When mama brought out the pinochle deck Jenny pulled
Herman aside and said, "Herman, I want you to stop
tearing down Mannie. And stop telling him his wife wears
the pants in the family."

He looked at her innocently. "What are you talking
about?"

"Don't pretend you don't know what I mean—you say it
all the time. Someday you may want to do business with us.
We'll be interested in a store to handle our leftover
merchandise. We'll be carrying nothing into the next
season." She saw his eyes light up. Bargains he understood. "But I tell you right now, you keep belittling
Mannie, and we won't even *consider* you as an outlet. Not
even for mama's sake."

"What's the matter?" Herman whined. "You can't take a
joke?"

"No. Not when it causes trouble in my home."

Though mama never asked a question about the store,
Jenny knew she snatched at every bit of news as the opening
day neared. She'd been horrified when she learned that
Maison Jennie would not be offering a piece-goods department. Didn't Jenny know that was the most important
department in *any* big store? The one that earned the major
share of profits? The piece-goods departments sold through
the store's dressmaker—and every major store maintained
an expert dressmaker—as well as to every private dressmaker in the city. But while waists and skirts could be
bought ready-made, they were hardly considered fashionable.

It was just this lack of a piece-goods department that
would make Maison Jennie unique. Like Neiman-Marcus,
Maison Jennie must cater not only to the very rich but to the

large middle-class buyers and to the burgeoning new class of working women who would buy one special outfit a season.

The opening of Maison Jennie was built up into a grand event to be covered by the press. It was announced that a share of the profits of the first day's sale would go to a local charity. Nicky gathered a group of beautiful young society matrons to serve as saleswomen and models.

At Mrs. Goldman's suggestion coffee was served from silver urns set up in several areas of the store and presided over by former Mardi Gras queens. Wearing a black crepe dress that was a replica of a French design, Jenny circulated among her prospective customers. She kept a sharp eye on the seven salesladies—she had chosen them with care and had coached each one to cater to every potential customer as though she were a member of royalty. In every aspect Maison Jennie was to be a smaller-scale replica of Neiman-Marcus.

Then, in the Sunday edition of the *Times-Piscayune*, Maison Jennie ran a large ad—in the style of Neiman-Marcus on its opening—to assure the buying public that despite the aura of catering to the wealthy, Maison Jennie's prices would be fair and much of their merchandise affordable for most of the ladies of New Orleans.

Society matrons, middle-class wives, eager young typists from the offices in the city flocked to the store. Any doubts Jenny might have harbored vanished within the first ten weeks of business. Maison Jennie was on the road to success.

To Jenny's surprise, Evvie stood up for herself when Mrs. Straus began insisting that working at the store was too much for her. Mrs. Straus's store—now in the hands of Herman and Mannie—was doing poorly. The two men blamed Jenny's earlier expansion for their problems, scoffing at the need to pay off their creditors—even after the bank reopened and paid off accounts to the last cent.

Three months after the opening of Maison Jennie Mannie stopped paying the house rent.

"You take care of it from your fancy salary," he snapped.

"You got enough for that." He didn't bother to mention where *his* salary would go.

At intervals Jenny gave her mother sums of money to pass on to Sophie to help with the grocery bills. Apparently Herman expected Sophie to feed a family of seven on almost nothing. It was understood, of course, that Sophie was not to know the money came from her sister.

Maison Jennie continued to prosper. Every garment that arrived in the store was put on a dressmaker's form and inspected. Any item that was not exactly right was returned immediately to the supplier. Jenny impressed upon the salesladies that they charged for perfection. Anything less was unacceptable.

Once a week Jenny met for a long conference with Mrs. Goldman, and they talked daily on the telephone. Like Mrs. Goldman in her day, Jenny was always on the selling floor or in the fitting room with customers. To the wealthy customers she explained that she ordered only the finest merchandise, chosen to make her ladies the best dressed in the country. To the middle class she explained the advantages of buying quality—better one superb outfit than three or four lesser ones. And to the working girls she extolled the virtues of the one special outfit that was worth minor sacrifices.

Meanwhile, Mannie and Herman battled to stay afloat. At the end of the year Jenny had made enough of a profit to sell off old stock to the other store at a pittance. She taught Mannie and Herman to cut out labels and hint to their customers that these were big bargains from "high-class New York department stores."

Six months later, when her prized saleslady moved to Baton Rouge to get married, Jenny offered Sophie a job at Maison Jennie. She knew how hard it was to get by on what Herman was able to bring home each week and she thought Sophie would be pleased. But Sophie was terrified at the prospect of bringing in money on her own.

"Herman would have a heart attack!"

"Not when he finds out what the store can pay you," Jenny said drily. When she named the figure Sophie's eyes lit up. "Karl and Carrie and Frederic are all in school already. Only Milton and Herbert are home. Give Annie Lou another dollar a week and she'll watch them, too. Mama will be happy to have them in the house." She had been trying to forget a remark she had heard mama make to an acquaintance last week—something about having "five wonderful grandchildren"—she seemed to have forgotten about Leon and Helen.

"But Jenny, do you think I could sell? What if I'm no good!"

Jenny was touched by Sophie's insecurity.

"Of course you can. I'll give you tips on how we handle customers. I've trained all our salesladies."

Sophie looked down at her figure, which showed the signs of five pregnancies in eight years and the rich heavy food Herman expected on his table.

"And I'm fat. All those ladies you've hired look like fashion models."

"You'll lose weight working, Sophie. And the right clothes will hide a lot of it for now."

"I don't know if Herman will let me." But her face betrayed her eagerness.

"He'll carry on. He'll make arrogant remarks about going ahead if you have to make a fool of yourself. But he'll be happy for the money."

Of the three Straus sisters, Jenny thought bitterly, not one had made a decent marriage. But that didn't mean they could not make something decent of their lives. She was happy Sophie was coming into the store.

Later that week Danny came to Jenny at the store and asked for a job.

"I thought you were happy at the men's shop," she said warily.

Danny shrugged.

"They're bringing in a new son-in-law, so I guess you could say I was fired." He flashed his ingratiating smile. "Anyhow, it'll be more fun to work at Maison Jennie. You know me. I love being around pretty women."

Jenny felt his insecurity beneath the bravado.

"Come to think of it," she said, "we do need a

floorwalker." This way Danny wouldn't have access to the cash register . . .

"That's me, Jenny. When do I start?"

"How much notice did they give you?"

"I'm free as of today. I had two weeks' notice," he said sheepishly. "I just didn't get around to admitting it. A blow to my pride to get fired—even for a new son-in-law."

Jenny paused. As much as she wanted to trust him, she couldn't help wondering if they'd caught Danny with his hand in the till. She decided to give him a chance.

"I want you to start tomorrow. But I'm warning you, Danny—you'll be putting in a full day's work. No fooling around."

Within two weeks she knew that her decision to hire Danny was a good one. Young and gallant and more than passably good-looking, he was an asset to the image of the store, escorting choice customers to their waiting carriages or automobiles, carrying their packages, and presiding over the afternoon tea run. Jenny had instituted the habit of having all business stop at three o'clock sharp so that every customer in the store could be served afternoon tea.

With Danny happily employed, mama told Jenny that her store could not provide an income for everyone. Mannie and Herman were again coming to blows and Sophie, as usual, bore the brunt of their hostility. What mama wanted was for Mannie to be absorbed in some capacity into Maison Jennie. Herman had brought money into her store— Mannie had come in with nothing.

"You do the hiring, Jenny. Hire Mannie."

"All right, Mama. But he'll have to stay off the selling floor."

"You can handle that."

At Mrs. Goldman's advice Jenny began keeping a list of weddings reported in the New Orleans newspapers so that discreet notes might be sent to husbands to remind them of approaching anniversaries. To her mother's and Mannie's horror—but with Mrs. Goldman's hearty approval—she even began to extend credit to choice customers. Greeting cards went out at Christmas and Easter, and on Hanukkah and Passover to their Jewish clientele. Jenny made a point of being seen, fashionably dressed, at the theater and opera, either alone with Nicky or with Nicky and Armand.

She cherished any words of encouragement from Marc via Nicky—he alone had been told about his grandmother's secret partnership. Jenny knew that he was immersed in his painting, ever striving to improve his work, but she wondered if he was happy.

Only once did Jenny and Armand come close to arguing, when he objected to Mrs. Goldman's insistence that her shares in the shop be willed to Nicky to insure Jenny's control of the store in the event of her death. Jenny knew that Nicky's parents and brother Benedict were irritated by Nicky's closeness to an upstart young woman merchant and if they knew about Mrs. Goldman's involvement in the store, they'd feel betrayed.

Jenny loved to see how much pleasure the success of Maison Jennie brought Mrs. Goldman. There was a lilt in her voice these days, excitement in her eyes. She and Jenny were responsible for the store's growing success; they were two partners, each immensely respecting the other.

If only Mrs. Goldman knew how much her one innocent remark had meant to Jenny: "Now why couldn't Marc have stayed here and married a bright, sweet, beautiful girl like you?"

Armand worried about increasing family friction if Mrs. Goldman should die and Nicky sided with Jenny, but Mrs. Goldman was adamant.

"I plan to live till I'm ninety," she declared. "But I want it in writing that Jenny will always have control of Maison Jennie."

Jenny was proud to have Sophie, Evvie and Danny in the store. Mannie seethed with resentment at being restricted to the back rooms. He and Herman were always making sarcastic references to Jenny's "highfalutin'" customers.

Jenny worked long hours at the store, took an hour out three times a week for French lessons, read at every odd moment, always saving her time with Leon and Helene. She was acutely conscious now that neither their father nor grandmother showed them any overt affection, and to compensate she lavished love on them, happy that they were close to Sophie's children. Carrie—spoiled by Herman and extremely difficult—was the one exception.

A few weeks before Leon's sixth birthday, Jenny took him to his first day at the private school Nicky had convinced her to enroll him in. Mannie, as usual, was outraged at the tuition and mama was annoyed that Leon was attending a private school while Sophie's children were going to public school.

As the profits poured in, Jenny decided to rent a house for the family in the Garden District. She remembered her mother scoffing, years earlier, when she had said that one day she hoped to live in that lush, affluent neighborhood. A house uptown in the Garden District would be a tangible proof that she realized her dreams. But the district was an area of family owned homes and houses for rentals were scarce.

At last Jenny found her house. Even before she walked inside with Nicky—who had discovered the vacancy through a family friend, Jenny knew she could live forever in the two-and-a-half-storied stuccoed house with its white columned gallery, set among tall magnolias, pecan and fig trees with crepe-myrtle, azaleas and rose bushes adorning the broad lawns.

Mama gave her grudging approval.

"Of course, it's nothing like the house *I* grew up in. But it's a pretty house. If Sophie wants to stay over with the children, we'll have plenty of room."

Somehow, Jenny made time to race around New Orleans with Nicky to choose furniture for the new house. This must be a place that would offer the same serene grace and charm of Maison Jennie. A house that Papa would have loved.

Almost shyly she invited her mother to help her pick furniture for her own room.

"It's your home," mama shrugged. "You pick."

It had become apparent to Jenny that her mother resented her success. If it were any of the other children, she would have been delighted. Jenny insisted that her mother go with her to a round of furniture stores and cabinetmakers. Hers was the choice bedroom in the house. Jenny longed to hear her mother say she was happy in the new house. That she was proud of her youngest daughter's success.

Mannie boasted about "my new house up in the Garden District" to anyone who would listen, though he made it clear that he didn't share her taste in furniture.

"It's too plain. You don't tell me how much you spent on everything, but I know where it came from. Those stores think everybody's made of money. I guarantee you could have got better for the same money." He made no effort to conceal his anger that Jenny did not hand over her weekly salary for him to distribute. He knew nothing of the partnership arrangement she shared, of the savings account that would someday—she hoped—buy the very house in which they lived. This was her hold on security for the future.

"It's a crazy life," he flung at her, "when the wife goes to pick furniture and don't ask her husband what he likes."

"Mannie," she said calmly, "may I remind you that in our first flat you chose all the furniture? You didn't ask my opinion once. Now it's my turn."

Evvie and the children adored the new house. Annie Lou was persuaded to become live-in help, not much coaxing necessary once she saw the two rooms in the dormered attic that would be hers. A part-time gardener was hired. Jenny knew that her mother secretly loved the beautiful flowers blossoming in the garden.

For the first time in her life Jenny felt secure. Then, in the midst of the Mardi Gras season—she received a neatly typed letter from a Vivian Fitzgerald.

> *I must talk privately with you on a matter of grave personal importance to you. Please write and let me know when this may be.*

Jenny read the brief letter several times. It had to have something to do with Danny. Mama was always fretting that he never brought his friends home, exasperated that he had not found a bride among Maison Jennie's wealthy customers, though she took it for granted that he would marry a Jewish girl.

Jenny decided not to dwell on what the mysterious note could mean, and she didn't want any ugly scenes. She would see this girl *before* going to mama. If her memory was right, the girl lived in a cheap boardinghouse in a rundown section of town. No point in talking to Danny first either. She had to handle the situation without involving mama. She wrote her a note asking that they meet at the store after closing time on Friday.

At 4:30 on Friday Jenny busied herself in her office at the rear of the store. The salesladies were leaving. Mannie made a habit of leaving the store an hour earlier, always pointing out that he came in an hour early to straighten out the stock. Tonight mama and Evvie would be at Sophie's for supper. Annie Lou would fix a stew for Mannie and keep it simmering on the stove until she came home. For now Mannie had abandoned the pinochle games with Herman. They now fought even over pinochle.

When she was certain everyone had left the store, Jenny went to stand by the door to admit her visitor. The store was dark except for the colorful display windows and her office at the rear. After a few minutes a small slight girl—she couldn't have been more than seventeen or eighteen—timidly approached, staring wistfully at a dress in the window.

It had to be Vivian Fitzgerald. And she was noticeably pregnant.

Forcing any premature conclusions from her mind, Jenny stepped forward to pull the door open.

"Vivian?"

"Yes. Are you Mrs. Adler?"

"Yes. Come in." Jenny ushered her inside and locked the door behind. "We can talk in my office."

They walked in silence through the dark aisles of the store until they were inside the office.

"Please sit down." Jenny settled herself behind her desk. Then, realizing that in this position she must seem intimidating, she stood up and pulled up a seat next to Vivian.

"If I knew any other way to handle my—my problem, I would not have come to you," Vivian said, her voice soft and tremulous. "I was raised in an orphanage in Baton Rouge. I came to New Orleans when they sent me out on my own because I thought it would be easier to find a job here."

"They taught you to type in the orphanage?" Danny must have refused to marry her.

"Yes. And I have a job." She lifted her head with pride. "They're pleased with me. But I can't stay there much longer." She paused. "Mrs. Adler, I'm four and a half months pregnant. I was alone in the city. So alone. And then I met Mannie—" The blood drained from Jenny's face. *Mannie*. Mannie and this sweet young girl?

"Excuse me," she said. "Did you say Mannie?"

"Mrs. Adler, he's the only man I've ever been with. When I met him, he told me he was a partner in a store in town. That he was unmarried. I was scared and lonely, and he was so friendly. He took me out to dinner, bought me presents. He said he had been orphaned as a little boy. But when I told him about the baby, it was like he became somebody I didn't know. He yelled at me for trying to trick him into marrying me." Her voice rose. "He said he was already married—that I was lying, it wasn't his baby." She lifted her eyes to Jenny's. "It has to be his baby. Like I told you, there's never been anybody else. I kept thinking he would ask me to marry him when he knew—I'm so ashamed. But I was so scared—and he made me feel safe. I would have done anything to keep on seeing him. But it was wrong to—Mrs. Adler, I'm so sorry—I didn't know he was married. I didn't know—"

A knot like a knife twisting in her stomach, Jenny looked sadly at this beautiful heartbroken young girl. "Vivian, it's going to be all right." How dare Mannie shirk this responsibility. *She* would not sit back and let this innocent girl suffer. Vivian Fitzgerald was carrying Leon and Helen's half-brother or half-sister. "I'll see you through this," she said, drawing the girl into her arms. "You won't be alone, Vivian."

CHAPTER
FOURTEEN

JENNY TOOK VIVIAN out for dinner to a small, quiet restaurant.

"I'll find a home where you can stay until after the baby is born," she said. "Everything will be taken care of. After the baby is born, you'll have to decide what to do. He could be put up for adoption . . ." But she recoiled from the thought of her own children's half sister or half brother being handed over to strangers. Maybe there was a way she could bring the baby into her own home.

"I won't give up my baby, Mrs. Adler," Vivian said defiantly. "I couldn't do that."

"Please call me Jenny. No, I didn't think you could."

"Are you going to tell Mannie about this?"

"No. And I don't want you ever to see him again. Not that I think you would want to," she added quickly. "What Mannie did was contemptible. But you're young—someday you'll meet someone else. This isn't the end of your life."

But what did this mean for *her* life? She'd already decided one thing—tonight she would move into a bedroom of her own. Never again would she share a bed with her husband.

Fleetingly she toyed with the thought of divorce, but like all other times she discarded the notion. Even if Mannie were free he wouldn't marry Vivian, and she couldn't bring herself to disgrace the family.

But mama must never know about Vivian and the baby. Somehow she'd find a way to blame *her*. Because she was a bad wife, mama would say. Mannie *had* to turn to someone else. How many times had mama told her she was an "unnatural wife and mother"?

Jenny arranged for Vivian to be cared for in a private home for unwed girls in the old French parish of St. Bernard—close enough to New Orleans so that she could visit.

She was aware of Mannie's nervous scrutiny when she moved out of their bedroom and into one of her own without a word of explanation. She wished she had the courage to face him with what she knew. Vivian wasn't just any Storyville prostitute—how dare he pretend to be unmarried, then retreat behind his marriage, denying that the baby was his! She would have less contempt for him if he had at least had the decency to ask for a divorce so that he could marry Vivian. Now his mere presence repelled her. Maybe she could set him up in his own store, have him out of her sight for at least a chunk of time. But she had no faith in his merchandising ability. It would be wiser to buy the house than try to put Mannie in charge of a store. She must build a future for the children. For mama and Evvie if—God forbid—something happened to her. Property was a safe investment.

One morning, as Jenny listened to a pair of ladies from Boston who had stopped off for Mardi Gras en route to Pasadena—she began to consider a daring new idea.

"Jenny, you would adore Pasadena," one of the ladies was saying. "The climate is marvelous. In one hour by electric train you go from a setting of orange blossoms and semitropical flowers into mountain snow under tall pines. Or you can spend an hour on a train and be at the seashore."

"There's no shope like Maison Jennie in Pasadena," the other lady said. "It would be lovely to spend some afternoons in town shopping in such a charming store."

She must go to Mrs. Goldman armed with facts, Jenny told herself. Not with vague talk about opening a branch shop in Pasadena. *She needed facts to show that it would be profitable.*

She left the store early and went to the library. Pasadena, she learned, was rapidly becoming a year-round resort. She left the library convinced that a branch of Maison Jennie in Pasadena could be a gold mine.

Jenny decided then and there to open up Maison Jennie Pasadena. She would send Mannie out to check the records of the shop once a month. He would make a complete inventory, balance inventory against the original stock, bring back a report of which items were moving, which stayed too long in the store. He would be away at least a week—maybe ten days, considering the traveling time. He'd be less sullen and nasty with the children because he'd feel important. And for a week or ten days out of each month she wouldn't have to see him.

Over lunch with Mrs. Goldman at Antoine's on Louis Street, while they dined sumptuously on lobster bisque, New Orleans pompano, and perfectly steamed rice, Jenny talked enthusiastically about the potential of a shop in a resort such as Pasadena. Mrs. Goldman listened, but Jenny sensed she was skeptical.

"I'll put up the investment money," Jenny offered. "We'll open a small shop."

"I just don't know, Jenny. How many people live in Pasadena?"

"Not that many. But we won't be selling only to the local people. Visitors from the east will be our major customers and they are some of the wealthiest people in the country. They stay at the most expensive hotels for months at a time. The official season is from November twenty-ninth until May twentieth, but tourists are coming all year round now."

"But Pasadena is a long trip. You can't very well run from one store to another."

"I'm sure that can be worked out." Jenny saw that Mrs. Goldman was wavering.

"In the store yesterday I talked with two ladies from Boston who came here for the Mardi Gras and who're going on now to the Green Hotel for two months. They'd love to find a shop like ours in Pasadena."

"Well," Mrs. Goldman began, "let's think it through." Jenny held her breath. "Our customers should be rich ladies from the east who're visiting the hotels. What do we do to insure they'll come into our store?"

"We could arrange for charity fashion shows at the resort hotels," Jenny said, "and of course we'll advertise. The ladies who come into the store will be excited about what we offer. They'll talk. Everybody will know about Maison Jennie Pasadena. We'll create a charming atmosphere, serve tea every afternoon, offer only the finest merchandise. Just as we do here in New Orleans."

"Jenny, how much does it rain in Pasadena? You know that rainy days are always the best shopping days. Isn't California supposed to be where the sun shines all the time? Rain bores people, my dear, and bored rich ladies spend money." Mrs. Goldman chuckled. "The not-so-rich buy, too, when they're bored. But not at Maison Jennie."

"Rich women buy when they're bored, Mrs. Goldman, whether it rains or not. They buy when they suspect their husbands are having affairs. They buy when they look in the mirror and see the years creeping up on them. They buy when they have a fight with their husbands." Mrs. Goldman laughed—Jenny was quoting her verbatim.

"And, my dear," she said, "they buy when their husbands visit the fancy houses. But you know what we're forgetting? They also buy because they love clothes and can afford them. When we go to Saratoga Springs or Hot Springs or to Europe—we buy because it's the thing to do on a holiday. To take back things to remind you of where you've been. You know, Jenny, you could be on to a good thing. I tell you what; we'll open a shop in Pasadena. We'll put up equal amounts of money." She winked. "Who knows? In ten years we may have half a dozen resort shops!"

At Nicky's house over dinner Jenny and Mrs. Goldman informed Armand of their plans to expand the business. He didn't think it was wise to open a shop so far from New Orleans, but Jenny had noticed that he often became annoyed when he wasn't consulted.

"Once again you didn't come to me for advice, ladies. Well, I suppose you're telling me to draw up the necessary papers." He couldn't hide the respect in his voice.

"My son Saul should have thought of this," Mrs.

Goldman said. "But he's too busy trying to make himself an important man in social circles. And Benedict," she chuckled. "At thirty-eight he's less a business man than little Louis."

Nicky kissed her cheek.

"You should be running Goldman's Department Store, grandma."

"If I had my way, I would be. But then I would miss all the fun of working with you, Jenny, my adopted grand-daughter."

Jenny took her partner home in the new Studebaker that Nicky had persuaded her to buy and had taught her to drive. She was grateful that Mrs. Goldman kept up a steady flow of conversation. Had she jumped too fast in laying out most of her money for the new store?

When she arrived home, Herman was playing pinochle with Mannie—their quarrels had become less frequent—and tonight, judging by the pile of dirty dishes in the sink, Herman, Sophie and the children had been over for supper. As usual he had let Sophie struggle home alone with the children, not caring that Sophie had worked all day in the store—the children were "the mother's responsibility." Mrs. Straus sat before the fireplace crocheting another doily. She peered at Jenny over her glasses.

"So. At last you're home. Evvie's already gone to bed. She was exhausted." Jenny knew better—Evvie had gone to bed to avoid listening to another few hours of complaining. "Leon and Helene are waiting for you to kiss them goodnight."

"I'll go right up to them." Leon was already in the second grade and in another year Helene would go to kindergarten—how the years slipped away!

The children finished their breathless accounts of their days at school, and Jenny kissed them goodnight.

"Mama—" Leon's voice stopped her at the door. "I had a fight at school today."

"Come on, Leon, no stalling. It's time to sleep." Already Helene's eyes were closed.

"No, mama. I really did." He grinned. "But I won. I pushed him down into the sandpile."

"What did you fight about?"

"He made me mad when he said that the Jews killed Christ." He didn't know about Christ, except that the name was somehow connected with Christmas. "They didn't, did they?"

"No, darling." In her own childhood she had encountered neighborhood children who jibed, "dirty little Jew" or "you're a Jew—you don't belong here." "Haven't I ever told you that Jesus Christ was himself born a Jew? A Roman governor called Pilate sentenced Jesus to die on a cross. In Rome at that time it was a form of execution often used. The Roman governor who sentenced him to die was not a Jew." This was exactly what papa had told her and what she had read in an encyclopedia at the Fisk Free Library on Lafayette Square, before it was moved three years ago to St. Charles Square. Would there ever be a generation of Jewish children not taunted by the ignorant?

Ten days after her lunch with Mrs. Goldman, Jenny arranged passage for Nicky and herself aboard the Sunset Limited. Run by the Southern Pacific line, the Sunset Limited would take them directly to Los Angeles and she had gotten accommodations in the Ladies Compartment Car, which had its own parlor, library, observation platform and maid in attendance.

To pass the time, Jenny coaxed Nicky into speaking only French when they were alone. Perhaps it was childish of her, but she envisioned herself one day living in Paris. Meeting Marc—with Nicky, of course, as their companion because both Marc and she were married. She'd see Marc's paintings hanging in a Paris gallery. She would be exquisitely dressed, poised—not the unsophisticated young girl Marc had been ashamed to introduce to his sister that summer nine years ago.

It was strange, she mused, that away from New Orleans she could think about Marc with no sense of guilt. It was as though she acquired an exhilarating freedom away from familiar surroundings. And now, knowing the truth about

Mannie and Vivian Fitzgerald, she felt divorced—in spirit at least—from her husband.

Did Marc ever ask himself what life would be like if *they* had married? But it wasn't meant to be. Marc needed the art world of Paris. Her family needed her.

At exactly 7:15 on a Monday evening Jenny and Nicky disembarked at the Los Angeles railroad station. As the Hotel Green office manager had advised, an omnibus was waiting to transfer them to the hotel. Looking north they saw mountains capped in snow, even while they felt the warm breezes of the Pacific. They rode past groves of lemons, oranges, olives, peach and apricot orchards, fields of many kinds of berries. They admired the graceful pepper trees, the flowers and hedges, the lovely homes set far back on sweeps of verdant lawns.

"Look," Nicky pointed as they approached a Moorish structure occupying six acres of magnificently landscaped grounds. "Hotel Green seems too ordinary a name for something so impressive."

Jenny leaned forward.

"I think the east wing was built in 1898. The west wing and the loggia added later. We were able to get rooms only because of a last minute cancellation. Did you know that they turn away hundreds of prospective guests every year?"

"Well, there you go!" Nicky said. "That's a sign the Pasadena shop was meant to be."

In the morning Jenny went directly to the real estate office which she had contacted earlier. There was so much to be done and she had only a few days—they were heading back to New Orleans on Saturday morning at 8:30 A.M.

Jenny was pleased with the way the business district looked. The streets were asphalt-paved and clearly well-lighted during the evening hours and most of the well-maintained commercial buildings were two or three stories high. She noted the prosperous-appearing clothing store of H. C. Hotaling, Glassock's Book and Art Store, Wetherly and Kayster's Shoe Store, the Bon Accord Dry Goods Store, Bertonnear and Sons, Fine Grocers. Several real estate and investment offices.

Jenny finally chose an available shop on the First National Bank block, at Colorado Street and Fair Oaks.

"I like it," Nicky said. "And it'll be good to be near the bank." She laughed. "After spending all their money at Maison Jennie those ladies can walk right over and get more cash."

The real estate broker was impressed with Jenny's plans. Contractors would be brought in immediately to carry out her instructions for redecorating—as in New Orleans, the store was to be done all in pale gray and lilac. She would start interviewing prospective employees in the broker's office on Wednesday and on Friday morning she would buy the furniture and fixtures, either at a local store or in nearby Los Angeles. In record time, Maison Jennie Pasadena would be launched.

On an August morning, moments after she had arrived at the store, Jenny received a phone call from the woman who managed the home where Vivian was staying.

"Mrs. Adler—Vivian has just gone into labor. You said you wanted to be told—"

"Yes. Thank you. Tell her I'll be there in a few hours." Instantly, Jenny had reorganized her schedule so that she could leave. During the past months she and Vivian had become very close and Jenny wanted to be there for her during the birth. She had even started taking material to her with the thought that sewing could help fill in the empty hours, and had discovered that the girl had a natural sense of color and style.

Thank God this was the time of month when Mannie went to the Pasadena shop—she couldn't bear to look at him while Vivian was in St. Bernard bringing *his* child into the world.

Early in the afternoon, on the pretext of a business appointment with Armand, Jenny left for St. Bernard. By the time she arrived, Vivian was in hard labor and attended by the doctor who served the temporary young residents of the house. She sat in the parlor with a half a dozen young pregnant girls, the air fraught with a tension that was only heightened by the sounds of Vivian's screams from upstairs.

Jenny had guessed it would be a difficult delivery—Vivian was small and the doctor had said it would be a large baby.

At last Mrs. Mulvany, who managed the home, came out on the second floor landing.

"Mrs. Adler, Vivian would like you with her."

Jenny flew up the stairs.

Pale and frightened, Vivian lay against a mound of pillows.

"Looks like the head's come." The doctor seemed to say it for Jenny's benefit, but it was hardly necessary—Jenny could see the baby's dark touseled head as she took Vivian's hand. Just at that moment Vivian screamed again. "It's those shoulders—they're very broad—" Involuntarily, it occurred to Jenny: *Mannie's shoulders.*

"Vivian, it's going to be all right." She tried not to pull away as the young girl's nails pressed into her hands.

The doctor was leaning forward now, his hands around the baby's head.

"Come on, girl, push again. Push hard."

"It'll be over soon, honey," Jenny whispered. "Don't quit now."

"No! No!" Vivian cried out. "Please, I can't stand anymore!"

One wild scream echoed through the room, and then Vivian lay still. Jenny watched a red-faced baby boy push his way into the world. For a moment, she held her breath as she looked for signs of Mannie—then she felt ashamed for thinking only of herself at a time like this.

She stayed with Vivian while Mrs. Mulvany washed the baby and the doctor waited for the afterbirth.

"Vivian, I think you should stay here for a few more days. I've found a place for you to live and as soon as you're able, you'll report to work in the office of a friend of mine. He needs a typist. I'll help you arrange for care for the baby. From now on," she smiled, "you're Mrs. Vivian Fitzgerald. A very young widow." Now Jenny reached for her purse and withdrew a small box. "If this doesn't fit, take it to the jewelry store and have it adjusted."

Vivian opened the box and stared at the gold wedding band nestled in bed of red velvet.

"Oh, Mrs. Adler—" Tears filled her eyes.

"You're going to be all right, Vivian." Jenny leaned forward and kissed her on the cheek. "The nightmare is over."

But would *she* ever be able to accept this child? Somehow, she felt partly to blame for the fact that he would be so alone in the world. If she had handled her marriage differently, could Vivian's agony—her son's shame—have been avoided?

Right after Mardi Gras 1912, with the Pasadena shop doing well under the managership of Carmen Mendoza—a charming middle-aged widow Jenny had hired on the California trip—Mrs. Goldman and Jenny agreed that it was time that Jenny did some buying in Paris. American women were fascinated by French designers—Carrie Neiman of Neiman-Marcus went to Paris every year. Once more Nicky—depressed that she had not yet become pregnant again—was to accompany Jenny, and once more Jenny faced her mother's loud objections, though at this point Mannie merely grunted his contempt for such gallivanting. Mannie enjoyed his monthly trips to the Pasadena store, always boasting to Herman that the store would not survive without him.

"Mama, Leon will be eight and Helene five. They're old enough to understand that I'm just going on a business trip—I'm not deserting them."

"I don't care." Mrs. Straus sniffed. "It's not natural. Later you'll understand you can't run off and leave your children with strangers for weeks at a time. Someday Leon and Helene will throw it in your face that you left them. Then you'll remember what I told you."

"Mama, we'll be gone three weeks, and I'm not leaving the children with strangers. Annie Lou is like a member of the family and you and Evvie will be here."

She refrained from mentioning Mannie. His trips to the Pasadena shop took him away from home ten days out of every month and when he was home, he was constantly battling with the children—nothing they did pleased him. Jenny knew it was because he didn't dare vent his resentment on her. His cowardice infuriated her.

"I never understood you, Jenny." Her mother's mouth tightened. "Always running off on business, sending the children's father all the way to California every month. What kind of wife does such things?"

Jenny closed her eyes. Thank God she was away from the house so much. She suspected that Evvie, too, was relieved to be away for the hours at the store every day. Lately mama seemed to be using Annie Lou as her audience.

Jenny and Nicky were scheduled to sail from New York to Bordeaux on the new French luxury liner the *France* in early April. Jenny arranged all the details of their week in Paris, pushing away the thought of what would happen when she came face to face with Marc. It had been almost ten years . . .

Two weeks before they were to take the train for New York, Nicky came to her with the news that she was pregnant.

"Nicky, that's wonderful!" She knew how much Nicky and Armand wanted a second child. "I'm so happy for you."

Nicky was glowing.

"Oh Jenny, I can't tell you how long I've waited for this. But there's one little problem. The doctor absolutely refuses to let me travel—he said I might miscarry if I do. So you go without me. Obviously you have to buy for the stores. And Marc would be so disappointed if you cancelled now."

"Nicky, how can I face him alone?" The prospect of seeing Marc alone terrified her. "I won't see him. It's absurd anyway. We're both married—we've changed—"

"Nonsense. You can't go to Paris and not see him. How could you deny the two of you that small pleasure? Anyway, you have to deliver a present from grandma." Jenny knew this was one of Nicky's inspirations of the moment. "She insists that at her age she won't cross the Atlantic again—and Marc won't come home until he has all of France at his feet." Jenny had heard that Marc was beginning to make a name for himself in the art world, but she knew he wouldn't be satisfied with just modest success.

"All right, I'll deliver the present. I'll call from the hotel and arrange to have lunch with Marc and his wife. The rest of the time I'll be racing around on business anyway."

Jenny couldn't shake the feeling that seeing Marc alone was a terrible mistake. What could they possibly have to say to each other now? She was a married woman with two children—a business woman, and she was acting like a silly, romantic girl. But maybe it was good that she would see Marc again. Maybe now she could wash the memory from her mind forever.

The lyrics of the traditional Mardi Gras song swept across her mind. *"If ever I cease to love—"* Would there ever be a day when she ceased to love Marc Goldman?

CHAPTER FIFTEEN

As the gleaming pullman sped away from New Orleans, Jenny tried to focus on the panorama of spring outside her compartment window—trees bursting into blossom, farmers planting cotton, preparing fields for sugar cane, birds of every description flitting about the fragrant air . . .

She felt an exhilarating sense of freedom punctuated by moments of panic. Away from New Orleans she could shed the responsibility of running Maison Jennie. But now she would not have Nicky's companionship and support . . .

She battled guilt, too, at the prospect of being away from Leon and Helene for three weeks. Her face softened as she envisioned their small, sweet faces—Leon, with papa's dark hair and eyes, Helene with golden hair and gray-green eyes . . . Sophie's four boys—though not Carrie, who bore a startling resemblance to her Aunt Jenny—resembled mama's side of the family.

Why did mama have to carry on so about her business trips? Other mothers went off on vacations for longer periods without their children and never gave it a second thought. Leon and Helene *knew* she loved them.

Still, this trip *was* different—she had never left them for so long. But nothing was going to happen to them, and she couldn't spend the rest of her life worrying about what might happen in her absence. Too many people were never able to enjoy today because they worried about tomorrow. The children were in Annie Lou's capable hands, surrounded by family. *They would be fine.*

When traveling with Nicky she had enjoyed leisurely

meals in the luxurious dining car attached to the pullman, but now Jenny clung to the privacy of her compartment. The time passed quickly as she read Edith Wharton's new novel and gazed at the passing sights.

Gradually she forced herself to concede that it wasn't the long train journey to New York, crossing the Atlantic alone or even the prospect of approaching such French fashion luminaries as Callot Soeurs, Lanvin, Poiret that intimidated her. It was meeting Marc.

Her schedule was such that she was able to go directly from the fine, new Pennsylvania Station in New York to her ship. The new French line ship, the *France*, had been dubbed "a castle on the Atlantic." Jenny was delighted with her *cabine de luxe*, listened in amazement to the stories told at the dinner table about the *de grande luxe* accomodations that provided three canopied beds in as many bedrooms, an Empire-style dining room, and a drawing room that was a replica of one in a Touraine chateau.

The ship provided elevators, a swimming bath, even a turkish bath. Jenny relished the *haute cuisine*, served in an exquisitely decorated two-level salon. She knew, too, that the attention she drew with her lovely wardrobe—her dresses designed with the new neat and slim silhouette, hats small and close to the head—could only end up helping business. Some of the gentlemen made her uncomfortable with their attentions, but she made a point of talking about her children and soon their interest faded. She savored this brief respite from reality.

Once aboard the train from Bordeaux to Paris she was again filled with misgivings about seeing Marc. What was the point? That brief part of her life was so long ago. She was a woman now—successful in business—the mother of two . . . no longer that young girl Marc loved—and who loved him. Marc was married to a woman for whom he had enormous respect, who helped him in his career as *she* could never have done. *Maybe Marc was just being polite when he spoke of his desire to see her again.*

Think about Paris! The famous French designers, the Louvre, the Champs Elysées, Notre Dame, Versailles

. . . Marc had written about the Café des Deux Magots, the artist studios on the Rue Odessa, and the excitement of Montmartre.

As the train approached the city, she stared out the window. The fields were becoming villages now. Soon she saw the shadowy outlines of the city bathed in gold.

Jenny's heart pounded as the train entered the thousand-foot-long tunnel of the Gâre Saint Lazare. *She was actually arriving in Paris.* In a little while she would be in her hotel room. Then what? Was she supposed to phone Marc or was he to call her?

As the train rolled into the station, she remembered that this was the busiest railroad station in the world—in one day as many as a quarter million people passed through. Before the train came to a full stop, she was on her feet, waiting at the door.

Disembarking passengers were met by porters in bright blue uniforms. Jenny followed her porter out to the waiting taxicabs.

She was amazed at the number of private automobiles in the streets—obviously the rich of Paris had abandoned the magnificent carriages, with their fine horses and liveried coachmen and footmen, for motorized taxis and buses.

Jenny remembered that the city offered its residents the Metro, the network of underground trains that were entered via the many *Metropolitains* located at key locations in Paris.

Grateful now for her French lessons, Jenny allowed herself—along with her luggage—to be escorted to a waiting taxi that would take her to the small but elegant hotel that Mrs. Goldman had recommended. Now she remembered—Nicky had told her to phone Marc the minute she arrived. He had promised to be her personal guide—but that was when he thought Nicky was to be their chaperone.

Leaning back in the seat of her taxi, Jenny debated whether to phone Marc right away or wait until the following morning. Perhaps she should put him at ease, make it clear she did not expect him to be her guide, that she was a woman with a working knowledge of the French language who could find her own way around the city.

I'm twenty-six years old. Why do I feel like I'm sixteen again? How can I be in Paris and not see him?

The chauffeur-driven Renault limousine deposited Marc and Simone at the Gâre Saint Lazare. He felt a familiar twinge of guilt about letting Simone go off to Aix-les-Bains alone, but she seemed determined.

"You know, it isn't too late to change your mind, Simone," he said, a hand at her elbow while they followed their porters through the crowds. "Why don't you just wait a few days and I'll go with you?"

Simone shook her head.

"No. I promise you, you would be bored to death there. If you're not taking the baths the only other thing to do is gamble, and I know how much *that* appeals to you." She slipped an arm through his. "Anyway, you'd be miserable away from your studio. So have your visit with Nicole's friend from New Orleans—Jenny, yes? It will do you good to talk to someone from home."

"I don't like leaving you alone when you're not feeling well." He had to admit, also, that he was nervous about seeing Jenny, unsure of his feelings. She was no longer the young girl in the miniature he had painted. All these years he had been cherishing a dream—how would the dream compare to reality? "Let's go back to the car, Simone. I'll arrange train tickets for a few days later."

"Marc, stop behaving as though I were ill. I'm simply tired. The baths will rejuvenate me." Her eyes anxiously searched his face. "Perhaps I was wrong in taking such a handsome young husband?"

"Simone, *I'm* the only one who's getting older. You're ageless. As beautiful as the day I first saw you at Mary Cassatt's party."

Simone laughed.

"Flattery will get you everywhere, my darling. I'll only be at Aix-les-Bains for three weeks. You'll be busy painting. The weeks will speed past."

"All right. But if you want me to come to you, wire me. I'll leave Paris immediately."

Once Simone had settled into her compartment, Marc

kissed her good-bye and slowly made his way back to the Renault.

He drove slowly back to the house. These years in Paris had passed so quickly, yet they had somehow strengthened his ties to his home and his family. His parents kept urging him to come home, even if only for a visit—but he just wasn't ready to yet. Simone wasn't the problem—in fact, she had often suggested a visit to the States. It was *he*. Mama and papa had not yet abandoned the hope that he would one day take over the store—and that could never be. Benedict had no real interest in the business and the sons of his two aunts who lived in New York were already in law and medicine. Marc smiled as he remembered Nicky telling him that Benedict was more interested in pursuing beautiful women than in helping the customers.

He knew, too, how his grandmother longed to see him. His face softened as he thought about the letters she still wrote him—long, loving missives filled with colorful stories about what was happening at home. It was hard to imagine Jenny and Grandma in business together . . . Strange, too, that Jenny and Nicky were so close . . . And yet it pleased him that this tie to a lost part of his life had been preserved.

As he approached the house his thoughts returned to the day ahead. It was Jenny's arrival that had sparked his ruminations. Unease settled like a knot in his stomach. She would be in Paris only a week. When would she call him? Would he recognize her? God, it was hard to believe it had been ten years . . .

He had made the trade; Jenny for Paris. But he had never been able to free himself of her—she had remained in a secret room in his heart. And yet he had remained loyal to Simone; Jenny was Jenny. His first love. His only love. Simone, in her fashion, filled another, very different need.

As he walked into the house, François met him in the foyer. "Monsieur, a Mademoiselle Jenny telephoned. Here is the number." Marc took the piece of paper. Slowly, carefully, he walked across the room and picked up the telephone.

* * *

She walked out into the tiny balcony off her hotel room.

At long last, she was in Paris. The scent of spring flowers filled the air. Chestnut trees lined the boulevards. Already the lights of Paris glittered like diamonds in the early evening. Her heart was pounding. Soon—very soon—she would meet with Marc. It didn't seem possible.

The phone rang. Slowly, she walked over and picked up the receiver.

"Hello—"

"Jenny—" It was Marc, talking as though they had spoken just yesterday. "Welcome to Paris."

"I can't believe I'm here." Somehow she managed a proper little laugh.

"Jenny, I can't wait to see you again." He paused. "To hear about everybody back in New Orleans, I mean. I trust everything with you is fine?"

"Oh, yes. Perhaps we could have lunch—"

"Dinner. Tonight. For your first night in Paris you must have dinner at Voison's." He hesitated. Did she know about Simone? "Simone left today for Aix-les-Bains. She asked me to apologize for her not being here to welcome you."

"Is she ill?"

"No, no. Just tired. She has a tendency to work herself into exhaustion." He chuckled. "Paris' social scene can be rather strenuous. I'll pick you up in an hour."

"I'll be ready."

Jenny turned toward her closet. What would she wear? Voison's was one of the finest restaurants in Paris. Everything about tonight had to be special.

She decided at last on a mauve-and-ivory silk Poiret, a tunic over a draped skirt that emphasized her narrow waist. Tonight she would wear her mink stole. She smiled to herself, remembering how shocked mama had been at her extravagance when she had bought it.

"You give yourself such airs. It must be because you're always with Nicky Lazar. Why can't you be that close to Evvie and Sophie?"

But she mustn't think of home now. She was a married woman having an innocent dinner with a married man—

with her best friend's brother. In sophisticated Paris this was accepted. Why not? What could happen that was wrong? That summer was probably only a memory to him. She would probably seem stupid and gauche to him now . . . he'd been living for years in Simone's elite world and she was just a storekeeper—even if she was now received in old New Orleans society.

The phone rang. Marc was in the lobby waiting for her. Trembling, she draped the stole around her shoulders. On her way out the door she caught a glimpse of herself— serious, frightened—in the mirrored walls. She forced a smile and walked out into the hallway toward the elevator.

When it reached the lobby, the Victorian, wrought-iron elevator stopped and the doors slid open. Jenny stepped onto the marble floor of the lobby, its walls hung with Gobelin tapestries. To her right, his back to her, stood a tall slender man in impeccable English tailoring. Was it Marc? It was his glossy dark curls, his way of holding his shoulders . . .

As though feeling the weight of her gaze he turned around. It *was*.

"Jenny!" Smiling, he strode toward her. "God, you're more beautiful than ever." He reached for her hand and brought it to his lips.

"You're looking very handsome and distinguished," she said lightly.

"I've been bursting with impatience for your arrival," he said. He pulled her hand through his arm while they walked to the waiting limousine. "I've thought of you so often."

She blushed. "And I am happy to see you, Marc. It's been a long time. But tell me about your painting, Marc." At least this was a safe topic. "I gather you're making quite a name for yourself—Nicky tells me you have exhibits regularly now."

Jenny sat in the limousine and listened to Marc talk about his current exhibit, and she was reminded of their many conversations when Marc rebelled against going back to Harvard.

"It isn't easy for an artist in Paris right now, Jenny—at

least not an artist who seeks something new, a break with the past."

Over dinner, Marc talked about his work with a passion and eloquence that brought tears to her eyes. It was this dedication—the very thread of Marc's existence—that had separated them. His art was his obsession, his mistress.

"You know what I just realized?" He put down his glass of wine. "I haven't stopped talking for a minute. Your first night in Paris, and I spend the entire time chattering on about myself."

"I'm enjoying every moment," Jenny said. New Orleans, home and family were part of another world.

"You know, there are always such interesting people here." He looked around the room. "You see that lovely woman over there—" Jenny followed his gaze. "That's the Duchess of Marlborough, who was Consuelo Vanderbilt of New York. And there's André Gide two tables beyond. He's a marvelous novelist, though, some say, rather shocking."

Marc pointed out an internationally known industrialist from England, a Baron Rothschild and the Aga Khan. But all the while the air was electric with the things left unsaid . . .

After dinner, Jenny let Marc take her on a night tour of Paris. He dismissed the chauffeur and they set forth arm-in-arm to explore the city.

In the Montmartre, near the Place Pigalle—amid a garish array of electric signs, pleasure-seeking revelers and the flashing headlights of cars, Marc took her to a small café.

"My first year in Paris I was here more often than in my room, Jenny. It was such a joy to me to be able to talk with other painters, to exchange ideas. And always," his voice dropped to a whisper, "you were with me."

"You never came to say good-bye." Her voice was filled with reproach. "You never wrote."

"I didn't dare." He reached across the table for her hand. "If I did, I knew I would be lost."

Jenny smiled, squeezed his hand. "It took time, Marc, but I understand why you had to come to Paris."

His expression darkened in anger.

"But why must life always be a matter of choosing? Why

must it always be, 'you can have this but you must give up that'?"

"I had responsibilities. I couldn't do what my heart told me to do."

He leaned toward her.

"Jenny, let us have this week together. I can't bear to let you out of my sight, even for a moment."

"It wouldn't be right—" She longed to throw herself into his arms . . . and she understood what he meant—this one week together would help them survive all the years ahead.

"Who would be hurt? No one would suspect—of course I ought to entertain a dear friend of my sister's. If we're seen around Paris together, it'll mean nothing—Simone knows that. And when we're alone together, no one will know. Your husband—" he stumbled over the word, "will never know. Jenny, please—let's have this one perfect week together."

"I came to buy for the store—" But her eyes betrayed her. *A whole week of days and nights with Marc . . .*

"I know why you're here. I'll take you everywhere you have to go. For one week let's pretend there's nobody else in our lives except each other. Jenny, my love, how can you deny us that?"

They went to Marc's house, where the only servant in residence had already retired for the night. Jenny saw instantly that this was one of the fine old houses of Paris.

"Tomorrow I'll send François off on vacation," he whispered, taking her hand and leading her up the wide curving staircase to his bedroom. She should feel wicked, Jenny told herself, but she didn't. She felt exhilarated, eager to be in the arms of the one man in the world she would ever love.

Marc opened the door to his bedroom, crossed the room and turned on a lamp which swathed the room in warm, muted light.

Jenny stepped inside gazing about admiringly.

"What a beautiful room!"

"You're beautiful." He pulled off her stole and draped it across the chair.

"My hotel," she whispered. "What will they think when I don't return tonight?"

"This is Paris, my darling." He took her face between his hands and brought his mouth down to hers.

All at once her arms were around him, her mouth parting.

"I don't have a thing to wear," she laughed shakily.

"You won't need a thing, my darling. Tomorrow I'll take you to the hotel to pick up your luggage."

Gently Marc removed her clothes, one by one, pausing to leave a trail of kisses where his hands had been. Jenny stood before him, eyes closed, head back. She shivered and Marc pulled her close.

"There's a chill in the air, Jenny. Let's get under the blankets."

She laughed softly as he led her to the bed.

"That sounds like a line from a Georges Feydeau play." He looked at her in surprise—that wasn't the kind of thing young Jenny would have said.

She lay back against a cluster of pillows under a white satin-covered down comforter and watched Marc undress. She loved his body . . . his broad shoulders, his slim waist and hips. And he was passionate. So passionate! Later she would look back and tonight would seem an impossible, beautiful dream.

"You can't know how often I imagined this night." He slid beneath the comforter and reached for her.

She was twenty-six years old, the mother of two, but she felt like a virgin. "Marc, please make love to me."

He lifted himself above her and gently, tenderly, entered her.

"I thought I'd never see you again," he murmured as they moved together. "I thought there would never be a night like this for us."

Six more nights like this. A few moments later their cries of satisfied passion blended in the still of the night.

They lay absolutely still in the darkness and then, slowly, he began to move within her again. Tonight would be a night to remember forever.

* * *

The following morning François was sent away for vacation. In the large, perfectly appointed kitchen—much like that of a fine restaurant—Jenny prepared breakfast, clad only in Marc's pajama jacket. For this precious packet of time she would be Marc's wife . . .

Immediately after breakfast—reminding herself that she was in Paris on business—Jenny went with Marc to call on M. Paul Poiret, the internationally known couturier who had freed women from the tyranny of the corset with dazzling, avant-garde styles made at his establishment in the Faubourg St. Honoré. She was momentarily startled that M. Poiret and Marc had already met but realized that her friendship with Marc added luster to her presence. No doubt the fashionable Simone was one of M. Poiret's steady customers.

Gradually Jenny's doubts were replaced by confidence and enthusiasm. She was spending a fortune, but the ladies at Maison Jennie in New Orleans and Pasadena would eagerly buy these masterpieces. She was pleased, too, at Marc's new respect for her—his little Jenny Straus from New Orleans was conducting business with the world's most fashionable tailor.

"Madame, you have chosen my favorite designs," M. Poiret said, his eyes admiring "Madame." "Your ladies in—how you say—New Orleans will be delighted."

Afterwards Marc took her to lunch at Pavillion d'Armenonville, one of the most charming of the restaurants in the Bois de Boulogne, the magnificent forest where all of Paris society sought to be seen in the spring. They sat in the shadowed coolness of the restaurant, where the green of the leaves was mirrored in the delicately blue-lacquered tables. Throughout the meal Marc would interrupt their conversation to introduce her to passers-by whose faces she knew only from magazines and newspapers.

That night they saw the exciting Ballet Russe, created by Serge Diaghilev and first seen in Paris—to wild acclaim—three years earlier. Jenny was entranced by the dancing of Vaslav Nijinsky, exhilarated as they left the glittering assemblage to walk out into the soft spring night air.

"We could go somewhere for supper, Jenny."

"Let's go back to the house. If you're hungry, I'll cook for you."

Marc slid an arm about her waist.

"I was hoping you'd suggest that. I can't bear sharing you with so many people."

Again they made love far into the night. In the morning Jenny awoke in Marc's arms.

"How long have you been awake?"

"Time doesn't count when we're together, Jenny."

At a respectably early hour Marc again took her to visit the establishments where she was to buy. When business was out of the way, they went to Montmartre—Marc's first home in Paris.

Hand in hand, they roamed the narrow, winding streets, stopping to eat or drink whenever the spirit moved them. Marc promised to take Jenny on the following afternoon to the gallery where his paintings were offered to prospective buyers.

That night, after they made love, Marc spoke of the troubles in Europe and Asia.

"The wealthy of Paris—of all Europe—live as though life was one long party. How can they be so blind? Italy is fighting Turkey to take over the Turkish colonies in Africa. The Chinese have overthrown the Manchus and set up a republic, but people are dying for the republic every day. We hear rumors of war between Bulgaria, Serbia and Greece on one side and Turkey on the other. Austria-Hungary warns of war if the Serbs take over ports on the Adriatic. Two months ago when Churchill spoke for 'home rule' in Belfast—protected by 3,000 soldiers—he was met at the railroad station with cries that 'We'll hang him from an apple tree.'"

"It seems strange for me to be in Europe and not see Vienna," Jenny said. "My mother was born and raised there. It's awful to think that there might be a war that would involve her family."

"We've never known a war at home in our lifetime. Though grandma has some keen memories of the War Between the States. My father was only eleven when the war ended, but he remembers. Jenny, if war breaks out in

Europe now—with all that has been developed in the way of weapons—it will be horrendous.

"Sssh." Jenny put a finger on his lips. "We won't think about it now. Not this week."

On her third afternoon in Paris Marc took Jenny to see his work. His paintings were truly like nothing she had ever seen.

"Marc, it's not because they're yours they are exquisite."

"Marc—" A smiling young man summoned him with a quiet gesture. "Monsieur would like to speak with you."

While Marc was out of the room, Jenny arranged to buy one of the paintings from the young man, swearing him to secrecy. The painting would be shipped to New Orleans shortly after her own departure, so that she would be in New Orleans to receive it.

"Marc, you've never sent a painting to your grandmother—"

"I don't think she'd like what I do."

"Don't be silly. She'll love it because it's yours. And Nicky tells me your mother boasts constantly about her son—the artist in Paris. Why don't you send her one, too?"

"All right," Marc chuckled. "Though somehow I doubt that they'll share your enthusiasm."

Jenny shook her head.

"Marc, you'll be terribly important one day. I'll be so proud that I know you."

"Jenny—" All at once he looked serious. "Promise me that you'll come to Paris for one week every year. I can survive the rest of the year if I know I'll see you for that one week."

She hesitated. "Marc, it's wrong—"

"No one will be hurt," he said quickly. "You'll come here on business. I'll find a way for us to be alone, where no one will know us. Don't deny us that, Jenny."

"Paris in the spring. Every spring. For one week. You're right—that's not too much to take for ourselves . . ."

When the day arrived to board the train for Bordeaux, Jenny insisted they say their good-byes at the house. She

didn't want to be part of a scene at the Gâre Saint Lazare—
Marc had a name to protect.

"It's better this way, Marc." She tried to be strong for
both their sakes, but she dreaded the long trip back to New
Orleans. Alone.

"I'll put your luggage into a taxi and have the driver
wait." She knew he hated this separation, perhaps even
more than the last.

For a few minutes she was alone in his house, remembering the moments they had shared in each room. She lived in
three worlds: the world of home and children, the world of
the store and the world she shared here with Marc.

She heard the opening of the heavy oak door that led into
the marble-floored foyer. Her heart pounding, she hurried to
join Marc for their last few minutes together.

"Jenny, I'll always love you." He pulled her into his
arms, lifting her face to his. "Darling little Jenny—my first
and only love."

"I'm very proud of you, Marc," she whispered, her eyes
luminous. "And I'll always love you."

He brushed her cheek with his lips.

"We'll be together next spring. Keep well, Jenny."

On the train to Bordeaux, aboard the luxury liner taking
her to New York and on the train that carried her toward
New Orleans Jenny wrestled with doubts about her promise
to see Marc every spring in Paris. If the truth ever came out,
they would both be destroyed.

But it wasn't for her marriage that she worried—in truth,
she and Mannie had never been man and wife. But for the
sake of her children she could not allow herself to be
disgraced. Nor could she bear the thought of hurting
Simone. *Was it too much of a risk to see Marc again?*

As the train pulled into New Orleans' Terminal Station,
Jenny's spirits lifted at the prospect of holding Leon and
Helene in her arms again, seeing their faces light up when
they opened the presents she had bought them in Paris.
Leon was old enough now to be impressed by the fact that
his mother had been abroad.

Nicky dashed over as she emerged from the train.

"I called the station to see when your train would arrive. The car's waiting."

"How're you feeling?" Jenny asked, gesturing to a porter to follow with her luggage.

"Sleepy all the time, but that'll be over soon. The doctor's not worried about me miscarrying anymore, thank God."

"How's grandma?" Everyone who knew Mrs. Goldman called her grandma.

"Fine. Full of energy, as usual. She's off with mama, meeting my aunts at Greenbrier for two weeks."

"Don't tell her yet—Marc's sending her a painting. I think she'll be pleased."

"Great! Listen, tell me about the trip. How was it? Never mind . . . Judging by the look on your face, it was wonderful. You have that glow, my darling."

"It was wonderful," Jenny said shyly. "And frightening . . ."

With Jenny's luggage heaped into the car, Nicky settled behind the wheel.

"All right, I want to hear everything. Marc, Paris, the buying. *Everything.*"

"Well—" Jenny paused. "Simone wasn't in Paris—she had just left for Aix-les-Bains." Nicky's eyes met hers. There was no need to say anymore.

"I'm happy for the two of you." Nicky's hand left the wheel to squeeze hers. "It was meant to be, Jenny."

CHAPTER SIXTEEN

THE MORNING AFTER her return Jenny was already back in the store—tense, restless, and now painfully aware of the void in her life. At least before Paris she could only *imagine* what marriage to Marc could have been. How foolish to believe that one week a year could somehow make their lives complete.

She had fought so hard to make a life for herself. She adored Leon and Helene. She loved running the store. But her future seemed bleak.

She wondered if Sophie was happy. She, too, enjoyed her job. She loved her children. But what kind of life was it tied to a loveless marriage? Jenny wished there was something she could do to make Sophie's life fuller.

"Sophie, I bought you a present in Paris. It's being shipped with the other merchandise. It's a Poiret."

Sophie looked uncomfortable.

"You bought *me* a Paris original? But Jenny, I'd have to lose forty pounds to wear one of those."

"Nonsense. Anyway, you can lose it if you really want to." Jenny knew that for Sophie this had been a losing battle, but Sophie was only thirty—she shouldn't look like a middle-aged matron. "I bought the dress to fit when you're thinner again."

Sophie sighed. "I don't know why I eat the way I do. I start the minute I get into the house, and I don't stop until I go to bed."

"You have two weeks paid vacation this summer," Jenny said. "Why don't you take the children and rent a place at the lake for two weeks? If you're not cooking for Herman, you'll probably lose weight without even trying."

"How much could I lose in two weeks? Besides, Herman would never agree to it."

"Don't ask. Just tell him. You have your salary—*you* can pay for it."

"Jenny," Sophie paused, looking embarrassed. "I give Herman my salary every week. He handles the family money."

Jenny was shocked. How could Sophie bear to be controlled by her husband like this?

"I tell you what, Sophie. I'll rent the cottage at the lake for mama for a month. You take the children and go with her for two weeks. The next two weeks Evvie will stay with mama. It'll do you all good to get out of the hot city. Herman can eat dinner with us." In addition to Annie Lou and the gardener they now had Dora to cook and help with the cleaning.

Sophie hesitated.

"I don't know if he'll agree—"

"Sophie, tell him *I'm* renting the cottage for mama. It'll cost you nothing. Think of it this way—he'll save money on food." *That* would certainly please Herman.

Jenny waited inpatiently for the Paris shipment, worried again that she had been too extravagant in her buying. She sent notes to special customers announcing the new department and placed lavish ads in the local papers. At last, the gowns arrived. Jenny placed them in strategic showplaces around the store and it was clear within a week that the Paris models were here to stay, both at Maison Jennie New Orleans and Pasadena. The ladies loved the idea of buying gowns available only to a select few . . .

"My husband will scream when he sees the bill this month," the women would confide, their faces glowing as they poured themselves into Poiret, Doucet and Paquin.

Jenny took time out to visit with Vivian, who was doing well in her job. Tiny Charlie was a healthy and happy baby. Still, whenever she held him in her arms, Jenny thought of Mannie and Vivian. They had created this child. *Her husband.* She vowed to provide for his education, just as she would for Leon and Helene.

When Vivian confided that she wanted to become a salesgirl, Jenny asked Nicky to talk to her father about an opening in Goldman's Department Store. The only way for a woman to rise in the business world was in a department store and a smart girl like Vivian, with a keen sense of style, could soon become a buyer.

Vivian was ecstatic when she heard that there was an opening in the sales department. She could hardly afford fine clothes on her salary, but she loved being around them and she knew she could be a good saleswoman. A little selfishly, Jenny was pleased with this turn of events—it couldn't hurt to have a source inside her competitor's store.

Early in June Jenny settled her mother, Sophie and Sophie's children in the cottage on Lake Pontchartrain. When Mrs. Straus began complaining about spending a month at a cottage without a maid, Jenny hired a woman to cook and clean for them. She rationalized the extravagance, convincing herself that this would be two weeks away from the kitchen for Sophie. Guiltily she realized she was looking forward to a month away from mama.

The month passed all to quickly, and soon Mrs. Straus—full of complaints about the cottage, the maid, their neighbors—had returned to the city. Jenny took Leon and Helene to spend a week at Armand and Nicky's cottage, where she phoned the store every day to make sure all was going well. Much to her relief—Sophie was proving to be efficient. But she had to admit that while she loved being with Leon and Helene and she loved the leisurely pace of country life, she missed her challenging days in the store.

The two nurses, with Helene and Leon and Louis in tow, disappeared along the shore of the lake while Jenny and Nicky—now very pregnant—sat for hours on the verandah overlooking the water, sometimes chattering and sometimes sitting in comfortable silence. The children would always return from their outings eager to report a dozen small delights. It was a wonderful, peaceful, fulfilling time.

On Sunday Nicky pleaded with Jenny to leave the children and Annie Lou for another two weeks.

"Louis adores having them here, Jenny, and you know I do."

"But what about when Armand comes up for the weekend? I can't imagine he'd want children underfoot."

Nicky's eyes were suddenly stormy.

"When Armand comes up, all he does is sleep. I don't know what to think, Jenny. He's sweet as he can be when we're together, but I just have this feeling he's seeing other women. I've even thought about divorcing him after the baby is born. But mama would die.

"Don't divorce him, Nicky. Maybe there are problems, but you two love each other. It will work out."

Nicky's face clouded in anger.

"But what kind of love is it that he has to sleep with other women? I admit right now he's afraid to come near me—the doctor scared him to death when I was first pregnant about me miscarrying. But I'm all right now."

"Nicky, remember what you said to me a long time ago—when we talked about Storyville?"

"No, not really."

"You said that going to Storyville was just a man's way. You said you were sure your father visited Storyville—that your mother didn't want to know about it. She felt it didn't concern her."

"But our mothers belong to another generation. And anyway," Nicky smiled, "I guess it was easier to accept when it wasn't me."

"Nicky," Jenny said, "if you love Armand, hang on to him. Maybe what I'm saying is that half a loaf is better than none. Maybe Armand just hasn't settled down to marriage yet."

"But we've been married eight years!"

"Maybe he needs longer. Love is very precious, Nicky. Don't let it go so quickly."

Feeling as though she was leaving part of herself behind, Jenny at last returned alone to the city. With the Pasadena store doing so well, she began to consider buying the house but the family couldn't know about it. She decided to talk to Armand first. Perhaps she could buy it in trust for the children.

Armand approved. He predicted that real estate in the Garden District would triple in value within ten years—in fact, he told her, his father was now buying up choice sites.

Jenny hadn't ever considered the prospect of getting rich on real estate. She went to the library and read past editions of the *Times-Democrat* and the *Daily Picayune*—they, too, foresaw a great future for the city. New buildings were under construction all over New Orleans. Hadn't Maison Blanche put a million and a half into their new twelve-story home already two years underway?

With Armand, his father and the newspaper editors as her board of directors, Jenny went to Mrs. Goldman with a daring plan to buy the building that housed Maison Jennie. They could use money from their growing nest egg and take a mortgage for the balance.

Armand entered into negotiations for the store property, and Jenny spent every waking moment looking for new angles to build sales in the two stores. Sophie had blossomed at the store—she had taken it upon herself to appear in the dressing rooms with accessories—a purse, a scarf, gloves, to complement whatever dress or suit a customer was trying on.

"That way we can sell a whole costume," she pointed out to her eager saleswomen, who now fought to earn the commissions that accompanied such sales. Jenny promoted her to assistant manager.

Evvie was put in charge of following up birth announcements, weddings, graduations and sending out notes of congratulations on Maison Jennie stationery. She also supervised a special department to help husbands and fathers select gifts for the women in their families.

Late in August Jenny was shocked to receive a letter of resignation from Carmen Mendoza, the manager of the Pasadena store. Gracious and unpretentious, Carmen had become one of Jenny's most trusted and valued employees. Jenny was bewildered by the letter, because Carmen gave no reason for her decision to quit the job that she had seemed to enjoy. She decided to meet with Carmen to discuss whatever was bothering her.

Driving home that evening with Evvie and Sophie—

whose family was coming to the house for supper—she decided on impulse to take Leon and Helene along with her. It was off season in Pasadena; she would have no problems reserving rooms on such short notice.

"The children have never been on a train, Sophie. I'll take Annie Lou along to be with them while I'm busy at the store, and if you think the smaller children will be too much for Karl and Carrie to watch over while Annie Lou is away with me, we'll ask her to find a friend to come in."

Sophie frowned.

"Karl I can count on, but not Carrie. She does whatever she wants."

"Oh, Sophie, Carrie's just high spirited," Evvie said fondly. "And she's so pretty everybody spoils her."

"But Herman's the worst! He spoils her all the time. I can't do a thing with her." Sophie sighed. "Mama spoils her too."

Driving up to the house they heard the screeching of children. On the front lawn Annie Lou was trying to separate Carrie and little Helene while Leon tugged at his sister.

"Carrie, stop that!" Sophie shrieked. "Helene's five years younger than you!"

"You always take her side!" Carrie turned on her mother. "You don't love me!"

Sophie stiffened. "Carrie, you know that's not true. Of course I love you. Now tell me, where are the boys?"

"You see?" Carrie flared. "You only love the boys. At least papa loves me."

Jenny regarded Carrie uneasily. Such an odd child . . .

"Let's all go inside and have some lemonade. It's so awfully hot." She held out her arms to Helene and Leon. "Don't I get a kiss?" She was aware that a wistful, teary Carrie had turned to her Aunt Evvie for comfort. She's deliberately doing this, Jenny thought angrily, to hurt Sophie.

Sophie's three younger boys played in the backyard under the doting eyes of their grandmother. It still hurt Jenny that Sophie's children—even Carrie—could do no wrong in mama's eyes while Leon and Helene were blamed for everything.

* * *

After supper Sophie and Herman and the children went home. Jenny first went up to Leon and Helene's bedroom to tuck them in and then to Annie Lou's quarters to tell her about the trip to Pasadena. She heartily approved.

"Miz Jenny, I think it's a right good idea. That Carrie—she's always pickin' on Leon and Helene. I'll be real glad when school starts again, and that one won't be under foot so much."

Jenny sighed.

"It's been such a hot summer for them, Annie. Next year we'll definitely have a cottage on the lake for the summer."

Annie Lou shook her head.

"Summer or winter don't make no difference with that Carrie. She jes' a bad child. She's gonna grow up and make trouble fo' everybody that comes in touch with her. It don't mean nothin' that she's beautiful like a little angel—she got the devil in her."

Leon and Helene loved sleeping on the train, having their meals in a dining car. Jenny was so proud when she noticed the admiring stares they drew from the other diners. If only papa had lived to see his beautiful grandchildren.

As soon as they were settled in their hotel, Jenny telephoned Carmen.

"Why, Mrs. Straus, I didn't know you were coming to Pasadena."

Jenny laughed.

"I thought I'd surprise you. Why don't you come to the hotel and have dinner with us in our suite? When Annie Lou puts the children to bed, we can talk."

They ate a superb meal that night, impeccably served by a hotel waiter in their sitting room, but Jenny sensed an uneasiness in Carmen. Why was she quitting when she had seemed to love her work? Perhaps Mannie had said something to her.

"Carmen, I can't bear the thought of your not being in charge of the store. What can I do to persuade you to stay?"

"Jenny, it's just that—well—" Carmen looked cornered. "I just can't—"

Instantly Jenny knew.

"Mannie's giving you trouble, isn't he?"

Carmen stared, the color rising in her cheeks. "I'm sorry, Mrs. Adler. It's just that the man's impossible. He talks to me as though I were a thief! I'm not used to that kind of treatment. And—" she hesitated. "There's the other problem. I hope you'll forgive me for saying so, but he—he bothers the girls. They don't want to come in to work when they know he's going to be there."

So that was it. Jenny listened, hating Mannie for again putting her in this humiliating position. "Things will change, Carmen. I'll make sure of it. He won't bother your girls anymore." She tried to seem calm, but inside she was seething. He had learned nothing form Vivian? Didn't he ever wonder about his other child? Was there no end to the hurt he would cause?

"Carmen, there will be no more problems, I promise."

"I—I'm glad, Mrs. Adler. I know he's only in the store for two or three days," Jenny did a few quick calculations. She knew where Mannie went the other days he was out of town. "But he makes it so miserable for everybody, Mrs. Adler."

"No more, Carmen, I promise. And tell the girls there'll be a raise for them at the first of the month. And a bonus for you. You've been wonderful."

Riding back on the Sunset Limited, Jenny prepared herself for the inevitable confrontation with Mannie. Ever since the night she met Vivian, nothing Mannie did could hurt her anymore. His weakness infuriated her. Sometimes she suspected that he hated her, too. But in the eyes of the world, she was Mrs. Adler. That would never change. If only he would show some affection toward the children! He seemed to resent her sending Leon to a private school, her dressing them in fine clothes. What kind of father begrudges his children a good life?

Arriving in the taxi that brought them from Terminal Station, Jenny was proud of this lovely two-and-a-half storied stuccoed house, with its lush and fragrant garden. How papa would have loved this house! Even mama loved it, though she would never admit it.

While Jenny paid the taxi driver, Leon and Helene charged toward the house with Annie Lou at their heels. Jenny followed them up the path, tensing as the front door opened and Danny walked out onto the gallery.

"Don't make so much noise," he called to the children. "Grandma's sleeping."

Jenny felt suddenly alarmed. Why was Danny home at this hour of the afternoon? And mama never slept in the afternoon . . .

"Danny, why is mama sleeping?"

"She's all right, don't get scared." Danny hoisted Helene into the air and kissed her, put her down, then kissed Leon.

"Uncle Danny, we slept on a train," Leon said proudly.

"And ate there, too," Helene said.

"Danny," Jenny said, "Why *are* you home in the middle of the afternoon?"

"Dora called me at the store." He kissed her and held open the screen door. "Get inside fast before the mosquitoes come in."

"Why did Dora call?"

"Mama had kind of a heat spell this morning. We keep telling her the fans have to be on when it's this hot, but you know mama. She figures it's a waste of money."

"Did you call Dr. Cohen?"

"He's out on the back porch now having some iced tea. I heard the taxi pull up and came out."

"Well, what did he say?"

"Nothing. A lot of people are suffering from the heat."

"Danny?" A querulous voice filtered down to the foyer. "What's all that noise down there?"

"It's just Jenny, mama," Danny called upstairs.

Evvie came out of their mother's bedroom.

"Mama wants you to come upstairs, but she said for Annie Lou to keep the children in the back where they won't disturb her."

Jenny went upstairs and opened the door to her mother's bedroom.

"Mama," she said tenderly as she sat on the edge of the bed. The ceiling fan whirred softly overhead.

"A fine way for you to come home," her mother sighed. "Finding me like this."

"Dr. Cohen says it's just a touch of the sun. You must keep the fans going on days like this."

"He doesn't want to scare me," Mrs. Straus said knowingly.

Evvie stood in the doorway. "You're all right now, mama. You just need some rest."

"I heard what he said." Jenny saw her mother's right hand tighten into a fist. "I'm not going deaf."

"Mama, don't excite yourself," Danny said as he walked in with Dr. Cohen. "Dr. Cohen said you have to learn to relax."

"Dr Cohen said," Mrs. Straus mimicked. "You heard. Evvie heard. He said I have a heart condition."

"Mama, he didn't," Evvie soothed. "He said that—"

"I said that she's in good health except that she lets her nerves get the better of her sometimes. And nobody in their right mind with fans in the house leaves them idle in this kind of weather. You have a very slight heart murmur, Mrs. Straus—it means nothing. I probably shouldn't even have mentioned it," he said drily. "You'll live another thirty-five years—you just have to learn to relax."

"It's easy for you to say—learn to relax . . ."

"Well, be that as it may, I have to be on my rounds," Dr. Cohen said briskly. "Stay in bed for another day, Mrs. Straus. Keep the fan going and drink lots of liquids."

"I'll tell Dora to fix a pitcher of iced tea," Danny said, following Dr. Cohen from the room.

Why couldn't mama relax? What was missing in her life? Papa *had* loved her. Yet there were times when Jenny wondered how long her mother's love had survived beyond the first year or two of marriage. All her talk about her life before papa in Vienna . . .

But they lived well now. Mama lacked nothing. Except for something she was unable to provide. Something intangible, something which perhaps she could never provide. Nicky's words came back to her . . . *"Jenny, why do you think you're responsible for the welfare of your entire family? They have to carry some of the load themselves."*

But papa was gone and the burden had passed to her. She

must learn not to be impatient with mama. Though mama rarely talked about her family she suspected their rejection of her was still painful. How cruel of them to have ignored letters mama wrote from America, saying that to them Louise Solomon—now Louise Straus—was dead.

"Evvie, my hair looks terrible. Brush it for me, darling."

"Yes, mama."

"I feel so relaxed when you brush my hair," Mrs. Straus said as Evvie helped her into a sitting position against the fat feather bolster across the headboard.

"Don't worry, mama. I'll brush it for you every morning." Jenny looked up sharply. What was this . . . Evvie was quitting her job?

"Evvie won't be working in the store anymore, Jenny," Mrs. Straus said with a faint smile. "She'll stay home to take care of me. A woman with a heart condition should not be left alone."

"Mama," Jenny said, "Dr. Cohen didn't say you had a heart condition."

"A heart murmur. Same thing."

"No, mama, it isn't."

Mrs. Straus waved her hand impatiently.

"Jenny, you're upsetting me. I have a heart condition. Evvie will stay with me. Is that too much to ask of my own child? But I wouldn't expect you to understand."

Jenny could see this wasn't going anywhere. "I think I'd better go call the store. Sophie said they were short of help yesterday—three saleswomen were out sick."

"Tell Sophie to come by and see me before she goes home. Maybe Herman should come over here with the children for supper. For what you pay her Dora can cook for a few extra."

Jenny paced the parlor waiting for Evvie to come downstairs again. Mama must not be allowed to do this. Working in the store had been so good for Evvie. She had loved being there. Every day she was becoming more of a whole person.

Though she had said nothing to Evvie yet—she had been waiting for the right moment—she had talked to Armand about the possibility of Evvie's divorcing Sidney. Armand said that it could be handled quietly. And Evvie was so pretty—there was no reason she couldn't find herself a husband worthy of her. But not if she was tied to mama.

She heard Evvie's footsteps on the staircase.

"Mama's asleep," Evvie said as she came into the parlor. "So. How was your trip?" Her forced gaiety told Jenny that she anticipated an argument.

"Evvie, you can't be serious about leaving the store."

"Mama wants me home, Jenny." Evvie avoided meeting her eyes. "She's scared."

"But Dr. Cohen says she's in good health. Why don't we bring in another doctor to confirm his opinion?"

"Mama wouldn't allow that. She respects Dr. Cohen."

"How can she respect him if she rejects his diagnosis? Evvie, we'll hire a companion for mama. You don't have to sacrifice your—"

"I'm not sacrificing anything. I liked working in the store, but I think it's more important to make mama happy."

"Evvie, you're twenty-eight years old. You can't throw away your life—"

"I'm not throwing away my life," Evvie snapped. "I'm doing what's right."

"But mama isn't sick!"

"She thinks she is. I have to do what mama asks of me. I can't take a chance on making her really sick." She hesitated. "Anyway, she does have that heart murmur."

"Dr. Cohen says it means nothing. She can live another thirty-five years."

"I pray that she does," Evvie said softly. "And that I'll be there to take care of her." She frowned at the sound of laughter at the side of the house. "I'll go tell Annie Lou to keep the children in the back. They mustn't wake up mama."

Jenny stood motionless. Clearly, she was fighting a losing battle. Mama had found a lifelong companion in Evvie.

CHAPTER
SEVENTEEN

J ENNY WAITED UNTIL she had been back home a few days before confronting Mannie with Carmen's accusations. As she had anticipated, he was outraged.

"What do you mean, she don't like the way I treat her? Who does she think she is? The Queen of England? She works for us! Maybe she wants I should ask her permission before I talk to her?"

"Don't act as though you think she's cheating on the accounts, Mannie. Carmen is a thoroughly honest woman. You have no right to be arrogant to her."

"Who's arrogant? She's crazy."

Jenny struggled to remain calm. Who was this cruel, boorish man? This man who was arrogant to his own children? To his wife? "Mannie, I *know* how arrogant you can be. And another thing—I want you to stay away from the salesgirls. They don't like you bothering them either."

In spite of her anger, Jenny almost enjoyed seeing Mannie's stunned expression. "Who's bothering them? They're crazy. I try to be nice to them, that's all. Figures. You're nice to a salesgirl, and right away you're bothering her!"

"Mannie, I'm not interested in your arguments. Either behave or I'll have to send somebody else to Pasadena. I have a good staff there and I intend to keep them."

Mannie's bravado was fading. He looked shaken.

"They won't leave so fast. Who pays as well as you do? Who gives them two weeks paid vacations?"

"Mannie, there will be no more discussion. I don't want any trouble in Pasadena."

"All right, all right!" He glared. "Queen Jenny has spoken."

As the weeks became months, Jenny accepted the fact that Evvie would not be coming back into the store. She had the gardener drive mama and Evvie around the city—mama had decided that Evvie was "too delicate" to learn to drive.

Early in November Nicky gave birth to a daughter and Jenny was convinced that tiny Stephanie was holding Nicky's marriage together. Armand was estatic. He bought a magnificent diamond necklace, and his parents gave them a title to a block of stores they owned on Canal Street in honor of their new grandchild.

On New Year's Day, 1913, Jenny went alone to Nicky's open house. None of Nicky's friends had ever met Mannie—and Jenny was determined to keep it that way.

As the lower floor crackled with the sounds of merriment, Nicky took Jenny upstairs to see Louis and Stephanie. Then she took Jenny to her own bedroom.

"Did you see the looks passing between Armand and that silly Lita Beauchamp?" she asked, fire in her eyes. "I just know he's having an affair with her. What should I do?"

Jenny laughed and kissed her. "Nicky, everybody knows Lita Beauchamp throws herself at every good-looking man in sight."

"I know Armand and he doesn't turn things down," Nicky said grimly. "For all her silliness she is gorgeous."

"Not as gorgeous as you. Anyway Armand loves you."

"My life is going to change," Nicky said defiantly. "I'm not going to sit at home and mope about it. From now on Nicole Lazar will be the busiest hostess in New Orleans. I won't have time to wonder about who's in Armand's bed besides me. And I'm going to start collecting paintings. All the new painters Marc is so enthusiastic about—Picasso, Matisse, Braque. He says they'll be worth a fortune some day."

"Why don't you come with me to New York and Paris in April?"

"Oh, I don't think so, Jenny. Stephanie is so young . . ."

"Stephanie will be five months old by then. And I bet Armand's mother would be delighted to move into the house for three weeks to watch the children. You need to get away, Nicky. Come on, say yes."

"Three weeks?"

"Including traveling time, two days in New York and six in Paris." She was counting the days until she was on her way to Paris and to Marc. She tried to be realistic—she could not expect a week alone with Marc again; but at least she would see him. For a precious little while her life would seem complete.

"I tell you what," Nicky said, "I'll talk to Armand's mother, maybe she'll be able to take care of Stephanie. Oh, Jenny, am I asking too much to expect Armand to be faithful to me? Sometimes I wish they'd burn down Storyville. That's a living testimony to the unfaithfulness of New Orleans husbands." She chuckled. "And sitting there right on top of Canal Street, where every tourist coming into town is sure to see it."

"Armand will change, Nicky."

"When he's fifty? I wish I had the guts to divorce him."

"Why don't you threaten him? That doesn't mean you have to follow through."

Nicky smiled.

"I guess I haven't the guts to do that, either."

Jenny watched with concern as a series of labor strikes paralyzed the work force in 1913. In New York City 150,000 garment workers walked out, and the strike spread to Boston. In Paterson, New Jersey, silk workers went on strike. But Maison Jennie treated its staff well and she was pleased by their loyalty.

Jenny was glad that Woodrow Wilson—a Democrat— had won the presidential election and would be inaugurated on March 4. Armand said that Wilson would cultivate the friendship of the Latin American countries and help them raise their wretched standard of living.

Late in March Jenny endured the usual reproaches from

her mother as she prepared for the trip to New York and Paris, and her usual guilt about leaving the children. But Leon and Helene were overjoyed when she promised them that she would take them with her when she went to Pasadena in August. She didn't mention that they might also visit Santa Barbara, the possible site of yet another Maison Jennie resort shop. Maybe then they would take Karl with them. Of Sophie's five children she felt closest to Karl, who loved music and art and the theater. But she couldn't just take Karl—Carrie would carry on like mad.

Jenny was grateful that Sophie was becoming so valuable at the store. She could leave her in charge for three weeks without a moment's thought. And for Sophie, too, the store was becoming home.

"I don't know how to handle Herman anymore," she confided a few days before Jenny was to leave on her buying trip. "He's furious that I hired a girl to come in to clean two days a week without asking him first—but how could I ask? I knew he'd say no. Of course he spoils Carrie to death—anything she wants she gets and he's impossible with the boys. Now he won't talk to anybody except Carrie. He sits at the table every night and talks to me through her. 'Carrie, tell your mother there's too much onion in the stew.' Karl gets the worst of it—nothing he does seems to please Herman."

Jenny gave her a hug.

"Sophie, I'm taking a house at the lake for the summer." She hadn't even told mama yet. "A large place. Let's arrange for the children to be up there most of the summer. You and I can drive up one night a week to see the children and on Saturdays we'll go up with Herman and Mannie. What do you think?"

"Oh, Jenny, I'd love it. And you can be sure Herman won't complain—" her smile was bitter. "You'll be feeding his children all summer."

I'll bet Danny would show up at the cottage a grand total of three times all summer, Jenny thought, and only then to see mama. Apparently he was doing well in the store, but according to mama he never brought anyone home. Who were his friends? And mama was impatient for him to find a nice girl—in a few months he would be twenty-five. In mama's eyes he should have a family already. But Jenny was happy that at least he enjoyed working in the fine store—let the rest come later.

Later that evening Nicky called.

"Jenny, I just got a letter from Marc and he says that Simone is ill at the country house so he'll have to come to the city to meet us and take us to the Paris house. I guess he'll be with us until the following morning. Then, once you've finished with the buying, he wants us to come up to the country."

Panic and guilt seized her.

"Nicky, I can't."

"We'll talk about it once we're there. I'm sure Marc wouldn't suggest it if he didn't think it would be comfortable for you."

"Oh, Nicky, I don't know—"

"Never mind," Nicky said confidently. "When we see him you'll change your mind. Anyway, why deprive yourself of being with him as much as you can?"

"Well, all right. I'm only agreeing to wait until Paris to see how I feel, so don't look so triumphant yet."

"Okay, okay. Anyway, I told Armand I meant to buy some paintings while we're there." Nicky laughed mischievously. "He thinks I'm out of my mind, but I know he'll humor me. With the fees he charges, he shouldn't be too uspset if I spend a few thousand on paintings."

Jenny lay sleepless far into the night. Soon she would see Marc. That in itself was hard to imagine. But staying with him at his house? She shuddered. Impossible. All this time she'd been able to rationalize her feelings, but she couldn't bear the thought of getting to know Simone. She had to find an excuse to stay in Paris.

On the morning of the day they were to leave Jenny hurried to the store to give Sophie some last-minute instructions.

"Jenny, you look exhausted," Sophie said. "Try to get

some rest on the trip. You'll never have the energy to do all that buying if you don't take it easy."

"God, you're right. I haven't been sleeping. I guess I've been preoccupied with the store. Did I tell you I'm thinking about opening another branch in Houston?"

"You mentioned it. But don't over-expand, Jenny. You're doing so well now."

Jenny smiled. How typical of sensible Sophie . . .

"I see an enormous future for Maison Jennie, Sophie. Before I'm satisfied, we'll have a chain of specialty shops, just you wait." She paused. "And I'm being taken in as a partner."

"Oh, Jenny, how wonderful!"

"The rest of the family isn't to know, Sophie, and your salary goes up the first of next month, so you'll be getting two pay envelopes. If you use your head, you'll start a savings account in your own name and bank the second envelope. Have some money for yourself that Herman doesn't know about. It'll make life easier."

For a moment Sophie looked frightened. But when she spoke, her voice was fierce. "I will. Then I'll have money for Karl's bar mitzvah in January. Herman's already complaining that we can't afford a big party."

Usually Jenny was able to unwind on the train. For those few days it seemed that she was in another world, cut off from the life she knew. But on this trip she was tense, haunted by her anticipation of what was to happen in Paris.

Nicky had been urged by her parents and grandmother to try to talk Marc into coming home for a visit. Jenny doubted that he would come. With an overwhelming sense of loss it suddenly occurred to her that he might never come home again . . .

But by the time they arrived in New York, Jenny was excited about being in Paris. And in a week Marc would be standing on the platform at the Gâre Saint Lazare waiting to greet them.

They spent two frenzied days doing nothing but buying clothes. They did take time out to go to Forty-second Street to see Grand Central Terminal, which had been opened to the public two months before. On their second night in New York, a manufacturer took them to dinner at the Ritz-Carlton and out to see a wonderful English dancing couple known as the Vernon Castles in a British musical, *The Sunshine Girl*, just opening in New York. The following day they set sail for Bordeaux.

By the time the ship arrived at the French seaport, Jenny was nearly torn apart by conflicting emotions. One moment she vowed she would see Marc only in Paris, the next she was determined to go to his country house—anything to spend every possible moment with him.

"Nicky, do I look all right?"

Nicky winked.

"Darling, if I weren't a girl, I'd fall in love with you."

"This is so crazy. What am I doing? I have a husband, two beautiful children." She reached for Nicky's hand. "I don't know if I'm strong enough to take this."

"Darling, don't be so melodramatic. Didn't you once tell me—'half a loaf is better than none'? Well, here's your half. Enjoy it."

Jenny's heart was pounding as they left the train with their luggage carried by porters. Her eyes scanned the crowd waiting in the arrivals section.

"There he is!" She clutched at Nicky's arm.

"Marc!" Nicky yelled, running toward him. "God, it's so good to see you!" She threw herself into his arms and kissed him warmly.

Jenny stood at a distance while Marc and Nicky exchanged greetings. Then they separated and he turned to her. For a long moment their eyes met.

"Jenny—" He drew her to him in what was meant to be a brotherly embrace and for an instant Jenny felt the wild pounding of his heart. "I've waited so long."

"I thought the days would never pass," she whispered.

Nicky cleared her throat.

"So Marc . . . how's Simone?"

"Better. But the doctors say it will take her a while to recover."

There was a chill in the April air as they walked quickly to the chauffeured Renault waiting outside. Marc helped

them and their luggage inside before getting in next to
Jenny.

Nicky chattered all the way to the beautiful house on the
Rue Marignan—first about her children, then Armand, their
grandmother and their parents. Marc seemed to be paying
attention, but Jenny could tell he wasn't concentrating. She
could feel the pressure of his elbow against hers, and even
though he would occasionally ask Nicky a question, she
knew he, too, was engrossed in her presence beside him.

"Here we are," he said lightly as they drew up before the
house. Jenny's throat tightened as she remembered the week
she had spent here—was it just last year? It seemed like a
lifetime ago . . .

"Oh, Marc, it's just as beautiful as I remember—" Nicky
turned around in the foyer. "Armand and I had the most
wonderful honeymoon here."

"I'm afraid I don't appreciate it as I should," Marc said.
"I'll tell you what: let's go out to dinner tonight at
Voison's." He looked at Jenny and they both remembered
their words a year ago . . . *"For your first night in Paris
you must have dinner at Voison's."*

"Okay. But let's come back to the house early," Nicky
said. "Jenny isn't, but I'm exhausted from all our traveling."

"Fine. But in the morning I have to return to the country
house. Why don't you phone me when you're through with
your buying jaunt? I'll drive down and take you back with
me."

Jenny knew that now was the time to say she wouldn't be
able to go to the country house, even for a day or two. She
could tell them she would be tied up buying. But she
couldn't bring herself to say it.

As Marc showed them their bedrooms on the second
floor, Jenny remembered that Marc's bedroom was next to
hers and she felt a pang of anticipation . . . *He wouldn't,*
she told herself—*they couldn't.* Could they?

A maid came up to unpack and draw her bath before
dinner. Jenny decided to wear the mauve and ivory silk
Poiret that she had worn on her first night in Paris last year.

But she wasn't trying to recreate that week, she reminded herself. This time it would be different.

Marc picked them up at seven sharp. Voison's was crowded, but Marc pointed out that they were eating early—later the room would be filled with international celebrities. Jenny remembered last year when Marc had pointed out the Duchess of Marlborough, André Gide, a Baron Rothschild.

"You know, I don't think Armand and I were here," Nicky said, peering around the room. "It's magnificent."

"I don't think you would have noticed," Marc said dryly. "You two had eyes only for each other."

Jenny watched Nicky's expression—first startled, then her face softening. Her marriage will be all right, Jenny told herself. Coming to Paris would be good for her.

After a long, delicious meal, during which several people stopped to ask about Simone's health, Marc led them to the waiting limousine and told Phillipe to drive them home. The city was bursting with life, fragrant with the scents of spring flowers and the perfumes of beautiful women.

"Let's have more coffee," Marc said once they were home again. The three of them walked arm-in-arm into the small sitting room where François had lighted a fire.

They seated themselves in front of the fireplace in gently curved, delicately framed chairs covered in Beauvais tapestries. The firelight cast flickering shadows around the room.

Throughout the evening, Jenny could feel the unspoken questions in the air—she suspected that Nicky was aware of the silent conversation between her and Marc beyond the pleasant banter of the evening.

Why was she so afraid to make love with Marc with Nicky across the hall? But it wasn't Nicky—it was Simone. Marc and she had waited a whole year for this week, and the idea of Simone, ill and unsuspecting, unnerved her. But was it wrong to take what they could?

She listened to Marc and Nicky talk about the new censorship in the London cinema, both of them amused by the banning of mixed bathing scenes on the beaches.

Marc was doing his best to keep the conversation light.

"Do you go to the cinema often in New Orleans?" Nicky laughed.

"In New Orleans, my darling brother, we call it going to the movies. And my personal favorite is Charlie Chaplin."

Nicky stifled a yawn as François arrived with the coffee tray. Try as she might, Jenny couldn't relax. Darling Nicky. Of course she was making every effort to let her and Marc be together as naturally as possible. But the air in the elegant Louis XV sitting room was fraught with tension.

"As soon as we've had our coffee," Nicky said lightly, "I'm going to sleep. Jenny and I will have breakfast with you before you leave, Marc. Be sure and wake me."

For a long moment Marc's eyes held Jenny's. He smiled.

Jenny and Nicky went to their rooms while Marc stayed downstairs, presumably to telephone Simone.

Her heart pounding, Jenny changed into an ivory chiffon-and-lace nightgown and drew on the matching negligée. But what if she had mistaken his intentions? Each minute that she waited seemed endless. At last she heard a faint knock at her door.

Her face radiant, all doubts in eclipse, she darted to the door.

"Jenny," he whispered, closing the door behind them. "My beautiful, wonderful Jenny—"

She awoke in Marc's arms, remembering the memory of her first morning in Paris exactly one year ago.

Marc kissed her.

"I wish I could stay in Paris with you, Jenny. But you'll finish your buying quickly, won't you? At least let's see each other for three or four days in the country."

"I'll buy as quickly as I can." She knew that in Marc's country house—with Simone under the same roof—they couldn't make love.

"I wish I could wake up every morning of my life like this," he said, reaching for her hand.

This time their lovemaking was heightened by the knowledge that they would not be together again for another year. Afterwards they lay entangled, savoring these last few moments.

Finally it was Marc who spoke.

"I must leave now, my love. Breakfast downstairs in half an hour?"

"Okay. I'll wake Nicky."

Marc left, and Jenny hurried through her dressing, grateful that the maid had been told not to come to her room unless she rang. She needed this time alone. When she went to Nicky's room, she found her dressed and reading by a window. She looked up from her book with a sly wink.

"Time for breakfast?"

"Just about. If we're to share it with Marc, we'd better go downstairs."

Jenny swept through her buying in record time, ever conscious that these were hours she could be with Marc. But, as always, she enjoyed admiring the rich fabrics, the beautiful lines of the designer clothes that would be shipped back to the New Orleans store and to the resort shop in Pasadena. Next time, she dreamt, she would be buying for yet another resort shop.

Nicky telephoned the country house when Jenny was through buying and within three hours Marc was in Paris to pick them up. On the drive through winding country roads Jenny tried to prepare herself for the meeting with Simone.

Both Jenny and Nicky were enchanted with the red-brick chateau, every window faced with marble, that sat a hundred yards from a rushing brook. Marc left the car for a houseman to park and led them into the spacious marble-floored foyer, above which hung a magnificent crystal chandelier. He talked briefly to a maid and then turned back to them.

"I'm afraid Simone is sleeping. She left word to apologize if she was not awake in time to welcome you."

Nicky laughed.

"Don't be silly. It's good for her to sleep anyway."

A maid took them to their bedrooms and told them there would be plenty of time for a bath since dinner wasn't to be served for at least an hour. Jenny was grateful for the chance to relax in a fragrant tub.

She spent an hour trying to decide what to wear and she was still in her negligée when Nicky came to her room, resplendent in a blue-green pussy-willow silk that she had bought from M. Poiret the day before.

"Nicky, I'm going crazy in here trying to decide. What do you think I should wear?"

"The new Poiret? Lilac does marvelous things for your eyes."

Simone didn't appear at the dinner table. Marc assured them that she was getting better, but he seemed distracted. After his second glass of wine he admitted that he had sent for Simone's doctor and in the middle of the meal—a gourmet feast—they heard the doctor's car, his greetings to a servant and his footsteps up the stairs to Simone's room.

In the morning Marc confessed that Simone seemed to have suffered a setback. Jenny gently insisted that the chauffeur drive Nicky and her back to Paris. This was not the time for visitors.

"Next spring will be better," Marc promised Jenny, holding her hand tightly for a moment before he helped her into the car. "Never forget, Jenny. I love you."

CHAPTER EIGHTEEN

THREE WEEKS AFTER their return to New Orleans, Nicky reported that she had received a letter from Marc. Apparently Simone was responding well to new treatment and was almost herself again, but because of the heat in Paris this summer she and Marc would be staying at the country house. Several years earlier, Simone had ordered a studio built for Marc there, so he could continue his work.

Late in May Jenny saw the family move into the lake house. Mannie decided to learn to drive, mostly because he needed something new to hold over Herman's head—this way he could talk about "my car." Jenny bought a second car—a Stanley Steamer, which of course instantly became "Mannie's car."

Jenny was convinced that within ten years half the families in the country would own automobiles, especially now that Henry Ford was setting up an assembly line to make inexpensive Model Ts. Mannie and Herman scoffed at Mr. Ford's revolutionary wage scale for his workers. Imagine—five dollars a day!

Jenny enjoyed the long drive to the lake house two or three times a week, again a bit of time that was far away from her daily world. Alone in the car her mind was swept clear of the endless detail that was part of running the store. For those few hours she could linger over memories of Marc.

Jenny discovered, too, that her solitary drives often sparked fresh ideas for the business. She was actively planning for a store in Santa Barbara which meant another stop for Mannie, who seemed to enjoy the traveling. The short distance between the two resorts would make things easy for him.

Early in August Sophie told Jenny, with some embarrassment, that she would be bringing the children back into New Orleans the following Sunday.

"Why?" Jenny asked, though she had a strong suspicion it was because Carrie was fighting with Leon and Helene.

"Oh, I don't know, Jenny. Herman claims Leon picks on Carrie," Sophie said unhappily. "I know it isn't true, but it'll be better if—"

"Then leave them at the cottage," Jenny said quickly. "This would be a good time for me to go to Santa Barbara. I've been in contact with the real estate brokers there and they have some stores they want me to look at. I'll take Leon and Helene with me." She hesitated. "Maybe Karl, too? It could be an advance bar mitzvah present." In January Karl was to be bar mitzvahed and Sophie had already started planning.

"Karl would love it, but no—I don't think so. Carrie would make life miserable for everybody if Karl went and she didn't."

"Sophie," Jenny said, "some day Carrie has to learn that she doesn't rule your household."

"I know. We do the best we can. I try to keep peace in the family, but she's impossible. Thank God I have the store."

Jenny planned to travel with the children to Pasadena first, and then north to Santa Barbara. She had no difficulty getting hotel reservations. In Santa Barbara they would stay at the elegant Potter Hotel, where the Carnegies, the Rockefellers, the Astors and the Peabodys stayed.

Leon and Helene, accompanied by Annie Lou, were delighted to be traveling again with their mother. It was a very special time for the four of them, and Jenny promised herself that they would make at least one trip a year together in the years ahead.

Now that the children were getting older, their nonexistent relationship with Mannie was especially disturbing. Sophie said he bragged about them every time he was together with Herman, but you certainly couldn't see any pride in the way he treated them. He was so consistently nasty and fault-finding that he often reduced Helene to tears. Sometimes Jenny saw Leon flinch at Mannie's table manners. When he started one of his tirades, Leon and Helene fled to their bedrooms.

On one of her brief visits to the Pasadena shop, Carmen confessed to Jenny that Mannie was acting up again.

"Jenny, I love the shop, but I don't know how much longer I can bear his comments. Couldn't you send somebody else?"

Jenny deliberated for a few moments. *She* could go check out the shop once a year. But she couldn't bear the thought of having Mannie underfoot every day of the year. She decided to be honest with Carmen.

"Carmen, Mannie doesn't have to come out here once a month. Frankly, I need him out of the house for those trips for my own sanity." Gratefully she noted Carmen's compassionate nod of understanding. "I'll talk to him again—this time I'll threaten to take his job away." She smiled bitterly. "I don't think Mannie wants that any more than I do. Write me after his next trip. Let's try to work this out."

"Thank you, Jenny."

The next day Jenny and the children moved on to Santa Barbara. The Potter Hotel was a rambling five-story 600-room palace situated right on the water, with 36 landscaped acres. A 500-foot avenue of palms led to the beach. There were acres of lilies and violets, 30,000 rose bushes, a mile of red geraniums.

The children were wide-eyed with delight when they discovered that thirteen movie companies were filming such popular serials as *The Perils of Pauline* in Santa Barbara. While Jenny talked to real estate brokers, Annie Lou took the children around town, where they were able to watch the Essanay Pictures company shoot a cowboy picture right on the city streets. The following day they greeted her on her return to the hotel with the news that they had seen Mary Pickford walking down the street in town.

Though it was off-season, Jenny was convinced Santa

Barbara was the perfect location for another Maison Jennie shop. She was about to despair of finding a store that would be adaptable to her needs, when a broker showed her a location that would be available within six or eight months. After considerable bargaining the owner agreed to make the necessary alterations.

It was an eight-year lease and she signed it with some qualms. They no longer had the luxury of a "testing period." But all indications were that this would be a real moneymaker. She wasn't just letting herself be persuaded because this meant yet another stop for Mannie—was she?

In September Jenny took Helene to her first day of school. She was so proud that she was able to provide fine schooling for her children. Helene was to begin dancing lessons this year and Leon was already studying the piano.

Sophie was running into difficulties in planning Karl's bar mitzvah party. Herman demanded a full accounting of every cent she spent. Sophie had been saving religiously for this event, but she would never admit to her private savings. She decided to say that Jenny was paying for the party as her bar mitzvah gift.

"Sophie, why don't you really let me pay for the party," Jenny said impulsively.

"No, Jenny, I couldn't. I love you for offering, but let me have the pleasure of knowing that I paid for Karl's bar mitzvah. It means a great deal to me."

"Of course." Jenny felt a surge of tenderness for Sophie. It was rare for any of the Straus women to use terms of endearment and Sophie especially was shy. "For his bar mitzvah present I'll start a bank account for him. We'll tell him that it's the beginning of his college money."

"Oh, Jenny, that's wonderful. But I hate having to lie to Herman."

"Don't think of it that way. Do what's best, Sophie—for the children and for you."

Early in February Jenny began to make plans for the buying trips to New York and Paris. Already work was underway on the Santa Barbara shop, so now she would be buying for three stores.

Nicky insisted that Jenny go alone to Paris this year but she fabricated a time when she would be there so that Marc could plan to be in Paris at the same time. Simone, Marc wrote, was now recovered from her illness, and would be in Cannes with friends that particular week.

Jenny could barely contain her excitement at the prospect of spending a whole week again with Marc in Paris. Then just two weeks before she was to board the train for New York, Jenny received a call from her banker, Mr. McFeeters.

"Mrs. Adler, I hope you'll forgive me for calling this way, but I'm afraid your checking account is heavily overdrawn. We've been honoring checks that have come in, but now the overdraft is becoming rather substantial."

"Mr. McFeeters, according to my figures I have a substantial balance." What kind of mistake could she have made?

"Perhaps you'd like to come in and go over this with me. Meanwhile we'll honor the check to Cranston Realty."

"But I haven't written a check to Cranston Realty. Please—don't go anywhere—I'll be there in twenty minutes."

Half an hour later, pale and shaken, Jenny was sitting across from Mr. McFeeters inspecting the checks presumably signed by her. The signature was very like her own, she had to admit, but it was *not* hers.

Mr. McFeeters drummed his fingertips on his desk.

"I think we had better call in the police, Mrs. Adler. Do you have any idea who would have access to your checkbook?"

"No, I really don't. But please don't call them. Not yet. Just give me until tomorrow morning—there's something I have to do."

Jenny returned to the store and made a list of the payees of the checks: Maison Blanche, Cranston Realty, a jewelry store. It came to three thousand dollars. The check to Cranston Realty caught her eye—it was a rent check. *Danny*. Maybe all those nights when Danny didn't come home—when he said he was sleeping over at his buddy's house—he was actually living in an apartment.

Grim, she went to Cranston Realty, pretending to be a stranger in the city.

"Excuse me, but I've lost my brother's address and I think I remember him saying he rented from Cranston Realty, so I thought perhaps you'd be able to give me the address."

The woman at the desk looked her over.

"What's his name?"

"Straus. Daniel Straus. I'm sorry to bother you about this—I know it was awfully careless of me." She watched as the woman began rummaging through the files.

"Ah!" she straightened up from the file cabinet, "here we are, Miss Straus. Daniel, right? I'll write it down for you."

Jenny left in search for Barrow Street. At last she stumbled on it—a pleasant little street off Canal. Danny's was an upstairs flat with a small gallery decorated with flower boxes of red and pink geraniums. From the payees of the other checks Jenny suspected that Danny was sharing the flat with a woman.

She rang the bell. No answer.

A door across the hall opened and a sour-faced woman holding her kimono closed across her sagging breasts stuck her head out.

"They ain't home." She inspected Jenny from head to toe. "You ain't one of her friends from Storyville?"

"Storyville?" Jenny stared blankly.

"It don't mean nothin' to me that they're married," the woman sniggered. "She's still Felice, who used to run a house in Storyville. Bein' married don't change that none."

"Thank you, I think I'll come back some other time," Jenny stammered, her face hot. *Danny was married to a girl from Storyville?*

Jenny hurried back to the store. Tears came to her eyes when she saw Danny helping a customer to a waiting limousine. How could he have married that whore—and then come to his family? What if one of the children had been exposed to some disease he might have brought home with him? How could she tell mama that Danny was married to a girl from Storyville?

Jenny sighed. Danny must have forged the checks to support that girl. But *she* had been the one who sent him to Storyville to make deliveries years ago. Now all Mannie's nasty remarks about Danny's reception in some of the houses in Storyville made sense. Why did it always seem that she was to blame?

Once she was back in her office with the door shut, Jenny phoned Josie in Storyville.

"Oh, yes," Josie said. "I thought I heard something about Felice getting married. But I had no idea who the lucky guy was. I first met Felice—when was it?—oh, about five years ago, I guess. After a year in one of the houses she opened up her own place—rumor had it she had a backer. I'll say one thing about Felice—she never took in a girl who was a virgin. She had a real firm rule about that."

Jenny left her office and went to summon Danny.

"In my office this minute," she said when he made a show of waiting to help a customer.

He knew she'd found out about the checks. She saw it in his eyes. But he *didn't* know she knew about his marriage.

"Danny, have you completely lost your mind?" she asked, slamming the door behind them. "I had a call from the bank today—"

"I'll pay it back, Jenny. I—I got caught at the pool halls. You know what they'd do to me if I didn't pay up—"

"Stop lying," she said with distaste. "I know you married that girl from Storyville—you're living with her."

He was ashen.

"I'm married to Felice, but she's not like those other girls, Jenny—you have to get to know her."

"I think I can do without that pleasure, thank you. How do you think mama will take this?"

"Oh, she'll scream and carry on. She'll be sure she's having a heart attack."

"We can't let her know. We don't know what it would do to her." With mama's nerves, something like this might—

just might—push her into a nervous breakdown. They couldn't take that chance.

"Jenny, I love Felice," he said defiantly. "I don't care how she lived before. I love her. I won't give her up. Not even for mama."

"We can't talk here," she said tiredly. The last thing she wanted was for the staff to hear about Danny's marriage. "I'll be at the flat tonight around nine. Meet me there, Danny. We have to talk this out."

Jenny knew the Paris trip would have to be postponed. She couldn't leave New Orleans in the midst of a family crisis. She'd cancel her reservations, plan to go to Paris in August instead. She'd talk to Nicky, have her write Marc immediately.

The next few hours seemed to drag endlessly. At last she was able to drive to Danny's flat. Though the night was pleasantly warm, her hands were cold as ice as she turned off the ignition and left the car. Jenny walked slowly up the stairs. She rang the bell at the door and waited.

The door opened. A tall, slight, pretty girl in a neat white shirtwaist and skirt stood before her.

"I'm Felice," she said, smiling hesitantly. "Please come in. Danny will be right back."

"Thank you." Jenny walked into the pleasantly furnished parlor. Felice was not the flashy Storyville girl she had expected.

"I sent Danny out to buy ice cream so that we could have a few minutes alone." There was a note of apology in her voice. "I know how you feel about Danny's marrying me. Not only a *shiksa*, but a girl from Storyville. I have to tell you—"

"You don't have to tell me anything," Jenny said.

"Yes, I do," Felice said urgently. "For Danny you must listen. I came to New Orleans five and a half years ago. When I was sixteen. I'd run away from home. I had to run away. When my father was drunk, he would beat me. When he was sober, he—he abused me. He didn't go to a red light district. He came into my bed. My mother was always too drunk to know. So I ran away. I was frightened and starving when I was offered a job in Storyville. After a year I opened my own house, financed by a—a patron. I paid off every cent he put up. I owe nobody anything now. I even have a couple of thousand put aside."

"Then you don't know that Danny has been forging checks to support you?" Jenny said. But she couldn't help being touched by Felice's story.

Felice turned pale.

"I have a little over two thousand in the bank. Will that cover the checks?"

Both women started at the sound of the doorbell.

"That's Danny," Felice said and hurried to open the door.

"I got chocolate," Danny said as he came in. "You've always liked chocolate best, right, Jenny?"

"I've told Felice about the checks," Jenny said carefully while Felice took the ice cream and went to the kitchen to serve it.

Danny flushed in anger.

"Did you have to do that?"

"Felice has to know," Jenny said. "You have to be honest with both of us, Danny. I've been doing a lot of thinking since we talked this afternoon. I can see only one way out of this. First of all, mama mustn't know about Felice. At least, not yet."

In spite of what had happened, Jenny liked Danny's wife.

"All right," Danny said, "I won't tell mama."

"Listen, Danny . . . you know I've been planning to open a store in Santa Barbara in a few weeks—you've heard me talk about it. We'll tell her that you're going to manage it. She'll be furious, of course—but if you insist what a wonderful opportunity it is, maybe she'll relax. A few weeks after you go out to Santa Barbara, you'll write mama that you've met a girl—"

"Felice!" Danny smiled. He crossed the room to take two dishes of ice cream from Felice, handed one to Jenny.

"Thanks—mmm this looks good." Jenny took a spoonful of ice cream. "Anyway, mama will be upset that she isn't Jewish, but as far as she knows, Felice is just a nice girl from Santa Barbara."

"Felice," Danny kissed her, laughing. "Sit down and eat

your ice cream before it melts—you're looking at Jenny like she's your fairy godmother!''

Jenny couldn't help but laugh—it seemed ridiculous to sit and eat ice cream while mapping out this grand deception just so two people who loved each other could get married.

"So you'll write mama in another few weeks that you've married this local girl. She'll carry on, but she'll get over it."

"Danny, I think we should tell Jenny that we can never have children." Felice's face was wistful. "Something happened four years ago. There was an operation. It went badly. The doctor said I can never have a baby."

"That's between the two of you," Jenny said gently.

"Jenny, stop talking and eat your ice cream," Danny said.

Later, Jenny warned herself, mama would somehow find a way to blame her for Danny's choice of a wife. She'd probably say it was because his sister had sent him away from home.

One thing was certain. Mama must never know that Danny's *shiksa* had not only been a girl in a Storyville house, but a madam as well.

CHAPTER
NINETEEN

JENNY TRIED TO pretend she wasn't disappointed about
having to postpone the Paris trip—now she really had good
reason to speed up the opening of the Santa Barbara shop.
She began drilling Danny about the details of operating the
business. There would be a strict accounting, and once a
month Mannie would come to Santa Barbara to check out
the records. Jenny was impressed with Danny's drive and
she had to admit that he could be an asset to the store—
especially when it came to his charm with the ladies.

Mrs. Straus went through her usual histrionics at the
prospect of Danny's moving so far away, but together Jenny
and Danny managed to convince her that this was a fine
business opportunity for him. Mannie sat by silently,
smoldering in jealousy.

Recently, things between Jenny and Mannie had de-
teriorated to the point where they barely spoke unless it was
about business. Mannie had taken to buying expensive suits
and without a word, a look of defiance in his eyes, handing
her the bill. Apparently the suits in Herman's shop were no
longer good enough for the fine Mannie. He smoked the
best Havana cigars, bought himself a solid gold watch, a
diamond stickpin. He had long ago abandoned contributing
to the cost of running the household. He was fat, pompous
and unbearably arrogant.

"Because Danny's always making eyes at the women,"
he said one night after dinner—one of the few times he and
Jenny were alone—"you think he can run a business."

"Mannie, I've been watching him—believe me, he'll be

all right. Anyway, I'm going to hire three good saleswomen and you'll check on the accounts every month. I do all the buying. I don't see how anything can go wrong."

In truth, Jenny had almost forgotten about the forging incident. Felice had insisted on giving her two thousand toward the checks Danny forged and she had promised herself she would give them a generous wedding present once they were settled in Santa Barbara.

Jenny went to Santa Barbara with Danny. He was now almost embarrassingly ingratiating and humble, and it was clear that he loved Felice. Jenny guessed she would be a good influence on him.

Once in Santa Barbara, Jenny took over. She interviewed saleswomen, stock supervisors and three assistant managers, and soon the entire staff for Maison Jenny Santa Barbara had been chosen. She visited the newspaper offices and arranged for ads to appear—the same "Grand Opening" featured in the New Orleans and Pasadena stores.

She helped Danny look for an apartment. The rental agent took them to a run-down building on West Sola Street and showed them three vacancies.

"What do you think, Jenny?" Danny leaned against the bathroom door. "Which one will Felice like?"

"I think the first one," she said after a moment. "But she should be here to make the choice herself."

"Oh, I'm sure whatever you like she'll say is fine. She's always saying there's nobody in the world like you."

With all details worked out for the opening of Maison Jennie Santa Barbara, Jenny and Danny returned to New Orleans. In two weeks Danny would return to Santa Barbara with Felice, and another Maison Jennie would open.

When Mannie came to Santa Barbara for the monthly check of accounts, he would not stay with Danny and Felice—he would stay at a boardinghouse. Since Mannie and Danny had never been on the best of terms, Jenny thought this was wise. And with Mannie in his current position, the situation was not likely to improve. But what really worried Jenny was that Mannie might recognize Felice from Storyville.

Marc continued to write—carefully, of course, in case someone other than Nicky should read his letters, and in his next he said that he would be in Paris the first week in August to supervise a new exhibit. Simone had said the heat in Paris would be too much for her, so she would stay at the country house. Jenny made arrangements to be in Paris the first week in August.

But there was another hitch in her plans: Carrie, used to getting her way, had been begging Jenny to take her to Paris. When Jenny refused, Carrie sulked, vowing revenge. As always, Sophie was helpless when it came to her daughter's whims.

"Honestly, Jenny, I don't know where Carrie gets the gall to ask you to take her to Paris. When I was her age I could barely ask someone to give me the right change! But if it's anyone's fault it's Herman's. He gives her anything she wants and God forbid he should do something nice for the boys."

Again Jenny rented a house by the lake. This summer, Herman insisted, Karl would stay in the city to help out in the store.

"It's enough for Karl to go up to the country on Saturday nights with me and his mother," Herman pronounced at supper one hot May night in Jenny's house just before Mrs. Straus and Evvie were to go to the lake. "At his age he ought to be working already. I don't like this craziness about high school." From across the room, Mannie nodded vigorously. Sophie stared at her plate, her lips pressed together. She had vowed years ago that her children would have the chance to acquire a profession.

Jenny watched Karl, who sat silently in the corner. It would kill him to leave school. Feeling Jenny's gaze, he turned to her and slowly she shook her head. He managed a shaky smile. Jenny and Sophie wouldn't let them take him out of school. He had to believe that.

"Let's have iced tea out on the gallery," Jenny said. This way the men and the children would settle outside and she'd have a few minutes alone with Sophie. "It's so hot in the house."

Mama insisted on going out to the kitchen to make sure Dora and Annie Lou put away the leftovers from the meal in the icebox and not in the garbage, and Evvie trailed behind. It was a ritual that had long since stopped bothering Annie Lou and Dora—they understood it was just mama's way.

Jenny and Sophie stood at one side of the deserted dining room, now quiet except for the low drone of the ceiling fan.

Sophie looked distraught.

"Jenny, I don't know what to do with Herman. Every night at dinner all he talks about is how he was already earning his own keep by the time he was nine. He refuses to realize this is a different world."

"You don't have to give in on that, Sophie. You can't."

"But he's the father—I can't very well ignore what he says."

"And you're the mother," Jenny said angrily. "You finished high school. Evvie and Danny finished high school." If only *she* had been able to finish school . . . "Sophie, you and I have to make a pact: our children must finish high school and go on to college."

"But it gets worse every year. I get home from the store, and all I hear are Herman's complaints." She smiled sadly. "At least, he's talking again. But sometimes I think it was better the other way. After supper, if he doesn't play pinochle with Mannie or his friend across the street he goes to bed. He turns his back to me and sleeps till morning. I'm glad that part of our marriage is over."

How sad, Jenny thought, that at thirty-two Sophie would never know what it was like to be with a man she loved.

"How old is Herman?"

"Forty-seven, but he acts twenty years older."

"Sophie, if Herman tries to force the boys out of school, we'll find a way to stop him. It's that simple. Someday Leon and Karl will be at the head of the Maison Jennie chain. And some day," she said softly, "there will be Maison Jennie stores all over the country." She paused. "But if they want to be something else besides storekeepers, they have to stay in school."

She didn't know exactly what it was about Karl that drew her to him—maybe it was because he looked so much like papa and Leon or maybe it was because he had papa's zest for living, his appreciation for beautiful materials, furniture, paintings . . .

Often Karl would come into her bedroom or the offie at the store just to look at the paintings—Marc's paintings—which she had been ordering from his gallery over the past few years.

When it came to the children, she and Sophie had to be strong. Their future depended upon it.

A few days before leaving for the lake house, Mrs. Straus received a letter from Danny saying he had met a girl in Santa Barbara and was thinking that maybe—just maybe—he would ask her to marry him. Needless to say, the prospect of another woman in Danny's life did not exactly thrill Mrs. Straus.

"Jenny, what kind of a girl is this? He says her name's Felice. That's not a Jewish name. Where do you think he met her?"

"I don't know, mama." Jenny suppressed a smile. Of course mama assumed the worst. "You know Danny—he meets all kinds of people."

"But he never talked about getting married before—and to a *shiksa?*"

"Mama, maybe it would be good for Danny to marry."

"A nice Jewish girl," Mrs. Straus said firmly. "Not this Felice whoever she is. Doesn't he know how he's upset me with this *mishagoss?* Please, Jenny, get me some water. I feel faint."

As the days dragged by, all Jenny could think about was her trip to New York and then Paris at the end of July. The prospect of five uncluttered days and nights aboard the *Mauretania*, and then seeing Marc were the only bright spots in an otherwise dim future.

Then, on June 29, the *Times-Picayune* carried a headline story of the assassination of Archduke Francis Ferdinand—heir to the throne of Austria-Hungary—and his wife. People were saying it could be the beginning of a war that had been brewing for twenty years.

Jenny remembered Marc talking, two summers ago,

about the upheavals in Europe. *"Jenny, if war breaks out in Europe—with all that has been developed in the way of weapons, it'll be horrendous."*

Even Nicky, usually optimistic, was concerned.

"Europe seems so far away from us, Jenny. And what do most Americans know about it—except for the museums and tourist things like the Eiffel Tower and Buckingham Palace and Roman Forum?"

"You know, you're right. I hear people talking about how we'll never have a war again because of the enormous military forces of the European countries. They're so confident nobody would risk starting a war under such circumstances. But Marc is worried—as are other thinking people in Europe—"

"Oh, God, Jenny, I wish Marc would come home. When you're over there, talk to him about it, will you?"

Ten days later Nicky received a letter from Marc. Over the years the three of them had developed an understanding that his letters to Nicky were meant for Jenny as well.

"Nicky, if you have any thoughts about a visit to Europe in the coming months, put them aside. Europe is on the brink of war. I'm convinced of it. If you are here when war breaks out, you might not be able to return home until it's over. We see frightening warnings on every side."

Jenny couldn't bear the thought of yet another delay. There were those who were sure the war would be over in six weeks, but that seemed like forever—why did fate always seem to keep her from Marc?

Then on July 26 the headlines on the *Times-Picayune* said, EUROPE TREMBLES ON THE BRINK OF WAR. Two days later everyone's worst fears became a reality, as Austria-Hungary declared war on Serbia. In less than a week Europe was in chaos. Germany had declared war on Russia, then on France. Germany had invaded Belgium and on the same day Great Britain declared war on Germany.

Jenny thought her mother would be worried about her family back in Vienna and she was—for about an hour. Then she seemed to forget all about it. Jenny was appalled. Mama's mother, her father, sisters and brothers, nieces and nephews, aunts and uncles—all the people she had talked about the years Jenny was growing up seemed to matter little to her now. Apparently she had swept the memories aside in favor of her daily complaining about how difficult her life was now.

The war was felt immediately in the United States.

On July 31 the New York Stock Exchange closed. The New Orleans Cotton Exchange followed suit. The port commerce that was the lifeblood of the city was dangerously crippled. Business all over the country was suffering. People all over were losing jobs.

Jenny was convinced that the Maison Jennie stores would survive, but she was worried about Marc—an American, living in Paris. Why didn't he come home?

Meanwhile, in Paris with the declaration of war all the banks closed. Money was to be had on the black market for 100 percent interest, the favorite places for negotiation being the open-air *pissotieres*. Those who could fled the country. Businesses closed. Unemployment was rampant. And Parisians lived every day with the knowledge that the Germans were marching toward their city.

At last, when German troops were within fifteen miles of Paris, General Joffre followed the advice of the governor of Paris, General Galliehi, and hastily formed a new army, putting it under the brilliant command of the master strategist Galliehi. The new French offensive—including 6,000 men transported to the battlefield in Paris taxicabs and trucks—pushed the Germans back from the Marne River to the Aisne River, thus ending the Germans' chance for a swift victory.

In honor of the "Miracle of the Marne," Simone gave a small dinner party at the Paris house. There was much celebrating, but everyone knew that in truth the prospect of peace "before the first first snowflake fell" was unlikely. Over dinner Simone offered her services to one of the heads of the French Red Cross.

"I must do something to help . . ." She noticed Marc's tense expression—for weeks he had been feeling guilty as he watched other men his age rushing into uniform.

"We're going to need all the help we can muster," a member of the French diplomatic corps said.

"Come now," Simone said, "enough of this depressing business. Let's talk of pleasant things. Perhaps we won't be taking off for the country house parties this season . . . but there'll be theater and opera. I doubt that we'll have the Ballets Russes, but we'll manage."

When Marc and Simone had said good-night to their dinner guests, they settled in the small sitting room off the library for a glass of sherry before going to bed— recommended by Simone's doctor to help her with her insomnia.

Simone watched Marc pour the wine into two delicate crystal glasses. "It was a good party, wasn't it, darling? If anything can be good in these awful times."

"You know, Simone, I'm afraid it'll be worse before it's better." As he handed Simone a glass, Marc couldn't help but notice how lovely she was. God, he was lucky.

"Marc, why don't you go back home for a while? This isn't your war."

"But you know I wouldn't leave you. And I don't think it's quite accurate to say it isn't my war. I've lived in Paris for a dozen years—I have obligations."

"But not to fight." Simone was pale. "You've always said you hated war. You said you could never bring yourself to kill."

"I could drive an ambulance," Marc said quietly. "At least that way I'd feel useful."

"You've already made up your mind, haven't you?" Simone put down her glass. "I heard you talking with Henri about the American college men who're signing up as ambulance drivers."

"Only if you approve, my darling. You know how I feel about leaving you alone."

Simone was still for a moment. Marc saw her hand tremble as she lifted the wine glass to her mouth.

"I'll be very frightened for you, Marc," she said quietly. "But also very proud."

* * *

Herman's concern over the business was approaching panic. In October he fired his only salesman and began insisting that Karl leave school and come to work in the store. One morning after a long, sleepless night of arguing with Herman, Sophie finally broke down and confided in Jenny.

"Herman's driving me crazy, Jenny. Now he's saying Karl has to leave school at the end of the week to help in the store."

"But he can't do that—what about Karl's education . . . all his dreams of becoming a lawyer?" Jenny couldn't bear the thought of sensitive young Karl indoctrinated to Herman's kind of selling.

"Jenny, he's the father. There's nothing I can do about it."

"We'll have mama talk to him—"

Sophie shook her head. "Mama's so scared of losing the business she's listening to everything Herman says."

Jenny sighed. Mama didn't have to worry about what was happening in the store—she was being supported by her children. She never once asked what mama did with the profits from her store—she hoped they weren't going under the mattress.

"How bad are things, Sophie?"

"God, Jenny, they don't look good. Herman's not even taking in enough to pay the rent. At this point we're living on my salary, and part of that's going into the store. I have money in the bank—but how can I tell Herman?"

"You must never tell him, it's as simple as that." Jenny frowned. "I think I know how to put a stop to his business of taking Karl out of school. I'll offer Herman an interest-free loan." She remembered the loan Herman had offered them when the bank closed. That had been his way of pushing himself into mama's store. Now, apparently, he considered it *his* store. "I'll make him a deal: he gets a loan if he stops this nonsense about taking Karl out of school."

Sophie smiled. "Oh, he'll go along. He'll do anything to keep the store open—in the store he's a king." She hesitated. "But do you think you should? With business so bad all over the country, Herman could lose that, too—"

"It's mama's store, too, you know. For mama and Karl I think it's the only way."

Suddenly Jenny remembered Nicky saying the family was her obsession. Maybe she was right.

Along with the rest of the world, New Orleans felt the pangs of war. Cotton, the backbone of Southern economy, had been piling up and unsold. Prices plummeted.

At last, on November 16, the New Orleans Cotton Exchange reopened. Twelve days later, the New York Stock Exchange reopened but only permitted the sale of bonds. Cotton was selling as low as five cents a pound. After talking to Mrs. Godman, Jenny decided to invest their surplus business funds in cotton, and she then put most of her own savings into cotton. She was not only pleased to be able to help the farmers, but was convinced that cotton prices would rise and it would be a profitable decision.

But, as always, her thoughts returned to Marc.

The mails from Paris had been more delayed than usual, and though Nicky and she clung to the hope that because Marc was an American he was safe, she couldn't help worrying.

In mid September Danny's letter to Mrs. Straus—announcing that he had been quietly married in a civil ceremony—arrived. He claimed that they had not come home for the wedding because of the store. Felice was an orphan, he wrote, and when they could make the necessary arrangements, she would convert to Judaism.

Mrs. Straus took to her bed for a week. As expected, she blamed Danny's marrying a *shiksa* on Jenny—after all, she had been the one to send him out to Santa Barbara. Away from family, of course, he'd been lonesome—and now he'd allowed this *shiksa* to hook him.

Evvie, too, was upset by Danny's marriage and Jenny couldn't understand why. Maybe it reminded Evvie of her own failed marriage—no one had ever heard a word from Sidney since he took off, and Jenny suspected that Evvie knew that he'd been the one who took off with mama's bankroll. In one of her harangues, mama must have let it slip.

All of this sharpened Jenny's concern about the apparent transformation in Evvie, but at this point it was useless to talk to her about anything, especially Jenny's feeling that Evvie would be happier if she came back into the store. Her mother and sister were bound together in an inseparable partnership.

At last, late in November Nicky received a long letter from Marc. Immediately she phoned Jenny.

"Come over and read it, Jenny. God, it looks like it was mailed weeks ago—"

"I have to finish up with a customer but I'll be there as soon as I can." Jenny had been pulled out of the fitting room with Mrs. Bradshaw, one of their best customers—and a lady who demanded Jenny's personal service.

Jenny returned to the fitting room, trying not to show her impatience.

"Jenny, you're sure this is right for me?" Mrs. Bradshaw twirled before her. "Now, be honest—you know I depend on you."

"The Poiret you have on now, yes." Jenny nodded. "It's much more flattering than the Doucet." Her wealthy customers especially appreciated her candor.

Despite her excitement about hearing news about Marc, as she drove to Nicky's house she couldn't help but worry about what he had said in his letter. Nicky had sounded unusually serious. But maybe she'd had a fight with Armand or something—according to Nicky, he'd been shocked by all the money Nicky was spending on paintings.

At last she arrived. Nicky must have been waiting by the window, because before she even had a chance to ring the bell Nicky threw open the door, startling her.

Pale, expressionless, Jenny stood quietly in the foyer. "That's only so we won't worry, Nicky—can't you see that? They drive right into the front lines to pick up the wounded."

"Don't think like that. Listen, let's have some lunch, okay?"

"Nicky, how can you eat? Can't you see that Marc's life is in danger?"

Nicky pushed her into the dining room. "Hush. We're going to have lunch. Then after lunch I'm going to drive over and tell mama and grandma. I have to be strong for them, Jenny."

"Dammit, Nicky—why couldn't Marc come home like other Americans?"

"Read the letter." She pulled it from a pocket of her skirt. "Flora, please tell Annette that we'll have lunch now."

Jenny took the letter and sat down in the sun-dappled dining room. Marc admitted he wasn't joining the French Ambulance Corps with any romantic illusions . . . *"I hate war—any war. But I've shared the best of Paris for twelve years—to live with myself I have to try to help save the lives of those who are fighting for it."*

If she had married Marc and gone to Paris with him, he would have come home with her when the war started. But she had let him go alone, and, since he had married a Frenchwoman, he felt—justifiably so—a part of France. So, he had become a part of this awful war.

"Armand and papa are sure the war will be over in six months, Jenny—please don't look like that." Nicky watched the maid serve them a superb shrimp-and-eggplant omelette. "We have to believe he will be all right—"

"But Marc doesn't think it will be over so soon, Nicky." She'd lost her appetite. Jenny reminded, "He thinks it'll go on for at least two years. Sometimes I think that if business weren't so bad people wouldn't even know there was a war."

In January Jenny went alone to New York for a quick buying trip. While she was able to bring in her "Paris originals," because of the war deliveries were often delayed and limited in quantity. European "society" as such had already come to an end and fashion seemed at a standstill.

The European textile mills were working half time or less. Many of the manufacturers wondered how much longer the fine materials that had been imported through the years would be available. What would American manufacturers do without the European dyes?

In New York Jenny visited her favorite manufacturers and found that the American mills were producing interesting new fabrics, that despite the war foreign mills were managing to ship to America—though in limited quantities. Jenny chose her merchandise carefully, often ordering special details to be added. She had an unerring eye for what would please her demanding customers.

Despite her heavy work schedule Jenny, along with Nicky, found time in the coming months to be active in the war-relief efforts. For both of them, it was Marc who prompted a feeling of special investment in ending this war. Both Mannie and Herman, born in a village in Germany, were hostile toward American sympathy for the Allies and Mrs. Straus refused to even discuss it.

Throughout the country German and Irish Americans were in support of the Central Powers, which included Germany, Austria-Hungary, Bulgaria and Turkey. Then, in May of 1915 the British liner *Lusitania*, with many Americans aboard, was torpedoed by a German submarine and Americans of all ethnic backgrounds were outraged.

"Benedict is screaming for us to enter the war," Nicky said one afternoon to Jenny, "and Armand agrees with Wilson that we should stay out."

"Of course Benedict doesn't mind us entering the war—he's too old for the draft." Jenny was worried about Danny—he was twenty-seven, and he would never be a father to keep him out of a war.

By summer the United States was entering a boom period. Cotton had risen to nine cents a pound and was expected to go even higher. The mills were working around the clock to fill orders from overseas. Steel was in huge demand. Munitions factories operated at capacity. A cry for preparedness was being heard across the country.

Money was in heavy circulation and stores all over were doing brisk business. Danny came home for a week with the news that the Santa Barbara shop was flourishing. He left Felice to keep an eye on the store in his absence and, of course, his mother was thrilled that she had her son all to herself.

After all, Felice was still "that *shiksa* who stole Danny when he was lonely."

After hearing the news about the Santa Barbara shop, Jenny and Mrs. Goldman decided to expand even further and Jenny went out to San Francisco to set up Maison Jennie San Francisco—another stop for Mannie, which would keep him on the road three weeks out of five.

Jenny let herself be swept up in Nicky's social world. Nicky was becoming one of the city's most popular hostesses and Jenny knew she had to keep busy—whenever she was alone, even for a moment, she worried about Marc. She knew it was unfair to expect him to write, but even two lines—some word that he was well—would put her mind at ease . . . For a while.

It was a cold and gray late February morning in 1916, and for twenty-four hours the Germans had been shelling Verdun, the fortress city on the Meuse River in northern France about fifty miles from the German border.

In truth, the so-called "fortress city" had been all but stripped of guns and troops. Now the German troops—both infantry and artillery—attacked on a twenty-mile front in an offensive designed to bring the French to heel. Verdun itself was surrounded by a ring of defenses and the French squadrons that had come to the aid of Verdun from the air had been chased from the sky.

Marc and his medic had been bringing in the wounded since eight o'clock the previous morning with no time out for sleep. The Germans had been relentlessly flattening out trenches and wire, and were causing heavy casualties. The countryside around the city was thick with the dust of tumbled earth.

"Marc, come on—we need a break. I can't take much more of this." Marc's co-worker, an American medic, had been a pre-med student at Columbia University, and was always getting tired before everyone else. Marc looked at him—his eyes were red from lack of sleep.

"We can't stop, Jim—not when the goddamn Boche are mowing down French soldiers. Let's go."

Marc drove back to the French lines, where he and Jim

leapt down from the ambulance, and, crouching low, searched the area for wounded.

Marc hurried to the side of a young soldier, obviously seriously wounded, lying in a ditch nearby.

"There's another." Marc pointed to a young soldier—probably no more than seventeen—writhing in pain a few feet beyond.

"Come on, let's come back for him," Jim said. "This one's bad. Let's get the hell out of here!" Bullets were flying as Marc and the medic carried the wounded soldier to the ambulance. While Jim administered first-aid, Marc hurried back for the young soldier, running blindly as bullets charged through the air. There was a cry from the young soldier—he'd been hit yet again. Marc pulled him into a hole and shielded him as he paused, catching his breath.

"It hurts," the soldier whispered. "Please, help me—I don't want to die."

All at once there was a blast, a flame. Marc felt a searing pain. Somehow *he had to get this boy back to the ambulance*. But he couldn't move . . . he couldn't see . . . he was losing consciousness . . .

CHAPTER TWENTY

NEW ORLEANS CELEBRATED Mardi Gras as usual, but the festivities seemed hollow and Jenny was relieved when at last the pageantry was over. Mardi Gras would always be a reminder of papa's death, and this year she couldn't feel festive when American soldiers were dying in Europe.

Every morning she called Nicky—even if she was going to see her later in the day—to find out if there had been any mail from Marc, and every day Nicky patiently reminded her of how difficult it was to get mail through . . . but there had been no news from Marc since early February, and already Passover was coming.

This morning the air was fragrant with the scent of early spring flowers as she drove Leon and Helene to school.

"Mama, you'll come to the play tomorrow morning?" Helene said as the car came to a stop before the school. "You promised."

"Of course, darling." She knew the children were relieved that Manny had given up an appearance at any of these affairs—he seemed to consider them the wife's obligation—and he always made comments that embarrassed them.

She kissed Helene on the forehead. "Don't I always come? I wouldn't dream of missing it." She kissed Leon, prodded them out the door and watched them join the other children gathering on the lush green lawn.

It was a tranquil morning and again Jenny was struck by the apparent calm of the city. It was as if the war didn't even exist. Somewhere, thousands of miles away, Marc's life could be in danger, and here people were going on with their daily lives without a thought or so it seemed . . . Sometimes the callousness of it overwhelmed her. French casualties alone were already over a million.

The store was her sanctuary. She let herself in and walked toward her office, feeling like she was coming home. Three walls of her office held paintings by Marc. The painting of "their" oak tree hung in her bedroom.

Walking back toward the office she heard an urgent pounding on the front door. She turned. It was Nicky. Her heart started pounding because she knew that could only mean one thing—*she must have received a letter from Marc*.

Shaking, suddenly cold, she opened the door. Nicky was pale, her eyes red.

"Nicky you look awful. Is it Marc?" She pulled her inside. "It is, isn't it? Please, say something . . ."

"Now, Jenny, it's okay, really. He's going to be all right. I got a letter this morning from Simone—he was wounded near Verdun."

"How bad is it?" Apparently Marc was unable to write.

"He'll have a long convalescence," Nicky warned. "A bone in his right leg was shattered. But the doctors seem to think he'll walk again."

"Where is he?" At least he was out of the war. But then she remembered hearing that German planes were bombing Red Cross hospitals. "Is he home yet?"

"Let's see . . . he must be by now. The letter was written sixteen days ago, and Simone said she expected him home any time. She's decided to open the chateau as a convalescent center for the Allied wounded. She's a good woman, Jenny."

"I'd feel better if we could hear from him directly. Maybe it's worse than Simone says—"

"No. I'm sure he's okay. Anyway, he's probably under heavy sedation. But by now I bet he's home. And the fighting is some distance away from the chateau."

"Well, that makes me feel a little better. But why can't

they just end this awful war? How many more must be killed or wounded before it's over?''

Jenny was relieved Marc wouldn't be returning to ambulance duty. She just prayed the war would end before he was put back in the fighting zone.

A few weeks later Marc wrote that he was trying to bring himself to paint again—he hoped it would help him pass the long hours while he was in the wheelchair. In the letters that followed Jenny sensed in him a freshened dedication to his work, a spark of life . . . it was as though the horror of the war brought a new dimension to his work. She shared his exhilaration, sensing that it would carry him through this difficult time.

In the summer of 1916 the mood of the country was preparedness. In May a huge New York parade was the first of a series throughout the country and in June in New Orleans, the *Times-Picayune* reported that forty thousand people joined a march in New Orleans that took four hours to pass city hall. During a Preparedness Day parade in San Francisco in July a bomb was thrown, killing ten and wounding forty.

In November Woodrow Wilson was elected for a second term, though the election returns were so close the outcome was uncertain for three days. Jenny and Nicky were ecstatic that Jeanette Rankin had been elected as congresswoman from Montana—the first woman to serve in the United States Congress.

Four days after his inauguration on March 4, 1917, Wilson announced that he would arm merchant vessels and the nation hovered on the brink of war. In Russia revolution erupted on March 8. A week later Czar Nicholas was forced to abdicate.

On April 2 the rumors that had ricocheted around the country for months became reality when Wilson went before congress to read a message that warned, ''The world must be safe for democracy.'' On April 6 the United States declared war on Germany.

* * *

America began to gird for war at a feverish pace. Mills and factories ran at peak capacity. Girls and women rushed into government offices in Washington for the unheard salaries of $1,100 a year and even higher. Women worked as mechanics, electricians, plumbers. They were employed in the factories and in the fields. They drove trains. The economy prospered.

In late May the family planned to attend Karl's graduation from high school. Herman was screaming that with jobs so plentiful, Karl should go to work immediately.

"Herman expects Karl to get a job and bring his pay envelope home to him," Sophie told Jenny grimly, as they walked into the steamy high-school auditorium where the graduation exercises were to be held. "He doesn't even want to hear about college in the fall."

"Maybe he'll change his mind, Sophie. Mannie seems to have softened on the subject—I think I even heard him say 'when my son goes to Harvard' the other day."

"Oh, I hope so. Karl doesn't talk back to his father, but I can tell he's angry. I don't mind him working this summer, but come fall I'd love to see him at Tulane. Money's not the problem—even Herman's doing well these days."

Jenny laughed.

"Well then, let's not think the worst yet. I want you all to come over to the house for cake and coffee after this and I'll start Mannie talking about when Leon goes off to college. I'll bet you a dollar Herman has a change of heart."

To Jenny's surprise it was Carrie—beautiful and precocious at fifteen—who was the one to bring up the subject of college that night. She was the only one of Herman's children who went to a private school. She was also the only one who had two closets full of clothes and took dancing lessons every week.

"Papa says if I get real good grades, he'll let me go to college when I graduate high school next year. Of course I wouldn't dream of staying here in New Orleans." Herman's mouth dropped open. "Somewhere back East."

"There'll be nothing so fancy for Karl," Sophie added,

glancing sharply at Jenny. "He'll live at home and work summers to pay for his tuition."

Mannie cleared his throat.

"When my Leon graduates, he'll go to Harvard. Nothing but the best for my son."

So it was settled. At last Sophie would see her oldest son in college.

"It won't be so bad to have a lawyer in the family," Herman said. "With a year of college already Karl can go into a law office and 'read law.' He don't have to go to law school."

Jenny saw Karl tense. He had always been a serious, introverted child, and she suspected that he kept his ambitions to himself. She remembered how intently he had studied the paintings in her office and in her bedroom—all by Marc—maybe his interest lay in art . . .

Early in June over nine million men between the ages of twenty-one and thirty—though the minimum age had originally been set at nineteen—registered for the draft. Including Danny. Jenny and Sophie whispered thanks that their sons were too young to fight. Mrs. Straus suddenly became anxious for Danny and Felice to have a baby. She hadn't even *met* Felice—and was obviously in no hurry to welcome her into the family—but a man with a family would not be drafted.

On June 26 the first American troops arrived in San Nazaire, France, under Major General Sibert. That same day, Jenny received a call from the store. When she picked it up, she heard Felice's voice, high-pitched with tension.

"Jenny, Danny went out and enlisted. He's already off at a training camp upstate."

"Why?" Jenny asked, stunned. Mama would be out of her mind with worry. "It's the last thing I would expect of him."

"I hoped you wouldn't have to know—" Felice said. "He's been gambling. I begged him to stop, but he wouldn't listen—you know Danny. They've been after him to pay up. They made threats. He was scared."

"You think he enlisted to get away from the gamblers?" Jenny tried to stay calm. "Is that what you're saying?"

"There's more. He—he took from the shop. The way I figure, it must have been close to four thousand dollars. I gave the receipts to him each week, and he was supposed to take it to the bank. When I looked at the bank book last night before I closed up, I could see he hadn't been depositing half of what he should. You have to understand, Jenny—he was just trying to keep gamblers off his back."

"You've been helping in the shop?" Jenny hadn't known—and Danny certainly hadn't said anything.

"I've been running the shop for months. Danny didn't care anything about selling. Oh, he came in for a while late in the morning and sometimes in the afternoon. Except the day or two each month when Mannie was here—then he was in the shop all the time and I stayed home. The first time Mannie was in Santa Barbara, Danny brought him home for supper." Jenny was at first startled, then relieved. Mannie had never said anything about meeting Felice. But clearly he hadn't recognized her from his visits to Storyville. "After that, he always said Mannie didn't have the time. I guess he was afraid I'd say something I shouldn't."

"The shop *has* been doing well—" Jenny said.

"And I love being there," Felice said eagerly. "I was so pleased the way business has been building up. Jenny, I don't know what got into Danny—gambling that way. If he wanted to manage the store, he could do that, too. I shouldn't have gone in to help. He figured I could handle everything."

"Don't blame yourself, Felice," Jenny said. "Someday Danny's got to grow up and take responsibility for his actions. He'll be twenty-nine years old in September." Jenny sighed. "I'm leaving in the morning for Santa Barbara. We'll figure out together what to do."

"Jenny, if you let me run the shop, I promise I'll pay back what Danny took—not all of it right away, but something each week. I thought we had something wonderful together, Danny and I—"

"Of course you'll continue running the store," Jenny said. It was partly her fault—she should have kept in closer touch with Felice. She should have known that just because Danny was married it didn't mean he would suddenly become responsible. "If the gamblers make any threats, tell them Danny's sister is coming out. I'll settle with them."

"It might be an awful lot."

Suddenly Jenny remembered stories of the Mafia in New Orleans twenty years ago. "Have they been threatening you, Felice?"

"They don't know yet that Danny's in the army. Three days ago Danny told me he was going fishing with a friend who has a shack in the hills. He said they'd be away two or three days. Then this morning he called and told me he had enlisted and was already in training camp. I don't know what they'll do when they find out Danny's taken off."

"Don't let them frighten you. Tell them Danny's sister will take care of his debts."

The next morning she left for Santa Barbara. Only Sophie knew why. Mama, Evvie and Sophie's children were staying at the lake house, which Jenny had bought this past winter from cotton profits. Leon and Helen had gone off with Nicky, her children and Nicky's nursemaid for two weeks at the "cottage" Armand's parents had just bought at Long Branch.

According to Nicky, the so-called cottages at Long Branch were really more like the mansions in Newport. Unlike Nicky's parents, Armand was determined that *his* children would play on Long Branch's beautiful sandy beach with other rich Jewish children and, ultimately, marry within the faith.

In Santa Barbara Jenny consoled her distraught sister-in-law. Already Danny's "creditors" were making ugly noises. According to Felice, such noises were to be taken seriously.

"Well, then," Jenny said grimly, "we'll see them together tonight." Felice had told her that Danny owed nearly five thousand dollars.

"You know, maybe being in the army is the best thing that ever happened to Danny. Now he won't have anyone to pick up after him. That's the way it was all his life, Jenny. First his mother and his sister, then me."

"Mama always did spoil him, didn't she? Maybe the army is what he needs."

It occurred to Jenny that they talked about the army so

casually, as if there weren't a war involved. Any day now Danny might be shipped to France—to fight.

"Mrs. Straus will be devastated if he's sent away," Felice said. "It's funny, I sometimes think that's what worries *him* most."

"Every mother with a son in uniform is upset," Jenny said. "Mama will just have to bear up."

Late that evening Jenny and Felice met with two of the hoodlums sent to collect Danny's debt. Jenny stood her ground when they tried to convince her that Danny owed seventy-five hundred dollars, and she made arrangements to pay the five thousand dollars in three-month increments.

When at last the door closed behind the men, Jenny turned to Felice. "If Danny ever does something like this again, Felice, throw him out of the house. I won't bail him out again. Not even for mama."

Jenny waited until after supper on her first evening back in New Orleans to tell her mother.

At first Mrs. Straus was quiet, and then her shrill voice shattered the silence.

"If you hadn't sent him out to Santa Barbara, it wouldn't have happened. You couldn't stand having Danny here because you know how much I love him. Your jealousy will kill my only son!"

"Mama," Jenny said, "where Danny was had nothing to do with his enlisting. He must have been carried away with patriotism."

"I know what it was—it must have been that wife of his. She must have encouraged it. She probably wanted to say she had a husband fighting for America."

"Felice is upset. Terribly. In fact the first leave that Danny gets, she told me she would bring him home to see you."

"Evvie, get my medicine." Mrs. Straus leaned back in her chair and closed her eyes. "I just know I'm going to have another attack."

"Jenny," Evvie said, "call Dr. Cohen." Jenny was shocked by the hatred in her sister's eyes. What had become of sweet, loving Evvie? "For God's sake, Jenny, don't stand there," she snapped. "Call him."

For the next three days Mrs. Straus stayed in her room, despite the heat. Finally, on the fourth morning, as Jenny was leaving for the store, she emerged from her room in her nightgown and kimono.

"Jenny, I want you to get Danny out of the army. I don't care how you do it—say his mother is dying. Say anything—"

"Mama, I can't do that."

"Of course you can. You're supposed to be so smart. You know all those important people? Let your fancy friends do something for us for a change."

"But, I don't know anybody connected with the army. I don't see how I—"

"Jenny, I just told you. I don't care what you do, but do something! Those rich women who fawn all over you—Sophie tells me about them. One of them must have a husband who can help. Or what about your friend Armand? His father is a judge now. Go out and talk to them. When your own children are grown and in danger, you'll know how I feel. I just hope I live to see it."

"All right, mama," she said. "I don't know what Judge Lazar can do, but I'll talk to him."

Jenny tried everything—she talked to Armand's father, she approached several sympathetic ladies among her customers. She even managed to persuade Dr. Cohen—against his better judgment—to give her a letter saying that her mother was seriously ill. The best she could do was to arrange a ten-day leave for Danny so that he could come home to visit his "dangerously ill" mother.

A week later Danny and Felice arrived in New Orleans. Jenny put her most trusted saleswoman in charge at the store. She breathed a sigh of relief when she saw that Mannie didn't recognize Felice.

"Danny, how could you do this to me?" Mrs. Straus said, clutching at him. "Maybe the war will end while you're here. Then I won't have to suffer this way."

Danny laughed, gently pushing her away.

"I'm at camp in northern California, mama—it's not exactly like I'm in the front lines—just pretend I'm as safe as if I were home with you."

Jenny had told her mother to be polite to Felice and so far she had obliged—she was smart enough to know that if she didn't, she might lose Danny.

"Felice, I hope we hear soon that you're expecting," Mrs. Straus said. "If you make Danny a father they might let him come home—"

"Danny—" Jenny said quickly, "Leon and Helene are dying to see you. Why don't you surprise them and go upstairs? For weeks they've talked about nothing but their brave uncle in uniform."

Danny spent every waking moment with his mother and Evvie, and Felice sensitively excused herself from the house as often as possible so that the three of them could be alone. She spent most of her days in the store with Jenny, absorbing everything she could about the business—and determined to use what she learned to make Maison Jenny Santa Barbara a source of pride to Jenny.

Knowing her presence would make Felice more comfortable, Jenny went home for supper each night. Mrs. Straus and Evvie were polite but distant with Felice. Only Sophie was friendly.

On Danny's last night, Jenny arranged a family dinner that was to include Sophie, Herman and their children.

"This is a beautiful family," Felice said wistfully, gazing around the table. "You're all very lucky."

Danny reached for her hand. "You're part of the family now, honey."

Out of the corner of her eye, Jenny saw her mother flinch. How typical, she thought—mama knows Danny loves Felice, and it's killing her.

"Danny," Jenny said, "Leon will be bar mitzvahed in December. Do you think you can get leave?"

"It's going to be some fancy affair," Mannie said, shooting a glance of malicious pleasure at Herman. "Jenny's spending a fortune."

Mrs. Straus sighed.

"I remember your bar mitzvah, Danny. Such a little thing we could manage. It was not long after your father died. You were robbed of the kind of bar mitzvah I meant for you to have."

"Will you be going to France?" Leon asked, his face bright in admiration for his hero uncle.

"Jenny, send Leon to his room!" Mrs. Straus snapped. "I don't want to look at his face when he can ask such things!"

"Mama, Leon didn't mean any harm."

"He's said too much—" she turned to Mannie. "You're the father. You send him to his room."

"Why don't I take all the children out to the gallery for their ice cream?" Jenny said. She wasn't going to let mama upset Leon. "Then you grownups can talk among yourselves. Who's ready for ice cream?" She turned to the children, seated together at one end of the table, and seven hands shot up.

Jenny followed the children out into the gallery, where Annie Lou brought out dishes of hand-churned boiled-custard ice cream. Leon was uncharacteristically quiet. It was time that Mannie and she moved with the children into a house of their own, Jenny told herself. Whether she owned this property or not, it would always be "mama's house."

But even as she considered it, she knew in her heart that they wouldn't leave—mama would take it as an insult.

CHAPTER
TWENTY-ONE

Americans learned to live with "heatless, meatless, sweetless and wheatless" days. Prices soared. In New Orleans camps rose in City Park Race Track, at the Fair Grounds, on Tulane University campus. Local ladies rushed to join the Red Cross. On October 10 the United States Navy insisted that Storyville be closed down on the grounds that it was a deterrent to the war effort.

It seemed to Jenny that she did nothing but wait anxiously for Marc's frustratingly sporadic letters. He sounded cheerful—apparently he considered himself fortunate to be alive—but Jenny worried about the seemingly endless surgery he was undergoing to restore his leg to full use. Still, she was pleased to hear that he was painting between operations.

In mid October Felice wrote she had received word that Danny was somewhere in France. Mrs. Straus—caught up in a fresh bout of hypochondria—had decided to leave Dr. Cohen for another doctor. She began running from one specialist to another, and as the bills began coming in, Jenny secretly asked each new doctor to charge her mother a small amount and bill the balance to her. If mama knew how much it really cost, Jenny told Sophie, she'd be outraged—she was oblivious to the realities of the outside world.

It was on November 3 that American troops first came under fire. Jenny told Mannie to hide the newspapers—they mustn't let mama see the headlines. *What if Danny had been with these American troops?*

Jenny felt guilty at the extravagant plans for Leon's bar mitzvah in the midst of war. Everyone's social life seemed to revolve around charity events and war work, and it had become fashionable to flaunt thriftiness. But arrangements for the bar mitzvah, on the last Saturday in December, had begun before America joined the fighting, and Leon and Helene were so excited—how could she disappoint them? She had promised Helene that, even though she was a girl, she would have as fancy a thirteenth birthday as Leon.

After hearing her mother's laments through the years about not being able to provide Danny with a fancy bar mitzvah, Jenny had decided that Leon would have the most extravagant bar mitzvah New Orleans had ever seen.

Mannie, of course, was thrilled. He felt he shared in his son's glory. Of course, as usual, he was constantly asking Jenny the price of everything—but this time it wasn't to reproach her. Now he had something new to gloat over in front of Herman. The bar mitzvah for Herman's second oldest son, Frederic, had been a modest affair because Sophie had decided to buy a Liberty Bond in his name instead to help pay for his college education. Already Frederic talked about becoming a lawyer.

It never ceased to amaze Jenny that, in his fashion, Mannie seemed to be enjoying life. He felt important and rich. He was proud of the big house in the Garden District and now the cottage Jenny had bought on the lake. He was even a little more patient with the children.

But her husband was still a mystery to her. Did he ever give a thought to Vivian? Charlie was already five years old. Jenny had bought Liberty Bonds in Charlie's name so that one day he—like his half-brother and half-sister—would be able to go to college.

Mrs. Straus's obvious disdain for the approaching festivities—expressed in her customary grimaces and silences—was a constant drain on Jenny's enthusiasm.

"How can you have such a fancy affair when your only brother is fighting in the war?" she said to Jenny one afternoon. "Why doesn't Daniel write to me? Why do I have to wait to hear what he's written to his wife?"

"Mama," Jenny said, "he's only been away two

months—he doesn't have much free time. Anyway you've already gotten two letters."

"Letters?" she snapped. "A few lines he writes. The wife he remembers. Not his mother."

Jenny decided to try a different tactic. "Mama, you still haven't come to the store to pick out your dress for the bar mitzvah. Evvie and you. Miss Emily will need time for the alterations."

Mrs. Straus rubbed her temples with her fingertips.

"I won't feel up to going to a bar mitzvah when my only son is fighting in the war."

Jenny stared from her mother to her sister. So, this is what mama and Evvie had been plotting—they were going to boycott Leon's bar mitzvah.

"You mean you're not coming?"

"Unless I feel much better, no. And," she added defiantly, "Evvie will stay with me."

"But mama, you're Leon's only grandparent—"

"He'll survive." She shrugged. "You're having two hundred people so he probably won't notice. And most of them I don't know—they're not even Jewish."

This must be what was really behind mama's decision. She had invited many of her best customers, knowing that mama would feel isolated. Mrs. Goldman had agreed that it was a necessity for the store—and Jenny was looking forward to having them there. This was yet another episode that highlighted the growing rift between her mother, Evvie and herself.

Jenny turned to her sister. "Evvie? Are you going to come?"

"You know I can't leave mama alone, Jenny." But her eyes were sad.

Poor Evvie. Was she to have no more of life than drives around town with mama, an occasional moving picture? Sitting on the gallery at the house or the cottage at the lake? Even taking mama out to dinner was a chore. They never even went to synagogue, though at home mama observed the holidays by lighting the Sabbath candles every Friday night.

"Somebody should always be with mama," Evvie said. "And not a maid. Mama should be with family."

On the following morning Jenny told Sophie that mama and Evvie would not be at the bar mitzvah.

"I'm not surprised," Sophie said. "All mama thinks about these days is Danny. If only he'd write more often—then she wouldn't spend all that time thinking the worst."

"Sophie, he's fighting a war. He can't sit down every night and write his mother."

"Why not? He writes his wife—" Sophie, too, disapproved of Danny's marriage to a *shiksa*. Apparently Felice's conversion hadn't had any effect on her in-laws.

"Sophie," Jenny said, "Felice telephones every time she hears from Danny and reads his letter. And anyway he's only written three times." Felice reported what Danny wrote about his daily life, and to Jenny she confided that he was determined to reshape his life once he was back home. He promised to come into the store and work side by side with her. He'd be a good husband. He planned to pay Jenny back the money she'd given the gamblers.

Sophie looked astonished. "Danny's in love with Felice, isn't he? He knew her only a few weeks when he married her, but he really does love her."

Jenny smiled. "Yes, he does."

Looking at Sophie—who had never been in love and probably never would be—Jenny resisted the urge to draw her sister into her arms. What were those lines by Tennyson? *"Tis better to have loved and lost than never to have loved at all."* Thank God Marc had come into her life. And she hadn't lost him . . . They were apart, but as long as they lived, they would love each other. That was all that mattered.

Jenny was pleased that the Saturday of Leon's bar mitzvah was a sunny day. Leon had been studying for months. Today the mother was in the shadows—it was the father and son who were honored. As she sat and listened to Leon read from the Torah all she could think was *papa should be here today*.

Jenny tried to ignore her mother's absence—Leon's parents and his sister, his five cousins and his Aunt Sophie were all there. After the services there would be a wonderful party in the ballroom of the YMHA, where many fine affairs took place.

While Mannie stayed behind to talk to the men at the synagogue, Jenny hurried to the site of the party to check on some final details before the guests began to arrive. It would be one of the most elaborate bar mitzvahs ever seen in New Orleans, Jenny told herself with pride—a day that Leon would remember forever.

At one o'clock the guests began to arrive. Jenny glowed with pride at how handsome Leon looked in his new suit, how pretty Helene was in her delicate green velvet dress. She herself wore one of her Paris originals from an earlier season—a cloud of mauve chiffon and velvet cut on Empire lines, the hem trimmed with seed pearls.

"Jenny, you look marvelous," Nicky whispered. "I'm so glad you decided to make this a big splash. Any excuse for a social event these days is welcome."

Two days after the bar mitzvah Felice telephoned Jenny at the store.

"Jenny, is that you?"

"Yes, Felice . . . are you all right?"

"Oh, God—Danny's been wounded. He's in a hospital near Paris."

No. No, not Danny . . . Jenny held her breath.

"Is it serious?"

"That's the awful part—I don't know. The telegram just says that he was wounded and is in a military hospital. How can we find out more?"

"I know someone who can help. I'll talk to him." Armand had connections in Washington. "We'll get word somehow." Jenny hesitated. "Do you want me to come out?"

"Oh, no, you don't have to do that." Felice's voice softened. "I'll be all right. It's just not knowing that's so awful."

"I'll do the best I can, Felice—just give me a few days. But I'm not going to tell mama until we know more."

Jenny remembered when Danny came down with the fever during the 1905 epidemic and mama had been furious with her because she had insisted he be taken to the hospital. "But Felice, don't imagine the worst. It could be just a minor injury that will keep him out of the front lines."

As when Marc was wounded, she clung to the hope that he would be safe from further fighting.

"You'll phone me the minute you know?"

"Right away, Felice—I promise."

As soon as she hung up, Jenny called Armand's office. Over the past few years Armand had become involved in various war-oriented committees. It was late afternoon before she was able to reach him.

"Have you talked to Nicky today?" he asked excitedly.

"Not yet. Why?" Then Jenny remembered that they were supposed to get together with a charity committee that evening.

"I'm leaving in the morning for Washington. I've been drafted for a government appointment. They want me there immediately."

"Is Nicky going with you?"

"No, I'll be there alone. It would be impossible to find a house for us there the way things are now—and I'd never be home with her. I'll come back to New Orleans whenever I can. You'll keep an eye on her for me, won't you?"

"Of course."

Jenny told him about Danny. Armand said he would check with the War Department in Washington and would phone as soon as he had some word. Jenny tried to tell herself it was futile to worry about Danny until they knew exactly what had happened.

She and Nicky arranged a charity fashion show—with wardrobe from Maison Jennie—for a new fundraising effort on behalf of war widows and orphans.

She shivered in the realization that now, somewhere near Paris, Danny lay in a hospital. No matter how often she had been furious with him, he was her brother and she loved him.

Danny had run to the army to escape the gamblers. As a married man, he would probably never have been drafted. Somehow mama would find a way to blame her for what had happened—she would say that it was *she* who had sent Danny out to Santa Barbara. Mama was convinced that it was "that girl Felice" who had pushed Danny into enlisting. How could they tell her about the gamblers, who might have done Danny even more harm?

On a dreary rainy afternoon several days later, Jenny was summoned from the selling floor to take a call from Armand.

"Do you have news about Danny?" she asked.

"Yes, Jenny," he said. "But I'm afraid it's not good news. He'll survive—*Danny had lost a leg*—but it's his left leg the doctors had to amputate."

"When do you suppose he'll be home?" Jenny said. A parade of images flashed across her mind: Danny as a boy playing baseball, riding a bicycle, charging around New Orleans on deliveries for mama's store . . .

"I gather it'll be a few months before he can leave the hospital," Armand said. "He'll be in a wheelchair for a while, then on crutches. Eventually he'll be fitted for an artificial leg. I imagine that will be handled here at home. He's not alone, Jenny. A lot of men will be coming home without a leg or an arm."

"Do you have an address for him?"

"Hold on—I think I have it somewhere on my desk."

After she hung up, Jenny sat motionless for a few moments, absorbed in her own feelings. She felt Danny's pain—and accompanying that was her own anger at this horrible war. How would she tell mama?

She couldn't tell Felice on the phone—she'd have to go to Santa Barbara. And she wouldn't tell mama yet. She mustn't tell anyone until Felice knew. Evvie would have to make sure mama was given a sedative before she was told.

The following day Jenny left for Santa Barbara on the pretense of meeting with a disgruntled employee. The trip seemed intolerably long, and she was haunted day and night by visions of Danny in his hospital bed.

At last she arrived in Santa Barbara. She took a taxi to the store. At the door she hesitated. Felice would know something terrible had happened by the mere fact that she was here. But Felice was strong—if anybody could pull Danny through the years ahead, it was she.

Felice was ringing up a sale at the register when Jenny walked in.

"You've heard news about Danny—" Felice rushed to Jenny's side.

"Yes, I did. But, Felice. He'll recover. Let's go into the office and I'll tell you."

Felice sat stiff-backed and at the edge of her chair, as though bracing herself for a blow, while Jenny told her what Armand had reported.

"Poor Danny," Felice whispered. "My poor baby—" Then her face tightened. "No. Danny's not a baby. He's a man. Now he'll have to be more of a man than he's ever been in his life. We must help him face reality. He's not the first man to walk with a wooden leg—nor will he be the last. Nobody must baby him, Jenny. I won't allow it."

Sophie was distraught when she heard the news, but Jenny was determined to remain calm.

"Sophie, our baby brother is a man. Felice will stand by him and he'll be all right, I'm sure of it."

"What about mama? Jenny, she'll have a nervous breakdown. You better tell her." Sophie shuddered. "I can't."

Together, Sophie and Jenny told Evvie, who first glared at Jenny and then broke into soundless sobs.

"Evvie, we're not going to tell mama for a while," Jenny said. "After all, Danny won't be home for months."

"But you have to tell her. How can you expect me to keep it from her? She'll look at me and she'll know."

Jenny decided that Evvie was right. It would be too difficult to keep Danny's injury a secret. Later that day, with Sophie and Evvie at her side, she sat her mother down and told her. She cried for several hours, and Jenny, relieved that she had made sure Leon and Helene were out of the house, called Dr. Cohen. With Jenny's help holding her still, he gave her a shot.

"Don't worry, Jenny," he said with a smile. "Soon, she'll sleep."

Once the doctor had left, Evvie turned to Jenny.

"You can go back to your store, Jenny." Her voice was icy. "I'll take care of mama."

CHAPTER
TWENTY-TWO

AFTER HEARING THE news about Danny, Mrs. Straus retreated to her bedroom and stayed there for over a week. When at last she did emerge she made a grand entrance and, standing at the top of the stairs, announced that she had decided to devote the rest of her life to caring for her son. It was, Jenny thought, as though she had forgotten that Danny had a wife. But it would be futile to try to make mama understand that now.

It was an unusually cold January and a shortage of coal didn't help matters. As she read the steady stream of articles about people freezing to death in Mexico City or ice-skating in San Antonio it seemed to Jenny that the newspapers took the weather as seriously as the war.

Danny hadn't written for several weeks, and Felice was worried. She tried to convince herself that it was because of his physical condition, but she couldn't help wonder if his injury had sent him into a depression. She wrote encouraging letters to him every night, as did Jenny. Mrs. Straus said she was too upset to write.

Felice was sure that, whatever happened, Danny would get through this. She did her best to convince Jenny of this. "Jenny, look at it this way . . . he's spent all his life up till now being spoiled by the family. He's tried all his life to shine for his mother, and yet he never really felt capable on his own. But I think—and hope to God my instincts are right—that before he went to France, Danny had finally freed himself from these obligations. We promised ourselves that we would build a life we could both respect—without trying to reach for the stars. Of course, we do have our dreams—"

"You will, Felice," Jenny said with conviction. "You're the best thing that ever happened to him."

Felice paused, embarrassed. "You know, we've talked about adopting a baby from Touro Orphanage in New Orleans." She laughed. "That way mama can't complain that Danny adopted a *shiksa*. How's she taking all this, anyway?"

Jenny sighed. "Not well. But I didn't expect that she would."

"Jenny, I promise you—Danny will be all right. He has a wife waiting for him. A business to run." Jenny had assured Felice that the job of running Maison Jennie Santa Barbara would still be theirs. "And when he feels ready, we'll start our family."

At last letters from Danny trickled in . . . first to Felice, then to Mrs. Straus. His letters to his mother were brief and reassuring. Mrs. Straus insisted he was just being brave for her sake, that surely he must be devastated. Only to Felice did he confess his darker feelings—the fear, the anger—but now he was looking forward to coming home and resuming his life—and he was ready to face the rough times ahead.

In his letters to Nicky, Marc reported that he was out of his wheelchair and on crutches, and that by spring he would be walking with a cane. He had left the hospital and was now recuperating in their chateau, which Simone continued to maintain as a convalescent home for Allied soldiers.

"Simone works like a dynamo," he wrote, *"and I'm worried about her health. But until this beastly war is over, she won't let up."*

In his next letter Marc wrote that he was spending hours every day painting, and that within a year he expected to have a gallery showing again. *"Hopefully in a Paris at peace."*

On March 23 Paris was rocked by the first attack by German artillery fired from eighty miles away. The world learned about the Big Berthas, built by the Krupp munitions firm to harass the capital of France.

In April the Allies formed a unified command under Marshal Foch, who became general-in-chief of the Allied forces in France. It was hoped that the German offensive could be stopped by the American troops that were arriving in huge numbers.

Jenny was worried about Marc. The Germans seemed determined to reach Paris, and in a recent letter Marc had said that he would be going into the city for painting supplies. According to the papers, German shells were killing Parisian civilians . . .

United States Marines fought heroically at Belleau Woods, on the road to Paris and lost nearly 7,800 men. American troops stopped the offensive at Chateau-Thierry, halting the Germans in their efforts to cross the Marne to Paris. Now the Allied offensive was stepped up.

Jenny read the papers carefully every morning. The German advance seemed to have been thwarted, but the number of Allied casualties was disheartening. Earlier in the year Vernon Castle, who had shot down two German planes when with the Royal Corps, died in a crash at Fort Worth, Texas, while training American pilots. Quentin Roosevelt, youngest son of ex-President Roosevelt, was shot down in battle.

Determined to appear carefree—though she lived in constant fear that Armand, engaged in secret government missions, might be killed in the line of duty—Nicky followed the latest style set by Irene Castle. She started tango lessons and took up smoking. At Nicky's and Helene's encouragement—after all, as the head of a growing chain of fashion stores, it was part of her job to be a trend setter—Jenny, too, bobbed her hair, but she couldn't stand the taste of cigarettes and doing the tango with Mannie wasn't an appealing prospect.

Beauty parlors were opening up all over the country, selling the powder, rouge, lipstick and mascara that were fast becoming a part of every woman's daily ritual. Jenny brought a makeup artist into the store to teach the fine points of makeup as well as the care of the skin with such products as cold creams, tissue builders, astringents and masks.

Sophie was increasingly disturbed by Carrie. Always rebellious, Carrie's most recent devotion was to movie "vamps" and the short skirts.

One hot Thursday morning in the store, over coffee, Sophie confided her worries to Jenny.

"I can't handle her, Jenny. I guess I never could. And Herman won't let me punish her for anything."

"What now?" Jenny said.

"When I went to wake her this morning, I saw cigarettes lying on her dresser."

Jenny had known Carrie was smoking, but she had figured there was no point in telling Sophie—Carrie would deny everything. "I know women are smoking now," Sophie said. "The way Carrie talks to me you'd think I was born in the Dark Ages. She even threw up to me that your friend Nicky smokes—but Jenny, Carrie's fifteen years old! Herman heard us fighting and, of course, refused to believe his little darling was capable of doing anything wrong. It was incredible—he actually believed her when she said they were Karl's. Now, I know Karl doesn't smoke—I asked him and I'm sure he wouldn't lie. Carrie does nothing *but* lie. What can I do about it? I could kill her the way she keeps shortening her skirts till they're practically up to her knees—And now Herman is convinced Karl's wasting good money on cigarettes. He always takes Carrie's word over everybody else's. Including mine."

Jenny gazed at her sister sympathetically.

"Sophie, you do the best you can—no mother could do more." Jenny always tried to be fair about Carrie, but she had to admit that she was not an endearing child. She sensed that Carrie didn't like *her* either—but she couldn't figure out why. According to Leon and Helene, Carrie had tried to get Helene drunk on wine, to get Leon to smoke with her—and as usual she had denied everything. "It's partly the times, Sophie," Jenny said. "The war seems to have changed values."

"Well, I hate it. I hate the way Carrie dashes around on those awful 'hourglass' high heels and her flesh-colored stockings and skirts shorter every time I look. Why, the girl could never sew on a button for herself—but she certainly has learned how to shorten those hems."

At the end of August, right after word reached the American newspapers that the Germans were retreating to the Hindenburg line, Jenny received a phone call from Felice. Jenny could tell by the lilt in her voice that it was good news.

"Jenny, I heard from Danny. He's at a hospital in Washington, D.C. He says he's on crutches now."

"Oh, Felice that's wonderful," Jenny said. "Do you want to go see him? Sophie can take over here. I could come out to relieve you."

"No, no—Danny told me not to come to Washington. He'll be home within the next ten days or two weeks. He's going to try to call tonight or tomorrow. Oh Jenny, I can't wait to see him!"

"Hey, I've got an idea—" Jenny said, laughing mischievously. "I'll tell mama he's in Washington, and I won't say when he'll be leaving. You'll let me know when he's ready to see her. Do you think you can leave Peggy in charge for a week or so?"

"Peggy will manage with no trouble," Felice said. "But we'll try to make it at a time when Mannie won't be here— he's not exactly one of her favorite people."

"Felice, I'm so glad he's coming home to us . . . to you. And I'm sure he's counting the days, too."

Felice stood in the twilight while Danny's train pulled into the Southern Pacific Railroad Station. From Danny's letters it seemed that he was in good spirits. She hoped it was true. But when he called her from Washington, she'd heard the tension in his voice.

The train pulled to a stop. While the others rushed forward, she hung back, almost afraid to see him. She had to be careful to say the right thing. Would it bother him that she would have to drive him home? She remembered how he had teased her when she'd insisted on learning to drive.

Now she'd have to do the driving—at least until he was fitted with a wooden leg.

People were disembarking but there was no sign of Danny. What if he wasn't on the train? But he'd probably wait to be the last—he would have to be helped down. How awful to feel so helpless! But he wouldn't be once he was fitted for a wooden leg. She had talked to Dr. Roberts—the local doctor who himself had a wooden leg. *He* practiced medicine, drove a car, was raising a family . . . *she and Danny would lead a normal life*.

There—was that him?—yes . . . Danny, being helped down from the train . . . in his uniform . . . one leg of his trousers pinned up. He looked thinner than usual, but as handsome as always.

"Danny!" She ran toward him. He stood still, his smile uncertain. A small knapsack lay on the ground beside him. He's as frightened of this encounter as I am, Felice thought in surprise. "Danny!" She kissed him with a passion and, startled, he pulled back.

"You're beautiful, Felice. You deserve better."

"I'm getting what I want. Come on—let's go to the car." She picked up the knapsack. "And guess what? I get to drive, too—" She saw the guarded look in his eyes. "For now, that is."

Slowly, self-consciously, Danny walked with her toward the car. Out of the corner of her eye Felice watched him. Was he in pain? He had refused to let her slow down for him—it must be exhausting to walk so fast on crutches. She had so much to learn.

"Did you write Jenny that I was coming home?" he asked.

"I called her. We've become friends, Danny—thanks to the phone! It's the most wonderful invention in the world! Jenny said she wouldn't tell your mother you were home until you were ready to make the trip to New Orleans."

Danny smiled. "Jenny's pretty smart, isn't she?"

"She certainly is. I took the day off from the store. Remember Peggy, the salesgirl we hired just before you left? Well, she turned out to be very good. She'll close up today. I've planned a special dinner with some champagne to celebrate—"

"Felice," Danny said gently, "any time you want to back out, I'll understand."

"Danny!" Felice teased. "If you think you're leaving me for somebody else, you'd better think again."

Danny was silent on the ride home, staring out the window, as if he were seeing everything for the first time. Now Felice was glad they lived on the first floor.

"I'll have to go to the government hospital in Los Angeles occasionally," Danny said. "But not for the next two weeks."

"That won't be a problem. Anyway it's not far—"

"You know what, Felice?" Danny said. "Sometimes I wondered if I'd ever get here."

"Don't think about it now, my love." Her eyes were luminous as she gazed at him. "You're home now, and it's wonderful. And soon you'll be able to handle the cash register again. When Marianne left the store to get married, I didn't bother hiring anybody else."

"Do you think that's going to work? I mean, what will your elegant customers think? A fellow with one pants leg pinned up—"

"Danny, you're a hero. Besides, you're the handsomest man I know—and you know how good that is for business in a shop that caters to women." She knew she was talking too fast, but she, too, was nervous.

When they arrived Felice purposely didn't offer to help Danny out of the car. As she watched him slowly, agonizingly unfold his leg and step out, she reminded herself that she would have to learn to stand back and let Danny risk falling. He needed, more than anything, to feel self-sufficient. Once inside the flat, Danny stood in the middle of the living room and gazed around him.

"God, Felice. If only you knew how many nights I lay awake in the hospital remembering you in these rooms, thinking about how it used to be for us."

There was something new in his voice—was it defeat? She knew one way to put his mind at rest. "Danny, how hungry are you? Can dinner wait a while? I thought maybe we could lie down for a while."

"Sure," he said, looking uncomfortable. "I guess."

"Good. Why don't you go inside and make yourself comfortable in the bedroom?" Her hand caressed his cheek. "I'll be there in a minute."

She had already hung the black chiffon nightgown—Danny's favorite—in the bathroom. Quickly she took off her clothes and pulled it on.

She walked into the bedroom. Her throat tightened as she noticed that he'd carefully puffed up the sheets around where his left leg had been. The room was dim, lit by only one lamp.

Danny cleared his throat.

"It's been a long time, honey—"

Felice turned off the lamp and slid beneath the sheet. Instantly his arms went around her, his mouth on hers. For a few moments they were content to kiss, to touch, just to be close. And then she let him move his hand lower. He groaned and lifted himself above her.

"Oh, God, how I've missed you," he whispered. "All those rotten months without you."

Afterwards, she lay in the curve of his arm, her face damp with tears of pleasure.

Tenderly, he kissed her cheek.

"I have to admit I was scared. I didn't know how it would be."

"Silly boy," she whispered, drawing him close. "Did you think losing a leg would make you less of a man?"

While Jenny waited at Terminal Station for Danny and Felice to arrive, she tried to sift through her conflicting emotions. On the one hand she was impatient to see her brother after his long ordeal, but on the other she dreaded the inevitable scene with their mother. At last the train pulled into the station and drew to a stop. Danny and Felice stepped out, Danny smiling. He looked happy.

Jenny held back the tears. Bless Felice . . .

Jenny asked Danny questions all the way back to the house. Within several months he would be fitted with an artificial leg and he would be able to walk without crutches or a cane. Now Jenny told him about Marc—he, too, would soon be walking on his own.

"How's mama taking this?" Danny asked uneasily.

Jenny smiled.

"You know mama."

"So she'll cry a little." Felice put her arms around Danny. "She'll be glad to see 'her baby boy.'"

Jenny parked in front of the house, and the three of them left the car. Danny stopped and gazed at the house.

"Boy, you've done all right for yourself, Jenny. I'd forgotten what a beautiful house this is."

"Danny!" Mama stood in the doorway, her arms outstretched. "My poor baby!"

She watched Danny slowly make his way up the stairs.

"Mama, I'm all right." He tried to shrug her off. "Really."

The family got together for dinner to celebrate Danny's homecoming. Jenny saw how pleased Danny was by his nephews' adulation of their "war hero"—but she noticed that Carrie seemed subdued. She probably resented not being the center of attention.

While they reminisced over dinner, even Mannie and Herman seemed mellow. Occasionally mama would break down and cry softly.

Jenny was annoyed at the way both Evvie and Mrs. Straus seemed to ignore Felice. And why was Evvie wearing her wedding ring? Then it occurred to her . . . it must be upsetting to Evvie that of the four sitting at the table, she was the only one without a marriage partner. But didn't Evvie know that Sophie's marriage and her own were only mockeries? Danny's, it seemed, was the only relationship built on love.

"Tonight, for my baby, I made your favorite," mama said as Dora brought in the apple strudel, hot from the oven and piled high with freshly whipped cream. "From now on I'll make dessert every night for you, Danny. Mama will take care of you."

"Mama," Danny said, "when you cook, I'm in heaven." He was being gallant, but Jenny saw the wariness in his eyes. "Just try to keep me from the table for the next five nights!" He winked at Felice.

Mrs. Straus sat completely still.

"What is this about five nights?"

"Well, mama, we can't stay here forever," Danny said. "Felice and I have to get back to Santa Barbara. We have a store to run."

"What do you mean?" Mama shot Felice a venomous glance. "*She* expects you to work? But that's impossible. You'll stay here with your mother. I won't let you work. Haven't you given enough?"

"Mama, I'm not helpless," Danny said. "I can earn a living."

"Darling, you don't have to be so brave. Why don't you just let me take care of you? I'll cook everything you like. You'll rest. Take life easy. Imagine, you working!"

"I want to work, mama," he said. "Felice and I have to go back to the store in Santa Barbara. Once a week I'll be driven into Los Angeles to the government hospital. In a few months I'll be fitted for a wooden leg. Except for the fact that I can't run or dance or ride a bicycle I'll be able to live a perfectly normal life."

Mrs. Straus stared from Danny to Felice, then turned to Evvie.

"Evvie, help me to my room." She brought her hand to her chest. "I have to lie down."

September came and New Orleans was hit by a vicious flu epidemic. By October the deaths in New Orleans soared to nearly a hundred a day. The hospitals were overcrowded. Doctors and nurses were dropping from exhaustion. Across the country boards of health ordered that schools, libraries, moving picture houses and other places of public gatherings be closed. Business was almost at a standstill.

Jenny confined Leon and Helene to the house, as did Sophie and Nicky with their children. Every morning they red the newspaper with fear in their hearts, trying to convince themselves that their children were safe. But, in spite of their false confidence, no one was free of the fear that maybe, just maybe a loved one would be stricken . . .

Mrs. Straus locked herself in her room, refusing to see anyone except Evvie. Convinced Leon and Helene were carrying influenza germs, she even warned Evvie not to come within six feet of the children.

By late October the epidemic seemed at last to be easing. The bans on public gatherings were lifted except, in some areas, for the public schools. Marc wrote, in letters long delayed in delivery, that the influenza epidemic in Europe was particularly hard on the soldiers—the casualties were staggering. By now, according to the news that came from Europe, Jenny knew the epidemic had run its course there. In New Orleans people were at last beginning to relax. But now the war returned to the forefront of everyone's thoughts.

One cool early November dawn, Jenny was jolted awake by what sounded like every whistle in New Orleans . . . Factory whistles, train whistles, whistles of the steamers in the harbor . . . then she heard the gunfire. She looked over at the clock. It was 4 A.M.

"Mama!" Her bedroom door flew open and Leon ran in. "Do you hear? The war's over! There are extras out in the street!"

"Mama!" Helene was a few steps behind her brother. "The war's over! This time it's real!" Four days ago the world had celebrated an end to the war, only to discover the news was premature.

"Thank God it's over. It's finally over!" *No more worrying that Marc's chateau might be bombed . . . no more going to bed at night afraid of what the next day might bring . . .*

Mannie hurried out into the street—in the silk pajamas he now fancied—to buy a copy of the *Times-Picayune* extra from a newsboy. With the children at her side Jenny hurried downstairs and out to the kitchen to put up coffee, but Annie Lou was already there, coffee pot in hand.

The phone rang. It was Nicky, jubilant.

"Oh, Jenny isn't it wonderful? Marc's safe now. And we can go to Paris in the spring!"

Jenny had barely hung up when Sophie called.

"Jenny isn't it wonderful news? I worried so that Karl might have to go if the war kept on for another two or three years. People were saying they were going to lower the draft age to nineteen, but now he's safe, thank God."

"Jenny?" Mama's voice filtered down the stairs. "What is all that noise about? Can't I ever get a decent night's sleep in this house?"

For the next several days New Orleans saw what the *Times-Picayune* was to call "the greatest celebration in the history of the city." From the gray dawn till far into the night the city celebrated the armistice. Bands played, people danced in the streets, there were fireworks displays, hundreds of parades, blowing of whistles and ringing of bells.

Jenny cherished the knowledge that Marc was safe. At last the world would be at peace. She prayed it would last.

CHAPTER
TWENTY-THREE

GRADUALLY THE EUPHORIA of armistice faded and New Orleans settled back into everyday life. For Carrie the best thing about armistice was that at last sugar rationing was over—now she could have all the sweets she wanted.

To Nicky's delight, Armand had returned from his Washington base with a repertoire of stories about his espionage efforts that would enliven many of Nicky's famous dinner parties. In spite of all their troubles, war had brought Nicky and Armand closer than they had ever been.

Jenny was already making arrangements for the trip to Paris. She told herself how important it was to bring the new Paris styles into the Maison Jennie stores—after all, fashion was undergoing such exciting changes. But in her heart she knew that what really thrilled her—what really kept her hopes alive all this time was the prospect of seeing Marc.

She had promised Sophie that she would give Carrie a Paris original as a high-school graduation present. That was in May. So, that meant she should go to Paris sometime in April. Sophie, meanwhile, worried about the rumors she heard about "petting parties" and though Carrie was silent on that subject, she insisted that boys wouldn't dance with girls who wore corsets. What was happening to the morals of the young?

Nicky would accompany Jenny to Paris—again—and would try to persuade Marc to come home for an extended visit. As Grandma Goldman had early taught Jenny, Nicky was invaluable in helping her buy. If she were doubtful about the saleability of a garment, she trusted Nicky's instincts.

Marc wrote that Paris went wild when President Wilson—having arrived for the peace conference—drove down the Champs Elysées in a car with President Poincaré. Everything American was in favor in France. Bobbed hair had crossed the Atlantic to become popular in Paris. American movies were arriving in the city. And Marc wrote that he couldn't wait to see Nicky in Paris. Jenny knew that eagerness included her.

Several days before they were to leave for New York, Nicky phoned Jenny and asked her over for lunch.

"I'll send the car for you," she said. "That'll save time." Nicky knew how busy Jenny was.

"One o'clock?" It was their customary time. "Will Grandma Goldman be there?"

"No, it's just us this time—Roland will be at the store at one sharp."

"I'll be waiting for the car," Jenny said, conscious of a certain evasiveness in Nicky's tones. Had something happened that she didn't want to talk about over the phone? *Was Marc all right?* She knew she wouldn't be able to relax until she learned what it was . . .

The car pulled up before Maison Jennie at exactly one o'clock. Jenny hurried over and slid into the back seat. Somehow she managed to exchange casual conversation with Roland, the Lazar houseman and chauffeur, all the while fretting over what Nicky had avoided telling her over the phone.

Nicky was waiting in the gallery.

"Arlette will call us when luncheon's ready, Jenny. Let's sit out here until then."

Jenny sat down. "You sounded upset on the phone, Nicky. What is it?"

"Well . . . I might as well just come out and say it. I got a letter from Marc this morning. Apparently Simone's suffered a collapse—he thinks it's a reaction to the years of running the convalescent center. I don't know. Anyway, the doctor's ordered her to spend the next four or five months resting in the sun in the south of France. They've rented a villa at Antibes."

"So I guess that means we'll miss seeing them." Jenny tried to hide her disappointment.

"Marc will meet us in Paris," Nicky said. "He'll stay until the following evening, when he'll take a train back to the villa." Nicky's eyes were compassionate. "Marc and you do have the devil of a time seeing each other, don't you?"

"We have no right to see each other," Jenny said quietly.

"Don't be ridiculous—you have every right. No one is hurt. You two share something precious for a little while—that's more than some people ever have."

"We must do something about making hotel arrangements," Jenny said. "Though I gather Paris is not exactly swarming with tourists this year—"

"Marc says we're to stay at their house. They've left a skeleton staff that'll be able to make us quite comfortable. Marc will have to come into Paris at intervals to confer about his new show." Her face lighted. "Jenny, he sounds so excited about it. Here—" She reached into her pocket for his letter. "Read for yourself."

Slowly Jenny read Marc's letter. Even the sight of his familiar handwriting seemed to bring him close.

She handed Nicky the letter after reading it.

"I'm thrilled that his work is going so well. But what a shame that Simone's health is poor." Guiltily, she realized that she was relieved she would not be seeing Marc's wife.

"Miz Nicky, lunch is ready," Arlette called from the doorway with a warm smile for Jenny. "My, you look pretty, Miz Jenny. But then you always do."

Churning with excitement Jenny headed for New York with Nicky, impatient that they would have to remain there for two days of hectic buying. But it wasn't all work. They were taken by a manufacturer to see the romantic operetta, *Apple Blossoms*, by Fritz Kreisler and Victor Jacoby, and were enthralled by the dancing of a brother and sister team, Fred and Adele Astaire.

The following morning they sailed for France. For

sentimental reasons—her trip to France had been aboard this vessel—Jenny had arranged for them to sail on the *France*. Both women were aware that several of the ocean liners were still involved in transporting American soldiers to home soil.

The *France* was one of the major liners that had survived the war, but the passenger list on this trip was shockingly small. Jenny was relieved that the socializing would be light—she was caught up in anticipation of seeing Marc again, even though they would be together for only two days. Not until she saw him with her own eyes would she be totally convinced that he had recovered from his injuries. She was proud of the decorations bestowed on him by the French government. Simone, too, had been honored for her efforts on behalf of the Allied soldiers.

Jenny tried to unwind aboard ship. The years were slipping by so quickly. Had it really been six years since she had seen Marc? Sometimes it seemed a century. And yet at other times she closed her eyes and could see herself in Paris with Marc as vividly as though it had been a few weeks ago.

"Jenny, you're so tense," Nicky said as they took a night stroll about the deck before retiring on this second evening aboard the *France*. "You're supposed to relax on an ocean voyage."

"I wish I could." The crescent moon in the cloudless night sky splashed silver about the deck. Stars shone brilliantly overhead. "Nicky, we're thirty-three years old—isn't it hard to believe?"

"So what?" Nicky said. "Grandma is well into her eighties, and she doesn't feel pressed by the years. Jenny, what are you worried about? You'll be going to Paris to buy fifty years from now."

"You know what, Nicky?" Jenny said. "Sophie had the family over to dinner at her house the night before we left New Orleans. Carrie sat there and said to me, 'for an older woman you still have a decent figure.' Can you believe it?"

"So *that's* what's bothering you." Nicky smiled. "Carrie has been jealous of you since she realized you're beautiful and successful. And rich." In addition to the large profits from the stores, Jenny had made a fortune on cotton during the war years—and though the family had no real conception of her worth, shrewd little Carrie had made accurate speculations. "We're not older women, Jenny . . . We'll be older women only when there's no living male around who looks at us with lust. And sugar, that's not either of us yet!"

"You know what it really is, Nicky? I'm scared of seeing Marc after all these years. He's seen so little of me through the years. I'm afraid all he's going to remember is a sixteen-year-old girl."

"Jenny, you're more attractive to Marc now than you were at sixteen. You've become a beautiful, sophisticated, knowledgeable woman. Who allows her family to push her around like a doormat? What do you care what that little snit Carrie says to you?"

"Marc's been through four years of war. Do you think he's changed?"

"Of course he's changed. But what he feels for you hasn't—it comes through in every letter."

"Do you think he'll hate my bobbed hair?"

Nicky threw back her head and laughed.

Jenny and Nicky spent long hours each day stretched on deck chairs, talking, drowsing or reading. As always when traveling Nicky brought along a supply of the latest novels—*My Antonia*, by Willa Cather, *Java Head*, by Joseph Hergesheimer, *The Magnificent Ambersons*, by Booth Tarkington, and a collection of short stories by Sherwood Anderson, entitled *Winesburg, Ohio*. But the ocean voyage this time was not the respite from reality that Jenny had anticipated. Fighting her impatience to be with Marc, she tried to concentrate on business . . .

In January Nicky had gone to Palm Beach with her mother and grandmother, and Grandma Goldman had been intrigued by the possibilities of a Maison Jennie in Palm Beach, where two men named Paris Singer and Addison Mizner were redesigning the already notable resort. A building boom was in progress and it seemed that Palm

Beach was destined to become—like Santa Barbara—a year-round resort. Grandma Goldman and she had explored the situation and had decided to open up Maison Jennie Palm Beach within the coming year.

From the ship Jenny and Nicky went directly to the boat train. Jenny gazed out the window, oblivious to the French countryside, seeing only Marc's face. Before the train had pulled to a stop in the Gâre Saint Lazare, she was on her feet.

"Jenny, you look about twenty right now," Nicky teased. "You come to Paris and turn back the clock."

Marc was waiting for them on the arrivals side of the station. Jenny's heart pounded as they moved forward to meet him. He looked marvelous . . . no cane. Not even a suggestion of a limp. A little older, but weren't they all?

"Jenny—" He pulled her to him in a brotherly embrace after he and Nicky had hugged. "Fate isn't kind to us, is it?"

"Don't say that, Marc. You came through the war in one piece. You don't know how I prayed for that."

"How is Simone?" Nicky asked.

"It'll be a slow recuperation," Marc said. "She exhausted herself during the war years. It was amazing the way she gave of herself. She was upset that, once again, she couldn't be here to welcome you."

It was bizarre, Jenny thought, to be standing here in the Gâre Saint Lazare talking to Marc about his wife when the three of them knew that within a few hours he would be making love to *her*. Already she trembled to be in his arms.

How many times through these years must she remind herself that Marc's marriage was not created out of love? He had great fondness for his wife—he owed her so much. As long as Simone didn't know the truth, she couldn't be hurt.

On the drive to the house Marc talked somberly about the recent changes in Paris. The gaiety and laughter, the excitement of pre-war Paris was missing. The French felt as though they had lost almost a whole generation to the war, and now they wondered if this sacrifice had gained them anything more than Alsace-Lorraine. But they were concerned for the future security of their country.

Painfully aware of how little time they had together, Marc suggested they dine at home. It was as though he could not bear to share Jenny with strangers—he seemed irritated even at the intrusions of the servants.

At nine o'clock Nicky suggested they retire. Nicky and Jenny went to their respective bedrooms. Jenny changed into the mauve chiffon nightgown made especially for the Paris visit. Marc had once said how much he liked to see her wearing mauve.

She crossed to a window, pushed aside the drapes and stared out into the soft spring night. When she was with Marc, her real life slipped into eclipse. She was no longer the hard-working business woman, mother of two, married to a man she disliked, struggling to keep her family together. With Marc she was simply a woman. A woman in love.

She started at the faint knock on the door. Glowing, she hurried across the Aubusson rug to the door.

"Jenny—" It was Marc. He closed the door behind him. "Jenny, my love—"

The next night Marc said good-bye to Nicky and Jenny at the house. The chauffeur would drive him to the Gâre Saint Lazare, where he would take the train for Antibes. Jenny tried not to cry as she watched him hurry across the sidewalk to the waiting limousine. This was to be the pattern of their lives. Could she bear it?

With Nicky at her side, she threw herself into buying for the stores. Already it was clear that the face of fashion was changing . . . new designers were appearing. She must visit the boutique of that woman everybody was talking about—what was her name? Jenny searched her mind for a moment. Oh yes, Gabrielle Chanel—her friends called her "Coco."

Though she and Nicky kept busy, Jenny was constantly aware of Marc's absence. It was clear that he would not be coming home to New Orleans anytime soon. For months Simone and he would be at Antibes. In the fall he would be all tied up with his new show. At last he was receiving the critical acclaim he deserved.

The years were speeding past—in two years Leon would be out of high school. She didn't feel old enough to have an almost grown son. With Marc especially she didn't feel old enough.

She would go back to New Orleans and look after her family and her business, Jenny told herself. But once a year—with luck on their side—she and Marc would live their dream.

CHAPTER
TWENTY-FOUR

LATE IN MAY the family gathered for Carrie's graduation from her expensive private school. Carrie wore the Paris original Jenny had given her and spent most of the day showing the label to everyone. Sophie, too, was dressed in a Paris original—and, after weeks of dieting, now elegant and almost beautiful. Carrie graduated at the top of her class—a fact that Herman insisted on bringing up throughout the day. But what he failed to mention was that the impetus for this was, more than anything, her healthy weekly allowance, not a great appetite for learning.

Carrie was, of course, given a lavish graduation party. Herman was convinced that the current business boom would go on forever. Though he never said anything, Sophie was sure he was squirreling away money every month, but she now felt secure with her own secret funds.

In September Carrie would begin her studies at Vassar. For years she had talked vaguely about becoming a teacher, but Sophie thought she was interested more in the excitement of going away to school in the East than in the idea of pursuing a career. Typical Carrie.

Karl, meanwhile, was doing well—though not spectacularly—at Tulane. Jenny suspected that he had looked at his uneducated, boorish father and was determined not to grow up in his image. Carrie went off triumphantly on a month-long graduation present trip to New York and Saratoga Springs with a classmate and the classmate's mother. Now Herman turned his attentions to his oldest son. One Friday night at a family dinner at Jenny's house—known in the

family as "mama's house"—he turned to Jenny magnanimously and said, "Jenny, talk to your friend Armand Lazar.
Karl has been for two years already at Tulane. He's ready to
become a law clerk. He don't need to bother with a little
summer job now."

"Two years at Tulane isn't enough," Jenny protested,
startled that Herman was on this track again. "Especially in
such a prestigious office as Armand's—they'd expect him to
have a degree."

"Herman, Karl goes back to Tulane in the fall." Sophie's
eyes flashed fire. "If we can afford to send Carrie to Vassar,
we can send Karl to Tulane."

"Sophie, use your head," Herman said with an air of
superiority. "Carrie's a beautiful girl. Before her first year at
college is over, she'll meet the brother of one of her rich
classmates. She'll be getting married. With Carrie a fancy
school is an investment."

"In two years Leon graduates high school," Mannie said
smugly. "Then he goes to Harvard."

"To be a lawyer," Herman said authoritatively, "Karl
can learn in a law office. Who needs to throw away money
on college? Someday he could even be a judge. Maybe a
senator. *Without* two more years of college."

"Danny should have gone to college," mama announced
to the table. "If his father had lived, he would have. Now
his life is over."

The following morning, when Sophie came in to work
she looked especially haggard, as if she'd been up all night.
These early morning hours—before the rest of the staff
came in—were a special private time both Jenny and Sophie
relished.

"You know, Jenny," she said, "sometimes when I go to
bed at night, I don't care if I don't wake up in the morning."

Never, Jenny thought involuntarily—no matter how bad
things were—had she ever had such a thought.

"Something must have happened with Herman,
Sophie—tell me . . ."

"It's always been Herman or Carrie." Sophie shrugged.
"Now it's Karl."

"He doesn't want to be a lawyer."

Sophie was startled.

"He told you?"

"No. I guessed. Karl never said he wanted to go into law. Herman just took it for granted." Jenny hesitated. "Is Karl interested in art school?"

Sophie nodded.

"Last night before we went to sleep, he told me he'd never wanted to be a lawyer. He doesn't even want to go back to Tulane."

"What does he want to do?" But Jenny knew the answer.

"You know how Karl's played around with painting the last three or four years. I thought of it as a nice hobby. Cultural. Now he says he wants to become an artist. I never thought of it as a profession. How many men make a living as artists?"

"Sophie, you have to give Karl the chance to find out." She remembered Marc's parents insisting he graduate from Harvard and come into the store. How different Marc's life—and hers—might have been if his parents had been understanding.

"Herman will have a stroke if I ask him to let Karl go to the art school in New York that he's talking about. The Art Students League. Karl says it's very well known." Sophie shook her head. "I don't mind telling you, Jenny, Herman's not the only one in this family who isn't thrilled with this art school business—"

"Sophie," Jenny said, "give Karl the chance to find out if he has a strong enough talent to make it as an artist. If he hasn't he'll come into the stores. He'll use his artistic talents there—he can become a window dresser for all the stores, or he can design our mailing pieces. I'm going out to Palm Beach next month—" she hadn't really decided this until she said it, but now it made sense . . . "So we'll have five stores and more to come—there will be plenty of work for Karl if he finds that being an artist is not what he wants. But let him have this chance, Sophie. If you don't, you may lose him. Tell Herman I've offered to pay Karl's way at the Art Students League in New York."

"He'll insist Karl find a job as a clerk in a law office," Sophie said gloomily. "I can hear him screaming now."

"Let him scream all he wants," Jenny said bluntly. "Karl won't listen." No more than Marc had. "Won't it be better for him to go with your approval than to have him run off to New York and struggle to work his way through art school? If he proves he's good, I'll ask Nicky's brother Marc to help him. I'm willing to finance a year of study in Paris if Karl does well in New York."

"I can afford to help him, Jenny—" Sophie smiled. "Thanks to you and Maison Jennie."

"Then you'll tell Karl he can go?"

"I'll tell Karl to tell his father that you've generously offered to finance him to two years of art studies in New York. And that he's accepted. It's better Herman should think you're laying out all that money."

"Tell Karl it's your money," Jenny said tenderly. "He'll understand why his father can't know. Let him understand that his mother is doing this for him."

Sophie waited until the family was almost through dinner to announce Jenny's offer. She had chosen tonight because Carrie was at a friend's house for the evening and Freddie was visiting with Leon—the boys were scheduled to leave for a Jewish summer camp in Maine on Monday where they would work as counselors.

"Who the hell does she think she is?" Herman yelled. "Your high and mighty sister wants to run this whole family? This is my son—not hers! *I* tell him what to do—not Jenny. You listen to me, Sophie—" The two younger boys—Milty and Herbie—accustomed to their father's outbursts, concentrated on their rice pudding.

"Papa, I'm going to New York to study art—with or without your permission," Karl interrupted. "If Aunt Jenny is willing to help me, I'm grateful."

"Two years, Herman," Sophie said. "If it doesn't work out for Karl, then Jenny will give him a good job with the stores."

"He should be a lawyer," Herman insisted, sullen. "I gave him two years at Tulane. You think I'm dumb," he accused Sophie. "I talked to people. With two years at Tulane he can get a job working as a law clerk. In a few years he could be a lawyer—instead of assing around with paints."

"Maybe Freddie will be a lawyer," Sophie said soothingly. "He's smart enough."

For two summers now Freddie had been working in his father's store—without being paid. Herman had been outraged when Sophie had suggested that he be put on the payroll, launching into the familiar tirade about working to support himself since he was nine. Since then Sophie had secretly been paying her second oldest son every week.

Herman pushed himself away from the table.

"Freddie will do what I tell him. I won't make the mistakes with him that I made with Karl. He'll know who's the boss in this house."

Jenny couldn't wait to leave for Palm Beach. She was scheduled to take off in three days. Her mother and Evvie, along with Helene and Sophie's two youngest boys and Carrie, would leave the same day for the summer cottage. Annie Lou had been promoted to the role of housekeeper, with private instructions to intercede between Helene and Carrie whenever necessary. As in past summers she and Sophie—with the exception of the week she would be in Palm Beach—would drive up two or three times during the week. Herman would go up on Saturday nights, as would Mannie on those Saturdays when he was in town.

Soaking in a cooling tub before dinner—already the weather was hot and humid—Jenny tried to analyze her restlessness. Seeing Marc had been wonderful—but disturbing. Being with him made her so aware of what her life might have been. Afterward it was always difficult to adjust to her everyday existence. But she would go out to Palm Beach, set up the new shop—she would be too busy to fret.

Vivian was excited about becoming the manager of the Palm Beach shop. Already promoted to head of the lingerie department at Goldman's Department Store, Vivian would be a tremendous asset—Vivian knew exactly why Goldman's was on the downgrade, had seen the mistakes that

Benedict made in buying, and she had a true sense of style. Mannie would not visit the Palm Beach store; Jenny decided that she would make the trek once a year.

Tonight Sophie was coming over for dinner. Herman insisted on staying at home—he was still sulking over Karl's departure for New York. Sophie would put dinner on the table for her family and then come over, ostensibly to discuss running the store during Jenny's absence—but Jenny knew that Sophie enjoyed these occasional dinners away from her family.

Out of the tub, warm again within minutes despite the ceiling fan in her bedroom, Jenny slipped into a simple cotton shift with the new cowl neckline that Paris was favoring and went out to sit on the gallery. Annie Lou brought her a tall frosty glass of iced tea.

"Why Annie Lou, thank you—this is just what I need." Jenny smiled as she took the glass. Mama would die if she knew about the bonuses she gave Annie Lou regularly. But Annie Lou was a treasure—a real member of the family.

A Model T pulled up before the house. Sophie, looking unusually slim, stepped out of the car and walked up to the gallery.

Jenny was glad that Sophie had insisted on learning to drive—ignoring Herman's fury that she was invading his masculine territory. Actually it was Carrie who had prevented her father from prevailing on this issue—she liked to be driven to her destinations, and when her father wasn't around, someone had to do it.

"You look nice and cool," Sophie said, settling herself in a rocker beside Jenny. "Isn't this heat awful? Carrie says mama can't wait until she and Evvie leave for the cottage."

"At least the early mornings and the nights are cool out there." Of course mama never said a word to her about enjoying the cottage—such information always filtered through the children.

Annie Lou appeared behind the screen door.

"Miz Sophie, you feel like some cold iced tea?"

"I'd love it, thanks, Annie Lou."

Annie Lou and Sophie chatted for a few minutes, then Annie Lou returned to the kitchen to see to dinner. From

Helene's bedroom upstairs came the sound of a phonograph record, with Helene singing along.

"It's going to be hot in Palm Beach this time of year," Sophie said. "But it's right on the ocean. I guess that will help."

"It's almost a ghost town from April to November," Jenny said with a wry smile. "I'll be rattling around in an eleven-room cottage—extremely modest by Palm Beach standards. The owners arranged for a couple to come in to clean and cook for the week I'll be there so I'll be comfortable and not have to worry about a hotel or restaurants."

"Mama said to come to the table." Evvie's voice, cold and harsh, intruded. "Dora's ready to serve."

"We'll be right there, Evvie," Jenny said with a cautious smile. Lately Evvie's hostility toward her had been especially unnerving.

"Now," Evvie snapped. "You've sat out here long enough gossiping about me."

"Evvie—" Sophie was startled by the accusation.

"Don't bother lying." Now her tone was quietly threatening. "I know how you two talk about me every time you get together. All day long at the store, probably."

"Evvie, that's just not true." *What was the matter with Evvie?*

"You and Sophie are always talking about me." Color flooded Evvie's milk-white skin, guarded religiously from the sun. "Your poor sister who's nothing but a deary old maid. Your sister who couldn't even hold on to her husband. I'm better off than either of you are!" Her voice was shrill. "I don't have to bother about some man creeping into my bed any time he wants." She whirled about and disappeared inside the house. Jenny and Sophie stared at each other.

"Jenny, what's happening to her?"

"A case of nerves, I guess. God, I don't know. Maybe this awful heat has got to her." She hesitated. "Maybe we ought to talk to Dr. Cohen about it."

But in her rush of preparing for the Palm Beach trip, Jenny didn't get a chance to talk to Dr. Cohen. Seeing Jenny off at the train, Sophie promised that she would call him. Maybe they were worrying unnecessarily, Jenny thought as she settled down in her compartment. One thing was certain—Evvie had to get out and socialize more—it was bad for her to be mama's shadow all the time.

En route to Palm Beach—with a palmetto fan constantly in her hand—Jenny forced herself to focus on the plans for the Palm Beach store. Work was indeed her salvation. From her many sources she had learned that the wealthy women who congregated in Palm Beach every season would be as demanding as royalty.

Her first objective was to convince the owners of the Royal Poinciana to allow her to set up a shop within the hotel, beside the branch shops of the finest stores on New York's Fifth Avenue. She had brought along correspondence from the top names in the Paris fashion world to convince any skeptics that she intended to provide the ultimate in style for the hotel's guests. And she had to find a year-round spot for Maison Jennie Palm Beach.

Every year, from mid December through February, Palm Beach was host to such society luminaries as the Biddles, the Nunns, the Phipps and the Vanderbilts. The ultrarich arrived in Palm Beach in their private railway cars, or aboard their yachts. Some even traveled by special train.

Jenny recalled hearing extravagant stories about the yacht business tycoon Pierre Lorillard who carried several Jerseys aboard just to make sure there would be fresh milk for his guests at all times, about Bromo-Seltzers's Isaac Emerson's yacht, which had an enormous wood-burning fireplace on deck to warm those who wished to view the stars on chilly evenings . . .

Jenny was met at the small railroad station by the fiftyish white woman who was to cook and clean during Jenny's brief residence in the Palm Beach house. Her husband, she explained, was the houseman and gardener. Taking Jenny to the house in a two-seater afromobile—a wicker chair attached to a large tricycle pedaled from the rear—she talked exuberantly about Palm Beach.

"I've been living here for forty years, but I never saw such building as is going on now. My folks came here to get away from the cold winters up in Minnesota. With their bare hands, almost, they cut themselves a farm out of the wilderness. Then Henry Flager came down—he was the biggest man at Standard Oil—after old John D. Rockefeller. He built the Royal Poinciana. By the time he got through adding wings, it had 1,600 rooms. Rich folks were falling all over themselves to be guests at the Poinciana. The next year he built the Breakers. Only then it was called the Palm Beach Inn."

They drove past a parade of boarded-up hotels and cottages. Still, there were a substantial number of houses that were occupied even in the summer, Jenny noted, though she realized that Maison Jennie Palm Beach would earn the largest share of its profits during the winter season.

At last the afromobile turned off into a private driveway and came to a halt beside a large, rambling, shingled house that sat right at the edge of the ocean. Jenny caught her breath at her first sight of the blue, pink and gold seascape before her. The Atlantic seeming to roll almost to the steps to the gallery.

Jenny threw herself into her work. First, she knew she would have to convince several people of the standing of the Maison Jennie shops. At last she was given the chance to locate in the Poinciana for a trial season. Then she sought out Palm Beach's enterprising architect, Addison Mizner, who was building a row of innovative shops on Worth Avenue. He agreed to rent Jenny one of the prestigious stores to open soon on Worth Avenue.

Every night Jenny was served dinner on the gallery in full view of the magnificent stretch of white sand and ocean. And every night her thoughts turned to Marc, living for the moment at Antibes, on another stretch of glorious beach.

She was glad she had come to Palm Beach. She needed this time alone, away from the family. She could sit here at dusk, watching the waves beat upon the shore, and think about those moments with Marc in Paris.

From what Nicky gathered, Marc was becoming quite a celebrity. Of course he never said anything in his letters but according to the Paris newspapers which Nicky had arranged to receive every week, he was gaining recognition as one of the new, rebellious young painters. Jenny was delighted and proud—yet a part of her feared that she would lose him completely to his career.

When Jenny returned to New Orleans, she found Sophie waiting for her at Terminal Station. Was it her imagination, or did Sophie seem particularly harried today?

"You look rested," Sophie said as they followed a porter to the car. "Even with all that tiring traveling. I guess the trip to Palm Beach was good for you."

"Sophie, I sat at the edge of the ocean every evening and was revived—I know, we grew up looking at the Mississippi. But there's something about the ocean that hypnotizes me. I've never felt so peaceful before."

"You'll be seeing it every year if the Palm Beach shop pays off."

Jenny smiled.

"The children all right?" Jenny asked. "I phoned them at the lake house Thursday night and talked to Helene and Carrie." Involuntarily she frowned in recall. "Carrie said mama was sleeping. It was only eight o'clock New Orleans time."

"Mama's upset." All at once Sophie was serious. "Jenny, Evvie's been acting strangely."

"Did you talk to Dr. Cohen?"

Sophie nodded.

"We had a long talk. He thinks Evvie ought to be sent to a sanitarium for a while. Mama won't hear of it. Evvie's been doing more odd things." Sophie paused. "The day after you left for Palm Beach, she went into your room at the lake house and slashed the pillows, the mattress, some of your clothes."

"Oh my God, Sophie—what about the children? Is it safe to leave them at the lake house? What if she turns on them?"

"I don't think there's anything to worry about—you know how much she's always loved them . . . anyway, Dr. Cohen thinks that all her hostility is aimed at you. But he has arranged for a nurse to stay with her, to keep her sedated. He wants you to try to convince mama that Evvie has to be sent away.''

"That will be a feat—you know mama will never agree. But I'll talk to Dr. Cohen tomorrow."

"Okay. Listen, Dora's making a special dinner to celebrate your homecoming." Sophie, as always, tried to make the best of things. "And I told Herman he could eat by himself tonight. Why don't you and I have supper together tonight? As long as there's food on the table, I don't think Herman will notice I'm not there. And of course he wouldn't dream of washing the dishes—he'll leave them in the sink until Mildred comes in tomorrow morning."

Later, as they shared a thick beef stew and red wine, Jenny couldn't help but feel it was odd to be having dinner alone with Sophie in the house. She missed the sounds of the children's voices. But it was relaxing to have some quiet.

They stayed mostly on "safe" topics. Jenny talked enthusiastically about the potential for the Palm Beach shop, knowing that Sophie, too, was caught up in the excitement of their expanding business, and for a little while they even forgot about Evvie.

CHAPTER
TWENTY-FIVE

At a little after five o'clock the following evening Jenny and Sophie sat in Dr. Cohen's office and listened to his explanation of Evvie's condition.

"I think it's imperative that your sister receive care in a sanitarium." He held up a hand as Jenny started to speak. "I know the problem with your mother—I understand she'll fight it . . . but it's not fair to Evvie to keep her under constant heavy sedation. And I'm afraid that's necessary to make sure she harms no one—including herself."

Was he talking about suicide? Jenny hadn't even considered the possibility. "Dr. Cohen, do you really think Evvie can be helped in a—in a place like that?" She couldn't imagine sweet, gentle Evvie locked up in one of those institutions.

Dr. Cohen sighed.

"I can't honestly say that Evvie can be helped. She's been sick for a lot longer than I think any of us realize. But we know so little about the mind. People make remarkable recoveries when you least expect it, and I recommend a fine sanitarium." Dr. Cohen hesitated. "Jenny, I don't think it's safe for Leon and Helene to be under the same roof with Evvie—they're at a very impressionable age. I just don't think it's wise."

"Okay, Dr. Cohen. Sophie and I are driving up to the cottage tonight. I'll talk to mama," Jenny promised.

"You know she won't agree to a sanitarium."

"When we're sure of that, then we'll figure out some other way," Jenny said firmly. She wanted Evvie to get the best care possible, but Leon and Helene could not be sacrificed. "Thank you, Dr. Cohen. I'll call you after I talk to mama."

They decided to go to Sophie's house to have dinner with Herman before heading for the lake.

"I made a big stew last night, Jenny," Sophie said as they emerged from the car. "I told Mildred to throw in some more potatoes and put it up to simmer before she leaves. We can eat and run as soon as I've done the dishes."

The table was set. Herman sat sprawled in a parlor chair with the evening newspapers. He didn't bother to look up as Jenny and Sophie came into the house.

"I'll help you get dinner on the table, Sophie." Jenny glanced at Herman's bulging belly, thankful that at least she didn't have to sit alone in the parlor with him. He always made a point of ignoring her anyway—apparently he hadn't forgiven her for supporting Karl's decision to study art.

Sophie piled their plates high with food—steaming noodles, rich, dark gravy and chunks of beef with mushrooms. While Jenny took the plates into the dining room, Sophie brought out the iced tea pitcher and the bread pudding.

Finally Herman put down his newspaper.

"So. What did the great doctor have to say about Evvie?"

"He said she should be in a sanitarium. And he is a good doctor, Herman." Sophie came out of the kitchen, drying her hands.

Herman grunted.

"Sure, it's easy for him to say—he doesn't have to pay the bills."

"That's right, Herman—and neither will you. I'll pay the bills," Jenny said.

For the rest of the meal Herman concentrated on his food. Sophie and Jennie discussed Maison Jennie Palm Beach in detail. It was as though the two women were alone at the table.

Finally, with the dishes washed, dried and put away, Jenny and Sophie went out to the car. Jenny was ready to leave the hot humid city behind—her eagerness to see

Helene was tainted by her trepidation at what awaited them back at the cottage . . .

It cooled off as they drove away from the city, the scent of summer flowers filling the air. Neither of the women spoke much, and tonight the trip seemed longer than usual. What if Helene and the boys had witnessed Evvie's erratic behavior? Even to an adult it was frightening.

When at last they approached the lake cottage, Jenny heard the light laughter of the children. *Thank God*.

The children—Helene, Milty and Herbie—were outside, probably chasing lightning bugs, their favorite after dinner pastime. At the sight of the car they came running over, all laughing and shouting at once. Jenny and Sophie were engulfed in a sea of welcoming hugs while Annie Lou waddled out to greet them.

"I sho is glad to see you safe, Miz Jenny. Nice to see you again, Miz Sophie." She paused. "Miz Jenny, you best stay in Mister Mannie's room tonight. That mattress in yo' room has gotta be thrown out. Miz Straus, she thinks it kin be fixed—but no way."

Jenny put down Helene.

"Where is mama?"

"She's takin' a nap. The nurse—she's with Miz Evvie."

"Did the children see what happened? Were they in the house?"

"They was out playin'. So nothin' happened to 'em if that's what you're wonderin'. But they couldn't help hearin' what was goin' on. It took your mother and me to hold her down till she fell asleep. That's when I made Miz Straus call Dr. Cohen. He sent the lady nurse out right away. Miz Evvie—she's been quiet since then."

Jenny and Sophie were sipping glasses of iced tea on the gallery when their mother woke up. They heard her talking to Annie Lou.

"Sophie's here and you didn't tell me? Honestly, Annie Lou, you've got to be more conscientious about these things. *Sophie's here*, Jenny thought. Not *Sophie and Jenny*.

Sophie stood up.

"Come on, Jenny. Let's go see mama."

Mrs. Straus stood in the soft light of the hall that divided the cottage from front to back, clutching at the kimono she wore over her summer nightgown. When she saw Sophie she came running forward.

"Sophie, what are we going to do about Evvie?"

Jenny stood by as Sophie and her mother hugged each other.

"Mama, we have to talk."

Reluctantly Mrs. Straus pulled away from Sophie. "All right," she sighed. "But in the kitchen. On the gallery all the neighbors will hear. We don't have to have everyone knowing our business."

The three women walked into the kitchen. As gently as possible, Jenny and Sophie tried to explain why Dr. Cohen felt it best that Evvie be sent away to a sanitarium.

Mrs. Straus sat in silence for a few minutes.

"Are you two through?"

Jenny and Sophie exchanged warning looks.

"Yes."

"Over my dead body Evvie goes to a sanitarium. You took Danny away from me when he needed me the most. When he lost his leg, you defended that woman who took him away from me. You won't do that to Evvie. It's your fault this happened to her!" Mrs. Straus's voice soared. "I told you she was delicate, but you made her work in the store. You know how weak she is—it was too much for her."

"Mama, Evvie hasn't been in the store for seven years—"

"Never mind—it's your fault. Everything wrong in my life has been your fault. Well this time I won't let you manipulate me—Evvie is staying here. With me."

"Annie Lou," Sophie said, "get me a glass of water and mama's pills. We'd better get her into bed."

Later that night, Jenny and Sophie sat on the gallery far into the night.

With Mrs. Straus up in arms, there was no choice of putting Evvie into a sanitarium. There had to be an answer . . .

"Sophie, there's only one way to handle this. I'll build a

little cottage at the edge of our property. Evvie will live there with a nurse. That way mama can see her twenty times a day if she likes."

Sophie took her hand.

"Jenny, there's something you've got to remember. It wasn't your fault, mama has to have somebody to blame."

"I know." Jenny forced a smile. "And I love you for saying that, Sophie. I'm so tired of always being the one to blame. But . . . poor Evvie's had it the roughest. I guess I'd sort of hoped for a miracle and mama would let us put Evvie away. Obviously I was being naive."

For the rest of the summer construction was underway on the tiny cottage that would be Evvie's home when she returned from the lake house. Jenny hoped that once she was living there, Dr. Cohen would recommend a specialist so that they would no longer have to keep her heavily sedated, but at this point Evvie's situation looked pretty bleak.

But there were some happy developments, too. A national magazine sent a woman reporter to New Orleans to interview Jenny as the subject of a story about women in merchandising—invaluable publicity for the store, and surprising to Jenny who couldn't imagine herself as something of a celebrity. She was proud, however, that they had chosen her as an example of the recently touted "independent woman" in the press, and she was thrilled that very soon the 19th amendment, granting women the right to vote, would become law.

The weeks sped past. Jenny was absorbed in the opening of Maison Jennie Royal Poinciana and Maison Jennie Palm Beach—both scheduled for early January. As always, everything had to be just right, and Jenny, keenly aware of the spending habits of the Palm Beach ladies, did a lot of reading of *Vogue* and *Harper's Bazaar*. She decided to place ads in these prestigious national magazines, to appear a month before the openings. Mrs. Goldman agreed.

Early in September Evvie—still kept under sedation— was moved into the cottage. For the first week Mrs. Straus insisted on staying there with her. At the end of the week she moved back into her room in the main house. Every day the two women sat in the privacy of the fenced-in cottage, Mrs. Straus talking to Evvie as though nothing had changed between them.

"Well, Sophie, at last mama has a willing ear," Jenny said wryly. "It doesn't seem to make a damn bit of difference that Evvie can't hear her and agree with everything she says." Sophie laughed.

"Maybe mama's found the perfect companion."

Eager to be in Palm Beach for the grand opening, Nicky talked Armand into spending a three-week winter vacation there—again Armand's mother would take care of the children. Nicky and Armand would leave a week before Jenny and stay at the Royal Poinciana, and Jenny would join them there later.

Right after Thanksgiving, Jenny saw Vivian and Charlie off to Palm Beach—Vivian was to oversee the final details of opening the shops. Charlie was all excited about the prospect of starting school in a city where it was warm enough to swim even in the winter.

Hugging Charlie to her for a final good-bye before Vivian and he boarded the train, the fact that this was Mannie's child brought back the old anger. He had to be the most unfeeling man alive to ignore the presence of his child. What did he think of Vivian? Didn't he wonder about her? Or had he just tried to forget the entire episode? The callousness of it frightened her. Well, Mannie and mama were alike in one respect; both could shut out bothersome events as though they had never happened.

Jenny looked out the window of her compartment as the train, carrying regular pullman and private cars, crossed the bridge over Lake Worth. Ahead, facing the lake—which was actually an extension of the Atlantic Ocean—she could see the immense six-story Royal Poinciana, with its two-story-tall, white, gracefully fluted columns forming an elegant colonnade.

Tomorrow would be New Year's Eve. Since mid-December hotel guests had been arriving. For weeks Nicky had been telling extravagant tales about New Year's Eve at the Royal Poinciana. While Jenny felt guilty about not being with the family, Leon and Helene seemed to understand that she had to be here for business.

Onshore, the train pulled into the immaculate little one-story special Royal Poinciana Station, and drew to a stop to let the passengers traveling in the public cars disembark. The private cars would follow the tracks around to the back of the hotel, where they would sit until their owners decided to depart.

Jenny watched a platoon of Negro bellmen, led by a bell captain in a striking blue uniform with gold epaulettes, march toward the train. From a second-story colonnade overlooking the station came the sound of music. An orchestra was playing to greet the afternoon arrivals.

The bellmen gathered around the vestibules of the pullman cars as the train porters put the steps in place and carried down the luggage. Jenny gazed at the hotel, painted a brilliant lemon yellow with white trim and green shutters.

"Jenny!" There was Nicky, waving and smiling as she made her way through the bustling porters. Jenny smiled and waved back.

A bellman had already taken Jenny's suitcases and her trunks were being removed from the baggage car and placed on carts drawn by mules. Nicky had warned that all the Palm Beach ladies were constantly changing their clothes, so Jenny had brought a lavish array of clothes even though she would only be here a week.

"Nicky—" Jenny hugged her—"I can see that you're enjoying Palm Beach. You look radiant. Is it the weather, or is it Armand?"

Nicky winked, laughed. "A little of both, my love . . ."

"Come on, Nicky, out with it—I can tell you're up to something."

"I'll tell you later. Right now let's get you settled into your suite." They fell in step behind the bellman. "Then we'll go over to the store. Armand is at the Everglades Club talking shop with a judge, so we can spend some time together. You know Armand—he never really escapes from business. Like you—"

"Have you checked on both shops? Vivian wrote that we

would be able to open Maison Jennie Palm Beach the day after the grand opening at the hotel." Immediately, Jenny had forgotten her happiness at seeing her old friend—she had two stores to open!

"Relax, relax . . . everything's on schedule. Vivian is a dynamo. You sure trained her well. And you don't have to worry about your customers—thanks to those ads in *Vogue* and *Harper's Bazaar*, they're practically breaking the doors down. And they're all buzzing about that magazine interview. That photograph of you is absolutely gorgeous—it makes you look like one of the models!"

"It ought to—" Jenny laughed. "It cost enough."

Jenny and Nicky followed the bellman up the broad stairs—carpeted in a beautiful sage green—to the main entrance to the hotel, its galleries extending a full block on either side and lined with green rocking chairs. They walked into the one-hundred-foot-wide rotunda—the main lobby—reaching two stories to a skylight.

Scattered about the rotunda were broad wicker chairs and couches, the seats upholstered in green velvet. A tremendous fan palm stood in the center with other palms, plants and flowers scattered around the room.

At the immense main lobby desk on the second floor of the rotunda Jenny was greeted as though she were a visiting princess. As Nicky rattled off names of current guests—a list that sounded like a page torn out of the social register— Jenny realized this was indeed a perfect spot for the latest Maison Jennie stores.

Once she was registered, she and Nicky followed the bellman to the gold-strap open-faced elevator. At the fourth floor they stepped out into one of the eight miles of hallway that crisscrossed the Poinciana.

"Nicky, didn't I hear someone say that the hotel has sixteen hundred guest rooms?" Jenny could just imagine the wealthy ladies from those sixteen hundred rooms flocking to Maison Jennie Royal Poinciana . . .

"That's right, darling—and you know what that means for us!"

The bellman opened the door and Jenny and Nicky walked inside. Through the open door to the bedroom Jenny saw that her trunk was already sitting on the foldout table at the foot of her bed.

Nicky spun around. "It's charming, isn't it?"

"It's lovely," Jenny said. "Everything you said it would be." The sitting room was done in blue velvet, the bedroom, furnished with a huge mahogany double bed, mahogany dressers and green wicker chairs. The wallpaper was a patterned green, the floor covered with a matching green Japanese matting. In the corner of the bedroom was a writing desk with a straight back chair and a telephone, Jenny noted in approval. Mannie was always accusing her of being a slave to the telephone but it was comforting to know that she was only a phone call away from Leon and Helene.

She tipped the bellman—rather extravagantly, she thought—and with a grateful smile he left. At last they were alone.

"Jenny, come over here—you've got to see this." Nicky walked to the mahogany nightstand beside the bed. "There *is* a private bathroom, of course. But for emergencies, *voila!*" With a flourish Nicky displayed the chamber pot. Designed expressly for the hotel, it was made of glistening white china trimmed with gold and with palm trees painted inside at the bottom, on the cover and the outside. Nicky giggled. "Now where else would you have your own bathroom and such an elegant chamber pot?"

"Nicky, I can't stand it anymore—you're bursting to tell me something—now what is it?"

Nicky hesitated.

"Well, I guess there was no way to tell you until now. I mean you were already on the train when we found out—"

"Found out what?"

"Yesterday when Armand and I came back from the tennis court, we found a message. You won't believe who're guests at the hotel right this minute." She took a deep breath. "Marc and Simone."

CHAPTER
TWENTY-SIX

J ENNY STARED AT Nicky. So . . . after all these years she would meet Marc's wife.

"Nicky, how did this happen?"

"Marc was coming home to New Orleans. He meant to surprise the family. Also, I guess he wanted to be sure that Simone didn't change her mind. Apparently he'd made plans before and she'd decided against the trip at the last minute. He didn't want to disappoint anybody—especially Grandma."

"Nicky, I still don't understand—"

"Just a day before Simone and Marc were to leave Paris, he received my letter saying that Armand and I would be in Palm Beach for three weeks. I also told him you'd be arriving today for a week's visit to supervise the opening of the new shops. You know how he's always eager for news about you—"

"I won't see him."

"Jenny, come on . . . there's no way you can avoid him. Everybody in the hotel is waiting for the opening of Maison Jennie Royal Poinciana. They're dying to meet you."

"Nicky, I'm not ready to meet Marc's wife . . . I'm not sure I ever will be." Jenny was trembling. Why was it that whenever she was beginning to feel secure something always happened to throw her off balance?

"Jenny," Nicky said softly, "it had to happen sometime."

"But not now! Not like this!" Jenny dropped to the edge

of the bed. She felt trapped. *Marc should have given her some warning*. This way she'd be busy with all the preparations for the store—she'd have no time to see him.

"You know, Jenny, you can't put off meeting Simone forever—you almost met her seven years ago." Nicky fished in her Marc Cross purse for a cigarette. "Remember? It was only because she was sick that she didn't meet us at the chateau."

"Yes, and I was terrified then, too. But now, to have them appear out of nowhere like this. How did they manage to get reservations, anyway?"

"Some friends of Simone who live in New York offered them their suite for the week—they'll be leaving for New Orleans the day before you, by the way. Marc wrote mama and grandma from New York that they would be coming home for a month's stay. I'm sure mama's planning all kinds of parties for them."

"Then you've seen them already?"

Nicky nodded.

"We had dinner with them last night and we're supposed to eat dinner with them every night they're here, though I'm not sure I'm ready for that. Apparently Simone likes to have breakfast and lunch in their suite—I guess she still gets tired early. You know, she's as charming as I remember when Armand and I met her on our honeymoon. But the years have caught up with her . . . don't get me wrong, she's still lovely—as much as a sixty-year-old woman with beautiful bone structure can be . . . and she's a lovely person, Jenny. Really." She squeezed Jenny's hand. "But Jenny, look at it this way—you're going to see Marc—isn't *that* exciting?"

"Of course, it'll be wonderful to see him," Jenny said slowly. "Sometimes I thought he would never come home again." But he *was* coming home—with his wife.

She couldn't imagine sitting through a whole meal with Marc, pretending they were casual acquaintances. Was it Marc or Simone who had suggested that they stop off at Palm Beach? Maybe he was as uncomfortable in this situation as she.

God, how she wanted to see him! But not like this

. . . not fearing every moment of betraying herself before his wife, terrified that Simone might look at her and guess the truth . . .

Nicky's voice cut into her thoughts. "Why don't you stop worrying, Jenny? Whatever happens will be for the best, I'm sure. Phone and ask for a maid to come up and unpack and press for you. Then we can go over to the hotel shop and visit with Vivian."

An hour later, Jenny and Nicky were hurrying across the rotunda into the hallway that led to the row of smart resort shops. When they reached Maison Jennie Poinciana she stopped and gazed with pride at the charmingly dressed windows, the immaculate, elegant entrance. Her thoughts went back to the day Grandma Goldman first offered to set her up in business.

"Look—" Nicky nudged her. "Here comes Vivian."

"Jenny!" Vivian pushed open the doors and threw her arms around her. "I've been so excited all day—I thought I'd fly off into space at any minute." Her eyes searched Jenny's. "Are the windows right? I tried to remember everything you said."

"They're perfect, Vivian. You've done a wonderful job." She was determined not to let her mood spoil Vivian's pleasure—she had brought off a formidable task beautifully. "And the walls are just the right shade of gray." She gazed around the shop in approval. "You even got just the right shade of lilac for the furniture."

"Oh, I'm so glad you like it—I mean I thought you would, but as time went on I got nervous. I sent the girls home early because we've been working late every night. They're all thrilled about the opening. Oh, yes—that case of champagne you sent arrived a week ago."

"The Chateau Mouton-Rothschild that Armand picked out for me," Jenny told Nicky. "You know I'd never trust myself on champagne." She turned to Vivian. "So. The buffet's all arranged?"

"All set." Vivian laughed. "It seems like the ladies of the hotel gather out front all the time—I bet you every model in the window has been sold—and not only to the ladies from Poinciana. From the Breakers, too."

"She's right, Jenny," Nicky said. "I know at least a dozen women who plan to buy the gray Coco Chanel."

Jenny remembered now that Henry Flager had to build the Breakers to handle the overflow of guests. It was connected to the Poinciana by the popular "mule train," a miniature trolley on tracks drawn by a mule. The Breakers—directly on the beach—provided a bathing casino for the guests of both hotels.

"How's Charlie?" Jenny brought herself back into the conversation.

"Wonderful." Vivian smiled, proud. "He loves the sun and sand."

"Listen, I'll be here first thing in the morning, Vivian, I promise. We'll go over every garment together. And I'd like to meet the salesgirls. You told them they'll be off at one P.M. tomorrow?"

Vivian nodded.

"Yes, Jenny. And they'll be in on January 2 at nine sharp. That'll give us three hours before the opening. All the publicity has been set up. The models will be New York and California debutantes of this season." She rattled off names that appeared regularly on the society pages of New York and San Francisco newspapers. "The newspapers have carried front page stores about percentage of the proceeds of grand opening day going to charity. They even carried a story about you along with the photograph from the magazine article. It reproduced beautifully."

"You know, Jenny," Nicky laughed, "it looks like you're becoming a celebrity."

Several hours later, Jenny stood in front of her chest trying to decide what to wear to dinner.

Remembering that Marc liked her in mauve, she chose a Chanel mauve chiffon dinner gown—classical, simple and elegant. At least let her meet Marc's wife looking her best . . .

Tonight they were to dine in the open court Grill Room, where a special dinner—the makings supplied by Park and

Tilford in New York—was offered—and billed in addition to the normal hotel fees. Armand and Nicky—he in white tie and tails and she in one of the exquisite Paris gowns from Maison Jennie New Orleans—arrived at Jenny's suite to escort her downstairs for dinner.

"Jenny, you're looking beautiful—" Armand always the gentleman, took her arm. "As always."

"By God, Jenny, you'll make every woman in the Grill Room look overdressed." Nicky laughed. "That gown is marvelous. And trust you to wear only a string of pearls with it. Most women would be aglitter with jewels."

Her heart pounding, Jenny followed Nicky and Armand downstairs to the Grill Room, where an orchestra—hidden behind tall palms—played soft background dinner music. To her relief, Marc and Simone had not yet arrived. Armand seated the two women one either side of him and launched into conversation about the New Year's Eve festivities. Jenny smiled and tried to listen, but her thoughts were elsewhere.

"There's Marc," Nicky said.

Jenny froze.

He was dressed in white tie and tails, talking solicitously to a tall, slender, smartly gowned woman in soft gray who looked like she could be his mother. *Simone*. Still beautiful, just as Nicky had said, in a heartbreakingly fragile way. And then Marc glanced toward their table and saw her.

Please, Marc, don't look at me like that . . .

Armand rose to his feet with a warm smile. Jenny forced a smile through the casual introductions. She heard herself saying all the right things, being gracious to Marc's wife . . . and yet she felt removed from the scene. Thank God Nicky was bubbling with high spirits.

Marc sat beside her. Simone sat beside her young sister-in-law.

Marc turned to her. "Everyone's talking about your new shop, Jenny. I gather it's going to be quite a success."

"Well, the press has been very kind. All the signs are good. I'm very excited about it." Jenny tried to avoid his eyes. *They had to sound casual*—as far as Simone knew she had met Marc only in France—on those two trips with

Nicky. "Nicky tells me you have a new show coming up in the fall."

She listened carefully while Marc talked about his work, thankful that they were on safe ground. Simone was talking to Nicky and Armand about running the chateau as a convalescent home for Allied soldiers.

Jenny adored gourmet food, but she was scarcely aware of the dinner—canapé caviar, planked pompano, saddle of lamb with mint sauce, asparagus, new potatoes and hearts of lettuce.

She told him about Karl, studying at the Art Students League in New York, knowing he would be sympathetic—and he was.

"Jenny," he said, "if Karl decides to continue study in Paris have him write me. I'll be happy to help him in any way I can."

At last dessert arrived . . . vanilla ice cream and petit fours with *café noir*. For a moment Jenny's eyes met Marc's . . . She knew he was remembering the endless cups of *café noir* they had shared in the French Market almost eighteen years ago. They had been so young. So in love. *Still in love?*

After dinner Armand suggested they go by afromobile to the Beach Club for the gambling.

"The Beach Club—Bradley's gambling house—is the most famous gambling house in the world next to Monte Carlo."

"I know," Simone said. "And it's far more exclusive than Monte Carlo. Friends in Paris have told me about it."

"Simone." Marc touched her arm. "I think you should rest."

"All right, darling—would you see me to our suite? Then you can join the others."

"No, no—we'll both call it a night." Marc turned to the others at the table, avoiding Jenny's eyes. "What do you say we visit Bradley's another time?"

But Nicky and Armand wanted to go and Jenny was talked into joining them. She knew she probably wouldn't be able to sleep anyway, and she told herself it would be good for business to be seen at the Beach Club. Already she realized that she was something of a minor celebrity. Some of the guests had recognized her and had rather blatantly inspected her gown when she came into the restaurant. So, if that's what they expected . . . "Jenny" of Maison Jennie would circulate among the guests of the country's most expensive resort.

In the morning Jenny had breakfast with Nicky and Armand in the colonnaded dining room and then hurried off to join Vivian in the shop while Nicky and Armand prepared to go to the beach. Later Marc would join them.

"Come on, Jenny," Nicky coaxed, "you know what they say about all work and no play. Why don't you take the mule train over and have a swim?"

"Maybe, but I really don't think I'll have the time, Nicky—I am opening a new shop, you know—you of all people should know that means a lot of work."

When Jenny arrived at the store the staff was gathered on the main floor waiting for her.

Jenny worked with them until one P.M., when they were to start their holiday. They checked every garment to make sure it was perfect . . . not a loose button, a stray thread . . . and she impressed upon each salesgirl the importance of behavior and appearance. Indeed, if Maison Jennie was to be a most special shop their service must be most special.

Jenny had lunch with Nicky and Armand. Immediately afterward, knowing that Marc and Simone were expected to arrive at any moment to sit on the verandah and talk until the two men went off to play golf, Jenny stood up to go by afromobile to the year-round shop. She had originally planned to meet Vivian there.

"Jenny," Nicky pulled her aside while Armand talked to a group of men, "meet us for tea at the Coconut Grove?"

"If I can—"

"Oh, of course you can—" Nicky dropped her voice. "Simone will be napping all afternoon because of the big party tonight. So it'll be just the four of us."

"All right. I—I'll try," Jenny said, her face hot. All this

time she'd rationalized her intrusion on Marc's marriage, with the knowledge that it was a match based more on practicality than love. But now that she had seen them together, she knew Simone loved him.

"Come on, Jenny," Nicky pressed. "Marc and Armand will be back from the golf course by four-thirty. Why don't you meet us at the Coconut Grove? Marc will be so pleased."

"I'll try, Nicky, okay? But I have to run." She hurried off in seach of an afromobile.

The prospect of sitting with Marc, Nicky and Armand in the Coconut Grove was an appealing one—but Jenny was determined not to succumb to temptation. She left the attractive little shop on Worth Avenue at exactly 4:30 P.M., telling herself that she would go straight up to her suite and rest until the New Year's Eve festivities began. But at the hotel entrance she hesitated. At this moment Marc was sitting in the Coconut Grove . . .

She wavered. For a little while she could be with Marc without fear of their betraying themselves. Armand, bless him, would never notice—he was too busy enjoying this respite from his busy practice and Nicky had, for once, been discreet.

But why not have this little bit of happiness? She turned and walked toward the Coconut Grove. As she approached the huge tea garden, set among lofty palms and decorated with myriad colored lights, she heard the lilting melody of Victor Herbert's "Kiss Me Again."

Her eyes scanned the sea of faces. There was Marc already on his feet. She hurried toward him. He took her hand.

"Jenny. I'm so glad you could come."

"Jenny listen . . . isn't the music beautiful?" Nicky, the eternal romantic, took Armand's hand.

"Oh, yes. I love Victor Herbert." And her eyes said to Marc *I love you.*

Nicky and Armand did most of the talking, but Jenny and Marc barely listened. In fact, they were oblivious to virtually everything around them in this glorious tea garden—everything, that is, except for the fact that they longed to be alone.

The orchestra began the poignant Herbert melody. "I'm Falling in Love with Someone" and under the table Marc's hand reached for hers. For a moment she panicked—then she realized that no one—except Nicky—was aware of what was going on. What would be the harm in it? For a little while let her have this small pleasure.

Dinner was, as Jenny anticipated, an extravagant affair . . . the ladies gorgeously gowned, wearing their most elaborate jewelry, the meal a sumptuous feast that started with a delicate duck liver pâté and ended with pears flambée. And, of course, champagne flowed throughout.

Simone was making every effort to enjoy the festivities, but Jenny suspected that she was tired. Every so often she caught a look of sorrow, a little regret beyond her brilliant smile.

Marc asked her to dance, but she declined.

"I'm afraid that's much to energetic for me, darling," she laughed. "Why don't you dance with one of these beautiful young ladies?"

With almost indecent alacrity Marc turned to Jenny and instantly, trembling, she was on her feet. At last, for a little while Marc would hold her in his arms.

"Jenny, I'm so proud of you," Marc said softly while they danced to a Strauss waltz. "You know, you're the most beautiful and accomplished woman here in this room."

Jenny felt her cheeks flush. "Oh, Marc, what I've done is nothing compared with you." She kept telling herself they shouldn't look at each other like this . . . not even on the dance floor . . . but she couldn't help it. He looked so handsome . . . "I'm so proud of what the critics are saying about your work."

"So," his arm tightened around her waist. "You'll come to Paris in the spring?"

"Yes, Marc," her voice was barely a whisper. "I promise."

At last midnight came and everyone in the enormous

ballroom raised a glass of champagne in honor of the new year. 1920. A new decade . . .

Five minutes later Simone and Marc excused themselves and left for their suite.

Jenny decided to leave, too.

"We'll see you to your suite," Armand said quickly.

"No, really, it's all right—I'll be fine." In truth, she felt that she needed every precious moment alone.

Back in her suite she thought about calling the children. It was not yet midnight there, and while she would love to hear their voices, instinct told her this just wasn't the right time. The phone might awaken mama and she'd assume something had happened to Danny. Maybe she'd just go to sleep and call them in the morning. Sleep would be difficult enough tonight . . .

She had promised Marc she would be coming to Paris this spring. Without a moment's hesitation . . . She must be mad. But, after all, she did have to do some buying this season, and she didn't trust anyone else to make the trip yet. But she had long sensed that once she met Marc's wife, she would have difficulty in continuing their relationship. Simone had become an obstacle to their love—now she was the intruder.

Finally, exhausted, Jenny fell asleep. When she woke up the next morning she realized that today she had no excuses to avoid socializing with Marc and Simone.

At the beach with Nicky and Armand she tensed at the approach of every man, at once hoping it was Marc and yet dreading another confrontation with him. Normally she relished the sight of the waves beating against the beach— for her it was akin to lovemaking. Today she couldn't wait for the day to be over. But Marc and Simone never appeared. She realized with some relief that they had probably decided to meet them only for dinner.

Later, over dinner, Simone was unusually quiet. It wasn't until they were finished dessert that she joined in the conversation.

"We would have liked to meet your husband, Jenny. What a shame he couldn't come to Palm Beach too."

"He's involved in business activities." Jenny couldn't bring herself to pretend regret.

"He must be so proud of your success."

"Oh, yes." Jenny forced a smile. Little did Simone know—her success was the greatest irritation in Mannie's life.

"You have two children, yes?" Simone looked at her with curiosity.

"I have a son and a daughter, and I adore them."

"Well, we're even then—" Simone said gaily. "I have Marc's paintings, and I adore *them*."

"You know, Marc," Nicky said, "Grandma shows your paintings to *everyone*. And Maison Jennie's favorite customers are allowed to see the paintings hanging in Jenny's office."

Marc turned to Jenny in astonishment.

"So you're the secret buyer!" He glowed with pleasure.

"Nicky," Jenny scolded, blushing underneath Simone's scrutiny, "now you've given me away."

"Someday, Jenny," Simone said softly, "Marc's paintings will be worth a fortune. Tell me, which ones do you have?"

As she named the paintings, Jenny sensed that Simone suspected. The last thing she wanted was to hurt this brave, loving woman.

"I'm very proud of my husband, Jenny," Simone said. "But I'm a very selfish woman. I wish to keep him beside me for the years I have left in this world." And from the look in her eyes Jenny was now certain that she knew.

She might go to Paris in the spring, but she wouldn't see Marc—it was time to cut him out of her life.

Marc stood at a window in their sitting room and gazed out at the moonlit water of the lake. Was it a mistake to have persuaded Simone to come down to Palm Beach? He had thought she would be amused, and—he had to admit it—he couldn't deny himself the chance to see Jenny.

"Marc—" He swung away from the window at the sound of Simone's voice. She stood in the doorway of the bedroom in a gray silk negligee, artfully designed to conceal the ravages of the years of illness.

"Would you like a glass of wine, Simone?" She had seemed unusually tired tonight—but lately, it seemed, she hadn't been sleeping well.

"No, darling. Just some talk." Despite her efforts to appear calm, he sensed her agitation.

"Are you feeling all right?"

"Oh, yes, I'm fine," she frowned. "No, I'm not fine. I'm scared. Marc, would you be terribly upset if we didn't go to New Orleans together? I'd like to return to Paris immediately. But there's no reason for you not to stay and then go on to New Orleans."

"Simone, I won't go without you." Determined not to let her see his disappointment, he took her hands and pulled her close. "If you want to go back to Paris, then we'll go together." The war years had taken so much from her. Maybe this trip *had* been too ambitious an undertaking.

"Marc, I can't bring myself to go to New Orleans and face your family. I'm old, and they'll hate me for marrying you."

"Don't be silly," Marc said. "They'll love you. Nicky loves you—"

"Nicky is a wonderful, adorable, open-minded young woman. But to your mother and father I'll be a contemporary. I can't face them, Marc."

Marc was silent for a long moment.

"Then we'll go back to Paris together. I'll make arrangements in the morning. We'll go to New Orleans another time."

CHAPTER
TWENTY-SEVEN

J ENNY TRIED TO enjoy the triumph of the grand opening of the Palm Beach shops, but she was haunted by her conviction that she now had to remove Marc from her life—even for those few days in Paris every year.

While she wrestled with the dilemma of making her annual buying pilgrimage to Paris without seeing Marc, the situation was solved for her. Marc wrote Nicky that he and Simone were leaving in early March for a long cruise to the Greek Islands and Egypt. They would not be returning to Paris until June.

In his letter Marc asked Nicky to write François, now their majordomo, telling him when Jenny and she would arrive in Paris. François would meet them at the Gâre Saint Lazare with the car. Simone and Marc expected Jenny and her to stay at the Paris house.

Hearing Helene excitedly tell a classmate that her mother would be going to Paris, Jenny decided to take Helene along. Leon—now in his junior year at high school—could not afford to lose the time beyond their normal spring vacation period. Later, Jenny promised. Mannie was outraged.

"A twelve-year-old girl has to go to Paris? You think you're Mrs. Astor?"

"I'm taking Helene with me," Jenny said quietly. "Thousands of girls her age have gone to Europe—it'll be a wonderful experience for her." Nicky was bringing Louis and Stephanie, also.

"Let her learn to work for a living," Mannie snarled. "You're raising a pair of snobs!"

"Helene and Leon will have everything I can afford to give them, Mannie . . ." She restrained herself from adding that Mannie lived far beyond what his own efforts would support. "All Herman and you can remember is how hard you had to work as small children. Helene and Leon can be spared that. Don't begrudge them that, Mannie."

"You teach them to look down on their father!" Mannie's voice rose and Jenny realized that Helene was listening at the head of the stairs. "But your time will come. Wait till they get so hoity-toity they thumb their noses at the mother!"

At the last minute Nicky decided that they would take Arlette along to keep an eye on the children while they shopped. She also reserved two drawing rooms on the train, knowing that she and Jenny would appreciate the solitude. She knew intuitively that this trip would not hold the same pleasure for Jenny as it had in the past.

Because of the children, there was a special excitement to their departure this year. She must remember, Jenny told herself, that everything was new to them—the train, the oceangoing liner, Paris itself . . .

It disturbed Jenny how often she thought about what would happen when Simone died. Lying sleepless in her berth as the train raced east she tried to analyze the situation. Even if she could imagine Marc being free, could she ever bring herself to divorce Mannie?

She suspected that—for a price—Mannie would agree to a divorce. But to mama that would be the ultimate disgrace. To many people, divorce was a disgrace. She couldn't put the children through that. Not until they were grown.

In Paris Jenny threw herself into buying for the six stores, trying to become absorbed in lines, fabrics, new trends in fashion. Occasionally she could forget that she was in Paris without Marc . . . but the loneliness always came back.

She did manage to set aside time for sightseeing with the

children and she loved seeing their excitement at this
wonderful new city.

Paris was full of Americans in this spring of 1920 . . .
the young trying to escape American morality, invading the
art schools, the music schools, talking about the volumes of
poetry or the novels they would write.

"It's the aftermath of the war," Nicky said as Jenny and
she sat at a sidewalk café on Faubourg Saint-Mártin.
"They're all sure our generation has made a mess of the
world."

"Nicky, what's happening to you?" Jenny clucked.
"You're the one who's always saying how young we are."
Suddenly Jenny realized that at thirty-four she didn't feel
young—she felt tired and ancient.

Nicky squinted in concentration. "You know, Jenny, I
look at these kids here and back home, and I can't believe
how cynical they are. We would never dare do the things
they do."

"Nicky, you, of all people . . ." Jenny laughed. "Of
course we did—we just didn't talk about it."

"You mean that man on the train to New York seven
years ago?" Nicky giggled. "And Marc and you? That's
different. Tell me this: Did you ever walk around with
condoms in your vanity?"

Jenny looked shocked.

"I didn't even know what they were at that age."

Suddenly Nicky was serious.

"Jenny—what is going to happen to you and Marc?"

"I just won't let myself think about it, Nicky. I guess I
don't dare."

"Come on—let's go back to the house." Nicky stood up.
"Tonight we're having dinner at Maxim's—that is if they'll
allow two unescorted women in the restaurant."

Jenny smiled.

"Tell them you're Marc Goldman's sister, then they're
sure to allow it."

She was glad this was their last night in Paris. Without
Marc, Paris was a ghost city.

* * *

Jenny was uneasy when her mother insisted that Evvie be taken back to the lake house, even though the nurse would be with her at all times. Jenny could have a fence put up at the back, and Evvie and Mrs. Straus and the nurse would sit out on the back porch. Why should Evvie have to suffer in the hot city?

Jenny asked Dr. Cohen. With Evvie under constant sedation he said it would probably be all right. Still, he seemed to be harboring some doubts.

"You don't like our having Evvie at the cottage, do you?" she asked.

"Well," he paused, "it's really more that I don't like your having the children there. I just don't think it's right."

"Well, then I'll rent a separate cottage for my mother and Evvie. That'll solve the problem."

Mrs. Straus was incensed when Jenny told her one hot night late in May that she and Evvie were to be installed in a separate house.

"Dr. Cohen insists, mama. It's not good for the children. Particularly the younger ones." She knew mama felt a special fondness for Milty and Herbie—young enough to be manipulated.

"Well, I think it's ridiculous. And where's all this money coming from? Herman and I don't see that kind of profits from the store."

"Mama, I'll take care of it," Jenny said patiently. Surely mama knew that. She just wanted to be reassured.

"You're putting Evvie and me out to pasture," Mrs. Straus accused, her eyes brooding. "Now I'll be alone all summer."

"We'll find a place close by—I promise." Jenny tried not to lose her patience. "You'll come to the house for dinner every night."

"Supper. You start a fancy job, and suddenly it's 'dinner,'" Mrs. Straus said.

Jenny decided to ignore that.

"Sophie told me that Carrie's coming home from school tomorrow. She wants us all to come over for supper tomorrow night."

Mrs. Straus looked bored.

"I guess Carrie didn't meet any special boy at that expensive college yet. Herman expected he'd be giving her a wedding present this summer."

"There's nobody special as far as Sophie knows." Jenny stood up. "I think I'll go up to bed. I'm tired from all this heat."

Jenny had not been looking forward to dinner at Sophie's. But at least Mannie was on the road this week. Whenever Mannie and Herman were together, they usually erupted into shouting matches. And Herman was growing more eccentric with each passing year. But Sophie seemed to have taught herself to ignore him . . . the boys tried to avoid him . . . and Carrie used him.

Watching Carrie tonight Jenny decided that Vassar had improved her niece's disposition. Tonight she was quiet, sweet, causing none of her usual fights with Leon or Helene. As she got older her resemblance to Jenny was startling.

"Jenny," Carrie said softly as the children and she prepared to leave, "will you be in the store around noon tomorrow?"

"Yes." Jenny knew Sophie hated having Carrie call her "Jenny," but Sophie was out in the kitchen wrapping up cookies for Leon and Helene to take home.

"I have to talk to you."

"Of course, Carrie." Jenny was curious. Carrie knew her mother would be away from the store between twelve and one. What did Carrie want to talk about that Sophie wasn't to hear?

The next morning was busy in the store and Jenny forgot about Carrie until she appeared at her office door a few minutes past twelve, after Sophie had left for lunch.

"Can we talk now?" Carrie asked softly, closing the door behind her—taking Jenny's acquiescence for granted.

"Sit down, Carrie," she said briskly. Today she was more wary of this new silken-voiced Carrie.

"Jenny, I'm pregnant."

Jenny went cold.

"Your mother doesn't know?"

Carrie shook her head.

"Well . . . who is this boy? Someone you met at college?"

"He doesn't know either."

"Don't you think you ought to tell him?"

"Why?" Carrie's eyes were beguilingly innocent. "I don't want to marry him."

"Of course you'll marry him. Who is he?"

"When I get married, it'll be somebody rich and important. He's a garage mechanic," she said with distaste. "He told me he went to Yale and came to Poughkeepsie for weekends because his folks lived there. He was always driving a swell car—how could I know he was lying?"

"Carrie, why did you come to me?"

"Because you'll know how I can get rid of it," Carrie told her. "I'm not going to have anybody's baby at my age."

Suddenly Jenny remembered Nicky's remark that one girl in ten at Carrie's age carried condoms in her vanity. *Why hadn't Carrie?*

"Carrie, if you've been sleeping with a boy, you've got to expect the consequences."

"I thought we were being careful." She shrugged. "I guess we got too carried away one time."

"You'll have to tell your mother."

"No." Their eyes met. "Mama doesn't have to know. Papa says you knew all those whores at Storyville. They'll tell you where I can find a doctor to take care of me."

"You'll have to discuss that with your mother." Jenny recoiled from Carrie's cold-blooded attitude toward her pregnancy. Imagine . . . barely a woman and already she's ready for an abortion.

"Jenny, please—you won't want mama to get all upset. You know how awful she'll take this. She'll be just sick."

"And what about you?" Jenny challenged. "Would it mean nothing to you to have an abortion?"

"I'll be smarter next time," Carrie said coolly. "Can't you just hear mama and papa and grandma carrying on if I had to tell them? I wouldn't marry him even if he wanted to. And I'll bet he wouldn't. He'd say it was somebody else's."

"Well, could it be?" Jenny hated herself for asking.

"I don't keep score, Jenny, if that's what you mean." Carrie's smile was defiant. But beneath her bravado, Jenny caught a glimmer of fear . . . "Don't you know, Jenny? My generation is out to live and let live. We don't ask questions—we just have fun."

"How far along are you?"

"About ten weeks. I figured I ought to finish out the school term. Papa would die if I didn't—all that money wasted."

Carrie was right, of course. Why should she subject Sophie to this kind of anguish if it wasn't necessary? Nobody could make Carrie do anything she didn't want to do and if she didn't find a decent doctor to perform an abortion, Jenny worried about what steps Carrie might take on her own.

"I don't like this, Carrie—"

"I'm not asking you to like it." Now Jenny felt Carrie's desperation. "Just send me to a doctor. Please—I've got the money . . ."

Two mornings later Jenny reluctantly drove Carrie to a private sanitarium where a competent staff performed abortions on some of New Orleans' most expensive whores—as well as some of its wealthy matrons. She sat in a well-furnished reception room while Carrie was ushered into one of a series of treatment rooms.

"You could come back later," the nurse said sympathetically.

"No, that's all right—I'll wait." Now that she was here, she was terrified of some slipup. How could she face Sophie if anything happened to Carrie?

It seemed hours before Carrie, pale and shaky, emerged.

"She'll be all right," the nurse said, an arm around Carrie's waist. "Just make sure she takes it easy for a couple of days."

Carrie and Jenny walked out to the car in silence.

"How do you feel, Carrie?

"It hurt," Carrie said in resentment. "He said it wouldn't."

"Nobody will be home now." The boys would not be out of school for two more hours. "Go straight to bed and stay there until dinner time. You can say the heat made you feel a little sick."

"Thanks, Jenny—I knew you'd come through." Jenny flinched at the arrogance behind Carrie's smile. "I knew I could depend on my dear old Aunt Jenny."

"I think the nurse thought you were my sister," Jenny said, smiling dryly. "And don't expect me to come through again, young lady. This is it. Next time you get caught, go to your father."

CHAPTER
TWENTY-EIGHT

THE SUMMER SPED past. Leon began his senior year at high school and Jenny's thoughts were full of plans for his college years. Leon threw himself into his studies, determined to pass the entrance examinations for Harvard.

As always, on Rosh Hashanah and Yom Kippur, Mannie and Herman forgot their differences and, with their sons, went together to the synagogue. After the services the two men and the boys joined the women at what was still called "Mama's house" for the post Yom Kippur dinner. Three generations sat down at a true groaning board. Jenny was sadly conscious of Evvie's empty chair.

Danny—walking with a barely perceptible limp and without crutches, had come home for the High Holidays, along with Felice and their adopted baby. But for Yom Kippur, Danny had gently rejected mama's insistence that he come again—alone. He was needed at the store and at home. His son, adopted from the Touro Orphanage, was taking his first steps.

Over dinner that night Jenny watched Leon's discomfort while his father boasted to Herman that there was no chance his son would be turned down at Harvard. It was as though Leon felt he had to be accepted or his parents would lose face in the eyes of his uncle. After all, Carrie was in her sophomore year at Vassar.

While Annie Lou and Dora cleared the table, the family sat in the parlor, Herman and Mannie already settling down to a pinochle game. The children went out to the back gallery for another helping of ice cream. Jenny watched

Leon walk out onto the wide front gallery. She followed him.

Here, the late September heat was somewhat less oppressive. Faint sounds of music drifted up from Evvie's little cottage—they had discovered that phonograph records soothed her whenever she became restless. The night air was sweet with the scent of roses and jasmine.

"Leon," Jenny said gently, "I can tell you're upset. What is it?"

"Why does papa have to carry on like that about my going to Harvard? Suppose I don't pass the examinations?" His fear touched and angered Jenny. Why did Mannie subject him to this?

"Leon . . ." she took his arm and turned him to face her. "If you don't pass, it won't be the end of the world." This was the tranquil mother she always sought to appear with the children. A flicker of guilt crossed her mind as she realized that she, too, hoped Leon would go to Harvard—because for three years Marc had been there. "Leon, you'll go to a good school," she said encouragingly. "You're bright and hard-working. Perhaps you'd like to go to Tulane, right here at home."

"No," Leon snapped. "I want to live on campus."

"Then you'll go away to college," Jenny said. "Wherever you decide, my darling." This she could give her son. Leon and Helene were what made her life worth living. "And if you decide to go to Harvard Business School afterward, that'll be fine, too."

"That's what I have in mind. I'd like to come into the business," he said seriously. "Summers while I'm at school I'd like to go out and work in a major department store to learn how they operate." His face was alight with a fervor she recognized. "I have so many crazy ideas about running a large store."

"Well, then, next vacation you'll work at Goldman's." She loved Leon's enthusiasm. "I haven't mentioned this to anyone, but I may be in a position to buy Goldman's Department Store. They're floundering badly. I'd like to take over the store, change its policy, its image—put it on its feet again. For Aunt Sophie's boys and you. I think

Helene will one day come into Maison Jennie. Together we'll build a merchandising dynasty." She saw her own excitement reflected in Leon. "Imagine, Leon . . . a nationwide chain of Maison Jennie stores . . . something that would have made your grandfather very happy."

The following day, churning with enthusiasm for this new project, Jenny met Mrs. Goldman for lunch. Jenny told her what she had been hearing about Goldman's troubles.

"I know." Mrs. Goldman looked tired. "Thank God, the family doesn't depend on the store for a living. It's the real estate today that counts."

"The rumor around town is that the store is to be put up for sale. Would it upset you if I make an offer?"

"No, Jenny." Mrs. Goldman's voice was tender. "There's nobody I would rather see taking over the store than you. But it will be sad for me to see the Goldman name no longer on a big department store in New Orleans."

"It'll remain Goldman's Department Store," Jenny said, shocked that Mrs. Goldman could believe otherwise. "Your husband and you built yourselves a permanent memorial in this city. The name of a memorial never changes."

"Jenny." Tears filled the indomitable old lady's eyes. "With you I have found myself another granddaughter."

With Leon and Helene Jenny went to Palm Beach between Christmas and New Year's for an annual check of the Poinciana and Palm Beach stores. It gave her a special pleasure to see the warmth between Leon and Helene and young Charlie, and she found herself wishing that they could know Charlie was their half brother. She saw this same wish in Vivian's eyes.

Vivian was doing a wonderful job with the Palm Beach shops and Jenny decided that in another year or two she would send Vivian to Paris to buy. How ironic that Mannie had brought her the most valuable member of the Maison Jennie staff.

While she and Nicky planned the New York and Paris buying jaunt, Jenny was confident word would come that Marc and Simone would be away. As she expected, Marc wrote that he and Simone were leaving for a three month tour of the Far East. He was hoping the trip would lift her spirits. So, the Paris house would be again at their disposal.

Carrie wrote, pleading with Jenny to take her along this year. She was bored with school and she had no intention of finishing out the term.

Troubled, Jenny went to Sophie with the letter.

"You're not taking her, Jenny," Sophie said bitterly. "Nothing satisfies that girl. She's failing all her courses—and you know how bright she is. Herman told her she's got to finish out the school year. She's forever writing him for money—and he sends it to her. Carrie gets everything she wants—and the boys get nothing."

"They've got you, Sophie. That's all they need."

As soon as she was back from Paris, Jenny focused on Leon's graduation in late May. Since she was the only one of the Straus children who had not been graduated from high school, this was a most important occasion, as important as the day when they would know if Leon had been accepted at Harvard.

As on the graduation of Karl and Carrie—and just last week, of Frederic—the whole family gathered to attend. Danny and Felice, along with their toddler son, came down for a quick three-day visit. Nicky and Armand would be there. Mrs. Goldman, too. Afterward there would be a party for the family.

Jenny personally inspected Leon's suit, his shirt, his shoes—today he was to look perfect.

"Darling, you look so handsome." She hugged him while Helene sighed in mock disgust from the doorway. "All right, let's go out to the car."

The three of them went downstairs. Mannie stood at the door, tapping his foot.

"Where's mama?" Jenny asked in surprise.

"She says she ain't going," Mannie reported, overly casual, but Jenny saw the fury in his eyes.

"Why not?" She tried to keep her voice even.

"Evvie's restless. She says she's gotta sit with her." He pulled the door open. "Come on, let's go."

"Wait a minute. I want to be sure Annie Lou has everything set for the party." Jenny hurried down the hall and out to the kitchen.

She *knew* Dora and Annie Lou were ready for the party. Dora had been baking for two days. But she didn't want the children to see how hurt and angry she was that their grandmother had elected to sit at home on the night of her grandson's graduation. Even on Leon's bar mitzvah she had managed to be busy . . .

She dallied briefly in the kitchen. Despite Prohibition, champagne was being chilled. Annie Lou and Dora were bustling proudly about in fresh, starched white uniforms, determined that everything would be just right for their "baby's" party.

Jenny joined the others in the car. From Evvie's cottage they could hear the drone of Mrs. Straus's voice. How could mama ignore her grandchild's accomplishment this way?

They found their seats in the auditorium, a sea of palmetto fans on this hot night. Sophie, Herman and the three younger boys were seated right behind them. Jenny waved to Nicky, Armand, Mrs. Goldman and the children when she spied them coming down the aisle. She had saved seats for them.

Jenny didn't hear the speeches . . . and she only had eyes for Leon. Occasionally she reached over and squeezed Helene's hand. Times like tonight made up for the bad ones.

After the ceremony they piled into cars and headed for the house. While everyone milled about the lower floor, laughing and talking, Jenny waited for her mother to appear. Finally, Evvie's nurse came over to relay the message that Mrs. Straus was spending the night in the cottage.

Grumbling that tomorrow was a working day, Herman insisted on leaving early with Sophie and the boys. Leon brought out the parchesi board and pieces and settled down to play with Helene, Louis and Stephanie.

Jenny was happy to relax over iced tea and talk with Nicky and Armand while Mrs. Goldman reminisced with Mannie about the days when her late husband had been a peddler in the Louisiana farm country. Mannie had peddled in Arizona and he was impressed that Mrs. Goldman had come to see Leon graduate and had come to the house afterward. Tonight Mannie was being almost civil, Jenny thought with amazement. Prematurely . . .

"In the old days the wives knew their places," he said loudly. Jenny stiffened. "You stayed home and raised your children. You didn't worry about being a big shot in the business."

Jenny saw Helene flush in anger, forgetting the parchesi game. Leon whispered nervously to her.

"Mr. Adler, I worked beside my husband in the store for thirty-five years," Mrs. Goldman said quietly. "I wasn't needed at home to cook and clean and watch the children. I delegated that to the help. My husband agreed that I belonged in the store, where I could make a real contribution to the family. When he was peddling, I stayed home. When he opened the store, I was right beside him. And my children didn't suffer for it."

His face flushed, Mannie rose to his feet.

"I have to make an early train in the morning," he mumbled. His train left at noon, Jenny remembered. "Goodnight, Mrs. Goldman."

Without bothering to say goodnight to Nicky and Armand he stalked out of the parlor. Stricken at Mannie's rudeness, anxious to puncture the awkward silence, Jenny reached for the iced tea pitcher.

"Let me bring in more iced tea," she said with synthetic cheerfulness. "This is getting all watered down." *How could Mannie be such a boor!*

"It's time an old lady went home and to bed," Mrs. Goldman said with a smile, pulling herself to her feet. "Jenny, it's been a wonderful evening."

Leon and Helene left the parchesi game and came forward eagerly to say goodnight. At least they'd enjoyed the party, Jenny consoled herself.

"Leon," Mrs. Goldman said, "I know you'll pass the examinations and go on to Harvard. My grandson Marc went to Harvard for three years." She chuckled. "He didn't go back for the fourth year, but he's done all right."

Jenny and the children accompanied Mrs. Goldman and the Lazars to their car. There were kisses all around, then Jenny and the children walked back into the house. She noticed that the cottage was dark already. Mama and Evvie had gone to sleep.

Protesting he wasn't sleepy, Leon went reluctantly upstairs to his room. Jenny knew he'd fall asleep the minute his head hit the pillow. Annie Lou and Dora had already retired. Jenny and Helene would wash the iced tea glasses and the spoons.

"Mama, why don't you divorce him?" Helene's anger exploded in the silent kitchen.

"Helene—" Jenny stared in dismay.

"You don't have to stay married to him. You're beautiful and smart—a lot of men would want to marry you. Why *do* you stay married to him?"

"Helene, you shouldn't talk that way," Jenny stammered. Did Leon feel this way, too? She had tried to give her children everything—but it wasn't within her power to give them a father they could respect.

"I don't care if he is my father," Helene said defiantly. "He's not nice. He's—he's crude." Somewhere Helene must have heard someone say that, Jenny thought in pain.

"Darling, marriage is supposed to be forever," she said lamely. "Wives and husbands have to learn to compromise—"

"Wives divorce their husbands these days. And not just actresses, either. Even a girl in my class—her mother divorced her father last year. And she got married again," Helene wound up triumphantly.

"Helene, we're not going to talk about this anymore. How would you like another sliver of Dora's strawberry shortcake? Everyone said it was delicious."

"All right." Helene was philosophical—a sliver of strawberry shortcake would be a minor consolation.

How could she divorce Mannie, Jenny asked herself as she sliced into the creamy shortcake. For mama that would be the last straw. First Danny, with his injury, then Evvie . . . how could she give mama another terrible blow?

* * *

A week after Leon's graduation Carrie came home from Vassar. She refused to go to the lake house this summer and when her mother suggested she help her father in the store—as Frederic was doing until he started college in the fall—she laughed.

"Mama, you can't expect me to work in that awful place. Not the class of trade papa caters to." She wrinkled her nose in distaste. "After a whole year of school I have a right to have some fun."

Sipping ice-cold Cokes one steamy June morning in the store, Sophie confided to Jenny that she was worried about Carrie. Apparently the girl slept all day and disappeared in the evenings with her rich young friends from her private-school days.

"Jenny, what can I do? She comes home at all hours of the night. I don't know where they go, what they do . . ."

Jenny understood Sophie's concern. Everybody was talking about this generation's lack of morals—their "petting parties," their devotion to the new "speakeasies" and the bathtub gin, their loud approval of "trial marriage." It was a bit unnerving, especially since Carrie was given to trying any new fad.

"I gave up trying to wait up for Carrie, Jenny. What's the use? Whenever I try to ask questions, she just tosses her head and walks away."

"Sophie, maybe it's just a phase. Is she going back to school in the fall?"

"She's leaving it up in the air because if she says she isn't, then Herman will talk to her about finding a job. This way she feels free as a bird." Sophie laughed grimly. "Oh—and now she's got a new bee in her bonnet. Her friend Denise—the one whose father is putting up that new bank building—is going to Paris in August. Instead of college Denise's father is giving her six months in Europe. Of course Carrie wants to go with her."

"I can't imagine Herman going for that," Jenny said. Sophie smiled.

"All he remembers is how desperate he was to get away from Europe—and now his daughter is dying to go there.

But the Europe Carrie wants to see is the one that Herman never knew. All the young people listen to these stories about the wild living in postwar Paris. I think it's wild enough right here."

By the end of June Jenny had finalized the arrangements to buy Goldman's Department Store. Already Leon was working there as a stock boy. She offered to find a place for Carrie in the store, but Carrie balked at the idea of working.

"Carrie just wants to lie around all day and run around all night," Sophie complained on a Saturday drive up to the lake house. "She can't bear to leave the city even for the weekend."

"Next week I'm going to have a talk with her," Herman's voice came from the back seat, startling Jenny and Sophie—they had thought he and Freddie were asleep. "She's gotta know her father ain't a millionaire."

On Sunday, while Jenny went boating with Helene and the boys, Sophie sat with their mother and Evvie. In the evening she brought Mrs. Straus to the house for dinner.

"Where's Carrie?" Mrs. Straus demanded, as she did every week. "Children today have no respect for their elders. Didn't you tell her that I wanted to see her?"

Jenny was relieved when Herman suggested they drive back Sunday evening rather than waiting until early Monday morning. She knew it was absurd, but she felt a kind of peace when she was in New Orleans—and mama was forty miles away, at the lake.

She dropped Sophie, Herman and Freddie off at their house and drove home. The house was dark. Just as she opened the door, the phone began to ring. She ran to answer it.

"Hello?"

"I called the lake house and they said you were coming home. What took you so long?" It was Carrie.

"It took the normal length of time, Carrie. Where are you?"

"Jenny, I need a lawyer . . . I'm in jail. It's crazy! Denise and I went out on a boat with these two fellows she met at a party. We didn't know they were bringing in booze on the boat. Now the police are saying we're accomplices!" She sounded like a scared little girl.

"Exactly where are you, Carrie?" Jenny realized she must be afraid to call Herman.

Jenny made a note of the police station and promised to call Armand immediately.

"Please, Jenny, don't tell mama."

"Carrie, don't be ridiculous—your mother has to know. If you're not involved, Armand will get you off."

First Jenny phoned Armand. He listened, then told her he'd dress and go directly to the police station. Now Jenny prepared herself to phone Sophie—she couldn't protect her from the truth any longer. It was enough that she had seen Carrie through the abortion; even now, she wondered if she'd been right to hide the truth from her sister.

She took a deep breath, picked up the phone and dialed.

"Hello, Sophie? It's me, Jenny. Now, don't panic. I'm sure it's just a misunderstanding, but, well, Carrie's in jail—"

"Jail?" Sophie's voice soared. "Herman, come here quick."

"I've talked to Armand, Sophie. He's already on his way over."

"Here's Herman, tell him where she is."

Jenny explained the situation to Herman, knowing how difficult this must be. Nobody in their families had ever been in jail, not even for an hour.

"Herman, let me talk to Sophie again."

"We're leaving right now," Sophie said.

"Would you like me to meet you there?"

"No . . . you go to bed, darling. This isn't your responsibility. We're the parents. We'll take care of this."

CHAPTER
TWENTY-NINE

As THEY DROVE away from the police station, Carrie clung to a corner of the back seat of the car. She could tell by the set of her father's head as he drove that she wouldn't be able to cry her way out of this situation. But it wasn't her fault, damn it. How could she knew they were running rum into New Orleans on the boat?

God, she wished she had a cigarette! Or a dry martini. Why did it have to end the way it did? Just when she was feeling so *good*. Seth had been telling her how gorgeous she was. From the minute they got on the boat he couldn't keep his hands off her He'd already had her down to her teddy when the police boat came. She'd been ready to go through the ceiling.

The car turned into their driveway.

"I'm fifty-four years old," her father said quietly as he stopped the car and reached for the door, "and nobody—nobody in my family ever saw the inside ot a jail."

"Papa, it wasn't my fault. Why can't you understand? Denise's father understands. He's even threatened to sue for false arrest."

"Let Denise's father sue," Herman shot back. Mama wasn't saying a thing, she noted, watching her mother walk ahead of them into the house. It was so hard sometimes to know what mama was thinking.

"Papa, we just went out with them because we were bored. Denise's father was very sympathetic. He said she can go to Paris as soon as he can get reservations for her—provided she can find a girl friend to go along. Janie Adams was supposed to go with her, but now she's engaged to this boy she met in Paris last summer, and he's coming over to meet her parents."

"She met a boy in Paris?" Her father handed Sophie the door-key. "She talks good French?"

"He's English." Carrie continued the fabrication. "Paris is just packed with rich English and American boys these summers. Why do you think so many American college girls go over there every summer?"

"How do you know a boy is rich or just a bum?" he challenged.

"Papa, that's easy," Carrie giggled. "The kind of clothes he wears. What kind of car he says he drives back home. It doesn't matter where he lives—students make a thing of living cheap in Paris. You wouldn't believe how far the American dollar goes there."

Carrie made a bet with herself that by tomorrow night this time she'd be able to call Denise and say she could go with her to Paris. Denise was telling her father she was dying to go to Paris because Carrie was going. Denise's father would let her go; he'd be glad to have her away from the city for a few months so he could run around with flappers half his age.

Jenny was nervous when Sophie came into the store on Tuesday morning to report that, wonder of wonders, Herman had agreed to finance Carrie in Paris for six months.

"She told him it was a wonderful way to perfect her French." Sophie smiled dryly. "She could do that with a job in the French Quarter. Herman figures it's cheaper than a year at Vassar, and maybe she'll find herself a rich American husband over there."

"How do *you* feel about Carrie's going to Paris?" Jenny was nervous at the thought of Carrie in Paris, away from all parental restraint—or rescue.

"It scares me to death," Sophie confessed. "But Carrie has a way of doing that wherever she is."

"Karl leaves for Paris in a few weeks, doesn't he?" Like Sophie, Jenny was proud of Karl—he had done so well at art school in New York that his instructors had encouraged further study in Paris.

"He's going next month. On the *Homeric*." Sophie smiled at Jenny's start of surprise. "I know—this summer is just running past. He's going with a friend from the Art Students League. He's already written to Nicky's brother. That's all right, isn't it?"

"Of course," Jenny said quickly. "Marc said he'd be happy to help Karl in any way he can. But tell Karl not to be surprised if he doesn't hear from Marc for a while—he and his wife are forever traveling somewhere."

Lately she had been worried that Marc was sacrificing his career now to chase around the globe with Simone, but between trips he managed to produce works that won praise from the critics.

Already she caught herself looking forward to her next trip to Paris. Much as she told herself she shouldn't see Marc again, she longed for the sight of his face, the sound of his voice. Palm Beach seemed years ago.

The reshaping of Goldman's required a great deal of work, but she was grateful for the distraction. Leon was accepted at Harvard, which thrilled her, of course. But she dreaded the separation. The summer that Freddie and he had spent at camp in Maine had seemed endless.

Now that he had decided to let Carrie go to Paris with Denise, Herman became more insufferable than ever. He boasted about his son studying in Paris, his daughter improving her French in Paris. A meal with Herman and Mannie trying to outdo each other was an exhausting experience.

Freddie was at Tulane. He seemed happy to be fulfilling his father's wish to have a lawyer in the family. Already Milty and Herbie were working after school at Goldman's, now "Aunt Jenny's store" and they seemed to have accepted a future in merchandising.

"Milty and Herbie have good business heads," Sophie told Jenny. "At last the children seem to know where they're going in life. Karl in art, Freddie in law, Milty and Herbie in business. Carrie will get tired of Paris, come home and marry. We've done all right by our children, Jenny."

* * *

Tourists had told them September was a beautiful month in Paris, Carrie recalled while she toyed with a vermouth cassis and waited for Denise on the *terrasse* of the Café du Dome. The sun was caressingly warm, and the chestnut trees cast gentle shadows on the boulevard. But in September the American college boys went home.

For two weeks now the ranks of college boys in Montparnasse had been thinning. For a while she and Denise had a ball with a parade of good-looking, heavy drinking boys who were willing to try anything and everything. Carrie giggled, remembering the boy from North Canton, Ohio, who had been happy to take on both Denise and her—until he discovered that Denise wanted everything they'd read about in the porno books . . .

"Honey, you don't need a man, you need a machine," he had said, utterly exhausted.

Carrie was growing bored with their sleazy fifth floor attic "studio" apartment—hot in the summer and probably freezing in the winter. But one of the stipulations of their staying in Paris for six months had been to "live cheap"— the checks from home provided for nothing better.

She and Denise should be staying at the Ritz or the Crillon or the Meurice . . . driving in the Bois de Boulogne in a white Hispano-Suiza . . . lunching at Sherry's, dining at Ciro's, listening to midnight music and a drink at Harry's . . .

"Waiting long?" Denise asked breathlessly, sinking into a chair across from Carrie.

"Too long." She jiggled her silk-stockinged crossed leg impatiently.

"Sorry, American Express was crowded. But I got the check from home. Shall we go to the Ritz bar again?" Her eyes glinted mischievously. Yesterday they had gone to the Ritz and been picked up by two Americans in their early thirties who claimed they were writers. After three drinks they had serenaded the girls with a maudlin rendition of "If You Would Care for Me." Both had been disasters in bed.

"No," Carrie said, "tonight we're accepting my brother's offer to take us to a real classy party."

"Carrie, your brother?" Denise said, frowning. "All Karl ever thinks or talks about is painting. What kind of party can he take us to?"

"Karl is kind of a protégé of this artist from back home. Marc Goldman. He's famous now. His sister and my aunt are best friends. His wife used to be a countess. Karl says they have a wonderful old house on Rue Marignan. She's awfully rich—"

"Then we'll go," Denise said exuberantly. "I'm so tired of hungry students and artists with no money. Maybe they'll have champagne. I used to think that in Paris people drank nothing but champagne." She frowned. "Do they speak English? Some of the French we picked up since we got here isn't for polite society."

"Marc Goldman come from New Orleans, silly . . . and his wife speaks several languages. Don't these French make you feel gauche when all you speak is English and *un peu* of their language?" She had barely passed French at Vassar.

Denise laughed.

"Sugar, in bed there's only one language."

Carrie dressed with care for the party at the Goldman house. None of her knee-length dresses tonight . . . For this she would wear the simple little mauve dress that Jenny had given her to wear to student-faculty affairs. Mama had said it cost a fortune. She had considered cutting it in the back for the backless look, but then she figured she'd need one outfit that wouldn't shock mama's generation.

She suspected that her father had written to Karl with orders to see that she met some "nice boys." She had little interest in the boys that Karl would know; they'd probably be as nutty as he was. But she might meet somebody fascinating at that kind of party.

"Denise, you cannot wear that smoking suit," Carrie objected as Denise came out of the bedroom. "You look like a character in *The Sheik*."

"What's so bad about that?" Denise pouted.

"Sweetie, Marc Goldman's wife is from an old French family. We're supposed to be chic, not shocking."

Twenty minutes early, Karl, breathless from the climb, knocked on the door.

"You're early," Carrie complained, puffing on a Gauloise.

"You're dressed," he said, obviously relieved. He had been worried that she might wear one of her flapper dresses.

"What are these parties like?" Denise—dressed to Carrie's satisfaction now in a simple black, strapless gown—seemed to be having second thoughts about an "old French family" party.

"It's the first party Countess Simone has given since I've been here," Karl said. "I've had dinner with them a few times."

"Karl," Carrie stubbed out her cigarette impatiently. "She's not a countess anymore. She's married to Marc Goldman from New Orleans."

"In Paris she's still Countess Simone," Karl insisted. "A very elegant lady."

"A very rich lady." Carrie laughed. "Which is probably why Marc Goldman married her. I heard mama say once that she's twenty years older than he is."

"Look, Carrie, you behave," Karl warned. "Mr. Goldman and his wife have been awfully nice to me. Aunt Jenny will be furious if she hears you put on one of your crazy acts."

"Of course I'll behave, Karl," Carrie drawled. "I wouldn't want to upset dear old Aunt Jenny."

Karl splurged and took them to the party in a taxi instead of by the metro. It was mean of Jenny never to take her to Paris when she came to buy, Carrie thought vindictively. What did Paris mean to silly little Helene?

Jenny and Nicole Lazar probably went everywhere when they were here. Papa said Jenny was one of the richest women in the state, though she'd never admit it. Pure luck, papa said, that Jenny piled up all that money.

She refused to admit she was impressed as she heard Karl talking in French with the taxi driver. "Come on," he said with a hit of nervousness.

"It's not chic to be early at a party," Denise snapped.

"We're not early," Karl said. "We're on time. And in France people don't try to arrive late at parties."

Carrie begrudgingly admired Marc's and Simone's four-story earlier-century mansion. Walking into the huge marble-floored foyer, lighted by an ornate crystal chandelier, she imagined herself as the mistress of such a house. Priceless antiques flanked the entrance to each room, the walls were adorned with old masters, the rugs, the thick Aubusson that Jenny was mad about. From Denise's expression it seemed that she, too, was suddenly impressed with this very different Paris from the one they knew.

"Karl, how are you?" A tall, dark-haired, mellow-voiced man had separated himself from a cluster of elegantly dressed men and women and was coming toward Karl with outstretched hands. *This was Marc Goldman?* She had not expected him to be so handsome. She had thought he would look older.

"Mr. Goldman," Karl said stiffly, "the countess said it would be all right to bring some friends—"

"Of course," Marc smiled, turning to Denise and Carrie. For an instant he stared at Carrie in disbelief. "You must be Jenny's niece," he said quietly. "You're the image of her."

Carrie flushed, thrilled at the attention.

"Everybody says that. I'll take it as a compliment, Mr. Goldman." She had forgotten that Jenny had met Marc in Paris.

"And this is Denise Freeman, Carrie's friend," Karl said. Marc turned to exchange a few words with her.

Carrie surveyed the scene. These all must be rich, important people—Marc Goldman's family back in New Orleans was rich; but not this kind of rich. That was probably why he'd married the older woman. He hadn't been famous then.

"Simone, come meet Karl's sister and her friend," Marc called, and Carrie focused on a tall, thin woman in black crepe and diamonds coming toward them. Twenty years ago she must have been beautiful. Now she was painfully slim, but expertly made up.

Within minutes Carrie lost her initial self-consciousness. Now she was the vivacious starry-eyed young Southern beauty who adored Paris. Most of the guests, as she had suspected, were bilingual. The men, as always, were attentive and admiring. With her scant understanding of the language, much of the conversation went over her head; but with her looks, she told herself, it didn't matter.

As the evening progressed she decided to focus her attentions on Marc and his wife. It would be fun to be part of their world—for a little while, anyway. Instinctively she knew that her resemblance to Jenny would be an asset. It annoyed her that Marc questioned her so thoroughly about Jenny. Why did he admire her so? Maybe there had been something between them . . . She remembered they had met in Palm Beach the first time Jenny went out there. No, that was ridiculous—Jenny was too much of a prude to let any man come near her. In New Orleans she brushed them off like flies.

At the end of the evening, Simone invited Carrie and Denise to lunch at Sherry's early the following week. Clearly the countess found the two young American girls charming.

"What are you up to with Marc Goldman and the countess?" Denise asked curiously once they were back in their flat. "Dripping all that Southern charm."

"Let's see how the rich Parisians live," Carrie shrugged. "Marc and his wife are loaded. Let them spend some of it on us."

Denise laughed.

"They'll get bored fast enough, I promise you—but I guess it'll be fun while it lasts. I've had enough Montmartre bistros to last me forever."

"He's awfully good looking," Carrie said with a coy smile. "You don't suppose he is faithful to her?"

"I never supposed," Denise said bluntly, faintly alarmed. "Carrie, don't try to start up something with Mr. Goldman. He's old enough to be your father—"

"He's fifteen years younger than my father. And I bet they don't sleep together."

"Your father and Marc Goldman?"

"Silly," Carrie chided. "Marc and Simone." Let Karl call him Mr. Goldman—to her he was already Marc.

"She looks as though she'd break in two if anybody blew

hard at her. But she does have a kind of indestructible class."

"Maybe they'll take us to see Mistinguett one night," Carrie said smugly. "I can tell the countess thinks I'm terribly sweet. If I look wistful, where do you bet she'll take us?"

Denise looked uncomfortable.

"I think you've got ideas that you ought to dump."

"Why? Because I think Marc's good looking? I've never made love with a forty-year-old man." Her eyes glinted in speculation. "I'll bet he knows everything in the book."

"Ugh . . . it would be like going to bed with your father."

"I don't feel very daughterly toward Marc Goldman. I think he's a challenge. And you know me, Denise. I can never pass up a challenge."

During the next few weeks Carrie spent every waking moment trying to charm Simone and Marc. She was warm, solicitous of Simone's health, knowing that Marc would be grateful, and she was aware of the way he watched her as she concocted some outrageous story to amuse Simone. She waited in growing irritation for him to contrive a way to see her alone, but she knew she excited him—it would just take him a little longer to realize it . . .

Early in December, at Harry's Bar, Simone told Carrie and Denise, when Marc went off to exchange a few words with an art critic friend—that she and Marc had decided just that morning to go off the next day for two weeks in Antibes.

"Marc thinks I need some sun after these past dreary weeks."

Carrie looked at her most beguilingly forlorn.

"We'll miss you."

"Would you like to stay at the house for the two weeks Marc and I are away?" Simone asked impulsively.

"We'll adore it!"

"What would you adore?" Marc, back in his seat, kissed Simone on the cheek.

"I just suggested that Carrie and Denise stay at our house

while we're away, darling. I thought they might enjoy a change of scene."

"I think that's a fine idea." For an instant he seemed disconcerted. "The staff's on duty anyway."

"Nicky and Jenny told us what a magnificent house you had, Marc," Carrie said, "but they didn't do it justice."

"Be at the house before noon tomorrow," Marc said, "so I can introduce you to the servants. You won't have to worry about a thing—they're in charge. Claudette even plans the meals. Just tell her when you like breakfast to be served and what time you'll be home for dinner."

Marc and Simone dropped the girls off at their studio. Tomorrow night, Carrie thought, we won't be climbing these narrow, murky stairs to our dingy little attic—we'll be sleeping in that gorgeous house on Rue Marignan.

"Carrie, can you believe the countess invited us to stay at her house?" Denise bubbled, breathless at the top of the stairs. "It's like living in a palace."

"It's kind of old-fashioned," Carrie shrugged. "If I owned it, I'd bring in Elsie de Wolfe to liven it up."

Carrie and Denise arrived at the house at eleven-thirty, each having brought only one suitcase—they could always run back to the studio if they ran out of clothes, Carrie pointed out.

Carrie was determined to have a moment alone with Marc. While Denise followed Simone on a tour of the bedrooms she went downstairs with him to meet the servants. Again she envisioned herself as the mistress of this house. When was Marc going to loosen up and kiss her? He had that hungry passionate look . . . Simone must be blind not to notice.

Maybe when Marc and Simone returned from Antibes, she'd ask him to go shopping with her to buy a present for papa. If they were alone, away from the house, he would be able to relax. She would take him up to the studio—when Denise was away, of course—for a glass of wine. It shouldn't be hard to get him into bed.

After Carrie had been introduced to the staff, Marc went off to tell François to bring around the car, and Carrie asked

Simone to come downstairs. At last, in a flurry of warm farewells, Marc and Simone left for the Gâre Saint Lazare.

"My mother will never believe this when I tell her," Denise said exuberantly. "We'll be living here for two whole weeks."

"Denise, it's time you stopped being the wide-eyed co-ed," Carrie said primly. "We've moved beyond college boys."

After the two girls had been served lunch, they had François take them for a drive through the Bois de Boulogne. It might not be a Hispano-Suiza, but a Renault limousine was pretty snazzy. They returned to the house and went up to their bedrooms to unpack, only to find that a maid had already unpacked and meticulously pressed each outfit.

"Back home Laura never unpacked for our guests," Denise said, wide-eyed. "But mama does always send her up to press."

They never had guests, Carrie mused. Not in all the years she was growing up did she ever remember anybody coming to stay with them. It would be fun to invite people to stay in a house like this—especially knowing they were just dying of envy.

Simone thought Karl was a fine boy, and had suggested they have him over for dinner several times while were away. She worried that he was so wrapped up in his painting he would forget to eat properly.

He arrived for dinner sharply at eight, ate quickly and rushed off to meet some of his art-student friends at a cheap bistro, where they'd argue half the night about who was the best of the new painters.

"Nobody knows where we are," Denise said self-consciously while they lingered before the fire in the small sitting room and sipped vintage wine.

"We don't want them to know," Carrie said smugly. "Not for now." She wanted to drown in luxury, enjoy every second of this richness without interruption.

"But Carrie, we've only got another five weeks in Paris—"

"Don't worry about that—later we'll worry."

François came into the sitting room to inquire if they wished anything else. The servants were retiring for the night.

"Thank you, no, François," Carrie said, relieved that he spoke English. "We're going upstairs shortly."

Walking up the stairs to her bedroom Carrie recounted in her mind all the American girls who had married European titles . . . Consuelo Vanderbilt had become the Duchess of Marlborough . . . Elsie de Wolfe was now Lady Mendl . . . Gloria Vanderbilt's sister had become Lady Furness. She would be quite happy to be Mrs. Marc Goldman.

Carrie prepared for bed, slipped between the soft silk sheets that Simone fancied. But she was too exhilarated to sleep. After a half hour of lying awake in the darkness, she switched on the lamp and lay back against the mound of pillows . . .

When Simone died Marc would be a very rich widower. And he was so famous—whenever they walked into a restaurant, headwaiters rushed to greet him, people at the tables recognized him . . . Wouldn't it be sensational to go back to New Orleans as his wife?

Restless, she pushed off the covers and got out of bed. All the servants, on the top floor, were asleep. It was just Denise and herself floating around the rest of the house. She reached for the negligee that a maid had placed across the foot of the bed and pulled it on. Something told her that Denise, too, was awake.

She went to Denise's room, knocked and open the door.

"I figured you couldn't sleep either," she giggled at Denise's start of surprise.

"I was thinking about Simone. She's so nice, Carrie. It's awful to think that she's so sick. Marc's terribly worried about her."

"She's been sick for years," Carrie dismissed it—not even to Denise would she confide her plans. "Come on, I'm bored—let's go look around." Denise stared uncomprehendingly. "Around the house, silly. I wonder which bedroom is Marc's?"

"Simone's is next to mine," Denise said, getting up. "She showed it to me. It's pretty luscious—"

"Let's go see."

The two girls poked around Simone's bedroom, both astonished at the array of gowns that hung in the specially designed closet. Not to mention the shoes, the hats, the purses . . .

"She had more clothes than a movie star," Denise said in awe. I'll bet she has as many dresses as Gloria Swanson."

"Where does that door lead?" Carrie pointed across the room. "That must be Marc's bedroom." She was annoyed that their bedrooms adjoined.

"Carrie, I don't think we ought to go in there."

"Don't be ridiculous. Let's go."

I can almost feel Marc in this room, Carrie thought, as she moved slowly toward the bed. She imagined herself seducing Marc beneath that satin bedspread, feeling like a younger Theda Bara . . .

"Carrie," Denise said nervously, "come on. I don't think this is right—let's get out of here."

"Why? The servants are all asleep. I want to look around."

She crossed to a rosewood commode sitting between a pair of tall, narrow windows. Denise stood at another window gazing out into the night.

"It's beginning to drizzle, Carrie."

"It'll stop by morning." Carrie opened a drawer, and began touching the fine silken undergarments piled neatly in stacks. Her fingers felt something hard. Curiously she pulled it from underneath the silken material.

For a moment Carrie thought that the miniature she held in her hand was of her. Then the hairstyle, the dress told her otherwise. It was Jenny, many years ago. How old was she then? Sixteen? Seventeen?

So . . . Marc did know Jenny back in New Orleans. Before Jenny had married Mannie. Before he had married Simone. Marc left Jenny behind and came to Paris, she thought with satisfaction. Obviously Jenny had not been able to hold him.

But she would.

CHAPTER
THIRTY

O<small>N THE DAY</small> that Marc and Simone were scheduled to return from Antibes Carrie dashed around Paris buying fresh flowers for Simone's room. During their absence she had meticulously screened the newspapers in search of small tidbits of social gossip that she knew would amuse Simone. She had decided that the only way to win Marc was to be so charming and kind that Marc would *have* to fall in love with her.

Carrie and François went to the station to meet the train while Denise posed for Karl—fully dressed, he had assured her . . . At the Gâre Saint Lazare she left François in the limousine and went to the arrivals section.

Exactly on time they emerged from the train, porters already reaching for their hand luggage.

"Simone!" Carrie rushed forward. "You look marvelous. That wonderful tan."

"I feel marvelous," Simone said, submitting to a kiss. She didn't look marvelous, Carrie thought. While the tan—so fashionable since favored by Coco Chanel—gave Simone a deceiving touch of color, her cheeks seemed to have sunk to the bones.

"How has Paris survived in our absence?" Marc asked, a hand at Simone's elbow.

Carrie noted a tenseness in Marc as the three of them went out to the waiting limousine. In minutes they were driving through the busy Paris streets toward the house. Earlier this morning Carrie and Denise had moved their things back to the attic studio—now more repulsive than ever to Carrie.

Tired from their journey, Simone went up to her bedroom immediately, but she insisted that Carrie stay and have lunch with Marc. She would have her own luncheon on a tray in bed.

While Marc and Carrie walked into the dining room, a maid came downstairs to express Simone's thanks for the flowers.

"That was thoughtful, Carrie," Marc said. "Simone loves flowers."

As they ate herb omelets and a tomato vinaigrette salad, Marc told them about the trip.

"I think the sun was good for Simone—"

"Marc, I do so admire Simone and you," Carrie said softly. "I mean, you have such a beautiful marriage." She let a little wistfulness creep into her voice. "That's rare, you know. My mother and father barely know the other is alive. And they're forever fighting when they're together. Nasty fighting . . ." She shivered, relishing the sympathy she was evoking in Marc.

"I'm so sorry, Carrie," he said gently.

"They're bitter and cynical," she went on. "When they fight, it's not like with Jenny and her husband—they scream at each other, even in front of the family, but everybody knows they're mad about each other." How upset Marc looked! All these years married to Simone, and he kept that miniature of Jenny hidden away. *But Jenny didn't deserve Marc.* "Half the men in New Orleans are in love with Jenny, and I suppose Mannie's right to be jealous of her. You know how the business takes her away on trips so often. Pasadena. Santa Barbara. San Francisco. New York. Palm Beach. But each time Jenny comes back home, they have the most wonderful reconciliations. Both of them just glow for days after she comes back from a trip."

She smiled to herself. If Marc had any romantic notions about going home and picking up with Jenny again once he was a widower, she'd certainly scotched that, hadn't she?

It was clear that Simone was failing fast. On Christmas Eve she was rushed to the hospital. Every day Carrie came to the hospital to visit with a bunch of fresh violets. The first week it seemed to Carrie that half of Paris came to see Simone. Then the doctors decided that she could only see her husband.

Marc was at the hospital constantly. Occasionally he was sent out to wait in the reception room—usually in mid afternoon, when her doctor arrived. Every afternoon Carrie came to sit with him and ask about Simone. Always with a bunch of violets.

One cold, gray afternoon, shortly after New Year's, Carrie couldn't find Marc in the reception room. The nurse told her that he was with Simone, and from her grave expression she suspected that Simone was critical.

She sat down at the edge of a chair, clutching the violets, aware of the poignant image she presented. She would sit just like this until Marc came down the hall.

She stiffened when she saw Simone's doctor, his face somber, talking briefly with the nurse on duty. She rose to her feet, feeling the drama in the air. Then she spied Marc walking slowly down the hall. His face drawn and pale, his shoulders stooped.

Still clutching the bunch of violets she hurried toward him.

"Marc?"

"She's gone, Carrie," he said gently. "We've lost Simone."

"Oh, Marc. Oh, no." Carrie broke into sobs, clinging to him. "Oh, Marc, I'm so sorry."

Jenny parked before Nicky's house and hurried to the door. She knew that Nicky would not have asked her to leave the store in the middle of the morning unless it was urgent.

Arlette greeted her.

"Miz Nicky is waitin' for you in the dinin' room, Miz Jenny."

Jenny walked quickly down the hall to the sunlit dining room. Nicky sat hunched over a cup of coffee, her eyes red and puffy.

"Nicky, what's happened?"

"It's Simone—" her voice shook. "I just received a cable. She died yesterday afternoon."

"Oh, Nicky—" Jenny sat down beside Nicky. She thought of Simone as she had last seen her. "Poor Marc—"

"He's known a long time that she was desperately ill, of course." Nicky reached for the silver coffee pot to pour for Jenny. "But I'm sure it was a dreadful shock anyway."

"I'm glad I had a chance to meet her in Palm Beach," Jenny said slowly. She remembered Simone's words to her. *"I'm very proud of my husband. But I'm a selfish woman. I wish to keep him beside me for the years I have left in this world."* She had been granted that wish.

"I suspect Marc will be coming home now." Nicky's eyes rested on Jenny. "His career is established. He can paint in New Orleans as well as in Paris. He's told me more than once how much he misses being home."

"We can only wait and see, Nicky." How often she'd dreamed of Marc returning to New Orleans . . . She knew what Nicky was trying to convey without words. At last Marc was free.

"Jenny, people are much more open since the war. Divorce isn't the scandal it used to be."

"Nicky, how can I even think about it at this moment? Simone hasn't been buried yet."

"Forgive me, but I want so desperately to see Marc and you happy."

"Marc will have a great deal to do in these next weeks." Her voice trembled. "Simone's estate is probably large. There'll be papers to be filed, the usual problems." She took a deep breath. "Why don't we wait until we hear what Marc plans to do with his life? Perhaps he'll come home. Perhaps he'll decide to stay in Paris."

"Marc will come home," Nicky said with conviction. "I wish you would at least talk with Armand about a divorce. You won't have to take action right away."

"When we know what Marc plans to do . . ." If he wrote her and said, "Jenny, I still love you, I want to marry you," maybe then she could brace herself to face a divorce. *She could.* After all, she was almost thirty-six years old. All she had known of love was that one summer, and the months they'd stolen since. *It was not enough.*

* * *

Carrie saw Denise, reproachful and hurt, off on the boat-train to LeHavre. Last night she had all but thrown Karl out of the studio when he insisted she had to go home with Denise. Mama had written to him, of course, and told him she refused to come on schedule. She had canceled her return reservations. The money would see her through at least another three months in Paris.

Carrie left the Gâre Saint Lazare and went directly to Marc's house. In the three weeks since Simone's death she had seen him every day. He couldn't bear the personal chores—disposing of Simone's clothes, writing notes of thanks to the countless friends who had sent flowers, sending out announcements of her death to other friends outside of Paris.

When she arrived at the house, François told her that Marc was again conferring with the lawyers. She went into the sitting room that had become her "office" to finish addressing notes. Marc had insisted that she be put on salary as his personal secretary, but she had demurred.

When the lawyers had gone, he came into the sitting room.

"I have to go to the chateau tomorrow," he said regretfully. "I'm putting it up for sale. I have an appointment with the real estate people. They already have a prospective buyer." He sighed. "I'll probably have to stay at least a week."

"Marc, let me go with you. I can help." Marc seemed startled. "Let me be your secretary while you're there," she coaxed. "There must be lots of things I could do."

"It'll be cold and dreary this time of year—"

"I don't mind. I have nothing else to do. Denise left for home this morning. I never see Karl—he's always busy with his painting. I know almost nobody in Paris."

"Well . . ." he wavered, "all right. But only if you let me put you on salary. If you're to be my secretary, it's only fair that you be paid."

"Marc, Simone and you have been so wonderful to me," she protested. "I'd feel awful being paid."

"That's my best offer," he said with a sad smile. "Take it or leave it."

"I'll take it," she said.

"Good. Your first chore as my secretary is to call Monsieur Gabin and tell him I'll be at the chateau for at least a week. If he needs to talk to me, call me there."

"I'll phone him right now."

Later in the day François took her to her studio and waited in the limousine to drive her back to the house with her suitcase. It had been decided that she would stay overnight at the house so they could leave early in the morning. François would drive them to the chateau.

The week that Marc had expected them to remain at the chateau became two. To Carrie's astonishment, Marc did need a secretary of sorts and she felt important making calls for him to Paris, checking with the gallery, with the Paris staff, with his attorney.

Every night they sat down together to dinner. She talked nostalgically about New Orleans and the changes in the city since he had been away. She had been a mere child when he left, but she made it sound as though she could remember all the recent changes in the city that he so missed.

"I am constantly amazed how much you are like Jenny," Marc said over dinner the night before they were to return to Paris. "It's incredible."

"Mama says I'm very much like Jenny was at my age, too—but, of course, she's so marvelously sophisticated and successful now. When she was in Palm Beach last year, some Mideastern ruler absolutely threw himself at her feet. The gossip columns were full of stories about them."

"Let's call it an early night," Marc said, suddenly brusque. Carrie knew it was because of what she'd said about Jenny. "We're leaving first thing in the morning."

"Do you have a deal with those people who're interested in the chateau?" she asked. "I know you're anxious to sell."

"Yes, they're buying it. Completely furnished. They're keeping the servants, thank God. I won't have to worry about that." He managed a wry smile. "You've been quite a help about that."

"I love doing things for you," she said softly, allowing her eyes to betray her. "These have been two wonderful weeks for me."

* * *

After dinner, they each went to their respective rooms. But tonight Marc couldn't sleep. He sat in a leather armchair before the smoldering fire, lost in thought.

Every time he looked at Carrie it was like looking at Jenny—so lovely, so charmingly young and sweet . . . so like Jenny that summer before he sailed for Europe.

He remembered Carrie's eyes when she said to him tonight, *"I love doing things for you. These have been two wonderful weeks for me."* Carrie had some young-girl idea that she was in love with him. He tried to dismiss it. She was just in love with the romance of Paris, wistful that Jenny had become a fascinating, sought-after woman. Pursued by even a Mideastern ruler, he thought, smiling to himself.

These last weeks Simone had insisted on talking about his future. He could hear her voice now . . .

"Darling, it's time for you to stop being an expatriate. When I'm gone, I want you to go home. I want you to remarry. You're young—so much of your life lies ahead of you."

He had meant to go back to New Orleans, not letting himself think about the future, but knowing that somehow Jenny had to be part of his life . . . Nicky had told him Jenny had no marriage, that she stayed married to her husband only out of loyalty to her family, fearful of disgracing them. But since the war divorce had lost its stigma and lately Nicky had been hinting that Jenny was wavering . . .

How could Nicky have allowed him to nurture such a fantasy about Jenny? He had clung to it all these years, seeing only what he wished to see. How little Carrie, so admiring of Jenny—never suspecting how he felt about her—had punctured his fantasy.

In his mind he relived their moments together since he had left New Orleans. How could Jenny have so convincingly pretended to love him—and then run home to those "wonderful reconciliations" with her husband? *Had* she pretended? Could Carrie be mistaken? No—he was no lovesick young boy. It was time to be realistic. With no conception of what it meant to him, Carrie had told the truth. Jenny was her aunt—and they were a close family. The Jenny he remembered no longer existed.

Carrie was determined to make herself indispensable to Marc as he tried to rearrange his life. But the weeks were passing. Papa was writing nasty letters. Carrie herself was growing impatient. Surely soon she would break through Marc's reserve—after all, no man was equal to a designing woman. Hadn't she read that in a novel?

She excited Marc. She saw it in his eyes. He was forty years old—didn't he need a woman in his life? She knew he was not one to pick up girls at the Ritz bar or to go to the "closed houses," as the French called whorehouses.

She stayed for dinner every night, knowing that Marc dreaded eating alone in the house that he had shared with Simone for nineteen years. One night early in March she was startled when Karl, too, appeared at the house, announcing he had been invited for dinner.

"Carrie, why don't you answer mama's letters?" he reproached. "She's worried sick about you."

"I wrote her that I had a job," Carrie said defensively. "You know I'm Marc's secretary." No need to tell Karl that she was making work for herself these days. Marc didn't seem to mind—he liked having her around when he wanted to talk.

"You wrote her seven weeks ago," Karl shot back. "She wants you to come home."

"I'll go when I'm ready." Carrie stared him down. "Here comes Marc," she whispered. "Don't you dare say anything about this."

The three of them went into the dining room and sat at the table. Marc was questioning Karl about his work, making suggestions, clearly pleased with his progress. A daring idea took hold in Carrie's mind. Maybe she shouldn't sit around any longer and wait for Marc to make a move. After all, this was 1922—women didn't have to be shrinking violets . . .

After dinner the three of them sat in the small sitting room before a cozy fire and talked over champagne.

"Karl, you must have friends waiting for you at some bistro," Marc teased affectionately. "I remember how it was when I was your age—don't let us keep you from them."

It amused Carrie that Marc and Karl seemed so close. Karl still called him Mr. Goldman. Now Karl was offering to see her to her studio.

"You go on, Karl. François always drives me home."

After Karl left, Carrie went into the little room that had become her office to get her coat, and with the coat over her arm she came back into the sitting room. Marc sat in his favorite tapestry-covered chair before the fire.

"Marc—" She managed a faint catch in her voice.

"Carrie, what is it?" Instantly Marc was concerned.

"I had a long talk with Karl before you came down to dinner." She crossed the room and stood by his chair. "Marc—" She touched his arm. "My parents are carrying on like crazy. They're insisting I come home right away. I don't want to leave Paris. I don't want to leave you!"

"Carrie," he said gently, "you knew that you'd have to go home soon."

"But I want to stay with you. Don't you understand? I'm in love with you—"

"Carrie—" His voice was uneven. "You're half my age."

"Does it matter?" Quickly, she leaned over and kissed him. His arms closed around her, and she knew this had been a smart move. She wouldn't go home to the studio tonight . . . She'd sleep with Marc . . . and tomorrow they'd talk about marriage.

She was glad she had found a gynecologist in New Orleans who had fitted her with one of his intrauterine rings. She had no intention of getting pregnant—not even by Marc Goldman.

CHAPTER THIRTY-ONE

As always when she arrived home from the store, Sophie headed straight for the hall table where Mildred put the mail every morning.

"I'm home, Mildred!" she called, which was the signal for Mildred to put the light under the pots on the stove and prepare to leave for the day.

"You got a letter from Paris, Miz Sophie," Mildred called back. "It's on the table."

"Thanks." Eagerly she looked through the pile of bills and ads until she was staring at Carrie's tight little scrawl. Bless Karl. He'd finally pushed Carrie into writing.

Leaving the rest of the mail on the table she started up the stairs to the bedroom, ripping open the envelope as she walked. She squinted at the expensive notepaper with a sigh of exasperation. In just these last few months it seemed, she had been finding it difficult to read without glasses. Jenny kept telling her to go to the optometrist. She sat on the edge of the bed and turned on the light.

Dear mama and papa:
  I know you'll be surprised and thrilled at my news. I was married yesterday afternoon to Marc Goldman, Nicky's brother. We didn't come home for a big wedding—and I know how that disappoints you, mama, but Marc's wife died just recently and it wouldn't have looked right. We had a civil ceremony in Paris. Marc and I will sail for New York the first Tuesday in April—

Sophie's face was luminous as she reread the brief letter. All her anxieties about Carrie's future were put to rest. Thank God, Carrie was married. *And married so well.* Her husband Jewish. After that business with those young bootleggers she had been a nervous wreck, wondering who Carrie would pick up next.

It would have been nice to give her only daughter a big wedding, Sophie thought wistfully. Every mother looks forward to her daughter's wedding. So instead, when Carrie came home with her husband, Herman and she would have a dinner party for their family and Marc's—for that Herman would be pleased to spend. He'd be all puffed up over having the Goldmans for *machatinistem.*

While she changed from her small black "store dress" into a flowered cotton housedress, tears welled in Sophie's eyes as she remembered holding Carrie in her arms minutes after she was born . . . seeing her as a feisty little girl . . . growing up . . . at her high school graduation . . . always beautiful and imperious and spoiled.

How she had worried through the years about Carrie! Guiltily she recalled those exasperated moments when she had told herself that Carrie was like no one on her side of the family. Indeed, except for the strong physical resemblance to Jenny, it seemed that she was all Herman's child.

Of course, Marc was twice Carrie's age—but Carrie needed a strong hand. Would people talk because he had remarried so soon after his wife's death? His first wife had been sick for years. According to Karl—who had been one of her admirers—Marc had been loving and kind, the perfect husband, right up until the day she died. Wasn't it funny that Karl never said a word in his last letters about Carrie becoming romantically involved with Nicky's brother? Her face softened. But then all Karl thought about was his painting.

Herman would be beside himself when he came home, she thought as she changed into house slippers. The trip to Paris had paid off. But first he would expect dinner on the table, so she'd better get downstairs.

"Miz Sophie, I'm goin'," Mildred called from the downstairs hall. "The vegetables is on the stove and the roast and potatoes in the oven. You can take the roast out in about thirty minutes."

"Thank you, Mildred. See you tomorrow."

"Ever'thing all right with Carrie?" Mildred asked.

"Just fine. I'll tell you about it tomorrow." It would take too much time now, and she was impatient to phone Jenny.

Sophie rushed downstairs to the telephone. Jenny would be as pleased for Carrie as she was—and she could go right over to the cottage and tell mama, who would be happy to know her grandchild was married.

She would call Jenny at the store—she always stayed an hour or so after it closed. She picked up the phone and dialed. It rang several times. Maybe Jenny had already left. Just as she was about to hang up, Jenny answered.

"Hello?" She sounded breathless—she must have been on her way out.

"Jenny, I'm so glad I caught you. I've just had a letter from Carrie—"

"Is she all right?" Jenny tried to hide her irritation—Sophie worried more about Carrie than all four boys combined. "Is she coming home?"

"Jenny, you won't believe it." Sophie's voice crackled with happiness. "Carrie is married!"

"Sophie, that's wonderful. Who is it? Is he an American?"

"Oh yes . . . you'll never guess . . . it's Marc Goldman."

She couldn't have heard right.

"Who?"

"Nicky's brother," Sophie said, jubilant. Jenny felt hands closing around her throat. Marc and Carrie? *No. She couldn't believe it. There was some ghastly mistake.*

"I just found the letter when I got home from the store. I know Marc's twenty years older, but you know Carrie needs somebody to hold her in check. Jenny, you've met Marc—what's he like?"

Jenny fought to keep her voice even.

"Marc's a charming man," she heard herself say. Marc must have lost his mind! "He's sensitive, gracious, bright. A perfect husband . . ."

"Karl likes him, too," Sophie said. "I know Herman

will be mad that Carrie didn't come home to let us give her a fancy wedding, but I can say it to you, Jenny, and nobody else—I'm just glad she picked somebody so fine."

"So . . . they'll live in Paris?"

"Oh no, that's the best part! They're coming home— they're sailing the first Tuesday in April, only ten days away . . . Oh Jenny, in less than two weeks my baby will be home . . . with her new husband."

They talked a few minutes longer—inconsequential chatter, and then at last Sophie said good-bye. Slowly, Jenny put down the receiver. The store was dark, empty. What kind of insane world was this, she asked herself in anguish. Marc, who had vowed he could never love another woman but her, had married her snip of a niece—and less than three months after Simone died. God, how she had longed for some word from him! Some word that a respectable period of time had elapsed for them to talk about their life together. She had promised herself she would divorce Mannie and she was sure that for a price he would agree.

She had to talk to Nicky.

"Nicky, Sophie just called me—" Her voice trembled.

"Jenny, I can't believe it!" Nicky sounded furious. "I just had a letter from Marc. How did that calculating little bitch trap him?"

"God, Nicky . . . I don't know. Sophie says they'll be home in two weeks. I'd like to leave a week earlier for Paris." She had been hoping that by the time they arrived in Paris, Marc would be ready to declare himself. Now he was coming home with a new bride. "I refuse to be here when they arrive, Nicky—I don't think I could bear it."

Nicky's voice was filled with compassion.

"Whenever you want to leave, Jenny, is fine with me. I could kill that brother of mine! How could he do something so outrageous?"

Jenny sat alone in the office and tried to pull herself together. It wasn't so terrible . . . After all, she had survived without Marc all these years. She could survive the years ahead. The children and the store would continue to be her life. It was quite simple, really. The Marc she had known was dead.

* * *

Marc sat at dusk in a deck chair aboard the *Paris*, the deck all but deserted at this hour when most of the first-class passengers were dressing for dinner. He was grateful for the solitude—he needed time to sort out his thoughts.

He had known within a week after his marriage that it was a terrible mistake. Simone had urged him to remarry and Carrie had been waiting, so lovely, so reminiscent of the one woman he had ever loved . . . She had thrown herself into his arms, but he couldn't blame her for what had happened—he should have known it wouldn't work. She was little more than an impressionable child.

He had stood with Carrie in the registry office and felt as though he was marrying Jenny. He had even persuaded her to choose a mauve suit by Lanvin for the ceremony because Jenny had worn mauve the first time he took her to dinner in Paris.

He had given Carrie *carte blanche* in shopping for a trousseau. She had bought backless gowns that brought stares of reproach from other passengers shipboard, the knee-high daytime dresses beloved by the flapper generation.

In bed Carrie was passionate. But he never felt he was making love to his wife. It was some girl he had picked up for a night. After they made love she turned away and fell asleep. To Carrie, it seemed, sex was no more than a heated physical exercise.

He knew he was of a different generation when he realized he was not the first man with whom Carrie had made love. Today's girls were unromantically frank. It jolted him when Carrie flirted with other men. To her generation, it seemed, the most urgent thing in life was to enjoy oneself.

As their crack pullman charged north toward New York from Atlanta, Jenny knew that Marc and Carrie were at the same time on another train bound for New Orleans. She knew she couldn't avoid facing Marc forever, but she had to delay it for as long as possible. Bless Nicky, she told herself, for not talking about Marc except in those painful moments when *she* brought it up.

They were scheduled to sail at midnight on Monday. She phoned Leon at Harvard and arranged for him to come down and stay in their hotel suite over the weekend, knowing that seeing Leon would be a kind of reassurance that her life was not entirely a shambles.

She spent two frenzied days in New York shopping. As usual, manufacturers entertained them with extravagant dinners and visits to the theater. They dined at the Brevoort at Fifth Avenue and Eighth Street on onion soup, escargot, and filet mignon *à la Bernaise*, with a dessert of pears flamed in liqueurs. On their second night in New York they were taken to a speakeasy favored by what was being dubbed "café society." The manufacturer assured them they could trust the drinks served here.

While Jenny warily sipped a concoction of gin, apricot brandy and grenadine, two socialites whom she knew from Palm Beach and Santa Barbara swooped down and greeted her. The manufacturer told her the meeting would probably be mentioned in tomorrow's newspapers—Maury Paul, who wrote a column as Cholly Knickerbocker, was making notes across the room.

When Leon arrived, Jenny and Nicky took him to the theater to see a powerful new play called *Anna Christie*, by Eugene O'Neill. Leon was indignant that five hundred copies of *Ulysses*, a pornographic novel by a writer named James Joyce, had been burned by U. S. Post Office officials.

Jenny dreaded their arrival in Paris. According to Nicky Marc had closed the Paris house, found jobs for the servants, and given the house to brokers. On this trip they would stay at the Meurice.

Jenny's moods swung between gaiety—when lone male passengers vied for her attention—and depression, when thoughts of Marc overwhelmed her. Nicky was concerned.

"Darling, don't look so distraught," she told Nicky the night before they were to arrive at LeHavre. "I won't jump overboard. I have too many responsibilities." But thank God for Nicky, who understood what she was going through.

Once in Paris, they kept busy every moment. But it was an empty, unhappy time for both women, and for Jenny especially, Paris was a ghost town. Marc had gone home to New Orleans . . . with his bride.

She was relieved when at last they were homeward bound. But as the train raced toward New Orleans, she wondered how she could face Marc. Still, she knew that she must. He was her niece's husband.

Armand met Jenny and Nicky at the station. Jenny looked with loving approval as they embraced warmly. After those early rocky years it seemed that Nicky's marriage was at last on sound footing.

"We're invited to a dinner for Carrie and Marc tomorrow night," Armand said as they settled themselves in his new Cadillac. "Carrie's mother insisted that the delayed wedding dinner be delayed even longer—until you two returned from Paris."

Nicky shot a warning glance at Jenny.

"How *is* my darling brother?"

"I'm not sure," Armand said, oddly somber. "I have a suspicion his wife is a little more than he bargained for. Maybe he was so numb after Simone's death he wasn't thinking straight."

Jenny couldn't bear to hear anymore.

"How's grandma?"

"She's fine," Armand said. "So thrilled to have Marc home. But she can't stand his new bride—the only good thing she has to say about her is that she's the image of you."

"I assume they're staying with mama and papa?" Nicky asked.

"No, they're at the St. Charles Hotel. Marc's searching for a house for them."

When Jenny arrived home she was swept up in a warm embrace by Helene. Her mother, rocking on the porch, accepted a kiss and said, "You certainly stayed away long enough, Jenny. Sophie wouldn't have the party for Carrie until you got home. Carrie says her husband is terribly rich—besides the Goldman money he inherited a fortune from his first wife. I always knew that child would do well for herself."

"Yes, mama, she's done very well indeed."

"I saw Carrie at Aunt Sophie's house the other night," Helene said, taking one of her mother's suitcases as the two of them started upstairs. "Aunt Sophie had grandma and me over for dinner with them. Papa was on the road. That Carrie's too much—she was wearing a dress almost up to her belly button!"

"Helene," Jenny reproached indulgently. "You *do* exaggerate."

"Carrie's 'fast,' mama—even Freddie thinks so."

"How do you like her husband?" Jenny asked impulsively.

"He's nice. He talked a lot about Karl."

All through the following day at the store, whenever she wasn't involved with business, Jenny thought about the dinner Sophie was giving for the two families. There would be eighteen—including Sophie's three boys and Helene—at the table. Sophie had gone out to buy special dishes. Annie Lou had taken over their silver. Annie Lou would stay all day to help Mildred with the cooking and to serve along with her.

How was she going to be able to sit at the same table with Marc and Carrie? Only Nicky knew her secret. Everyone else thought she had simply met Marc in Paris . . . stayed at his house . . . that she had met Marc and Simone in Palm Beach. That was all any of the others knew. That must be all they ever knew.

She left the store early to dress for dinner. She had ordered Sophie to leave at noon. This was the most important social occasion in Sophie's life. She was entertaining her daughter's in-laws. Nothing must spoil the dinner.

Jenny debated about what to wear. She stood before her closet, touching the mauve-and-ivory silk Poiret that she had worn exactly ten years ago tonight—when she dined with Marc in Paris for the first time . . . at Voison's. It was still in fashion. That was the marvelous thing about those classic designer styles.

She decided on the mauve-and-ivory silk gown. Next, she debated about whether the night was cool enough to wear her mink stole. She had worn that, too, her first night in Paris . . . She started at a knock on the door.

"Yes?"

The door opened. Mannie stood there in one of his expensive suits, a diamond stickpin in his tie . . . his stomach hanging over his belt. He chewed on a Havana cigar.

"Mama's getting nervous. She said to come on downstairs."

"I'll be right there, Mannie."

Helene peeked around the door. "Oh, mama, you look beautiful.

"Thank you, darling. So do you." She pulled Helene close and held her for a moment.

"Jenny!" Her mother's voice drifted querulously upstairs. "Hurry. I don't want to be late."

When they arrived at Sophie's house, it seemed to Jenny that every light on both floors was on. Armand's Cadillac already sat out front. She urged Nicky to be early—she needed moral support.

"I don't know why Danny couldn't have come down from Santa Barbara," Mrs. Straus said as Jenny helped her out of the car. "His wife probably talked him out of it."

Mama had been looking forward to tonight's party— Jenny never remembered her mother looking so well. She held herself with an aristocratic air that seemed a throwback to her childhood in Vienna. The dress she wore was chic and becoming. She would be horrified if she knew what the Lanvin original cost, even wholesale.

Tonight, Jenny thought with compassion, mama was moving back—briefly—into the past. The Goldmans were rich and social, and her granddaughter was now one of them.

Armand and Nicky, Benedict and his wife were already gathered in the parlor along with Herman. Neither Marc and Carrie, nor his parents and grandmother had arrived. With a starched white apron over her black uniform, bought especially for the occasion, Mildred was circulating among the guests with glasses of champagne. Seeming self-conscious at all this splendor Frederic and Milty went over to talk with their grandmother. Herbie took Helene off to see the new litter of kittens.

Mr. and Mrs. Goldman and Grandma Goldman arrived. Jenny and her secret business partner hugged.

"Jenny, I've missed you," Grandma Goldman said. "Have lunch with me tomorrow."

"I'd love it, Mrs. Goldman." Jenny knew that Mrs. Goldman's son and daughter-in-law thought it odd that they were so close. Grandma Goldman didn't care at all.

While Jenny stood with her hand in Mrs. Goldman's, she heard the doorbell ring. Annie Lou was going to the door. It would be Marc and Carrie. Everyone else was here. She braced herself for the sound of his voice. The sight of his face.

"Grandma," Marc said jovially and strode toward them. He pulled his grandmother to him for a close embrace. Jenny dropped her eyes, forced a smile. "Grandma, you are the most beautiful lady here." Only now did he allow his eyes to move to Jenny. She was startled by the intensity of his gaze. "Jenny—" He extended a hand. She gave him her own. "Beautiful as ever," he said quietly. "Mauve becomes you."

"Thank you."

"Hello, Aunt Jenny." Carrie came forward, her smile oddly malicious. Carrie had not called her Aunt Jenny since she was fourteen.

"Hello, Carrie."

"Darling, I think you've met everybody except Uncle Mannie," Carrie said sweetly, dropping a hand on Marc's arm. "Uncle Mannie," she called, "come over here and meet my husband."

Jenny saw the startled look on Marc's face when Mannie came forward. The look was quickly replaced by one of warmth as he extended a hand. She had given Marc an unvarnished portrait of her husband . . . Had he expected Mannie to be a handsome, polished gentleman?

"Let's go in to dinner now," Herman called out importantly. Gone was the more plebeian "supper."

At Jenny's request, Sophie had seated her between Armand and Benedict. She had not expected Marc to be sitting directly across from her. Marc smiled, but his eyes were unhappy. She remembered what Armand had said about Marc on the drive from the station. Was he already regretting his marriage? *It was too late for that.*

By mid-morning Jenny was exhausted. She had slept little last night after coming home from the party. How had Marc let himself be caught in a marriage with Carrie? Nicky said he must have been blinded by Carrie's resemblance to *her.*

Now she remembered that Marc seemed troubled by Nicky's coolness toward him. Their mother had suggested that Nicky should give a party to present Carrie to their circle and Nicky had flatly refused. Only Denise, now engaged to a young dentist, had given a party for Carrie.

Was Marc worried that Nicky might drop some embarrassing remark to his parents? That she might tell them he'd had a longtime affair with his new aunt? *Why did she let him invade her thoughts this way?*

She had to do something—she couldn't sit here like this going over it. She'd go to the selling floor and see how the staff was doing. She stood up and walked across the room. Before she reached the door, she heard a faint knock.

"Come in, please."

The door opened. Marc stood there with a tentative smile. He looked as though he, too, had not slept . . .

"I need some help, Jenny . . . about a gift for grandma."

"Why not ask Sophie to help you?" *How dare he come here this way?* "She's excellent at personal service."

"Jenny, I have to talk to you." He closed the door behind him.

"We have nothing to talk about, Marc." She clenched her fists to conceal her trembling.

"Jenny, I've made a fool of myself. Within three days of our marriage, I knew it was a nightmarish mistake—"

"I don't want to hear this, Marc," she said steadily.

"Jenny, I have to tell you. Carrie looked so like you—I must have been crazy. I've never stopped loving you."

"I don't want to hear this. We're never to discuss what happened between us. *It never happened, Marc.* You're my niece's husband. Nothing more. Not ever."

CHAPTER THIRTY-TWO

IN A BRILLIANT green chiffon shift by Coco Chanel, Carrie sat, long silk-stockinged legs crossed daringly high, in the reception room of Dr. Rice's office. For a few moments she had enjoyed scrutinizing the rabbitskin rug that dominated the floor. Large squares of white and black fur and the rug edged with a border of white and black. He said his wife had brought it back from Paris.

Carrie sighed. She was so bored in New Orleans with almost everybody away for the summer. Marc had rented that silly cottage on Lake Pontchartrain, and he drove out there every day to paint. She had no intention of staying out there for the summer, so he'd rented that big house.

He was being real mean not to take her to Bar Harbor or Newport or some place like that. He said they didn't like Jews there, but with their kind of money they'd find plenty of people happy to entertain them.

"Mrs. Goldman, you can go in now," Dr. Rice's nurse said politely.

Leaving behind the scent of her expensive Coty perfume, Carrie walked into the office and closed the door behind her.

"Sugar, what are you doing here?" Harlan Rice asked with an uplifted eyebrow. At thirty-seven, Harland was handsome and highly successful, numbering much of New Orleans' social set among his patients. "I thought I was seeing you at your place tomorrow."

"Life's too short to wait." Carrie moved in to him. He was almost as old as Marc, but he had young ideas. "I brought a bottle of gin and me to brighten your afternoon. Lock the door, honey. We don't want to be interrupted."

Harlan crossed the tiny room and locked the door, quietly turning the key so that his nurse in the reception room wouldn't hear. He went back to his desk and picked up the phone, watching while Carrie provocatively began taking off her clothes.

"Miss Barnes, I'm in consultation. No calls, please." He put down the phone and walked over to Carrie. "You are a hot little number," he said, pulling her toward him.

"What are you going to do about it?" she asked, nuzzling against him.

"Start a real conflagration."

She spun out of his arms.

"Want a drink?"

"With you who needs gin?" His slightly parted lips settled on hers while a hand moved beneath the silken teddy.

She drove Harlan Rice right through the roof, Carrie thought with satisfaction. He was one of the fanciest doctors in town, but all she had to do was part her legs and he'd do anything she asked . . .

"Come over to the couch," he said thickly, pulling her by one hand. "And get out of that thing."

It disturbed Jenny that Nicky was estranged from Marc because of her. Over lunch in late July, when Nicky came into town from the lake house for a day's shopping, she tried to talk to her about reconciling with Marc.

"I don't care, Jenny . . . I think he's acted like an ass," Nicky declared. "He knows it, too. Carrie and he are fighting like mad. I don't imagine Marc's heard the rumor, but it's all over town that she's having an affair with Dr. Rice. So he's spending most of his time at the cottage he rented on the lake. He paints there all day and half the night."

Marc ran to his studio and she ran to the store, Jenny thought sadly.

"I wonder if Sophie knows," Jenny thought aloud. "Not that it would make any difference. Carrie wouldn't stop seeing Harlan Rice just because her mother told her to."

"I hope Marc finds out," Nicky said viciously. "I wish he'd throw that little slut right out of the house. Even if she is your niece . . ."

"You know what they always say," Jenny tried for flippancy. "The husband is always the last to know."

Mannie left Santa Barbara and headed by train for New Orleans, knowing he'd make his customary detour to a little town about ninety miles upriver. There was a whore in that cathouse run by Lola Jackson who always set his teeth on edge . . . Once a month, for over a year now, he had made this detour.

He arrived at Lola's house shortly before nine. Taking a taxi from the railroad station he had to listen to a long account about the record rainfall they'd had in the past week.

"That old river's really takin' a beatin'," the driver said. "I just hope to hell we don't have any trouble. We ain't prepared in this town. It ain't like down in New Orleans."

"No guarantee down in New Orleans," Mannie shrugged. "If the river's gonna overflow, it'll overflow."

Lola welcomed him warmly. Mannie flashed his roll, knowing she'd be impressed.

"Eula's upstairs waiting for you, honey," Lola purred. "You staying all night?" It was an unnecessary question—he always stayed all night.

"Yep," Mannie said peeling off three fifty-dollar bills. Already he was hot, imagining Eula parading around in those black silk stockings and nothing else. She had the best pair of tits in the parish.

Eula knew just what he liked. She had only complained once when he used his belt on her. But money made all the difference in the world.

"Mannie, I thought you'd never get here this month," Eula scolded, her kimono falling open to display her black-stockinged long legs. "You want the phonograph record?"

"Yeah, put it on," he said, his hands already at his belt. "Eula, I missed you."

When they had finished, Mannie collapsed on the bed. After an hour with Eula, he always felt good.

"Go downstairs and get a bottle," he ordered, again pulling out a bill. "We got a whole night ahead of us." He frowned. "What's all that hollering downstairs?"

Eula opened the door.

"Eula, get Mannie and come on up to the attic," Lola called, excitedly racing up a flight of stairs. "That damn river is spilling right over its banks. The water's already rushing down the street!"

"Mannie, put on your pants and come on!" Eula threw his trousers onto the bed. "Come on, Mannie!"

The hallway was filled with the sounds of panic—men and girls pouring out of the rooms, shouting, fighting to get to the attic.

"Wait a minute . . . we better make it up to the roof," one of the men said. "At the rate that water's rushing down this whole house could be afloat in ten minutes!"

A dozen took refuge on the uncomfortably pitched roof. In the hot cloudy night they could hear the rush of water below.

"Dammit," Mannie said. "I left my wallet in the room!"

"Mannie, where you goin'?" Eula screamed.

"Where do you think? I gotta get my wallet!"

He let himself into the attic. As he stumbled down the stairs toward Eula's room he saw the water gushing up to meet him, but it was too late. On the roof they heard his terrified screams as the water engulfed him, swept him down into the darkness of the house. Then there was only silence.

Early on Wednesday morning, numb with shock, Jenny drove the ninety miles upriver to identify Mannie's body. Yesterday the water had receded. A business card in the jacket of his suit had been dried out. The authorities knew whom to notify.

At the morgue she steeled herself to make the necessary identification. Mannie was the children's father. Shouldn't she feel some grief? She made arrangements for the body to be brought to New Orleans. In accordance with the Jewish faith immediate burial was necessary.

With Helene on one side of her and Sophie on the other

she watched while Mannie's coffin was placed in the above-ground vault, as demanded by New Orleans law. She had not asked Leon to come home—she knew he could not arrive from Harvard in time for the funeral.

Mrs. Straus was horrified when Jenny decided not to sit *shivah*. It had been a long time since Mannie had been her husband. For Helene to sit for her father would have been hypocrisy. The irony of her situation did not escape Jenny. Now it was she who was free and Marc who was tied to a bad marriage.

Jenny's life was changed little by Mannie's death. It was Marc's presence in the city that kept her constantly on edge. No matter how many times she told herself what she had felt for Marc was over, she knew she lied. She would go to her grave loving Marc Goldman.

At painful intervals she was forced into social situations with Marc. She knew his anguish matched her own . . . but Marc allowed this to happen—and there was no turning back. Nicky was increasingly frustrated that Marc seemed to close his eyes to Carrie's continued affair with Harlan Rice but Jenny suspected he didn't know about it . . . As always, he buried himself in his work.

Early in October Nicky asked Jenny to a surprise ninetieth birthday party for their grandmother. Reluctantly Jenny accepted.

A week before the party Marc phoned Jenny.

"I know about the party," she said quickly, as always nervous at an encounter with him. "I'll be there."

"I need some advice, Jenny." Marc sounded sincerely anxious. "I've painted grandma's portrait without her sitting for me. I'm not truly a portrait painter and now I have some misgivings about it. I'm afraid she'll be unhappy with it, but she'd never admit it. I can't ask Nicky," he said. "She would never tell me the painting was bad. But I know you wouldn't lie to me, Jenny. Will you please come to the cottage and tell me what you think about the portrait? It won't take long. For grandma, please, Jenny."

"All right," she agreed after a moment. This was not some trick on Marc's part to see her alone. She knew him too well to believe that. Just as she knew that, somehow,

Carrie had connived to marry him. "I can drive out late this afternoon. About five. Is that all right?"

"That'll be fine." He sounded relieved.

"How long will it take me?" she asked. "And how do I get there?"

Jenny drove out to Marc's studio cottage in the unseasonably chilly October afternoon. By the time she arrived, the sky was heavily overcast. She parked and walked to the cottage, her heart pounding. Maybe she shouldn't have come . . .

"Jenny—" Marc smiled at her from the doorway. "It looks as though it's going to pour. I was hoping you'd arrive before the rain."

"Show me the portrait, please." It was absurd to be trembling this way because she was alone with Marc. "I really should start right back to the city."

"It's right here." Marc led her into a large sprawling sitting room with a beamed ceiling and a huge fireplace. The furniture was casual wicker with colorful chintz upholstery, the draperies a matching chintz. "In the corner there by the window," Marc pointed. "The light's not too good now." He squinted in annoyance and crossed to turn on a lamp.

Jenny stood before the portrait of Mrs. Goldman and inspected the likeness. Tears welled in her eyes. It was as though Grandma Goldman was in the room with them. Marc had painted his grandmother's portrait with love and a fine artist's eye for detail.

"It's beautiful, Marc." She managed a tremulous smile. "Grandma Goldman will love it."

"She won't be upset that I've shown all her wrinkles?"

"Grandma Goldman is proud of every line on her face," Jenny said. "And she'll be proud of this portrait."

Marc looked immensely relieved.

"Thanks, Jenny. It's not really my field . . . I've only tried portraits twice in my life." The look in his eyes was so revealing that Jenny dropped her own in sudden confusion. "Grandma's and one other that has been with me for almost twenty years." He paused, and then as though in sudden decision walked to a small commode. He unlocked a drawer. "My first portrait, Jenny." He reached into the drawer, pulled out the miniature, and handed it to her.

Jenny held the miniature in one hand. Her mouth parted in astonishment. Her heart pounded. It was her as a young girl. She recognized the dress—one she had worn that summer with Marc.

"So you see, Jenny, you've always been with me," he told her softly. His eyes saying much more.

"I—I've got to get back to the city."

As she spoke, the storm that had been threatening was unleashed. Lightning crackled in the sky. Thunder rumbled, seeming to shake the cottage. Rain pelted the earth.

Marc dashed about the room. "Are your car windows closed?"

"Oh, God, that's right . . . I forgot." Jenny started toward the entrance hall.

"I'll get them," Marc said.

Back in the cottage Marc shed his sodden jacket and focused on starting a blaze in the grate. It seemed as though the temperature had dropped twenty degrees within a few minutes.

"I'll put up coffee for us," he said. "This is like a tropical storm. It'll be over soon."

Jenny sat in one of the pair of wicker armchairs that flanked the fireplace. She would sit here and have coffee with Marc. When the rain stopped, she would drive back to New Orleans. That was all there would be. But it was unnerving to be here alone in the cottage with him. All the neighboring cottages had been closed up for the season. She doubted that there was another cottage occupied anywhere on the lake.

The rain came down in torrents. In a little while it would let up, Jenny promised herself. It was usually that way with autumn rainstorms. Already the aroma of fresh coffee perking drifted through the cottage. Now Marc came into the room with a plate of croissants.

"I bought these in the French Market early this morning . . ." Even as he spoke he remembered—as did she—their early morning walks in the French Market twenty summers ago. "I popped them into the oven to warm up. The coffee will be ready in a few moments."

"Perhaps I should phone the house and say I may be late—"

"I'm sorry, you can't. There's no phone. I didn't have one put in because I didn't want to be interrupted when I was working."

"No one will be upset if I'm a little late." Jenny tried for a casual air. "Helene is having dinner and spending the night with a classmate. My mother will assume I've been delayed at the store."

"Try the croissants," Marc said. "I'll go get the coffee."

Carrie lay back against a mound of silken pillows, a satin-lined lace coverlet hiding her nakedness while she watched Harlan rush into his clothes.

"I have to be at the hospital in twenty minutes." He frowned at his watch. "I make late rounds after dinner."

"You're sorry I called you," Carrie pouted, but her eyes were smug. Harlan came any time she called.

"Baby, you know better than that," he said, shoving his shirttail into his trousers. "But I do have a practice to keep up, you know."

"Phone the hospital and say you have an emergency." She tossed aside the coverlet. "We'll have a drink, and maybe then you'll—"

"I don't need a drink around you." His eyes trailed over her . . . "I have to get to the hospital, Carrie."

"I'll be all alone till midnight," she purred. "Marc stays out there at the cottage till all hours." She pulled herself into a sitting position and wrapped her arms about her knees. Knowing how provocative the spill of her breasts was. "Did you talk to Irma about a divorce?"

"I tried last night," Harlan said. "But she got hysterical. I'll make her listen to me, I promise, Carrie." Harlan knew she wouldn't divorce Marc until she was sure he was free. "I'll call you later, baby, okay?"

After Harlan left Carrie pulled on a black chiffon nightgown and matching negligee. She strolled out into the Spanish-style parlor, rummaged in a cabinet for her box of

Pihan chocolates and stretched full length on the burgundy velvet sofa. For a few minutes she was content to pick out and nibble the chocolates.

But the stillness began to irritate her. She laid aside the chocolates and went to put a record on the phonograph. It was funny how she had never cared about jazz, which was supposed to have been born in New Orleans, until she went to Paris.

While Kid Ory and his band poured jazz into the room, Carrie lay prone upon the sofa. She swore aloud at the sound of the doorbell. She'd dismissed the servants at six o'clock, to be sure they were gone before Harlan came over. She sauntered out into the foyer and toward the door. Maybe Harlan had changed his mind and come back . . . She pulled open the heavy oak door.

Her mouth dropped open. She had never met Harlan's wife, but she recognized Irma Rice from her photographs on the society pages. At this moment Irma Rice was highly agitated.

"Yes?" Carrie asked with an effort at puzzled inquiry.

"You rotten little bitch!" Irma Rice said as she came into the foyer and slammed the door behind her. "I knew you were seeing Harlan. It was all over town. And now he dares to ask me for a divorce so he can marry you!" With trembling hands she was opening her gray velvet purse.

"Mrs. Rice, I'm married." Carrie tried to brazen her way out of this situation. "I have no intention of divorcing my husband."

"It doesn't matter now!" Irma pulled a revolver from her purse. "You won't have Harlan! You won't have anybody!"

Carrie screamed as the first bullet tore into her body. She screamed again as she fell to the floor with blood gushing from the wound in her chest. Irma Rice fired until the gun was empty. Then she darted from the house.

No one heard the shots or Carrie's screams. Kid Ory and his band was the only sound that spilled out into the night stillness of the Garden District street.

CHAPTER
THIRTY-THREE

Wʜᴇɴ ᴛʜᴇ ʀᴀɪɴ had not let up in an hour, Jenny insisted she would have to drive home despite the storm. She was upset now that she had agreed to come out to the cottage. It was unnerving to be here alone with Marc.

"This rain might continue all night." Jenny rose to her feet.

"But Jenny, it's dangerous—"

"I'll be careful, Marc, really. I have to get home . . ."

"Then let me drive in with you. I can't let you go out in this alone."

Marc banked the fire with ashes, went out to his bedroom for a raincoat, and joined her in the entrance hall. He opened the door so that Jenny could rush out to the car before he turned off the hall lights, then put out a restraining hand.

"We can't leave in this. The road's flooded. We'd never get through."

"But I can't stay here all night." Jenny stared out at the flooded road. The water was spilling over onto the front lawn of the house and seeping up to the steps.

"We'll have to wait for the water to recede," Marc said gently. "There's been a tremendous amount of rainfall."

"It might take hours!" She had dashed out here without thinking clearly—it wasn't unusual for this road to be washed out in a heavy rain.

"Jenny, I'm telling you, the car can't get through. We'll just have to wait."

Nobody would worry about her at home, Jenny com-

333

forted herself. Mama always had dinner in the cottage with Evvie. When she came home, she went right up to her room. Helene was away for the night. Dora and Annie Lou would leave dinner on the stove for her and go up to their rooms. Nobody would worry . . .

"As long as we have to stay," Marc said, "let's go out to the kitchen and see what we can rustle up for dinner. I always keep some staples around." He was already taking off his raincoat. "But first let me start up the fire again."

With a blaze going once more, Jenny and Marc went out to the kitchen. Jenny remembered her first trip to Paris when she had stayed with Marc at the house on Rue Marignan and made breakfast for them. Tonight, Marc whipped up fluffy mushroom omelets, and hashed brown potatoes made from leftovers in the ice box. Jenny put two croissants into the oven and made fresh coffee. They ate slowly, talking comfortably as they lingered over the rich omelettes and buttery croissants. It was when they were doing the dishes that Marc suddenly said, "Jenny, I have to tell you about Carrie and me . . ."

"Marc, no. I—I don't want to hear about—"

"Jenny, I know how you feel. And I understand. But at least let me tell you how it happened. The stories Carrie fed me about Mannie and you . . . and I was so worried then about Simone—I wasn't really thinking clearly. I believed all those lies—"

"It doesn't make any difference, Marc," Jenny said slowly. "But tell me what Carrie said to you. I think I ought to know."

A Studebaker drove up before the Spanish-type house in the Garden District that was temporarily home for Marc and Carrie Goldman. The air lush with autumn flowers drenched from the recent thunder shower.

"I don't know why we have to stop by for a drink with Carrie," Jason, Denise's boyfriend—soon to be her husband—said. Denise knew he didn't like Carrie—he thought she was a bad influence.

"Come on, Jason—I promised we would. Anyway, we won't stay long."

"All right. One drink—but that's all."

Denise knew he only drank to be sociable.

"One drink. You are a darling . . ." She leaned forward and kissed him.

They left the car and walked to the house.

"Why is it so dark?" Denise said, putting her arm through Jason's.

"Maybe Carrie went out—"

"Not when she asked us to stop by for a drink some time this evening. Unless she's—um, entertaining," she said delicately, stopping dead.

"Look, we're here. We should at least find out. If she's, as you put it, 'entertaining,'" Jason smiled dryly, "she'll get rid of us fast enough."

They went to the door. Jason pushed the bell. There was no sound of anyone approaching from within. He rang the bell again.

"Forget it—maybe she's in bed," Jason said, turning away from the door.

"Wait."

Denise reached for the doorknob. The door was unlocked. She pushed it wide and walked into the foyer.

"Carrie? Oh my God!" There was Carrie, lying on the floor in a pool of blood. Denise started screaming.

"Don't look, honey." Jason pulled her around to him, buried her face against his chest. "Just don't look . . ."

"Jason, is she dead?"

"I think so. We have to call the police."

In the first pink streaks of dawn Jenny noted that the water had receded. The road was passable. All night she and Marc had sat before the fireplace without touching. Talking. Admitting their love but knowing they had to deny it. At the moment Marc dozed.

"Marc," she said urgently and he started. "Marc, the water's receded. I can drive back to the city now."

He sat up, rubbing his eyes.

"Will you be all right alone?"

"Of course."

"I think I'll stay here," he said.

"But won't—won't Carrie worry?"

"Jenny, when did Carrie worry about anybody except herself?" He smiled. "Drive carefully, darling. I'll grab a few hours sleep here and go back to work."

Marc saw Jenny to her car, watched her drive off, and went back into the cottage and to the bedroom. But he couldn't sleep. The minute he'd set eyes on Jenny's husband he'd known all of Carrie's stories about their marriage were lies . . .

He walked out into the kitchen to put up a fresh pot of coffee. He heard a car drive up. Maybe Jenny had changed her mind . . . He charged out of the kitchen and down the hall to open the door.

Two men were emerging from a New Orleans police car.

"Are you Marc Goldman?" one of them asked.

"Yes?" He looked from one to the other in bewilderment.

"You're under arrest, Mr. Goldman," the second detective said.

Marc stared from one to the other uncomprehendingly. "For what?"

"For the murder of your wife."

Jenny parked the car and walked toward the house. She turned cold at the sounds of anguished crying inside the house. Mama? Had something happened to mama? She ran up the stairs and pulled open the door.

"Mama?" she called. "Mama, what is it?"

Annie Lou and Dora came into the hall.

"Oh Miz Jenny, it's so awful!" Dora wailed.

"We didn't know where you was, Miz Jenny," Annie Lou rocked back and forth in grief.

"Mama?" Jenny's face was ashen.

"Your mama's been over with Miz Sophie all night. Ever since they found Miz Carrie like that."

"Annie Lou, tell me! What happened to Carrie?"

"She done been kilt," Dora managed to say. "She wuz murdered last night. They think her husband did it. He jes' disappeared."

Jenny rushed to the telephone. She was sure Armand and Nicky were awake.

"Hello," Nicky answered, sounding distraught and scared.

"Nicky, I've just come home. I was caught in the storm out by the lake—"

"Jenny, Marc has been arrested!" Nicky's words tumbled over each other. "The police just brought him in." They must have taken the short-cut, Jenny thought subconsciously—she'd been afraid it might be washed out. "Armand is on his way over there now. Do you know about Carrie?"

"I just heard. Nicky, Marc couldn't have done it. I was with him from late yesterday afternoon until forty minutes ago. At his lake cottage. Didn't he tell the police?"

"Marc wouldn't do that, Jenny—"

"Then I will. I'm going right over now."

Driving to the police station Jenny warned herself that her presence at Marc's cottage overnight would be misinterpreted. There would be a public scandal. But it didn't matter. All that mattered was saving him . . .

She parked before the police station and started toward the entrance, flinching as she caught sight of the morning newspaper's headline:

Beautiful Young Society Matron Murdered.

Inside the station she identified herself and explained that she had evidence regarding Marc Goldman. Immediately she was ushered into a room where Marc was being questioned while Armand hovered beside him.

Marc gazed in astonishment at her. It was clear that he had said nothing to the police about her presence at the cottage—he wanted to protect her reputation.

"I'd like to make a statement, please." Her voice was clear and firm. "I was with Mr. Goldman since before six yesterday evening until daybreak. We were caught together out by the lake."

Jenny signed a statement. The police released Marc but requested that he remain within the city for possible further questioning. Armand used his influence—and that of his father, the judge, to persuade the police to withhold the circumstances of Marc's release from the newspapers.

Hopefully the case could be solved before it became necessary to make Jenny's statement public.

"Marc, you'll come home with me," Armand said. Knowing Marc could not go back to the house where Carrie had been murdered. "I think you could use some sleep. You look terrible."

"I'll go to my sister's house," Jenny said, only now reacting to the horror of Carrie's murder. "Sophie will need me."

Early in the afternoon Marc came to consult with Carrie's parents about the funeral. Everything would be the way her parents wished, he said gently.

"Why did it happen?" Sophie cried out for the hundredth time. "Who would want to kill my beautiful little girl?" Later Sophie would know and understand, Jenny thought. But not now. Not yet . . .

"The police will find whoever did it," Marc promised. "It's taking priority over everything in the city."

"I'll tear the bastard apart with my two hands," Herman said. "My little angel. Who would do this to her?"

Knowing it was too painful for Sophie, Jenny went with Marc to talk to the rabbi, to choose the simple marble tomb. On the following morning, overcast and humid, Jenny stood beside Sophie, holding her sister's hand while the rabbi read the service. Helene, wide-eyed and hurt, stood on her other side and clung to her arm—as she had at her father's funeral . . .

Herman sobbed inconsolably, surrounded by Carrie's three younger brothers. Marc stood at one side with his family, his face white and drawn. Annie Lou, Dora and Mildred clung together and wailed in their grief.

Mrs. Straus had taken to her bed. She stayed at home in the care of a nurse. Jenny was determined that Annie Lou and Dora, who had watched Carrie grow up and worried over her, could pay their respects.

At last the service was over. For one poignant moment Marc's eyes met Jenny's. Then he joined his family as they walked to their waiting cars. Jenny returned with Sophie and her family to the house, where Sophie, Herman and the boys were to sit *shivah*. All of the Maison Jennie stores were closed for the day.

Late in the afternoon Jenny and Helene returned to their own house. The nurse came out to report that Mrs. Straus was sleeping. She had slept most of the day. Annie Lou and Dora went sorrowfully out to the kitchen.

"You want some coffee, Miz Jenny?" Annie Lou asked lovingly.

"That would be nice, Annie Lou."

"And I'll bring you a glass of cold milk, Helene," Annie Lou said, wiping tears from her eyes. "That po' little baby. I can't believe she's gone."

While Jenny sipped at her coffee, Nicky phoned.

"They know who killed Carrie," Nicky reported. "She came into the police station and confessed—it was Harlan Rice's wife."

"She knew!" Carrie had hurt so many people . . .

"Irma told the police that Harlan asked her for a divorce so he could marry Carrie. I guess Carrie was waiting to make sure he got his divorce before she asked Marc for one."

"What's going to happen to Mrs. Rice?" Jenny asked.

"She's being committed to a mental institution. Armand says she'll probably be released in a year or two. Harlan made a dramatic declaration that he would devote the rest of his life caring for his wife."

"How's Marc?" Jenny asked.

"He's sleeping now. Later he's going over to the house with Armand to pack up his things and bring them over here. He'll stay with us for a while."

"I'm glad. He'll need you."

"He'll need you more, Jenny."

"Nicky, how can you talk like that?" Her voice softened, but the bitterness was still there . . . "In death Carrie separated us forever."

At the end of the period of *shivah* Jenny prodded Sophie back to her job. She knew that more than anything else at this time Sophie needed to be kept busy. She had four sons to think about—she couldn't afford to give in to grief.

This year Mrs. Goldman's birthday had come and gone

without a party. It didn't seem right to celebrate Mrs. Goldman's ninetieth birthday when her twenty-year-old granddaughter-by-marriage had just been laid to rest . . . and without asking Jenny knew that Marc had not presented the birthday portrait to his grandmother.

The weeks sped past as Jenny threw herself into the business. She was grateful that Goldman's Department Store, undergoing a complete face change under her guidance, required so much of her time. In this fashion, she was able to involve Sophie in additional responsibilities at Maison Jennie.

Six weeks after Carrie was murdered Marc came into the store. Sophie told him that Jenny was in the dressing room with a special customer. She took him back into Jenny's office to wait for her. Puzzled at Marc's presence in the store she went into the dressing room area.

"Jenny?" she called at the entrance.

Jenny emerged from one of the luxurious dressing rooms.

"What is it, Sophie?"

"Marc is here. He'd like to talk to you. I put him in your office."

Jenny paused.

"Tell him I'll be there in a minute." Her smile was tentative.

When she walked into her office five minutes later, Marc stood at a window gazing out into the sunlight.

"Hello, Marc."

"Jenny," he turned, smiling. "Come out with me for lunch, will you? We have to talk about grandma's birthday," he said quickly, seeing that she was about to decline. "Nicky thinks that three months is long enough to wait. I said I'd have to talk to you." It was only three months since Carrie's death . . . "Grandma's ninetieth-and-one-quarter birthday party," he said with an attempt at humor, but his eyes were serious. "Please, Jenny—it's only lunch . . . ."

"All right, Marc."

But even as they walked out of the store, she regretted accepting his invitation. Surely Sophie suspected that something was going on between them . . . Marc had a way of looking at her that told the world how they felt about each other.

At Antoine's, over a delicious lunch of crabmeat mousse and chocolate tarts, Marc talked gaily about the birthday party, about his work . . . and then at last he abandoned pretense.

"Jenny, life is not over for us because Carrie is dead. We're both free—"

"No, Marc. We're not free. Not after what's happened."

"We *are,*" he said stubbornly. "And I want to marry you, Jennie. I won't let you keep us apart."

"How would it look?" Jenny stammered. Yet the thought of being Marc's wife . . . Could it really happen after all these years?

"I don't give a damn how it looks." He reached out for her hand. "Considering that Carrie and I were married barely eight months, it'll be quite respectable for us to marry six months after her death."

"Marc, I can't do that to Sophie. To mama . . ." How could she even consider it?

"You're not doing anything to them. You're doing something for yourself—and for me. Jenny, without you I'll never be fully alive. We'll wait six months. We'll say nothing to anyone until then. But in six months we'll tell them we plan to be married."

"Marc, I want that more than anything else in the world. You know that . . . but I need time."

"How long?"

"A week," she said shakily.

"All right. Think about it for a week. Then we'll make plans." In his mind it was all settled.

Dazed, Jenny returned to the store. She knew that her whole life would light up if she married Marc . . . but how could she be so selfish? For the rest of the day she grappled with the decision. Yes, she would marry him. No, she wouldn't. How could she tell Sophie and mama she was marrying Carrie's widower?

At eleven that night, unable to sleep, she phoned Marc.

"Marc, yes," she whispered in a haze of happiness. "I'll marry you. In six months. But we can't tell the family until then. Only Nicky."

The days turned into weeks. Jenny went out to lunch

every day, usually to meet Marc at some obscure little restaurant where they could spend an hour together without being recognized. If any of the family saw them, they could always say they were planning Grandma Goldman's surprise party.

On a crisp early December day Marc insisted on lunch at Galatoire's—he had just arranged for his first gallery showing in New York and he wanted to celebrate.

"Oh Marc, I'm so proud of you!"

"It won't be for a few months," he told her. "By then we'll be married. You'll go to New York with me."

Jenny knew that Sophie was aware of the lunches with Marc—she had told Sophie about the surprise birthday party.

Today when she came back from lunch, she saw a speculative look in Sophie's eyes.

"Jenny, you look happy," Sophie said. "God knows, you deserve it."

"It's such a beautiful day—I love being outside for a little bit every day."

"It doesn't have anything to do with Marc, does it?" Sophie asked with a gentle smile.

"Would that upset you?"

"No, darling." Sophie's face was tender. "Anything that makes you happy will make me happy."

"It's too early to say anything." Jenny's eyes held hers.

"I know. But time will pass."

Tonight when Jenny came home from the store, she discovered that her mother was having dinner with Helene and her.

"How's Evvie today?" she asked her mother.

Mrs. Straus shrugged. "The same."

She turned to Helene. "So . . . tell me about school." Mama had something on her mind—later she would talk.

Jenny listened carefully while Helene reported on school activities.

"Mother, is it all right if I go over to study with Peggy?" Helene asked. Her friend Peggy lived three houses away.

"Okay . . . but be home promptly by ten," Jenny stipulated.

As soon as dinner was over, Helene dashed upstairs for her school books and left.

"Jenny, I have to talk to you." Her mother's voice was ominous. "After Annie Lou and Dora go up to their rooms."

"Of course, mama." Had somebody seen Marc and her at Galatoire's? Had somebody told mama she was seeing Marc? She braced herself for a confrontation.

Mrs. Straus was sitting in the parlor, crocheting. Jenny tried to pretend interest in the copy of Willa Cather's new novel which Nicky had lent her, but tonight the words danced before her eyes.

Mrs. Straus put down her crocheting. Annie Lou and Dora were upstairs.

"Jenny, how could you? How could you disgrace the family by sneaking around corners to see Carrie's husband?" *Marc wasn't Carrie's husband. He was Carrie's widower.* "Herman called and told me. He was outraged! A customer of his saw you today at Galatoire's. He came into the store and told Herman. He told Herman you'd been seen all over town with Marc. I demand you put a stop to this instantly!" Mrs. Straus's voice rose. "Do you hear me, Jenny?"

"I hear you, mama." Jenny took a deep breath. "But no, I won't stop seeing Marc. I'll go on seeing him because there's nothing wrong in—"

"Your niece's husband!" Mrs. Straus screeched.

"Carrie's widower, mama. Marc is free."

"It's indecent!"

"Marc and I are going to be married." Now was the time to tell her. "Not right away but—"

"I won't have it! You can't do that to the family!" Mrs. Straus stood up, white and trembling. "How could I face people? How could I live with that disgrace?"

All at once mama stood before her in a searing clarity. All mama cared about was herself. Not how Marc and she might feel about each other. *Only herself.* Guilt slid from her shoulders. She felt almost lightheaded, free . . .

"Mama, I love Marc."

"Love?" Her mother made it sound an obscene word.

"Love is a fairy tale for silly young girls. You're almost thirty-seven years old. You just lost your husband. How dare you talk about marrying again!"

"I knew Marc twenty years ago, mama. I would have married him then if I had not felt it was my responsibility to stay here to look after you and Evvie and Danny instead of going to Paris with him. You're right—I'm almost thirty-seven. And for almost twenty-three of those years—ever since papa died—I've come last in this family. It's over, mama." Happiness surged through her. "It's my time now. I'm marrying Marc in six months."

"You're selfish and unfeeling!" her mother shrieked. "You've always been an unnatural daughter. You think of nobody but yourself!"

"No, mama," Jenny corrected, "you're selfish and unfeeling. You think only of yourself. You've never once thought about the sacrifices I've made. You don't care. Even my children come second to you—after Sophie's children. But that doesn't matter anymore because from now on I'm living my life. Marc and I will marry. We'll build a house for ourselves and my children here in New Orleans. Marc will be my husband and a father to my children. *I will be a person, mama.* Not your doormat. I will continue to love and respect you," she said calmly. "I will always be your daughter. But first I will be Jenny Goldman."

Jenny left Mrs. Straus standing in the parlor and walked out of the house. She would drive to Nicky's house, and she would tell Marc—and Nicky and Armand—that in six months Jenny Adler would become Jenny Goldman.

At almost thirty-seven she had indeed become her own woman.